500 MILES
FROM YOU

Also by Jenny Colgan

The Bookshop on the Shore

Christmas on the Island

The Endless Beach

Christmas at Little Beach Street Bakery

The Bookshop on the Corner

Summer at Little Beach Street Bakery

The Loveliest Chocolate Shop in Paris

Welcome to Rosie Hopkins' Sweetshop of Dreams

Meet Me at the Cupcake Café

The Good, the Bad and the Dumped

Diamonds Are a Girl's Best Friend

Operation Sunshine

West End Girls

Where Have All the Boys Gone?

Do You Remember the First Time?

Working Wonders

Looking for Andrew McCarthy

My Very '90s Romance

Amanda's Wedding

500 MILES FROM YOU

a novel

Jenny Colgan

WILLIAM MORROW
An Imprint of HarperCollinsPublishers

Originally published in the United Kingdom in 2020 by Sphere.

FIRST U.S. EDITION

Designed by Diahann Sturge
Illustrations courtesy of the author
Title page and part title image © Aerial-motion / Shutterstock, Inc.

Library of Congress Cataloging-in-Publication Data has been applied for.

ISBN 978-0-06-291124-7 (paperback)
ISBN 978-0-06-2911142-1 (hardcover library edition)

LSC 10 9 8 7 6 5 4 3 2 1

This book is dedicated with love and gratitude to organ donors everywhere. You are the true heroes of so many stories.

There are two teachers in the school,
   One has a gentle voice and low,
   And smiles upon her scholars, as
    She softly passes to and fro.
  Her name is Love; 'tis very plain
She shuns the sharper teacher, Pain.

Or so I sometimes think; and then,
  At other times, they meet and kiss,
  And look so strangely like, that I
    Am puzzled to tell how it is,
Or whence the change which makes it vain
   To guess if it be—Love, or Pain.

—SUSAN COOLIDGE, *WHAT KATY DID*

500 MILES
FROM YOU

Part I

Chapter 1

It should have started with ominous dark crows, great murmurations and flutterings, bad omens taking to the sky; with thick storm clouds rolling in, clocks striking thirteen.

In fact, it started with an extremely undignified argument with an old lady over a bar of chocolate.

"But you have a bar of Dairy Milk right there in your hand!"

Mrs. Marks looked up at her, heavy and glowering, from the cracked brown leather sofa. "I do not!"

"Behind your back!"

Like a tiny child, Mrs. Marks refused to remove her hand, just shook her head mutinously.

Lissa Westcott put down the medical equipment she'd been packing away and strode back into the center of the room, exasperated. "You thought I'd gone! You thought I was leaving the room and you were making a grab for a hidden Dairy Milk!"

Mrs. Marks fixed her with beady eyes. "What the bleedin' hell are you then, the chocolate police?"

"No. Yes!" said Lissa, rather desperately.

She held out her hand. Mrs. Marks finally handed it over. It was, in fact, a Bournville.

"Ha!" said Mrs. Marks.

Lissa looked at her.

Old Mrs. Marks lived on the fourteenth floor of a South London tower block where the lifts were often broken. Her foot was gradually giving in to diabetes, and Lissa was trying her absolute hardest to save it. She glanced out from the dingy, fussy room with dusty fake flowers everywhere, over at the grand views of the river to the north, at the great towers of the City, glinting in the light, bright and beautiful, clean and full of money, like a vast array of glittering palaces, completely out of reach, though less than two miles away.

"We've just been talking about your diet for twenty minutes!" she said to the poor woman who was practically a shut-in, with only her daughter to visit her. Watching *EastEnders* with family-sized bars of chocolate was one of the few pleasures she had left, but it wasn't doing her any good. "I don't want to be coming up here one day and finding you in a coma," Lissa went on, as severely as she dared.

Mrs. Marks just laughed at her. "Oh, don't you worry about me, duck. Whatever will be will be."

"That's not how health care works!" said Lissa, glancing at her watch. She was due in Peckham in twenty minutes. Driving in London was an absolute fool's errand, but she didn't have any choice; she couldn't carry drugs on the tube.

Lissa was an NPL: a nurse practitioner liaison. She followed up on hospital discharges who had trouble attending outpatient departments in the hopes that they didn't become readmissions. Or, she said in her more cynical moments, did half of what community nurses did when they still had the budget and half of what GPs used to do when they could still be asked to leave the office. Originally trained as an accident and emergency nurse, she loved her current job, which involved rather fewer drunks spewing up on her than A&E did—particularly the bits of it when she got chocolate.

Her hopes, though, in Mrs. Marks's case, were not at their highest.

"You're not exactly a sylph yourself," said Mrs. Marks.

"You sound like my mum," complained Lissa, who had her mother's curvy frame, to her mother's occasionally vocal and occasionally silent disappointment.

"You take it then," said Mrs. Marks grudgingly.

Lissa made a face. "I hate dark chocolate," she said. But she took it anyway. "Please," she said again. "Please. I'd hate them to admit you again. Next time you might lose your foot. Seriously."

In response, Mrs. Marks sighed and indicated the entire old brown three-piece suite. Lissa put her hands down the backs of the cushions and found chocolate bars behind every one.

"I'm donating them to the food bank," she said. "Do you want me to buy them off you?"

Mrs. Marks waved her away. "No," she said. "But if I do end up back in that place again, I'll blame you."

"Deal," said Lissa.

IT WAS CHILLY for mid-March as she left the tall building, but the sun was shining behind a faint cloud of smog in the air, and

Lissa could sense spring coming, somewhere on the horizon. She prayed, as she always did, that nobody had seen the medical personnel sticker on her car and attempted to break into it in case she'd left any drugs in there, and contemplated the new Korean barbecue place she was due to meet some friends in later. It looked good on Instagram, but this wasn't necessarily a good thing and sometimes quite the opposite if it was just full of people photographing cold food.

She noticed the boys loitering on the sidewalk, which was nothing unusual. It was hard to tell with some teenage boys, whether they should be at school; they were so big these days. The best thing to do was keep her head down, hide her ringlets in a tight braid or a scarf, and just keep moving past them. She remained profoundly glad of the unflattering green trousers she wore as part of her uniform that rendered her practically invisible.

These boys, however, weren't talking to her; they were arguing with one another. Just the normal teenage beefs, showing off, puffing out their chests like peacocks. They were a mix of races, with tiny little wispy beards and mustaches, lanky legs and too-pointy elbows, a strong smell of Lynx Africa, and massive trainers the size of boats. It was slightly endearing in its way, watching them try to pretend they knew how to be men. But intimidating too, and she was about to give them a wide berth when she realized she recognized one of them. In fact, it made her wince. It was one of Ezra's cousins. Ezra, beautiful Ezra, whose graceful body and lovely face made him irresistible whenever he got back in touch and messaged her.

Unfortunately, Ezra was well aware of this, which was why he felt obliged to spread himself pretty thinly all around South London. Every time he ghosted her Lissa swore blind she'd never fall for it again. She was not much better at keeping that promise than she was about not eating Mrs. Marks's chocolate.

But she'd met Kai by accident—Ezra had never introduced her to his family—down in Brixton market one morning when they were grabbing breakfast supplies. He was a bright, mouthy fifteen-year-old and should, Lissa thought with a sigh, really be in school. She wouldn't mention that.

"Kai!" She raised her hand.

Just as she did so, he turned to face her, his open mouth already starting to grin as he recognized her, and then, out of the blue, there was a sudden roar of an engine, a screech of brakes, a glint in the sky as something was thrown up, a sickening sound.

Chapter 2

Five hundred and eighty-three miles north by northwest, in the small village of Kirrinfief, on the shores of Loch Ness, a cool March wind was blowing off the water, rippling the white tops of the little waves, and the clouds were hanging heavy off the peaks of the purple mountains.

Cormac MacPherson, the town's NPL, glanced at his watch. Joan the GP was over on the other side of the moor tending to a hiatal hernia. In a human, Cormac assumed, although with Joan it could be hard to tell. She rarely traveled anywhere without being surrounded by a dust cloud of wire fox terriers. So Jake, the local ambulance paramedic, had corralled him in to help with a DNR on a very old lady. Jake knew Cormac could never say no to someone in distress and took wide advantage of his soft nature. They had sat with the family and made sure Edie was as comfortable as possible to the end, in the bed in the little cottage she'd been born in ninety years before. As these things went, it had not been bad.

Now they were heading out for a well-deserved pint.

"Not a bad way to go," said Jake philosophically as they headed down the cobbles, the air cool on their faces.

"Mm-hmm," said Cormac, glancing at his phone.

"Emer on you again?" Jake glanced over.

"Aw crap, she came over to make me a surprise dinner."

"That's terrifying."

"It's not terrifying," protested Cormac weakly. "It's sweet."

"She must know you're out on calls all the time."

"I said I was off duty."

"Yeah, well," said Jake, not looking remotely embarrassed. "Might as well have a pint now, though."

Cormac glanced at his watch and shook his head, just as a door opened from the little row of terraced houses they were passing; the sitting rooms came straight onto the street.

"Jake! Cormac!" came a soft voice. "I didnae want tae—"

"Bother the doctor," finished Jake for her. "Yup, we know."

Chapter 3

A glint of something in the air. An incredible cacophony of sound.

She had seen it only briefly, out of the corner of her eye: she had been watching the boys yelling, gauging with that innate city sense whether they were dangerous and whether it was likely to escalate—Lissa had a good antenna for trouble, having mopped up the effects of so much of it—when she heard what sounded like a car speeding.

At first she'd ignored it, but then she realized that rather than slowing as it rounded the corner into the housing development, it had sped up. She had turned around instinctively to where her own car was to make sure it didn't crash into it, and by the time she turned back, there was a huge howling screech from the wheels as it mounted the curb—deliberately mounted the curb—and she saw . . . the only thing she saw was the glint of a phone, bouncing up in the air, spinning, catching the light, almost lovely, so slow . . .

And then everything happened so fast and there was a twist and a turn of a hideous shape; a thumping noise, horrible, wet, and loud, reverberating around her head; something unthinkable following the phone; and the car's wheels, still moving, engine still revving, and the even harder cracking noise as the huge, unthinkable shape hit the ground, lay there, twisted, misshapen. Lissa couldn't actually believe what she was looking at, that it could not—absolutely could not—be Kai, and she lifted her eyes and found herself staring straight into the face of the driver, whose mouth was drawn back in a snarl, or a leer, or something; something, thought Lissa, through her incomprehension, through her panic, that she couldn't figure out, not at all, as it screamed something about "staying out of Leaf Field"—and then the car revved and sped on.

THERE WAS A moment's silence, then the yelling started: disbelief, fury; and suddenly Lissa found herself clicking into action, found her training propping her up, propelling her forward.

"I'm a nurse. Move away please, I can help."

She expected to have to clear a path, but the other youths bounced upward, shouting their heads off, and dashed screaming in pursuit of the car.

"Dial 999!" Lissa shouted as she knelt down to examine Kai, pulling her phone out of her pocket. She had no idea if the lads could catch the car and was terrified they'd get hit again; there was only one way out of the development, it would have to double back at some point—but she had to prioritize.

She looked down at the figure on the pavement, his head sideways on the sunbaked stone, next to cigarette ends strewn in the gutter.

"DARLING."

He was beautiful, fifteen years old. Lissa couldn't get over it. Not that that mattered, of course; of course it didn't. It had absolutely nothing to do with it. But as she bent desperately trying to save him, as she finally, *finally*, heard the sirens she'd been waiting for, she couldn't get over it: the sheer heart-stopping beauty of the young soft skin, the curve of the neck, the dark hair. He was a child. She couldn't bear to think of how the family was going to take it. She cursed herself; her best friend had deleted Ezra's number from her phone, for her own good. She couldn't even call him.

Even when the paramedics arrived she didn't stop CPR. She carried on compressing, using the heels of her hands as they joined her, monitoring the oxygen, grabbing the adrenaline to shoot into his heart. She knew the paramedics and they trusted her and brought her along, Ashkan working with her, Kerry driving like a fiend as the blue lights screamed over the traffic, even if that clogged up the overwhelmingly crowded London roads, too stuffed full of lorries, vans, Ubers, motorbikes— everything jammed up so tight they could barely find room to pull over to let an ambulance through.

But on this trip, they all knew, deep down, blue lights wouldn't matter. No matter how quickly they moved, how urgently they shouted and cleared the way. Back at the crime scene, a policewoman would be kneeling down in a pool of blood on the pavement, concerned citizens gathering around, but anyone who could have been involved was long gone into the cacophonous city. The sun had gone down and now everything felt chilled.

Kai suddenly contorted, bounced in the air as Ashkan shouted, "Clear!" and Lissa had jumped back instinctively, watching him twitch, wondering if the policewoman sitting in the blood had started the weary business of figuring out who he was, had started the weary, unbearable process of contacting his family.

Lissa let the training take over completely, wouldn't let herself think, automatically putting the oxygen mask back on the boy's lips, still blue; injecting another shot of adrenaline; loading another pint of blood above his arm—all of them desperately hoping he could hold on, hold on just until they got there. None of them spoke apart from the basic terms of the attempt to resuscitate and trying to get more blood into him than was leaving him.

Attempts to resuscitate are, even with the most extraordinarily advanced equipment in the world, much more unsuccessful than not. People see miracle returns from the dead on TV all the time. They didn't see this: the blood pumping out as fast as it could be pumped in; the lack of response in the pupils every time they checked; the artificial twitching and stimulation of the young body; the barked commands and steady listening for independent breath—the hot chaos of it all as the ambulance swerved and howled through the thick London rush hour, only one of many screaming sirens, helicopters, dispatches, attending to pain and blood.

"The doctors are going to call it," predicted Ashkan, glancing at his watch.

"You can't," said Lissa.

Ashkan swore. The pointlessness of it. A hit-and-run that looked deliberate. On a child. He turned away and tuned in to the police radio for a bit, then even half smiled.

"They got him," he said grimly. "The rest of the lads jumped on the car, wouldn't let it leave. Smashed in his windows. It must have felt like a zombie attack."

It didn't register with Lissa at all.

"Carry on. More blood! Now!" said Lissa fiercely, and redoubled her efforts, hissing into the boy's ear, "Come *on,* Kai! Wake up! *Wake up!*"

THEY HAD ARRIVED at Guy's Hospital: the ambulance doors were hurled open without ceremony and two porters and an A&E doctor jumped aboard.

"Move," said the young doctor, who looked about nine.

"I'm not finished here," said Lissa strongly, as she continued to work the oxygen mask, shined light in his eyes, checked for vitals.

"Yes, you are," said the doctor. "Let me look at him."

"I can do it!" said Lissa. His face. His beautiful face. He was a child, a child asleep, still warm—or was that their efforts?—still sleeping, dreaming, losing his homework, wishing he were a footballer or a rock star.

"Stand back!"

"*I can do it!*"

Lissa didn't realize she had screamed, didn't realize everyone stopped to look at her, as Ashkan pulled her back gently, his face a mask of concern. The junior doctor was already moving in, ignoring her.

"Step back."

"I just . . ."

It was unheard of for a nurse to defy a doctor in this way, even if this particular doctor looked like he'd drawn his mustache on with a pen that morning.

"Step back!"

But she couldn't; she could only stand, as if she had absolutely no idea where she was, her arms reaching out uselessly, muttering, "Kai . . . Kai . . ." into thin air, still believing fervently, even as the doctor looked at his watch, shook his head, even as the blood was no longer dripping on the floor, was getting ready to pool, to congeal. The only thread to life was her.

"I can just . . . try one more time . . ."

"GET HER OUT of here," the young doctor was muttering as the porters tried to move the body onto the gurney. Several other medics appeared.

"Is next of kin here?" yelled one of them, and Lissa recognized in horror the people—perfectly nice, professional people—whom, in day-to-day life, she admired hugely. The transplant team.

"He's not even dead, you *vultures*," she found herself screaming, and Ashkan really did move then, bodily pulled her out of the ambulance as she swore and thrashed away. "He's not even . . . !"

"I'm calling it," said the doctor. "Take him to the HDU."

This was where they held transplant patients, in a twilight world between life and death, just holding on for long enough to get the necessary signatures, to beg and plead that a life taken in vain would not be entirely in vain.

"18:38," he said. "Can we move it fast? We've a . . ." And his voice sounded so very, very weary. ". . . hit-and-run incoming."

Lissa collapsed onto the pavement as it started to rain and burst into tears, deep racking sobs. She was a professional, had been doing this for four years, had seen road accidents, murders, every kind of horrible thing it was possible to see.

But it was a boy she knew whose name was Kai who broke her, at 6:38 P.M., on a totally normal Tuesday night.

Chapter 4

Ashkan tried to move her.

"Mate," he hissed under his breath. "Mate, you have to move. They're going to haul you into the nutter room."

There were no gentle words among the London Ambulance Service when it came to Occupational Health and the therapy unit. As far as they were concerned, ambulance paramedics were a gang of outlaws, pirates, screaming through the streets on a mission to save. Once you started wobbling the lip about it, like every other bugger would, well then. What was the point of you? Someone had to scrape people off the ground; someone had to hold the line. If you started crying and needing therapy and basket weaving, well, then you were no use. Nobody denied that it was a tough gig. That was the point of it. If you couldn't hack it, you weren't much use. A&E teams relied on each other like little else.

Lissa was finding it impossible even to get up, even as the rain crept down the collar of her heavy green jacket.

"Everything okay?" said Dev, the station controller, coming over, his kind face concerned, his glasses as usual up around his bald head—they were always wherever he wouldn't be able to find them as soon as he needed them, including dangling around his neck or in his pocket.

"Fine!" said Ashkan breezily.

Lissa was aware they were there, that they were around, but somehow she couldn't concentrate, couldn't really focus on what they were asking of her or why she was sitting on wet pavement. It was like her body didn't belong to her at all, like she was somewhere else and everything was going on without her and the person sitting on the wet pavement was somebody else.

Dev looked concerned. "Lissa? Were you on the hit-and-run?"

"She knew the lad," said Ashkan. "Bad bloody luck. Bit of a shock."

Lissa couldn't even nod her head to respond. The police took her to the station to pick out the perpetrator from a lineup, and for a statement, which she gave blindly. Ashkan waited for her, even though his shift had ended.

"Come on," said Ashkan gently. "Let's fill you up with tea."

He frog-marched her back to the hospital, and Lissa let him, as if her legs were moving without any input from her at all, as if they belonged to someone else.

The ground-floor canteen was quiet this time of night: on-duty doctors keeping an eye on their beepers and phones; one poor soul fast asleep by a potted plant, his head looking uncomfortable on a wicker divider; a clutch of porters playing cards; and a few nervous-looking family members, not sure they were in the right place, glancing around. The catering staff had gone for the day; it was just vending machines and hideous coffee in plastic cups with plastic stirrers. Ashkan brought back two teas and gave both of them to Lissa, pulling out his own flask of vegetable juice he squeezed himself. Ashkan took his health extremely seriously and usually headed straight for the gym at the end of his shift. Lissa had always teased him about how vain he was—he spent longer on his shiny black quiff than she did on her spirally curls, although, to be fair, they were liable to turn into frizz in the wet, so she just got them out of the way in a tight ponytail. Plus, the fewer things that stood out about her physically, the less abuse she normally had to take from people not quite in their right minds by the time they showed up at A&E.

Lissa took the tea, feeling it burn her fingers through the thin plastic—Ashkan was harshly opposed to single-use plastic, so his doing this was a clear sign of how concerned he was. She understood all of this—kind of—from a long, long way away. She could sense how worried he was. But somehow she just didn't care. About anything. Because that boy was dead, and nothing mattered, and she felt half dead herself.

The harsh strip lights felt purgatorial; the rain-spattered windows showed nothing but themselves back to them. Lissa wondered for a second if they had all died in that ambulance. Her eyes were drawn to the door as a bent-over woman entered, her face anxiously scanning everybody in the room. When she saw Lissa, she blinked.

The woman who approached them couldn't have been much older than Lissa, was surely only in her thirties. But the expression on her face was that of someone who'd lived a million lives.

Chapter 5

The woman was pulling her cardigan around herself, shuddering in the cold wind, the rain spattering from the south.

"Och, hello there, Cormac."

"Hello there yourself, Mrs. Coudrie."

There was a pause. "Could you just . . . I really don't want to bother the doctor."

He turned to Jake. "Off you go," he said. "I can get myself home."

Jake grimaced. "Is it wee Islay?"

The woman nodded.

"Aye, aye, I'll come along," said Jake, with the resigned voice of a man who knows that his dream of a lovely foaming pint and possibly a quick flirt with Ginty MacGuire has almost certainly just vanished forever.

Chapter 6

Lissa lifted her eyes to the strange woman's. The lady's face was drawn with pain.

"Excuse me," she said.

It was as if someone were speaking from far away. Lissa managed to blink. "Yes?"

"I'm . . . I'm Kai Mitchell's mother?"

She said it so quaveringly, as if she wasn't absolutely sure whether she was or whether she could still describe herself as such. Perhaps, Lissa found herself thinking, she wasn't a mother anymore. She must be Ezra's auntie.

Ashkan jumped up and offered her a chair.

"No," she said gravely. "No, thank you. I don't want to sit." She looked around the chilly clinical cafeteria. "I'm not staying."

Ashkan leaned over. "I am so, so sorry for your loss."

She held up her hand. "I'm not. I'm furious."

Lissa nodded, something stirring within her. "Me too," she said.

Ashkan shot her a warning glance that she ignored. Instead she stood up.

"I'm furious too."

"I just wanted to know," said the woman. Behind her, at the door, stood a cluster of frightened, upset people: friends and family. Outside, Lissa knew, would be cameras, journalists, the media, desperate to spin another narrative of death.

In here, in this now-silent room, was just a desolate mother.

"You have people helping you?" said Ashkan, looking over. "You won't be alone."

"Yes, I *will*," said the woman. "Were you with him?"

Ashkan indicated Lissa. "She was with him the most. She did the most."

"I didn't do enough," said Lissa dully. If she'd been braver. If she'd realized the car was going too fast, shouted a warning. If she'd paid more attention.

"You need to know we did everything we could. We tried . . ." said Ashkan—they couldn't be too careful, not these days, with lawyers hanging around like carrion crows.

But the woman wasn't listening to him. She had stepped forward and was taking Lissa's cold hands.

"You held his hand?"

Lissa nodded.

"This hand held his hand?"

"We tried," said Lissa.

And suddenly the two women were weeping in each other's arms, clinging to each other. Ashkan was very unhappy. This wasn't appropriate, not at all. He wasn't sure what to do.

"I'm so sorry," Lissa sobbed.

"Did he say anything?"

Lissa desperately wanted to say he had asked for her or said to tell her that he loved her. But she couldn't.

"He was . . . he was already so unwell," she said.

The woman nodded. "Oh well," she said. "I'm glad . . . I'm glad someone was with him."

Lissa nodded, wishing she could do more.

"All those people shouting at me," said the woman, looking confused. "You know, they want to chop him up! They were shouting at me! To chop him up! To cut up the body of my son! Before he's even cold! To cut bits off him!"

Ashkan winced. The transplant people were so desperate, so determined—and if he had good organs, oh, what a difference they would make to people.

Lissa seemed to snap out of herself a little then and straightened up. "What did you say?" she asked.

Chapter 7

The cottage was nearly identical to the one they'd just left but furnished in a neutral, modern style, with a wood-burning stove and large prints of the children in black and white on the walls.

"Hello there, Islay," Cormac said cheerily. "Why aren't you asleep, then?"

The tween was lying on the bed, blue and breathing heavily. Nonetheless she attempted a grin for Cormac and a slightly flirtatious look for Jake, who was generally a hit with the ladies.

"Ach, you've looked better," said Cormac, understating the case. The child had severe cardiomyopathy, and absolutely nothing seemed to be helping. The pacemaker was just the latest in a line of therapies that were failing her.

"I was thinking about maybe taking her in," said her mother. They were extremely familiar with the hospital in Inverness.

"Well, let's have a listen," said Cormac, taking out his stethoscope. "Those beta-blockers not working on you, Islay?"

Trying to be helpful, the child shook her head, just a fraction. How used she was; how tired she was of the constant invasion, the constant questions. She looked so weary. Cormac felt his own heart sink. He'd left the army to get away from the endless trauma cases, but this, in its own way, was just as difficult. Jake took her blood pressure and frowned.

"Well?" said Mrs. Coudrie.

"I'll talk to Joan," said Jake. "This"—he wrote down the number on a piece of paper, but Elspeth Coudrie already knew it by heart—"is when we'd blue-light. But I think we'll see what Joan has in her armory."

Cormac patted Islay on the hand. "I know you want to stay up all night watching Mr. Drake on the television."

Islay rolled her eyes. "It's Drake," she wheezed. "Not Mr. Drake. And I don't like him anyway."

"That's good," said Cormac. "He's too old for you."

Islay tried to smile.

"But the best thing you could do is get some sleep," said Cormac.

This wasn't true. The best—and rapidly turning into the only—thing she could do was to get a heart transplant. If only it were that simple.

"Imagine," said Mrs. Coudrie, as Jake finished his call and Islay tried to get comfortable. "Imagine waiting for someone else's child to die. Imagine hoping that they will."

"I DON'T KNOW!" said Kai's mother, her voice hysterical. "They were all yelling. And I just wanted to see my boy. He's my boy! And they wanted to chop him up."

Lissa took the woman's hands. "Did you say no?" she said softly.

"I didn't know what I was saying!" said the woman, looking up at her. "Yes. I think I said no."

"Do you know," said Lissa very softly and quietly, as if trying to soothe a child. "Do you know what would be the most wonderful thing you could do for Kai, and Kai could do for the world?"

"But they want to chop him up! My boy! My beautiful boy!"

"He'd be giving his life for others," she said. "That . . . that is very beautiful."

The woman gently touched a small crucifix around her neck.

"He could save a life," insisted Lissa.

"But my beautiful boy . . ."

"Would be a hero. A hero beyond heroes. Forever."

The tears didn't stop falling. Mrs. Mitchell stood back. "Is it too late to say yes?"

Lissa shook her head, even though she wasn't sure, even though it might be.

"Come, please," she said. "Please. Can you come with me? Quickly?"

And together they ran back through the long corridors, the devil at their heels, Lissa terrified they would be too late, that they would have unplugged their machines, gone on their way, their tragic work unsuccessful.

They clattered into the resuscitation ward, panting, terrified. *Thank God, thank God, thank God for all the cuts* was the only thing she could think. The staff had taken a break; the next shift, which would remove the tubes and make up the body, had not yet been called in—and there he still was, still connected.

They both froze. Kai's mother made a sound, an animal noise, as if it were all happening over again.

"You can do this," said Lissa. "You can do this."

The officious young transplant woman was summoned with a beep and came bustling down the corridor, the fussiness in her face transformed, suddenly, into something like hope.

"Mrs. Mitchell?"

The woman nodded blankly. She sat by his bed again, stroking the beautiful, still-warm skin. "She made me come back."

"I didn't!" said Lissa. And looking at the boy, so close to sleeping, she could absolutely understand the instinctive horror at cutting him up, parceling him out, using him for parts.

"Give me the thing to sign," said Mrs. Mitchell. "Quickly please. I don't want to change my mind again."

The nurse brought the paperwork over. "You have to understand—"

"That it's binding, yes, yes, I know that. Quick, I said!"

"No," said the transplant nurse, straightening up. "I just really want you to understand. What you are doing is the bravest, the most wonderful thing you can do."

Mrs. Mitchell stared at her, her mouth hanging open. "You sound," she said, "like you want me to be *pleased*."

Chapter 8

Kim-Ange was up and waiting for Lissa, after she'd pulled off her clothes, taken out her contacts, put on her thick, black-rimmed glasses, and gotten into her tracksuit bottoms. Lissa couldn't deny being pleased to see her. Living in the nurses' home, while hardly the lap of luxury—it was a grimy old sixties block near the hospital—was still much cheaper than trying to rent privately in London, or even getting the train in every day from where her parents lived in Hertfordshire, and it had the added benefit, even if it was noisy and the showers were peeling and the kitchens got very grim, of there always being someone to talk to if you'd had a bad day. A really, really, really bad day.

Kim-Ange had her hands up.

"I know," she said, her face a mask of sadness. She was holding up a bottle of some mysterious plum-colored substance. That was the good thing and bad thing about nurses' homes: word got around.

"It was Ezra's . . ."

"I know that too." Kim-Ange swallowed. "He's been seeing Yazzie."

"Ah," said Lissa, even in her exhaustion and misery registering that Ezra had been spreading himself around the exact same place she actually lived.

She felt utterly hollow inside.

Kim-Ange waved the bottle. "Come try this."

Ever since she'd found an old cocktail cabinet in a dumpster that she'd hoicked home single-handedly, Kim-Ange had been on a mission to invent something new, which meant experimenting with a lot of things that were disgusting. Lissa didn't care that evening, though.

"So, how bad are you feeling about it?" said Kim-Ange, eyeing her shrewdly. "Tracksuit bottoms bad? I mean, you know other people can see you."

Kim-Ange had extremely high sartorial standards. She herself was wearing a long pink-and-red nightdress, matching robe, marabou slippers, and a full face of makeup.

"Yes," said Lissa. "It was a hit-and-run. Possibly deliberate. Fifteen years old."

"It barely made the news," said Kim-Ange.

Lissa sighed. "Give me the purple elixir of joy and/or misery then," she said, holding out her mug, and Kim-Ange filled it up. "Oh my God, that's revolting," Lissa choked out, collapsing onto her bed. Then she took another sip. "Still bad."

There was a pause and she tried again.

"Okay, now it's not so bad."

"There we are," said Kim-Ange, pleased. "A three-sipper. One of my best yet!" She started absent-mindedly folding Lissa's clothes.

"They're going to call me in too," said Lissa after a while.

"Disciplinary, I think. I didn't get out of the way of the doctors. I messed up with the transplant protocol."

"You stopped a transplant?!"

"No, I made one happen."

"Oh, that is terrible." Kim-Ange snorted. "And don't tell me, did you have a baby doctor who didn't know his arse from his elbow and couldn't tap a vein in either of them?"

"No, I crossed the line," said Lissa.

"Thank God there's such a plethora of highly trained para-medical staff they could fill your job from," said Kim-Ange, looking mischievous.

Lissa half smiled. "How short are they at the moment?"

"Four grade eights," said Kim-Ange. "Haha, they'll never get rid of you. I mean, seriously. What else did you do? Did you have full sex in the ambulance?"

"*Kim-Ange!*"

"I'll take that as a maybe."

"No!"

"Did you steal the car afterward?"

Lissa bit her lip. "Stop it."

"No, seriously, I am trying to work out ways they'd actually let you go. Did you make the ambulance stop at the KFC drive-through on the way to the hospital?"

"No."

"There you go then. It'll be a telling-off."

"I hate those too."

Kim-Ange rolled her eyes. "That's right, terrifying NHS management sitting on their fat arses ticking boxes all day.

They are pretty tough and scary, right enough. I heard they don't even cry when they get a paper cut."

"Tell me about your day," said Lissa, changing the subject. "Hang on, didn't you have a date tonight?"

Kim-Ange approached Tinder with more or less as much tenacity as her job in cardiology. *"Hmm,"* she said.

"Oh no!" Lissa scrolled down her phone. "But look at you on Insta! You look amazing!"

"I do," said Kim-Ange.

Lissa looked at her, then back at the picture, then up at Kim-Ange again. "Stop doing that!"

"What?" said Kim-Ange innocently.

"Giving yourself a waist. It looks really weird."

"Beautiful weird?"

"I'm taking FaceTune off your phone. You have gone *too far.* You look like a shark has bitten a chunk out of you."

"Piss off!"

"You're beautiful as you are," said Lissa. "So, don't tell me. He was a shark-bite fetishist and then you turned up *without* a chunk out of you?"

"No." Kim-Ange sighed. "He just kept going on and on about kimchi."

"Oh, you're kidding," said Lissa. "Did you tell him you're from Margate?"

"Yup. That's when he started telling me I really ought to get to know my own culture."

Lissa laughed and rolled over on the bed, stuffing her face into her pillow. "*No!* Know-your-culture bro strikes again! *Nooo!!*"

Kim-Ange checked her waist in the mirror and breathed in, quite hard.

"What else did he say?" said Lissa from behind the pillow.

"Oh! He went to Cambodia on his gap year."

"So?"

"So! Obviously I would want to hear *all about that*!"

Lissa screwed up her face, then pulled out her phone. "Oh well. Let's see what everyone else is up to."

"You mean, let's see where everyone else is FaceTuning themselves."

"And lip-filler watch."

"On it," said Kim-Ange, and she refilled their glasses with the filthy purple alcohol and they sat down and scrolled through the absurdly overfiltered pictures of everyone they'd ever known, and then for good measure they made their own ridiculously overfiltered FaceTuned pic that turned them both into busty size 6s with giant fish lips, stuck their figures onto a background of a golden beach, and posted it. Immediately the likes started pouring in.

"Oh, for *God's* sake," said Lissa, rolling her eyes.

"Now everyone's going to ask me how Hawaii was," said Kim-Ange, getting up to go to bed.

"Tell them you got sponsored by a luxury holiday site to go for free for the 'Gram," suggested Lissa.

"I will, I will." And Kim-Ange kissed her on the cheek and Lissa went to bed, feeling slightly better, or, at least, a little drunk.

Chapter 9

Cormac wasn't entirely disappointed to notice that Emer had gone by the time he got home. There was a text on his phone he didn't read the whole of, but it definitely included the phrase "you're like a really shit Batman." He was pondering this when, for the third time that evening, Jake rang.

Cormac hurried out into the street.

"That was quick," said Jake suspiciously. "I take it she left."

"Don't you start," said Cormac.

"Ah," said Jake. "The thing about lady problems is . . ."

"Don't start," said Cormac. "And for the third time, *I'm not even on call.*"

"I know," Jake said, and tried, and failed, to suppress a smile.

Cormac gave him a sideways look. It wasn't like any call to be great fun. Unless, in Jake's case, a supermodel had gotten herself stuck in the bath or something ridiculous like that. "What?"

"I thought you might like this one."

"*What?*"

"It's your young Islay."

Cormac's heart started beating extremely quickly. "What about her?"

"It's only come up. Ten minutes ago."

"You are *kidding*," said Cormac.

Jake shook his head. "Nope. Some poor kid down south."

"The right age?"

"Fifteen."

"Oh God," said Cormac. Then: "*Oh God.*"

"I know." Jake whistled through his teeth. "I never thought we'd get there."

Heart and lung transplants were so rare, and the chances of success so slim, that the heart was transplanted only into patients who desperately needed it.

"It's the right size: he was tiny. Couple more years growing, and they can do it together."

Cormac had watched the clock run down on patients before, had been fully expecting it to happen again.

"Chuffing hell," he said. "That is absolutely *brilliant* news."

"Want to come with me to get her?" said Jake.

Cormac did. And he clasped his hand on Jake's shoulder as they climbed into the van, Tim the silent driver pulling away.

LISSA COULDN'T SLEEP.

Outside the nurses' block, with its single-glazed windows, was the ongoing sound of London, rumbling away. Normally Lissa didn't mind it, quite liked it, in fact: the steady, reassuring noise of lorry deliveries; bottles being recycled from pubs; bin pickups; sirens; shouting. It was the city she'd been born in, the city she'd always known. It was her lullaby.

But tonight, it was getting right on her nerves, as she lay there, eyes dry and wide, wondering how many other Kais were out there, how many other boys wouldn't make it home to their mothers.

Normally in her job she followed people into their homes. Alive people who got better, hopefully, or at least reached a stage of acceptance and learned to deal with whatever hand of cards they'd been dealt.

This had happened the wrong way around, and all she could see was a dripping pool of blood and wide staring eyes and someone who could have been her brother, could have been anyone she'd been at school with . . .

Every lorry stopping on the road sounded like danger; a car's screeching brakes made her stiffen. She could feel the adrenaline shoot through her, without warning, feel it spurting through her system even as one bit of her was chanting, *Must rest, must rest,* and her phone glowed on the table, counting down the minutes until she had to get up; even as she could see the sky lightening through her cheap, thin standard-issue curtains. She groaned, turned over in bed, stuffed her head under the pillow, feeling simultaneously grimly alert and as if all her limbs were pinned down by stones, and the night ground on.

Chapter 10

Joan had arrived by the time the boys got back there to Islay's house. All the lights were blazing in the quiet village street. Mrs. Murray, who ran the village shop, lived next door and had gotten up to see what all the fuss was about, just in case she missed any vitally important gossip.

She didn't consider what she did to be gossip, but instead an intensely important life force to the surrounding area and, in fact, a moral source for good, practically heroic—hence her standing in her eiderdown dressing gown outside her (spotless) front step at one o'clock in the morning. Plus, everyone had known wee Islay from a bairn, knew it wisnae fair, the poor lass. When all the other kids were running themselves ragged down at Zahira's nursery, she'd had to be kept home like a china doll sat on a shelf, never moving, jumping, running— everything children wanted to do. She was made of porcelain and couldn't be let out. It was a real hardship, to live somewhere as beautiful as Kirrinfief, which had the loch close by, the mountains, and as much freedom and space to play in as a child could dream of, and be stuck indoors all the time watching TV or playing with her iPad.

And here were all the medical folk of the town—Joan *and* Cormac *and* Jake—as well, my goodness, a full house. But they were smiling and chatting and everyone was excited, and the next minute out came Islay herself, being wheeled on a stretcher, sitting up, a tube in her nose to keep her blood supplied with oxygen.

"I can't believe it," Islay's mother was saying, clutching her hands to her chest. Gregor, her dad, was blinking hard, trying to shush her, that it was very early days, that these things weren't always a definite, that there were false alarms.

"Wheels up!" shouted Jake into his walkie-talkie, face beaming.

"Och, listen to you," said Cormac, helping him wheel the bed. "With your fancy language! What are you, on *Air Force One?*"

"They're sending a plane with the heart in it."

"Who is?"

"British Airways! They volunteered!"

"They volunteered to fly here?"

"I think they had to move a plane," said Jake. "Anyway, they're rushing it."

Cormac shook his head. "That's amazing. That's just amazing."

He patted Islay on the shoulder.

"Can you believe this? They're rolling the red carpet right out for you."

They hopped in the ambulance, Jake in the front, Cormac and Islay's parents in the back. Even though Islay was thirteen, she was still clinging to an old, raggedy toy seal she must have had since she was a baby.

Jake had every new gadget on his phone and pulled up an app that identified planes that flew overhead. They ignored him at first, then gathered around, in amazement, watching as the only flight in the air at that hour—BA 978, noted as "special cargo"—blipped its way up the country from London. They fell into silence. Jake gave the phone to Islay to hold and started up the ambulance.

THE TRIP THROUGH the pitch-black countryside seemed to take forever. Jake had the headlights on high beam, given the unlikeliness of bumping into anyone—at least until 4:30, when the farmers started getting up—and every hedgerow, it seemed, contained a pair of suddenly glowing eyes. Creatures stirred by the road: hooting owls, a shiver of starlings taking off from a tree, a quick rustling in the gorse or the high grass as small creatures rumbled through, past almost before you knew it. Cormac imagined the ambulance, the only little pool of light in the whole world, as it shot past distant darkened farmhouses and vast fields of sleeping cows, one occasionally stirring itself sleepily to watch as the precious cargo sped by; the animals of the Highlands, it felt to Cormac—ridiculously, of course—standing aside respectfully to let them through, nothing standing in their way, as a girl sat on a bed, tracing a plane through the night skies.

Chapter 11

The sun rose at six A.M., approaching the March equinox, and Cormac was there to see it, partly because he'd gotten caught up in making sure the operation went all right and partly because he had to wait for Jake, who had to sleep an acceptable amount of time before he was allowed to drive the ambulance back again.

He didn't mind. He'd sat with the parents for a while, then, as Joan was still back in Kirrinfief, he took the calls from the hospital office in London, after explaining who he was. He was a little intimidated, talking to the world-class teaching hospital—it felt a little like taking an exam—but he explained as much of Islay's backstory and state of mind as he could and felt he was more or less doing all right.

The plane had landed at a little after one o'clock, and another ambulance was dispatched and sent screaming through the streets, with absolutely no cares whom it woke in the process.

Cormac had watched as they'd jumped out the back, running. The icebox was so small, so inconsequential looking. It looked like nothing, even as it contained the whole world.

How amazing. And also the sheer luck: the tissue matching,

the exactness of the match. He watched as they dashed in, said a wee prayer. Wondered, briefly, about the person who had sacrificed his life to give it, and to think how very, very lucky they were. Or should be.

LISSA GAVE UP at six. It was light. She closed her heavy, crusty eyes, opened them again, and thought at least she could get in first in the shower, wash it all away. That was one good thing about the nurses' accommodations: it was triumphantly overheated, which meant almost limitless amounts of hot water, as long as you didn't mind the low water pressure that made it dribble.

She stood under the shower, hair tied up, for as long as she could. She probably should have turned it to cold to wake herself up, but she couldn't bear it. Her whole body hung down. She was weary and bedraggled and grimy to her bones, even as she stood in the shower, and was absolutely dreading the case meeting, whatever Kim-Ange said.

Chapter 12

The next week was awful for Lissa. She received a written warning, but more than that, she could see people pointing and talking about her. The young doctor had apparently been furious.

She tried to bury herself in her work and going out with friends. But she couldn't sleep. Not at all. Every time she lay down, she saw that young boy's beautiful face bleeding out. She heard herself screaming at him, saw the ambulance lights flash against the wet pavement. She called Ezra, but he wasn't answering anyone. She couldn't blame him.

During her years in A&E, she'd become hardened to practically anything. But when it was someone you knew: that was different. She got crankier and more careless, was so exhausted she was in tears half the time; not even Kim-Ange could cheer her up, even when she dated a man who liked to go to conventions dressed as a rhinoceros and wanted to know whether Kim-Ange had ever considered doing the same and whether she would like to.

Lissa felt sick, but that was nothing new these days. Beyond not sleeping well at all, she felt her heart race at the smallest thing. She wasn't doing well at work either; she could tell. Her regulars had all noticed and remarked upon it, missing her normal cheery demeanor.

But the spark had gone out of her. She was terrified of everything now: loud noises, even the ambulance sirens she heard every five minutes going in and out of hospitals; sudden movements. It felt like her heart was bursting out of her chest; every time she tried to get some rest, she was bolt upright again, in agony. She tried sleeping pills, but they made her feel worse, foggy and disconnected, and she was scared she'd be asked to drive the car while taking them.

Kai's funeral was exactly what Lissa had feared: a massive community outburst of misery and sadness and rage. His entire school, his church, and the whole of his housing development, it seemed, turned up to pay their respects, singing and crying, spilling out of the large church and onto the street. It was a paroxysm of agony and grief, even as his mother tried to stay dignified and the pastor tried to calm the anger obvious in the crowd at the terrible waste. Ezra didn't even look at her.

At the church she linked arms with Kim-Ange, whose large presence was always a comfort. Today Kim-Ange's hair was bright burgundy, but thankfully she was wearing black rather than the orange and purple she favored. Okay, it was a fuzzy-wuzzy coat that made her look like an enormous black bear, but Lissa found it comforting nevertheless and leaned in as they approached the incredibly busy church. You could hear the hubbub a mile away. Traffic had stopped. People were standing crying in the street.

They found a tiny spot on a pew. Nobody ever liked to budge up to Kim-Ange. This bothered Kim-Ange not a bit, and she scooched her sizable bottom along the pew as far as she could and patted the seat beside her.

"Come on, darling."

Lissa sat down. She was trembling and checked her pocket with the tissues, just to make sure it was all right. She was going through a lot of tissues these days.

There was a lot of noise and hustle and bustle; it seemed half the world was there. But suddenly there was a hush, as the doors at the back of the church opened. It was like a wedding, Lissa thought, her heart racing. Only of course so, so wrong.

The choir stood to the side, their numbers absolutely packed too. On a note, very softly and sweetly they began to gently sing, "Swing low, sweet chariot," and the pallbearers began a slow, long march down the aisle, carrying a pure white coffin.

Lissa collapsed. She was sobbing so hard she couldn't breathe. This wasn't her boy, wasn't her tragedy. She was drawing attention to herself. This was awful, completely inappropriate. People were looking at her crossly, and she didn't know what to do, even as she sounded louder than the choir. Someone tutted. Righteous and noisy grief was expected from contemporaries, and family, and young people. Not from a thirty-year-old young professional who didn't even know the family.

Kim-Ange looked at her, made a decision, and half dragged, half hauled her outside and set her down, quite roughly, on a park bench. There were still mourners trying to get in who watched them with interest.

"Breathe," said Kim-Ange, and when Lissa didn't respond, she pushed her head between her knees. "Breathe!"

The brusque tone, oddly, was just what Lissa needed. Being told what to do without having to think about it. The panic attack was intense, but gradually, her heart rate slowed, the blood came to her head, and she started to feel ever so slightly better.

"Sister," said Kim-Ange, rubbing Lissa's back as she finally came back to herself, "this cannot go on. This absolutely cannot go on. Also the walls in our rooms are really thin and I can hear you getting up and pacing about half the night and it's extremely annoying. But I am mostly thinking about you. Although also, when you have a shower at five A.M., you make a lot of noise. But also, for you, this cannot go on."

Chapter 13

Lissa liked the HR director, Valerie Mnotse, always had; she considered her a friend and mentor, supportive of her career choices when working in the community was often seen as second best.

Valerie got it. She understood the importance of connecting the hospital with the people who used it, and how the better the care they got at home, the less likely they were to boomerang straight back to the hospital and clog up A&E, whether because they were so endlessly confused with the labyrinthine system or because they felt bad but couldn't get a GP appointment. But this morning, Valerie looked grave.

"Health care in London is always difficult," she started carefully.

Lissa was about to fire back that she wasn't burned out, she was fine, she was a good nurse, she knew she was . . . but she found, suddenly, that she couldn't get the words out—couldn't get any words out—because she was going to cry again.

No. She couldn't. She couldn't cry in front of Valerie, the most immaculate, punctilious woman she knew. She had to be strong. She'd defied her family to go to nursing school, get her university qualifications. She'd done it by herself and worked in some of the toughest, most deprived wards in the entire country, in the whole of Europe. She could do it. She could . . .

"It's all right to cry," said Valerie, pushing over a box of tissues.

Lissa felt the tears leak down her face and was furious with herself. If she showed weakness, they were going to move her, she knew it. Lissa nodded slowly as Valerie picked up her phone.

"Could you send Juan in? Thanks."

A slight man Lissa had seen around came in, looking neutral and nodding to her. She was terrified suddenly. "What's happening? Am I getting fired?"

"No, you're not getting fired," said Valerie. "If we had the resources, we'd sign you off. But we don't."

"I don't need to be signed off! I'm fine!"

"We think," said Juan softly, "that you might need to recalibrate."

"That I might need to what?"

"We want you to see someone," said Juan. "We've assigned you a counselor from Occupational Health. And . . ."

"We think maybe a quieter beat," said Valerie. "Just for three months. Just to give you a chance to breathe, to have another look at your approach."

"We really feel this program works well," said Juan. "We're desperately trying not to lose you. You must see that."

He handed her a leaflet with pictures of lovely rolling green fields on it, sun going down behind some cows.

"What's this?" said Lissa sullenly.

"Just . . . about your options. We do swaps with rural practitioners who want to broaden their skills. Like a student exchange."

"I'm not a student!"

"We've found the program mutually beneficial," said Juan.

"Lissa," said Valerie quite firmly, "I'd highly recommend you give it some very serious thought."

Chapter 14

Islay's recovery was going well, and Cormac called the London hospital to update them. Transplants happened in total secrecy and Cormac knew better than to ask. But what accident involving a fifteen-year-old could be anything other than a dreadful tragedy?

Instead he conveyed as soberly as possible that patient B had come through the operation and was currently in intensive care; that the prognosis was good, maybe even extremely good; and that everything was proceeding as usefully as possible.

The voice at the other end of the phone paused. "And you're the NPL?" he said, looking something up on his computer.

"Uh-huh," said Cormac.

"Cormac MacPherson?"

"Aye."

"Because I'm looking at your HR form here."

"Are you now," said Cormac, instantly wary.

"You haven't always been an NPL, have you?"

Cormac hesitated. He hadn't been expecting this at all. "No. I was an army medic. Why?"

"Have you heard of the exchange program?"

"The what?"

"The three-month exchange program. You could move up a grade. We have a place opening up here."

"I'm not moving to London!"

"The idea is to bolster the skills of people in different areas. So if you've always worked in a rural district, you might benefit from some more acute specialization, that kind of thing. And vice versa."

"You mean you're looking for somewhere to dump your burnouts," said Cormac tartly. He might live in a village, but he wasn't its idiot.

There was a wry chuckle at the other end of the line. "I think you'd be good down here," came the voice. "Let me send you the brochure."

"Aye, whatever," said Cormac, who then hung up and thought no more about it.

He headed home and had a long shower. He found himself missing having someone to talk to, the black-humored camaraderie of the army. He wondered if the London front lines were like that. Probably.

He went out into the village to pick up some of the good local butter they did up at Lennox's farm. Lennox wasn't much of a talker, but the farm produce was spot-on. He picked up some local bacon too. It would make quite the sandwich.

KIRRINFIEF WAS A village arranged around a central cobbled square, with a war memorial in the middle, Eck's pub on the corner, Mrs. Murray's general store, a hunting and fishing shop, three antique/bits-and-bobs stores, a bakery, and, most days, a little bus that stopped to sell books. It was nestled in the hills, hidden away near Loch Ness but not on the main tourist routes. Any tourists who did stumble upon it, though, were generally taken by its atmosphere—an air of a timeless place, a Brigadoon—which wouldn't last long as soon as they heard old Eck and Wullie shouting from outside the pub, although they meant well really. The sleeper train from London to Fort William ran close by; otherwise, Kirrinfief was a haven of peace and tranquility, and that was just how people liked it. Well. Mostly.

Cormac stalked across the square. It was a cold but sunny day; too early for lambing, but a few ambitious crocuses were pushing their way up in between the cobbles. He got three steps before an old lady stopped him. "Ooh, Cormac, what was all that kerfuffle with young Islay?"

He smiled politely. "Och, you know I canny talk about that, Mrs. Norrie."

"Yes, well, everybody already knows," she said rather sniffily.

"Well then."

Mrs. Murray in the shop was even more direct. "Why did I see that young Emer in here earlier sniffing and buying three bars of Dairy Milk?" she said. "That's not like her, young slim thing that she is. Three! Were they for you?"

"No," said Cormac.

"Well then," said Mrs. Murray, as if that proved something. "How's your ma?"

"She's good," said Cormac slowly. He hadn't seen her in a

fortnight, which was a long time around here. His brother Rawdon had been commended for something, and she'd wanted to
talk about that in a rather emphatic way.

"Still fussing you about your job?"

"I'll just take this cheese," said Cormac, smiling heartily.
The shop was so overstuffed with things he had to lean over the
counter away from the newspapers. "Thanks, Mrs. Murray."

"Oh well," said Mrs. Murray, who took rather a lot quite
personally, as Cormac escaped.

He got home to an email from London. The brochure had
a picture of bright high skyscrapers. "Secondments in a fast-
moving environment!" he read. "Experience a high-paced community in central London and sharpen your clinical skills!"

Cormac had been to central London with a girlfriend long
ago. They'd gone to the Imperial War Museum; eaten at a steak
house, where they'd had to sit in the window and get gawked
at by other tourists and where the food was absolutely awful;
then gone to see a West End show about a lady murderer that
had made him fall asleep fifteen minutes in. That relationship
hadn't lasted much longer either.

Chapter 15

Valerie had sent Lissa home for the day—which was anxiety-creating enough in itself—and Lissa found the crowds on Tottenham Court Road rather overwhelming. She stumbled over the vast, polluted Euston Road, escaping the honking into the relative quiet of Regent's Park. It was too warm for this early in the spring. It should have felt good, the sunshine, but it didn't: it felt ominous and scary, as if the world were shifting and changing beneath her feet. Every teenage boy she passed, every loud laugh he made, shoving around with his mates, crowding her off the pavement, playing his music too loud—every single one made her flinch, made her want to grab him, hard, shout at him in his face to be safe, to keep safe, to stay indoors, to not draw attention to himself.

But they were teenage boys. It was part of their makeup to yell, to beef, to get into each other's faces. They felt invincible. Indeed, their towering size, their massive trainers; they *looked* invincible.

But they were as fragile as day-old lambs.

Lissa hurried on. She could feel her breathing speeding up again, her heart pounding in her chest, and tried to calm herself down. She sat near a bright wave of daffodils, concentrated on breathing in through her nose and out through her mouth as much as she could, in and out, slowly and not rushing, trying to get her equilibrium back, even as she wanted to scream, to scream to everyone: *The world isn't safe. It isn't safe.*

She swallowed hard. Maybe Valerie and Juan were right. She couldn't work like this, couldn't think like this. But it would pass, wouldn't it? Would it?

She took out the leaflet they had given her. With its soothing view of rolling hills, it looked more like a funeral-planning leaflet. Oh God. The funeral. She couldn't bear it. If she felt this bad, what on earth was life like now for his mother? How did you go on? How could anybody go on?

She turned open the leaflet.

Chapter 16

Jake and Cormac went to have a pint in the pub, nodding hello to Eck and Wullie and petting the cheerful sheepdog who lived there and who appeared in perfect and glossy health despite living on a major dietary supplement of beer nuts and pickled onion crisps. It was a chilly evening, but the sun had come down purple in the sky, which was a pretty sight to render anyone more or less cheerful about the world. They'd even persuaded their friend Lennox in for half an hour, although it would literally be half an hour, and he'd be glancing at his watch for half of it. He had a wee lad at home and wouldn't miss bath time for the world.

Jake was staring at Cormac, aghast.

"Run this past me again," he said. "They're offering you cheap accommodation in the middle of London for three months *and* a London bonus on your pay packet, to hang out in London, work a bit, and do whatever the hell you want, without every old lady you meet in the street asking if you wouldn't mind looking up her bum?"

Cormac frowned. "They don't do that."

"Mrs. MacGonnagall does that!"

"She does, aye." Cormac drained his pint.

"Seriously, you're so lucky. They should do that scheme with ambulance drivers!"

"Ha, that'd be a lot of use."

"What do you mean?"

"'Hello, welcome to London, off you go to Oxford Street . . .' 'Och, aye, sorry, where would that be now?'"

Jake sighed. "Oh. Aye. Even more reason why you'd be absolutely mad not to go. The women in London, oh my God."

"How do you know?"

Jake shrugged. "In the papers, aye?"

Cormac looked at him suspiciously, but Jake was refusing to look his way. "Have you been reading *Grazia* again?"

Jake sniffed. "This is the chance of a lifetime, man. Kirrinfief, it's all right."

In the corner, Eck's dog let out a massive fart right next to the fire then looked around with an innocent expression on, as if it couldn't possibly have been him.

"Uh-huh."

"But *London*! On a cheap rent! Hot summers and amazing women and everything going on and famous people and stuff off the telly and that!"

"Well, I'll be working."

"Yeah. Looking after hot models with toe injuries from wearing really, really high heels," said Jake sadly, who had clearly given this quite an astonishing amount of thought. "Seriously, mate. You're insane. You'll be back in three months. What's going to change for you in three months?"

Cormac stared out the window. The clouds had been low today. Rain threatened for tomorrow. Being somewhere sunny with models in it suddenly seemed rather exciting.

"Plus, you know, since you got back . . ."

Cormac gave him a sharp look. "What are you saying?"

"Nothing," said Jake hastily. You didn't talk about Cormac leaving the army. You just didn't. "I just mean, it's quiet."

Cormac looked at Lennox, who as usual wasn't saying much. "What do you think?"

That was a pretty stupid question. Lennox had been to agricultural college, then come straight back to the farm he'd been born on. The most surprising thing Lennox had ever done was get together with the clever nerdy English girl who ran the local bookshop, and even then she'd been renting one of his farm buildings. Literally all he'd had to do was fall across the road.

Lennox shrugged. "Not for me," he said, to absolutely nobody's surprise.

Above the crackling fire, the old clock ticked mournfully on.

"But you're just a bairn. You've no ties, nothing holding you back. Why wouldn't you?" He stood up. "And send me back some lads, will you? Brexit's put a bloody big hole in my harvesting teams, I'll tell you that for nothing."

And with that he put down his glass, smiled, and went home to his lovely Nina and their perfect darling baby boy, deeply happy in his soul that as far as he was concerned he never need decide to go anywhere else other than home ever again.

Part II

Chapter 17

There are few places lonelier than a crowded station platform five hundred miles away from home, where you know nobody but a lot of people are trying to get past you, or get you out of the way.

Cormac had taken the sleeper train down. He thought he wouldn't sleep, given he had so much to think about, but the comfortable bed and the rocking motion of the carriage, as well as the nip of whisky he'd bought from the onboard bar, had all combined to send him off into a surprisingly deep sleep, punctuated by dreams that had him swimming or riding a horse—anything involving motion.

Euston station at 7:30 in the morning was absolutely heaving: grimy with dirt, full of smartly dressed people moving—why did they all have to walk so fast?

He looked around them, standing under a huge four-faced clock, feeling ridiculously out of place. He must have stood out a mile to anyone with his freckled complexion, his messy sandy-brown hair, his corduroy trousers. Perhaps he would have to rethink the trousers. His mum had bought them for him, telling him that's what everyone wore in Edinburgh. Why she

thought Edinburgh was the height of fashion sophistication
he wasn't entirely sure. Nobody here was wearing corduroy.
She was happy he had gone anyway. It wasn't easy, bearing the
weight of his mother's disappointment. Another good reason to
take some time away.

Anyway, everyone here was wearing expensive suits or
skinny jeans or baggy pants and all sorts of weird and wonderful colors you didn't see much of in Kirrinfief. And Jake hadn't,
it turned out, been lying about the women; some of them did
indeed look like models, all made up, with bright blond or pink
or blue hair, strange eyebrows (Cormac was not the expert on
eyebrows), and incredibly outlandish clothes. The whole thing
was bewildering. How did all these people know where they
were going? Why didn't they all bang into each other? Why were
they all holding to-go cups with green drinks in them?

Cormac scratched his chin and slowly—clumsily, rather, with
his heavy rucksack—went in search of a London Underground
map, narrowly missing clouting a tiny girl clip-clopping her
way around him, who let out a sigh louder and more pointed
than he would have expected from such a small woman.

KIM-ANGE HAD GIVEN her a big kiss as Lissa set off.

"Into exile," Lissa had moaned, looking sadly around the
little room she was leaving behind.

"Don't be stupid," said Kim-Ange, bundling a cake into
Lissa's bag. "It's not for long! It'll be an adventure."

"I'm being suspended," said Lissa. "They never want me back."

"Of course they do," said Kim-Ange. "You're definitely the second-best nurse on this floor."

Lissa rolled her eyes. "Oh God," she said. "I've never lived in the countryside. What's it going to be like?"

"Think of it this way," said Kim-Ange. "When anyone phones you don't want to, you can just tell them your reception is cutting out."

Lissa nodded. "I suppose."

Kim-Ange hugged her. "Honestly. It'll be great. Peace and quiet. Get some sleep. Read some books. Build a massive Instagram brand of you looking at misty moors. Think of it as a holiday. And come back and be fabulous with me please. *And* think of me. I'm the one that's going to get some wittering country idiot being Scotch next to me!"

Lissa managed a wan smile. "I'm sure he'll be perfectly nice."

"*Oh*, you're sure. You're sure, are you? I don't even want a boy on this floor." She sniffed noisily, and Lissa gave her a hug.

"Thanks, Kim-Ange," she said.

"The sacrifices I make! You'll miss me every day!"

"I will miss you every day," promised Lissa, and meant it.

Chapter 18

Lissa looked at the paperwork again, carefully, anxiously, so terrified she'd get something wrong. She was taking on the caseload of one Cormac MacPherson, who was also lending her his home.

They each had a secure NHS log-in that they could exchange patient data on, only with each other, so they could achieve continuity of care, and would be expected to debrief every day for three months. They also had to write a weekly report for HR—apparently, she discovered, they were guinea pigs for the entire scheme. At the bottom of the first page, Juan had added, "Good luck, Lissa—I think this will be a wonderful experience."

Lissa was not thinking this. Not at all. She felt banished, pied off, reduced to being put out of sight out of mind, as if she'd gone crazy and needed to be hidden out of the way. She loved London; it was the air she breathed. The idea of being stuck out in the country was ridiculous.

She'd googled Cormac MacPherson, but his Facebook page was private and gave absolutely nothing away. He didn't seem to be on the internet much, which was strange enough in this day and age. She'd spent more time looking at Kirrinfief on Google Earth. It was tiny!

She'd never spent much time in the country; London was all she'd ever known. She'd never been to Scotland at all.

But Lissa needed—absolutely, desperately needed—the insomnia to stop, as well as the nightmares from when she finally drifted off into a shallow, tainted half-sleep. During the day she felt grit under her eyelids, and she could not control her breath when she saw a bunch of lads on the street or heard a shout or, worst of all, a car backfiring or accelerating. If going to this godforsaken place would help her get over that, then it was worth a shot. She would have vastly preferred to be at her granny's in Antigua, but that wasn't an option the NHS was notably keen on offering her. So the wild north it was.

Chapter 19

Cormac was, he rapidly realized, somehow just too big for London. He'd played rugby for the army, and it had never really left him. It wasn't just that he was tall, although he was—there were plenty of big-looking people; aye, there were plenty of people, full stop. More people, surely, he thought, than were strictly necessary or even viable. More people than you could figure out had gotten crammed into these hot, sticky streets that smelled of food and smoke and choking exhaust fumes. Didn't they notice how revolting the air was? Maybe not. London clung to you, put greasy fingerprints all over you.

The nurses' home was a tall, peeling eight-story building situated outside of a tube by a roundabout in what Cormac would learn to call South London.

There didn't appear to be any automatically obvious way to get through the roundabout, which was, on closer examination, actually two roundabouts, each with four lanes of traffic. The air was a haze. Cormac thought back to what he had imagined he'd find the first time he came to London. It had definitely involved lots of parks with swans in them. And also, Buckingham Palace.

He sighed and tried several times to reach the block through subway passages lined with people asleep on flattened cardboard boxes, in filthy sleeping bags, and finally made it to Nightingale House. The glass was security protected. He rang the bell, and a large man saw him from inside and buzzed him in.

"Hi," said Cormac nervously. "I'm the secondment for . . ." For a split second he forgot her name. "Alyssa Westcott? I'm taking over her room?"

The man stared at him, unperturbed, then ran his finger down a grubby list of printed names.

"Neh," he said.

Cormac looked to the side, then tried again. "I'm not Alyssa," he said. "I'm Cormac MacPherson."

There was another very long pause.

"Yeh," said the man, lifting a heavy finger from the page and sighing deeply.

"So, youse having a good day?" said Cormac cheerily.

The man looked at him, humphing as he got out of his chair—which creaked alarmingly—and stretched up to a long line of keys.

"I just got down on the sleeper. Didn't think I'd sleep much, but actually it was great . . ." Cormac left space at the end of his sentence, but the man wasn't responding. This was very odd.

In Kirrinfief, if you went up to Inverness for the afternoon that would provoke a fairly long conversation in the grocers about what you'd seen and whom you'd met and whether you'd been to the big cinema, which had something called a Nando's. Going on the sleeper was a next-level adventure; it would have involved the input and discussion of anyone in the shop. The train had narrowly avoided a crash about three years ago and people still talked about it.

By contrast, this man didn't respond at all, as if Cormac weren't there or hadn't said anything.

"So, anyway. It's . . . Well, this place looks interesting . . ." Cormac was stuttering on, but in an increasingly confused fashion. He felt like a dog wagging his tail and getting roundly ignored. He was just making conversation, that was all, what people did. What was this guy's problem?

The man grunted and put down a set of keys and gave him a bunch of forms to fill in, all the while avoiding eye contact. Perhaps, Cormac thought, there was something wrong with him. Yes. That had to be it.

He handed over his passport for photocopying and paid the deposit, worrying again whether he'd left the cottage clean and tidy enough for the girl who was moving in there.

Lined with old random chairs, the lobby was the kind of place that smelled of smoke even though nobody had been allowed to smoke in there for years. Cormac leafed through an old copy of *Nursing Times* while the man, still ignoring him rather than making conversation like a human being, shifted his bulk around photocopying and laboriously noting down all of Cormac's details. It couldn't be pleasant, Cormac decided, being trapped inside that booth all day.

Meanwhile, the bell buzzed and nurses came and went, loud and confident. He was used to being surrounded by women doing this job, but this was a lot by even his standards. Cormac felt slightly intimidated. Where he'd done his training, everyone had been local, more or less, and he'd known a couple of people from school and everyone was friendly. This looked like a glamorous menagerie of bold, colorful women calling, laughing, with a mix of great barking accents, saying, "Yeah, awight," and sounding like they were on *EastEnders* or from across the world. He tried not to stare. It was more different types of people than he'd ever seen.

A few people gave him a glance as they passed, but most of them assumed he was someone's boyfriend, a visitor waiting for someone. He wondered whom he'd be living next to.

Finally the man inside the glass box grunted and pushed his paperwork back toward him.

"Which room?" asked Cormac, figuring that surely this was the one question that would need an actual spoken answer, but the man only put a burly finger on a cheap plastic tag attached to one of the keys: 238.

"Brilliant," said Cormac, who was not normally a sarcastic person. "Thanks so much! For everything!"

But the man hadn't heard, or wouldn't hear, because this was London, and Cormac picked up his rucksack again and headed for the old creaking lift.

THERE WERE TWELVE rooms on either side of the central lift, with a large kitchen at each end—rather grotty—and two sets of bathrooms. The facility was obviously old, but the windows were big, looking out across the roundabout and onto North London and the river itself. Cormac fiddled with the lock and entered the little student room.

He didn't know what he'd expected—he supposed something left over—but the room was almost completely bare. There was a north-facing window, a single bed, a sink with a mirror above it, harsh-brown carpet, and a cheap wardrobe with a few hangers inside it. He worried then if he should have cleared everything out of the cottage—he'd left the books, the dishes, and the rugs. Was that not right? But it was only for three months; he wasn't clearing out his entire life.

This person had, though. There was nothing here at all.

Chapter 20

After such a long journey, Lissa was absolutely sure she'd gone too far, or at least was going around in circles. She could distantly appreciate the hills dotted with lambs, the deep blue of the loch, the shadows cast by the crags on the fields, the farmers out plowing new seed—she understood in the abstract that these things were nice—but looking through the dirty bus window was a bit like watching it on television, as if she were seeing it from a distance.

And now she was worried she'd missed her stop, and she would put any money on Uber not working out here, and everyone was looking at her funny (she was convinced) and the bus driver was trying to chat her up, and this was just awful and doing her anxiety no good at all.

Finally, after about half an hour, during which she simply sat on her hands, trying to breathe, trying not to let everything get on top of her, the bus driver, who'd been trying to engage her in conversation for the last forty minutes and didn't understand why she didn't know making conversation with the bus driver was very much the least you could do on a bus, stopped in Kirrinfief Square, where he normally liked to take a short break and buy a book, and smiled at his last passenger, the pretty girl with the curly hair who looked terrified.

"Come on noo, lass, you've made it!" he said encouragingly.

Lissa stared at him; she didn't understand a word. The driver nodded toward the door, and Lissa jumped up and sidled past him. Was this it? She lugged her heavy bag and jumped down the steps, ignoring the driver offering to take her case and not remembering to thank him either, which didn't change Iain's idea of English people one iota, frankly.

But Lissa was too nervous to care. She tried to shake herself. She never used to be like this! She'd traveled in South America one summer when she'd been a nursing student, traveled through strange countries, drunk tequila and danced in strange bars in strange neighborhoods. What had happened to that girl? In one terrible moment she had gone. In the scheme of things, of course, she was the lucky one. She felt guilty that she even felt bad, when she had lost nothing and others had lost everything.

But still. She missed that girl. Here she was in a little village in a perfectly safe environment, and the hand gripping her rolling suitcase was shaking.

LISSA MADE IT to the park bench. The sun was out, but the wind felt incredibly cold. You never really noticed the wind in London, except when you crossed the Thames. The Millennium Bridge, a short walk from the nurses' quarters, was always breezy.

Here on Kirrinfief's pretty, open cobbled square, she could

feel the full force of its chill and pulled her new puffer jacket closer around her. The houses were higgledy-piggledy, in gray stone, with doors that led right out onto the pavement; there wasn't a straight roof to be found. Smoke puffed out of several chimneys. There was a cozy old pub on the corner, with hanging baskets outside, and a bright red-painted grocers with mops and brooms propped up against the window. A pale blue bus was parked in the corner, selling books. Lissa tried to imagine sitting and reading a book again. It seemed incredibly unlikely, managing to slow her brain down, managing to concentrate for long enough without breaking the spell. And she couldn't read anything triggering or upsetting . . .

Something else lost.

She looked at her watch. The local GP was supposed to be meeting her, talking her through the job. Bit of a jack-of-all-trades, by the sound of things, provisions being so patchy and far apart. In London it sometimes felt like there was a hospital every hundred yards. It didn't seem like that was the case here.

She looked around again, up the hill, where long streets of narrow terraced houses weaved their way upward, backed against the deep green of the mountains. To her left she could catch the sun glinting off Loch Ness. That was a bit mad. She wondered if it was rude to ask about the monster. She could see it was a pretty spot. But what did people *do* here? What on earth . . . How did you pass your days without restaurants and theaters and nightclubs and shopping and exhibitions and cocktail bars?

Suddenly, the oldest, dirtiest car Lissa had ever seen charged around the square at top speed. It was a big old Volvo in a very unappetizing shade of brown, and the back of it appeared to be full of straw and dogs. It screeched to a halt before her and a tall, imposing woman stepped out, wearing a tweed skirt and a dark green polo. She had fine features and her skin was weather-beaten, but she wore no makeup, her hair gray and cut into a bob, more or less. Lissa had the oddest sense looking at her that she hadn't changed her style since her first day at primary school. As premonitions go, she was spot-on. The dogs, meanwhile, were going berserk.

"*Hello!*" barked Dr. Joan Davenport.

Lissa frowned slightly and felt her heart rate jump up and her nerves pile in. "Um," said Lissa.

"Are you Alyssa Westcott?"

"Um, Lissa?"

Joan looked like she couldn't care less about that. "Well, you're my charge, it appears. I did ask for a boy."

Lissa was confused.

"Just my little joke! Never mind! Nobody reads, I get it, I get it."

"Are you the GP?" said Lissa, as Joan started around the vehicle.

"Huh? Well, of course. Did Cormac not explain?"

Lissa didn't know how to tell Joan that she'd been too anxious and full of worry to contact Cormac to ask the questions she needed to; she'd barely replied to his email at all, as if ignoring what was coming would somehow make it go away.

She shook her head, and Joan looked at her keenly. Her bluff manner wasn't put on—that was just who she was—but it didn't mean she wasn't perceptive.

"You've had a tough time," she observed.

Lissa dragged the bag behind her and stared at the ground. "I'm fine," she said. "I'm perfectly fit to work."

Joan glanced at her again. "Well, we'll try and keep your workload light. I'm sure they'll keep Cormac busy!"

Joan opened the back door of her ancient car and three scruffy terriers jumped out.

"Yesss!" she said, her tone instantly changing from brusque welcome to motherly concern.

"There we are, Montgomery, my angel! Jasper! Jasper! Come here, my lovely boy! Pepper! Pepper! Come here!"

But it was too late. All three dogs were immediately leaping up, covering Lissa with their mucky paws. She was frozen in fear. She had learned on her rounds to be very wary of dogs; many dogs in London were bred to be guard dogs and righteously defended their property whenever she walked up the path. And these hairy beasts seemed completely uncontrollable. As she tried to make them go down, she saw Joan looking at her, the stern face completely gone.

"Aren't they wonderful?" she said. "You're lucky. They like you."

Lissa did not feel in the least bit lucky as she attempted to gingerly pat one on its fuzzy head.

"You'd better get used to dogs if you're going to work a country beat," observed Joan.

And almost completely surrounded by panting dogs—a state

Joan appeared to consider entirely desirable—Lissa followed Joan up behind the square to a whitewashed stone house, separate from the others, with a brass plate on the wall announcing the GP surgery.

"Is it just you?" said Lissa, worried. "Do you take the dogs in?"

"No," said Joan. "Bloody Health and Safety."

She whistled, surprisingly loudly, and the dogs left Lissa alone and slunk around the back of the house. Lissa peered after them and saw a rather pretty medium-sized garden and three dog kennels. The idea of a GP surgery having a garden tickled her.

"And it's just you?"

Joan nodded. "Yes. Small population in the village, plus hamlets and homesteads. I spend a lot of time in the car, and so will you."

"Oh yes," said Lissa. "They said there'd be a car . . ."

She pondered Joan's terrible brown vehicle for a second. How bad was her car going to be? In fact, as Joan showed her behind the surgery, it was a perfectly nice little Ford.

"Of course you'll want to cycle most places," said Joan. "Lot easier than getting the cars up the road."

"Cycle?" said Lissa. "What about the drug box?"

"Try not to leave it by the postbox," said Joan dryly, "and I'm pretty sure you'll be fine."

They entered through the back into Joan's office, and she started riffling through her daily files, then looked up as she remembered something. "Are you going to need time off for therapy? How are they even doing that?"

Lissa winced even to hear the word. She wanted to shout, wanted to tell everyone: This wasn't the real her! She existed in the world! She was fun and carefree! The real her was cool! Not some traumatized wreck! Not, she realized, a patient. She looked after patients. The idea that she needed looking after . . . she couldn't bear it.

"I'm to see someone over Skype," she admitted grudgingly.

Joan sniffed loudly. "Of course, London would be full of therapists. Lots of crazy English. You know what you really need?"

Lots of people had told Lissa what they thought she needed— a love affair, to get drunk, to go on holiday, to fall in love, to travel the world— and she hadn't enjoyed any of that either. She weighed up what she thought Joan's response would be.

"Is it a dog?" she said.

Joan smiled. "Well, that and a bit of fresh air, I would say. Lots of walks, lots of being out in the countryside. That's a cure for just about anything."

Lissa looked out the window, where it had clouded over ominously. "Doesn't it rain all the time here?" she said.

"So what?" said Joan, stumped at the question.

She went back to her files and pulled some out.

"Cormac will send you his case notes," said Joan. "These are just the current ones dished out."

"So what kind of thing do you see around here, then?" said Lissa.

"Oh, the usual. Some diabetes care. Bit of stoma work. Vaccinations. Old. Farming accidents."

"What?" said Lissa.

"People lose bits to tractors. More often than you'd think. That kind of thing."

"What kind of bits?"

"Sticky-out bits," said Joan matter-of-factly, walking into the waiting room and throwing open the unlocked door.

Lissa twirled around. "You leave your *door* open?!"

"Well, they're very welcome to the *Homes and Gardens* back issues and the broken toy garage."

Lissa stepped through in wonder. The old front room of the house was the waiting room, and it was thankfully rather cleaner than Joan's car, although she suspected faintly that the dogs still did indeed get in here from time to time. There were toys, posters warning against smoking and drinking—nothing notably different from London, except that every other inch of the walls was covered in pictures of dogs and horses; there was a stag's head on one wall and a stuffed greyhound in a glass case in the corner.

Lissa started when she saw it.

"Ah, yes. Cosmo." Joan sighed. "Wonderful, wonderful animal. Could never let him go."

"Doesn't it scare the children?"

"Don't be ridiculous! They love him!"

Lissa stared at the glassy eyes. "Are you sure?"

Joan snorted. "Here," she said, indicating a whitewashed room, thankfully free of taxidermied pets. "This is Cormac's office."

"He gets an office to himself?"

"Aye. He's got one up at the hospital too."

"You're kidding!"

Lissa normally did all her notes back in her room, and if she was lucky she got to squeeze into a staff room at one of the bigger practices every now and again.

Joan blinked. "There's six rooms upstairs we don't use at all."

"Cor," said Lissa. "In London this would be worth, like, millions."

"Yes," sniffed Joan with a tone of utter disdain. "But it would be *in London*."

Chapter 21

Cormac looked around. His room was tiny—more of a cell than a room, really—long, narrow, cheerless. How did people live like this? Where did they go when they needed to stretch their legs? There was not a piece of green to be seen anywhere out the window, just concrete and cars and more concrete and the occasional spindly, sickly-looking bare tree, roped off from the pavement. He watched the people below him streaming across the roundabout when the lights went green, taking big steps and little ones, as the endless circling traffic and lines of buses and cabs stopped and started and belched smog and stopped again. It was dizzying. How did people stop? How did they calm down and take a deep breath? He opened the window. The air was harsh with exhaust fumes and the noise was incredible. He quickly shut the window again and poured himself a glass of water from the sink. Then he poured it away. It was lukewarm and chalky and hard and absolutely revolting. Perhaps it was just the pipes, he thought. Maybe it was just old pipes.

He looked at his watch. It was only ten in the morning and

he didn't report for work until the following day. There were millions of people in the city, and he didn't know a single one of them. He'd never been surrounded by so many people in his entire life, and he'd never felt so lonely.

There was a loud knock on the door.

JOAN GAVE HER the list of appointments for the next day and the keys to the cottage.

"I have surgery," she said. "You'll be all right getting on, won't you?"

Lissa wasn't sure about this but nodded her head.

"Are you always this quiet?" said Joan. "You're like that other English girl."

"There's another English girl?"

"Oh, we're infested with them."

"You're English! Well, you sound English."

Joan fixed her with a horrified glance. "I'm from Edinburgh! This is how we talk."

Lissa couldn't see why it could possibly matter whether you had an English accent and wondered whether saying something like that wasn't rather . . . racist . . . but she tried to smile politely and listen to Joan's directions, even as they vanished from her brain as soon as she found herself outside the white surgery.

CORMAC WOULDN'T HAVE been entirely surprised if his mum and her friends from the church community Zumba group had appeared there with nine boxes of Tunnock's tea cakes; but, in fact, the apparition that greeted him was even less expected.

The most extraordinary person Cormac had ever seen was standing in the doorframe. Was larger than the doorframe, Cormac realized. At least six feet, with big, burly shoulders; a huge swath of beautiful shiny, long black hair braided around her head; a fully made-up face, including pink and yellow eye shadow and vast amounts of sticky pink lip gloss—all balanced over an extremely roomy pair of blue scrubs and a pair of pink glittery trainers.

"*Hello!*" said the voice with a broad Estuary accent. "*Ooh!* She didn't say you were a fittie!"

Cormac considered himself a fairly easygoing character on the whole, but he wasn't the least bit sure where to look.

"I'm Kim-Ange," continued the creature, entering the room. "She didn't tell you about me? I thought you guys were emailing each other."

"I've . . . sent her one email," said Cormac.

"I'm not surprised she wanted to keep you to herself!" said Kim-Ange. "We tried to look you up. You know your Facebook profile is absolute crap."

"Aye . . . I don't really do Facebook."

"You don't do Instagram either! And why not?"

Kim-Ange sat down on his bed in a familiar fashion, even as it creaked beneath her weight.

"Um . . . well, I see most of the people I want to see. And

I don't really see the point of it otherwise, unless you want to show off and all that."

"That," said Kim-Ange, "is annoyingly sensible. And misses out on the joy of showing off."

Cormac shook his head.

"But you've heard of the internet? They have the internet in Scotland?"

"As long as we've positioned the ram's horns in the right direction. So . . . you're a nurse?"

"No, I just love the fabulous outfit," said Kim-Ange, looking down at her dull scrubs in distaste.

"Which specialty?"

"Cardiology."

"Oh, I bet you're useful. Lot of . . ." Cormac had been about to say that there was a lot of heaving heavy people about, which there was, but realized just in time that this would not be the right thing to say, as Kim-Ange gave him a look.

"Because of my warm and empathetic manner?"

"Um, yes," said Cormac, blushing bright red to the roots of his sandy hair.

It was just a glance. But Kim-Ange caught it. She was absolutely attuned to being able to figure out whether people were allies or not. Abuse from strangers she could handle—had to, every single day of her life. But sometimes it was nice just to make a friend. She had come in to invite him to a nurses' drinks party. She almost changed her mind.

Cormac had never met anyone like her before. He'd never

given anything much thought beyond what he knew. His stuttered hesitation and hastily constructed excuse about being tired were simply confusion on his part but were taken for something rather worse by Kim-Ange. She turned on her surprisingly dainty feet with a quick, tight smile and left the room, leaving Cormac with the horrible certainty that he'd been there five minutes and he'd already done something very, very wrong.

Chapter 22

If Kirrinfief had been a tiny bit bigger, Lissa would have gotten immediately lost, but not understanding Joan's directions had given her a chance to wander a little.

There was a small stream at the village's edge that fed into the loch, and down there she found another large, impressive house that formed the nursery (well, she assumed it was the nursery; children were screaming their heads off in the garden and chasing each other with sticks, so it was either the nursery or something she really didn't want to get involved in at this stage) and a tiny redbrick school that looked incredibly cute; and along the road a little farther, out of the village altogether on a grassy verge, stood the cottage.

Okay. She knew what her job paid. Cormac got paid less than her because she got central London weighting. But even with that, and even living in subsidized accommodation—even with both those things—she could never, ever, ever afford a place of her own, certainly not one as beautiful as this.

It wasn't flashy, or incredible, or like something you'd see in an interior-decorating magazine, nothing like that. It was a cottage, roughly whitewashed in the same style as the bigger

house with the GP surgery. It had a roof that had obviously
once been thatch but was now slate, with two dormer windows
in it; a red wooden front door with a protruding porch that
had a shoe rack, presumably for Wellingtons, and an umbrella
box with two walking sticks leaning out of it in a friendly way.
There were two windows at the sides of the door, giving it the
friendly visage of a house a child might draw, and a stone step
straight onto the pavement.

Behind it was a small, tidy garden with a vegetable patch
planted neatly. Imagine, thought Lissa, having time to tend a
vegetable patch. She had never met anyone in her life with the
time: not her family, always busy; not her fellow nurses, some
of whom worked two jobs to get through nursing college and
the university courses that were required these days; not her
school friends. She barely knew anyone with a garden, not to
mention a vegetable patch. She had assumed this nurse guy
was . . . well, she hadn't really thought about him at all after
they'd failed to find much on Facebook. This was something
that was happening to her, after all. She really, really hoped he
didn't expect her to keep his vegetable patch alive. Because she
really didn't have a clue how.

She added it to her worry stack, went back around the front,
and turned the rusty key in the old lock, both nervous and
rather excited.

The door creaked open straight onto a cozy sitting room—
no hallway or corridor at all.

A wood-burning stove sat in the middle of the side wall,
with an old fireplace surround; a leather sofa and a floral sofa

bunched companionably around it. On the other side was a dinner table that looked underutilized, and through the back was a small, functional kitchen on a wobbly-built extension with several glass windows overlooking the back garden. Behind the house was the stream, cutting through the bottom of the garden, and then . . . nothing.

Beyond the wooden fence were fields leading to woods straight ahead, and the mountains loomed behind them. If there hadn't been an electricity tower in the distance, she could have been in any time from the past three centuries. It was really rather extraordinary.

She turned back to go upstairs. She was slightly worried about entering a strange man's bedroom as she mounted the small staircase. She needn't have worried. There were two tiny rooms underneath the eaves, a tongue-and-groove bathroom in between them, and she was obviously expected to sleep in the spare, which suited her fine. The whole place was spotlessly clean. She wondered about him again. Gay? Some male nurses were, but that didn't mean anything. A pickup artist? She couldn't imagine many players would choose to live in a cottage in the middle of nowhere, though.

Lissa hauled her bag up the narrow stairs and considered unpacking. The house was freezing and she couldn't figure out where the central heating was. It hadn't occurred to her that it might not have heating. Hang on. How was that going to work?

Back downstairs she found a folder full of instructions for anything and everything—the hot water heater, the fact that she had to light the log burner and that would heat everything else. There were no instructions on how to light the log burner. This was obviously something he assumed everybody knew how to do. She opened the back door and glanced outside, and sure enough, just next to the kitchen extension was a huge pile of chopped-up logs that gave off a warm, aromatic smell. In the kitchen were a small packet of fire starters and a box of matches. She stared at them for a long time, feeling as if civilization had ended and she was going to have to get on with life as the last person on earth. She felt the now-familiar feeling of panic creep up on her.

Then there was a knock at the door.

Chapter 23

Cormac figured he should probably go out and look at a bit of London. He took the tube up to Leicester Square, walked into the M&M's shop while wondering what on earth the point of that was, considered going to see a film until he saw the cost of a ticket, and ended up having a very poor meal in the window of a steak house, exactly as he had the last time. He didn't feel it was going very well.

How's it going? Jake had texted him. Met any supermodels yet?

Cormac rolled his eyes. I think I managed to insult someone already, he said. I'm not sure how I'm going to get on here.

Aye, well, everyone in London's a weirdo, typed Jake, man of the world. Was it a woman?

Think so, typed Cormac tentatively.

Did you apologize?

No.

Well, do that then!

I'm not sure what I'm apologizing for.

That NEVER MATTERS with women.

So Cormac set out to find the local supermarket next to his digs, quite pleased to have an errand.

He found it extremely confusing—there was no square sausage or Irn-Bru, the crisps were different—and in general it was not entirely unlike the time he'd been to Spain and wasn't sure what to ask for whenever he was hungry, and once he'd ordered some toast with butter and everyone had laughed at him because he'd asked for toast with a donkey on it.

Anyway. He had made a mistake on his very first day and thought he'd take Kim-Ange a small gift. The shop didn't sell tablet candies or Tunnock's tea cakes or Edinburgh Rock or soor plooms or Oddfellows, so he was slightly puzzled as to what she might like but eventually went for a box of Dairy Milk and knocked on her door.

She opened it up, looking magnificent in her Japanese robe.

"Och." Cormac pushed his hair out of his face, trying to look sorry. "I thought . . . I thought we maybe got off on the wrong foot," he added.

Kim-Ange sniffed and folded her arms and raised a black eyebrow, all at the same time.

"I'm . . . from a very small village."

"That has never heard of the internet or the outside world. We established that."

Cormac looked down at the chocolates. "Well, I'll just leave these here," he said. English people were, he had concluded, very, very confusing.

"I'm lactose intolerant," said Kim-Ange.

"I'll throw them in the bin then," said Cormac, picking them up and retreating.

Kim-Ange stuck her arm out of the doorway and snatched the box. "Well," she said quickly, "it comes and goes."

And she shut the door, making sure she didn't betray even a hint of a smile.

Chapter 24

As soon as he'd knocked on the door of Cormac's cottage, Jake realized that turning up unannounced to greet a strange woman who'd just arrived in town might be seen as a bit . . . well . . . odd.

But on the other hand, he told himself, he was going to have to work with her after all. Might as well be friendly. Yeah. Friendly. Just checking in.

The sun was going down behind the meadow as Jake looked around. Ach, come on, surely she was going to like it here all right. It was gorgeous. And with someone like him to show her the sights . . .

Of course that wouldn't be appropriate. At all. But Jake liked playing the odds, and there were few enough girls in the area—several mostly liked him, which was fine, but they were hardly a challenge when he thought about it—and Ginty MacGuire still had her eye on him, just like she had in fifth year, and she was about the prettiest girl in Kirrinfief, even if she was also a pain in the tonsils, so, you know, they'd probably get around to that one of these days. But no harm in checking to see if there was any competition . . .

"Yeah?" a loud English voice shouted at him from the other side of the door, instead of just yelling "come in."

This was unheard of. Jake considered opening the door and just walking in, as he'd have done if Cormac were home, but (thankfully) discarded that idea (Lissa would have hit him with a lamp she'd already eyed up).

"Hi . . . uh, it's Jake Inglis? I'm the paramedic. Did Cormac not mention me?"

Lissa cursed. This was the second time she was in trouble for not actually reading the stuff Cormac had so thoughtfully typed up for her and therefore following the most basic of his instructions. She hadn't left him anything, had just assumed that her entire world was pretty obvious. Was that what anxiety did to you? she thought. Made you so focused on the tumult inside you that you couldn't focus on anyone else, not properly?

Tentatively, she opened the door a crack. It wasn't locked, she realized. Presumably if he was going to murder her he'd just have walked in.

Jake, perceiving what she was thinking, stepped back.

"Just me," he said. "Except, of course, you don't know me, so saying 'just me' isn't much use. Ha. Aye. And also I'm not in my uniform, so . . ."

Get it together, he thought. This wasn't like him at all. But he hadn't expected . . . he hadn't thought of what to expect, truly. Not this pretty, curvy girl wearing old jeans, with ringlets coming out from her head at all angles, beautiful big freckles dotting her cheeks, and tired dark eyes. She looked a bit cross. He wondered immediately what she'd look like with a bit of effort and maybe a smile.

He tried one himself. "Hello again," he said. "Jake Inglis."

"Yeah, you said that," said the girl, frowning. "Sorry. I thought I didn't start till tomorrow."

"Oh, you don't," said Jake. "I thought it would be polite to come and introduce myself . . ."

Suddenly it didn't feel particularly polite to either of them, with twilight falling and the occasional owl hooting in the woods.

". . . but I suppose I'll see you about."

"Okay, thanks," said Lissa. She was thinking how weird, rude, and standoffish she was being. But she just couldn't . . . What was she supposed to do, make jolly conversation with a stranger? Nobody in London would do this in a million years.

"Well, let me know if you need anything—I promised Cormac I'd look out for the house if anything came up."

"Okay, thanks, that's kind," said Lissa, feeling her heart beat completely impractically. *He's just being kind!* she tried to tell herself. *Nothing bad is going to happen! This is normal.*

She found herself closing the door in his face anyway.

Oh well, thought Jake. *You win some you lose some.*

Just as he was pulling out in his silver SUV, he heard her voice behind him.

"Sorry," she said, and she did sound genuinely sorry, anguished almost. She was, Jake concluded, extremely odd.

"Aye, nae bother," he said, stopping the car.

"No, I mean . . . could you possibly . . ." She pulled at her curly hair. It really was quite something. "Could you . . . ? Do you know how to light a fire?"

Jake slapped at his forehead. "Did he not leave you instructions? For God's sake, what a bampot."

He jumped out of the car again.

"I mean, there's lots of wood . . . but . . ."

"But that's the only way to heat the house," said Jake.

Lissa sighed. "I was afraid of that."

"And the water." He looked at her. "Were you just going to sit in the cold all night?"

Lissa tried to smile and looked rather rueful. "Um, I don't . . . I hadn't really thought about it."

"Because it's going to be below zero tonight." He grinned cheerfully. "Just as well I turned up then."

Lissa bit her lip, nerves returning. "Suppose."

Jake disappeared and returned with an armful of the neatly chopped logs.

"He's left you well prepared. Good stuff too."

He handed her one and she stared at him blankly.

"Smell it!" he said, and she took a tentative sniff. It had a deep, oaky aroma she couldn't quite place.

"Whisky barrel," he said. "When they don't use them anymore. They burn like hell and smell delicious. Right, watch this."

And he showed her how to open the wood burner and pile the logs up like Jenga, to create a chimney inside the fireplace itself. Then he lit a fire starter, popped it down the middle of the logs, pushed open the flues, and clunked shut the door. The entire thing was blazing merrily in ninety seconds flat.

"You may have to write that down for me," said Lissa.

"Yeah, best thing is not to let it go out," he said, showing her the basket of peat to the side, with which she could damp it down through the night like a blanket and let it smolder. "Then you'll be cozy all the time. Works all right this place, once it's up and running."

And he gave her a quick, charming smile, and before she even had the chance to get nervous or offer him a cup of tea— if she had any tea, which she didn't—he'd bid her good night.

IT TURNED OUT that Jake had been right: the cottage did heat up surprisingly quickly. There weren't any lamps, just a bright overhead light that reminded Lissa of the hospital, so she just sat as the evening grew pitch dark, staring listlessly into the flickering flames. Then she opened her phone and looked for Deliveroo choices.

Blinking in amazement, she took in the terrible, terrible news. There were none.

Chapter 25

Cormac gave himself an hour to get to the hospital the next morning, not understanding the layout of London at all, and was surprised to find himself there thirty-five minutes later. It was the oddest thing, he'd found, getting onto the packed tube train and, just by habit, looking around for a face he recognized. Did you get over this? Everyone, regardless of color or how they were dressed, had the same expression on their face: a sort of studied disconnectedness, a complete inability to meet anyone else's eyes. Even the schoolchildren had it. It must be an animalistic self-protection mechanism, he reckoned. Like dogs. Don't make eye contact, because you don't know anyone; you don't know how they'll react to you. What a strange way to live. Cormac couldn't really remember an existence where he didn't know most people and they knew him. How did people cope? Wasn't everyone incredibly lonely all the time?

He liked Juan from HR at once, the diminutive form in a suit, phone going off constantly. Juan had smiled apologetically, said that it was great he was here, could he fill in a weekly questionnaire that someone would almost definitely not read, and, by the way, if there were another seventy or eighty full-time nonagency NP staff available just like him up in the Highlands, would he mind terribly bringing them with him next time as they were a bit short-staffed? Oh, and 147 midwives.

Cormac had smiled, realizing what Juan was really saying: *Please, please get on with things and don't bother me.* Which suited him just fine, if Alyssa Westcott would just get in touch with him. He knew Jake was going around to see she was all right, and even if he hadn't known that, he would have guessed it, because that was precisely the kind of thing Jake would do, but, rather to his surprise, Jake hadn't contacted him. That wasn't like him at all. Normally he had a score out of ten for any woman between the ages of eighteen and about sixty-five, more if you included Helen Mirren. Maybe this Alyssa was just awful.

He opened up the case notes the hospital had sent him—the kind Alyssa was meant to be annotating for him—and thanked goodness for the GPS system.

DRIVING IN LONDON, however, he was not remotely prepared for. Cormac had been driving on his mates' farms since he was fifteen years old, like most Kirrinfief boys, and he could drive a tractor and had had a go on a baler. And once he hit the open road, particularly for work, it was hills of empty long roads, single-track lanes up to visit farms, vistas of dappled mountain shadows so stunning that sometimes he would simply stop in a lay-by, push open the door of the little car, breathe in the sweet and bracing air, and eat his cheese and pickle sandwiches staring out at the unpeopled view, feeling very pleased with his lot.

None of this was the least preparation for crazed London traffic, with furious cabbies and delivery vans on insane schedules and huge SUVs doing the school run and red buses swaying everywhere; with tourists stepping straight out into the middle of the road while keeping their eyes fast on the opposite way, expecting the traffic to come from the right; with cyclists zipping through every gap in the road like darting birds. The exhaust fumes, the confusing lane system, the vast roundabouts, the endless honking, the stop-starting.

It was terrifying. And there was nowhere to stop, no quiet lay-bys; red markings on the roadside meant you couldn't stop at all, just try to rotate your head 360 degrees at all times to try to clock who was coming at you and where from.

Eventually Cormac pulled into a large supermarket car park and took a deep breath. This was going to have to be gotten used to. These roads were insane. He took another deep breath and checked his GPS. Okay. There was a housing development not far from here called Rosebud, and all the names of the buildings were flowers. He needed to be on floor 19, Daffodil House.

DAFFODIL HOUSE WAS the least likely thing to be named after daffodils he could imagine. It was a massively high tower block, one of seven in the development cutting great bruised scars across the sky. As a child he'd wondered what it would be like to live up high, rather than in their little terraced house. It sounded very exciting and glamorous.

Daffodil House was not like that at all.

There was deprivation in the Highlands, of course. Cormac had known houses without indoor plumbing. There were places that relied entirely on foraged wood to keep warm. And then there were the usual ravages of all economies: drink, of course; horse racing; family breakdown.

But there were always the hills, the mountains, the lochs, and the trees. There was work, even if it wasn't always the best paid. The schools still had plenty of outdoor space to play. You could still cycle your bike into the village and feel most people knew who you were, or walk into your local bakery and get a hello and a French cake for 75 pence, and rich or poor, that was one of the best things Cormac knew.

Whereas here. There was an unpleasantly dark and dirty little convenience store with heavy bars on the windows and the security grilles halfway down. A huge dog was chained up outside and barked at him, setting off another few dogs barking around the place. Everything was grimy; nothing seemed friendly. Cormac was good with dogs—they didn't put that on the job description but should have—but even he didn't feel like extending his hand to be sniffed by this fearsome-looking beast who was showing his teeth at him.

"Good dog," he muttered, heading on.

The lobby smelled absolutely dreadful, a concentrated mixture of hash and urine that made Cormac's eyes sting. He'd been buzzed in, but the trundling old lift took a very long time to come. There was graffiti everywhere. As he waited, an old lady came in pulling a shopping trolley on wheels.

"Morning!" said Cormac, standing back to let her go ahead.

"Fuck off," she said instantly, and they had to stand for what to Cormac felt like another five years before the lift finally arrived, smelling, if anything, actually worse. Two men got out, obviously in the middle of a fight about something, or so it sounded to Cormac.

"Yeah, roight, fing is you cahnt . . ." trailed behind them as they swaggered past, all aftershave and wide knees. They glanced at him as he got in the lift, and he kept staring straight ahead.

On the nineteenth floor the scent of dope was still pretty strong, but it was now mingled with food and cooking smells, some of which were good, some less so. He paced up the hallway, which was covered in dirty linoleum. Most of the lights were broken and there was no natural light at all. Cormac didn't want to admit it, but he was nervous. His admiration for his counterpart was rising in leaps and bounds.

He could hear music playing behind the door of number 16 and he knocked gingerly, then louder when it became obvious nobody could hear him. Eventually he rapped loud enough that the noise was turned down inside and a tumble of voices answered the door. He glanced down at his notes as a burly man pulled the door open, surrounded by children.

"Mergim Kavaja?" said Cormac as best he could.

The man frowned at him.

"MerGIM KaVAja?" Cormac tried again, with the emphases on different syllables.

The man continued to frown at him suspiciously as a loud stream of questions in a woman's voice came from behind him.

He shouted back noisily, and Cormac simply showed him the name printed on the file, at which he sniffed and pushed open the door.

The tiny flat, with its thin walls and cheap doors, was clean but full. Undeniably full. Through open doors, Cormac saw mattresses on the floors of each room, and in the sitting room, bedding was piled beside two ancient worsted sofas. Men and boys sat around the living room, and where there was space they sat with their heads pressed against the wall. There was a smell of cooking as well as a lot of drying clothes, sweat, deodorant. The shower was running, the washing machine.

"Mergim!" said the man, somehow making it sound totally different from what Cormac had said, and in the corner a man raised his hand. They spoke to each other in an unintelligible string, then the first man turned back to Cormac.

"Doctor," he said, pointing at him.

"Actually I'm a nurse," said Cormac, but everyone ignored him as he approached Mergim, who was sitting in the only armchair and had his leg up, his cheap tracksuit bottoms turned up to reveal a skinny white leg thick with black hair.

What Cormac saw was an absolute mess. He looked at it, blinking, for a minute. He had stitches to take out, but the wound itself was a total mystery; it wavered up and around like a whirlpool or a drunk.

"What did you do to yourself?" he asked, undeniably interested. He'd never seen anything like it.

Mergim—he was twenty-four, according to Cormac's file—didn't say anything, looked inquiringly out into the throng.

Eventually a slender man with glasses who had been sitting to the side reading a comic in English got up, sighing. He hissed something at Mergim—probably along the lines of "Speak English!" Cormac guessed—and reluctantly came over.

"Hello," he said. "I Zlobdan. I speak English. Everyone else is"—he shot them a look—"very lazy men. Idiots."

"Aye," said Cormac. They didn't look lazy to him. They looked knackered, dusty from building sites, presumably, on-and-off shift work, sharing beds if the amount of trainers was anything to go by. "So what happened?"

"He have accident. With drill on-site."

"Okay," said Cormac, taking a closer look at the wound. There were stitches all over the place, gaping holes that had puckered then healed like that. It was fortunate he was young. In an old person, the skin wouldn't have been strong enough, would have stayed like that. "He get stitched up here by . . . ?"

Zlobdan indicated one of the men, who blushed red.

"Is he a doctor?"

"No! He idiot!"

"Why didn't he go to the hospital?"

"Because they are lazy idiots and didn't realize health is free here."

"You're European, though, right?"

"Yes! Albanian!"

"And you didn't know that?"

"I know that! Not lazy idiots know that!"

Zlobdan gave the pair a look of withering scorn, and the poor man who'd done the stitching stared at the floor, still blushing.

"I sent him to hospital. After *all the screaming*."

Cormac's lips almost twitched, contemplating how difficult it must be to share a tiny apartment with at least a dozen other men with whom you had nothing in common.

"We pay tax!" said Zlobdan fiercely.

"I know," said Cormac, holding up his hands. "It's okay, I'm just here to take the stitches out."

He opened his box and took out his disinfectant wipes. Everyone was eyeing him up intensely; it was rather disconcerting. He wondered if there wasn't much to watch on Albanian TV.

He snapped on the rubber gloves, then fingered the wound. It was a shame; it was a great creeping mess that almost certainly wouldn't have been if they'd cleaned it out properly and got a professional in. He looked at Mergim, who had now gone white.

"It's okay," he said. "I'm just going to take them out."

"Drugs?" said Zlobdan.

"There's no need," said Cormac, slightly sadly. The nerve endings would have been killed in the botched job, unfortunately. It would all be scar tissue from now on in.

Zlobdan said something to Mergim, who looked as if he was starting to cry. A bearlike man stepped forward and drew out a plain bottle filled with what smelled to Cormac like paint thinner. He passed it to Mergim, who took a huge swig, wincing as he swallowed. The bearlike man took the bottle back, had a large swig himself, then put it back down.

"Um," said Cormac, taking out the scissors. "Honestly, you really don't have to worry."

He took out a small pair of forceps and gripped the end of the metal stitch in his right hand and gently started to unlace it.

There was a huge bang. One of the big bearded lads at the back had fainted out cold. There was a lot of conversation about it, and, sighing wearily, the bearlike man took his bottle of spirits and went over to revive him.

"Okay!" said Cormac, after he went over and attended to the other man, including giving him a stitch in the back of his head, which the others had watched him do with interest, debating what he was doing in their own language. The men had nudged the big chap who'd done the original stitching on Mergim, obviously admonishing him to watch and learn.

"Everyone out!" Cormac said as he tried to get back to his first patient. He realized as he ordered everybody out that there was nowhere else to go in the minuscule apartment. The men crammed themselves politely into the hallway and stood tensely, as if they were watching a football match.

"Tell him to look out the window," said Cormac, not wanting another fainting on his hands. Zlobdan promptly did so, as Mergim started shaking. Cormac leaned his arm on his patient's leg to keep it still and deftly pulled the metal stitches cleanly through the nerve-dead flesh. There was a little threading in and out, but the entire process was finished in less than a minute.

When Zlobdan announced to the room that he was finished, there was a pause—and then a huge round of applause. Mergim burst into tears; the rest flooded in, and Cormac found himself picked up and hugged. The bottle was offered to him, and he found it quite difficult to refuse. He told Zlobdan to explain that he had to drive a car, and Zlobdan thought that worrying about drinking before driving a car was the funniest thing he'd ever heard. One of the men produced a drawing of a huge, angry spider in a web, which Zlobdan explained Mergim was going to get as a tattoo; and Cormac, affixing the bandage, explained that he couldn't get a tattoo for another three months. When Zlobdan lifted an eyebrow, Cormac said, "Tell him if he does we'll have to take the leg off," which was hypothetically, potentially true, even if it was profoundly unlikely. And when Zlobdan had explained to them once more that they didn't have to pay, Mergim came out of the kitchen and handed Cormac a heavy plum cake.

And Cormac left to the man tearfully shaking his head over and over and cheering, as if Cormac had performed a miracle, and he felt both acutely ridiculous, given the tiny job he'd done, and rather pleased with himself. He heard the music start up again as he let himself back into the stinky lift, with an exhausted-looking young woman pushing a filthy double buggy and coping with a whining toddler at her side too, covered in snot, in a T-shirt too thin for the brisk spring day.

He opened the door for her on the way out.

"Can I give you a hand with the buggy?" he asked, seeing her struggle.

"Fuck off, Social Work," she barked at him, and the day went on.

Chapter 26

It was the silence she'd noticed as she sat down the previous evening on the deep and comfortable little sleigh bed in the slope-roofed spare room, with its gray washed boards and faded blue-and-yellow rug. Well, no, it wasn't silent, in fact; there were rustles outside; she could hear the wind, unusually, moving through the trees and the distant squawk of—what, a bird? An animal? She didn't know.

Lissa prepared herself for not being able to sleep. She was in a strange bed a very long way from home, cast into exile. She had a million new things to do tomorrow: a new case list to take on, a new set of worries as well as the ongoing ones—everything circling in her brain. She was never going to be able to sleep, everything was so strange and odd: the sweet-smelling air, the comforting crackle of the whisky wood in the fire, the faint tinkling of the stream in the bottom of the garden . . .

When she woke up nine and a half hours later, she hadn't even taken her contact lenses out.

SHE WAS TOO late to make breakfast or do anything, in her surprise, other than jump into the shower and, in her haste, use some of the old shampoo already there. It smelled of almonds.

She threw on her uniform, put on her glasses, tied up her damp hair. Of course there wouldn't be any food; she was an idiot for not having planned all of this yesterday. Automatically she went to open the fridge door anyway—then stopped, as her hand didn't find the handle. That was odd. She tried it again, then smiled to herself. The door opened on the other side. It was a left-handed fridge. She supposed it wasn't that strange in the scheme of things—one in ten—but she was left-handed too and had always considered such a thing the height of luxury. If he had a left-handed fridge, he would have left-handed scissors too! And can opener! It was oddly thrilling. She glanced around, but there wasn't a picture of him—or anyone, or anything, in fact—up anywhere in the cozy little sitting room. *Typical man,* she thought. She had to email him; she glanced at her watch. Nope. No time. Dammit, and he'd have had Zlobdan's mob this morning, whom she'd come up against before. Could always do with a bit of prior warning. She glanced at her phone; there was a long message from him telling her what she should be doing.

Finding a half-empty tin of dry cornflakes at the back of the cupboard, she grabbed a handful and looked at the message crossly. Well, wasn't *he* organized. Show-off. There was quite a lot to it. She'd look at it later.

LISSA SQUINTED AT the address, but it wasn't making much more sense than it did before. She was parked on a narrow single-lane track, having a fight with the GPS and having lost her phone connection, which meant she couldn't read the email Cormac had sent her that presumably explained exactly what to do and where she was meant to be going to meet this patient. Oddly this was making her cross with Cormac rather than, for example, herself.

She got out of the car and was struck once more by just how incredibly quiet everything was. She could see in the distance figures up and about on the hills—farmers, she imagined. Shepherds. Were shepherds still a thing? She supposed they were. She looked closer. The white shapes on the hillsides had smaller white shapes prancing along beside them. Perhaps they were lambs. It looked like something out of a children's storybook; an old orange farmhouse set back from the road that she'd passed as she came in, with its red barn, looked like something you'd read about to a very small person.

Lissa had never in her life given her food a second thought beyond checking it was organic, sometimes, when she felt flush enough. She never cooked at all; why would you in London? Her mother hadn't cooked, had said it would put her in a domestic servitude role, whereas her job was to break out of feminine stereotypes. Which was why the nursing had never really gone down too well.

Anyway. Lissa wasn't going to think about that right now. Instead she drove back into the center of the village, parking right in front of the bakery, to her utter amazement. There were no yellow lines or anything. She took a photograph to send to Kim-Ange, but she couldn't make it send.

Nothing seemed to have a street name, or at least not one she recognized. There was something called "The Binns," something else that looked like "Lamb's Entry," which she didn't like the look of in the slightest. Why they put a farm name in the case notes, when there were no directions to farms and they didn't show up on Google Maps, was unhelpful to say the least.

She looked in the window of the bakery. There were lots of things she hadn't seen before, including signs advertising "Puddledub!" and "Lorne!," neither of which meant much to her, but she went in nonetheless. It was incredibly cozy and warm inside, and a cheery-looking woman looked up.

"Hello," she said, taking in Lissa's uniform. "Och! You're yon lass that's up here doing Cormac's job for three months! Amazing, welcome, it's lovely to see you. Now listen, do you want me to put you down for a regular ginger delivery? And also the provost says could you join the Highland Games Committee? But he says that to anyone who turns up, you don't have to say yes just to be polite, okay? Dinnae mind it."

Lissa had understood about one word in six of this and was seriously unnerved by why this woman was jabbering away to her and how on earth she knew so much.

"So, listen, if you join the Kirrinfief Facebook you can find out everything that's going on. There's a barn dance coming up, if you're not married—are you married? Cormac didn't think so, said there was only one person coming, and then Mrs. Ochil said, 'Well, maybe she's just trying to take a break from her man for a wee bit—you know men, can hardly blame her, and maybe he's got one of them big jobs down in London or you know.' I know you're from London and it's all lesbians there too I suppose . . . Can I still call them lesbians? My son says I get it wrong all the time . . ."

Her face looked worried, as Lissa stood like a stone, completely unresponsive.

". . . um," said the woman, running out of steam. She met a lot of tourists in the summertime, but they were usually more than happy to chat, to ask about walking trails and Highland cows, and to buy bags of shortbread and tablet and big sandwiches overspilling with coleslaw. She wasn't used to this. London, she supposed gloomily. She'd been once on a coach trip with her friend Agnes, and neither of them had thought very much of it, was her settled opinion.

Lissa tried not to panic—the woman was only trying to be friendly, she wasn't some spy sent to track her down, the stupid voice in her head had to shut up.

"Um . . ." Lissa stared, bright red, at the food behind the counter.

A young laborer, unshaven and ready for the day in heavy work boots, came in with a cheery grin, shouted, "Hi, Deirds," and ordered five steak bridies, two macaroni pies, and four cheese scones, and Deirds asked him did he lose a bet, and he replied yes, indeed he did, but it could have been worse, it being the last thing he had asked for. When her attention turned to Lissa again she nervously asked for a cheese scone and was there the possibility of a coffee? Deirdre said of course and simply made her a Nescafé rather than asking her which of ninety-five different varieties she'd like to try and charged her

80 pence for the privilege and handed her a scorching plastic cup, and Lissa muttered her thanks and got out of there as soon as possible.

"That's the new girl?" said the laborer, Teddy. "She's pretty."

"Pretty rude," sniffed Deirdre. "Honestly. Why English people can't give you the time of day is beyond me."

"It's because they're evil oppressors," said Teddy, who had grown up in a staunchly independent family and was very clear as to what he thought of the visiting influx, which was why he kept working the land rather than somewhere nice and cozy inside in a tourist operation.

"Aye, she's just never been made welcome afore," said Deirdre. "When Agnes and I were in yon London . . ."

Teddy was only twenty-two, but he was no stranger to Deirdre's rant about how much she disliked yon London, and although he never minded to go there himself—evil oppressor central—he knew he'd better get out to the lower field before Lennox gave him a kick up the arse. He was a great boss, Lennox, didn't interfere as long as the work was done, but you'd do no good getting on his wrong side during lambing season, anyone knew that, so he bade Deirdre good morning and headed on his way, observing the strange English girl sitting in her car, looking as miserable as someone attempting to eat a warm cheese scone fresh out of the oven could possibly look, as word was already spreading about the village about her snotty ways, and if she hadn't been an evil oppressor, Teddy would have felt sorry for her.

LISSA FINALLY FIGURED out which was the Collins farm by asking another passerby who, madly, also immediately knew who she was and was eager to engage her in conversation, and asked if she wanted to join the village choir. She was pretty sure that wasn't in Cormac MacPherson's notes; he hadn't mentioned that she'd be expected to have a full personal conversation with literally everybody she met and not much guidance about how to get around. The fact that she wouldn't have gotten all the necessary relevant information about how to get around by cheerfully talking to everyone she met had simply never occurred to Cormac; how else did people live?

The farm was small, a few cows and chickens mostly, the farmyard a churn of mud and the track leading up to it single lane and full of potholes. It did, however, crest a vast hill, and she suddenly caught a glimpse of the valley and the village down below, beneath the shadows of the crags, a straight train line on one side and the great expanse of Loch Ness on the other. She stared at it for a long while. It must be so strange to grow up here. All this space, all this fresh air. Did they like it? She supposed they must. How strange.

Blinking, she stepped out of the car, up to her ankles in mud.

"Hello?" she shouted out. The farmhouse itself was quiet, old gray stone and empty-looking windows. It was perched high up in the hills and the cold wind whistled through her, completely unprotected above the low stone walls, but the view was utterly breathtaking. She felt as if she were in the middle of a living, breathing painting in a million shades of green.

For the first time in a while she wasn't constantly aware of whether her heart was jumping in her chest, wasn't worried about loud noises or someone creeping up on her. This vast canvas spread in front of her. This landscape with birds rising from scattered seed and tiny bounding spots of fluff on distant hillsides, mirroring the little clouds scudding quickly past in the cold bright blue sky. Lissa shut her eyes and took a deep breath.

So it was ironic, really, that the very next second she jumped out of her skin.

Chapter 27

The traffic wasn't getting any less frightening, Cormac noticed. He thought there was meant to be something called a "rush hour," but it didn't seem to exist here. It was like that all the time.

The next address was a tower block too, but a very different one.

Right on the south bank of the river, on a street called, mysteriously, Shad Thames, stood a high warehouse building and, at the very top of it, as if it had been plonked down, a white-paneled house in the shape of a lighthouse, with a weathercock on the top of it, surrounded by terraces overlooking the Tower of London and the sparkling river.

Inside, it was the most extraordinary place Cormac had ever seen. It was immaculate, beautifully furnished in a minimalistic way. Large, expensive-looking paintings lined the walls, even though from the mirrors on three sides of the room the view was reward enough. It was a beautiful day in London, warm enough that Cormac's hi-vis jacket was an encumbrance, but the apartment was perfectly temperature controlled. Fresh flowers were lined up on every available surface. There weren't many drugs in Kirrinfief, but Cormac had dealt with a few overdoses as a student on placement. He'd never, ever met a junkie who kept flowers in a vase.

Barnabas Collier leaned against an island in the vast kitchen, having buzzed him up. At first Cormac couldn't imagine what on earth he was doing there. His patient was standing with a glass of something he'd just taken from a massive American fridge. He was incredibly handsome: floppy hair over the high planes of his face, long green eyes. Slim and fit looking. It felt like a setup or a strange blind date gone a bit wrong.

"Hello," said Barnabas warmly, shaking his hand. He was wearing lots of what was clearly an extremely expensive cologne. "Coffee? Water? Wine?"

"I'm fine, thanks," said Cormac, then he frowned and glanced at his hospital notes. Why couldn't Lissa have filled him in? There was nothing but the basics here . . . "Sorry, it says here we have a wound treatment?"

"Yah," said Barnabas, yawning ostentatiously and pouring himself another large glass of Chablis from the fridge. "Sorry, don't mind if I do? Rather a hair of the dog—I was at a Serpentine party last night, and goodness, you know how they are."

Cormac very much did not and smiled awkwardly.

"So," said Barnabas, leading him through to the sitting area. It had windows on three sides, two balconies, and a vast gray modular sofa; a huge flat-screen television hung on the wall. Cormac didn't know many junkies who had those either. "You're a very rugged young man. One of our Celtic cousins?"

"Scottish," said Cormac shortly.

"Ooh, lovely. Although I do miss busy Lissa . . . Is she well?"
Cormac shrugged. "Never met her."

"Oh, that is *such* a shame. Seriously, my tastes are"—he gave
Cormac a long-lashed look—"very broad, but she is sweet as a
peach."

He sighed and sat down. Cormac frowned. This man didn't
seem terribly ill at all.

"Sorry, but . . . why isn't this being handled by your GP?"

Barnabas sighed. "Oh yes . . . we had a little bit of a
rumpus . . ." He smiled at the memory. "Goodness me, she was
quite the . . . well. Mustn't be disrespectful."

"Did you get struck off the list?" said Cormac, amazed.

"Oh, darling, we both got struck off," said Barnabas, smiling
cruelly. "Ho hum. *And* I'm banned from Bupa. Hence the riff-
raff like you, darling." He lifted up his glass. "Are you *sure* you
don't want a little glass of this? Just emptying Daddy's cellar . . .
It's quite tremendous."

"No, thank you," said Cormac. "In fact, I've got lots of—"

"Yes, yes, more patients, I know."

Barnabas stood up and unbuckled his trousers. He was
wearing Calvin Klein underpants, and although too thin, he
was in beautiful shape: a narrow waist, long legs, a broad back.
He looked like a statue on the beautiful sofa and gave a "I just
can't help being so gorgeous" look directly at Cormac.

"Aye, aye," said Cormac. His attention focused on a small
lump on the side of Barnabas's underpants, and he put on

gloves to take a look at it. He had a good idea what it was, but he was utterly horrified when he finally unwrapped the bandage. Suddenly it became clear why Barnabas needed so much aftershave.

What was revealed wasn't merely a wound.

It was a hole, directly into his groin. Even Cormac, who had seen a few things—a man gored by a stag for starters; a tankful of soldiers picked off by snipers—had never seen anything quite like this.

"I know," said Barnabas, continuing to drawl. "A *little* dramatic. Although it's quite the party piece."

The thing was vicious, infected, oozing, incredibly deep.

"Why aren't you in hospital?!"

Barnabas rolled his eyes. "They won't give me the good stuff and they time everything."

"You need a skin graft!"

"Yeeeaass . . ." said Barnabas, staring out the window and gulping his wine, and suddenly the full horror of what was actually happening struck Cormac forcibly.

Barnabas wasn't getting help because he didn't want it. A direct route into his body was actually fairly useful to feed his habit. The two men looked at each other, Cormac trying his best to hide his horror and disgust.

"And they still want to fuck me, can you believe it?" said Barnabas languidly.

The pain of it, Cormac thought. The amount of drugs he must need.

"I'll need to clean it out," he said, gulping.

"Yes, please," said Barnabas. "I do pretty well, but it tends to make me faint."

He slurped more of his wine, and Cormac got to work, glancing at the beautiful telescope and the great hanging works of art and out the vast floor-to-ceiling windows, the Thames in full flow, dredgers, commuting boats, sightseeing boats, and huge tugs full of slurry traversing up and down the great expanse underneath the bridges. It was a profound and extraordinary sight; the city lay at your feet, yours for the taking, everything you could possibly want. And what this beautiful dissipated young man had wanted was to stuff himself so full of drugs that he had created an entire hole in his body.

Cormac hadn't really come up against money before—even the local laird was more or less skint, or certainly dressed as though he was. This hushed, thick-carpeted world was new to him.

He didn't like it at all.

He refilled Barnabas's glass at his request (Barnabas slugged it as if it were water), then he anesthetized the area—Barnabas laughed at the idea of that doing him any good at all—and cleaned and swabbed it, then filled it with packing and taped it together as best he could. It was nothing like enough.

"You need to be in hospital," he said urgently. "If you get sepsis, it could kill you."

"Certainly not," said Barnabas. "I'm having far too good a time." He waved his arm around. "You should join us tonight, there's a Shoreditch restaurant opening. Some filthy fusion thing, but the champagne should be good."

Cormac looked at him in amazement. "You've just met me!"

"I know!" said Barnabas. "It'll be adorable! You'll be like my pet nurse. I can pay you. Better than what you're on, wouldn't be hard. Look after me. Keep it clean. You wouldn't even have to sleep with me!"

Cormac frowned. "Don't talk to me like that. Don't talk to anyone like that."

Barnabas pouted. "Most people want to sleep with me."

Cormac blinked. "Where's your mum and dad?" he said quietly.

Barnabas shrugged. "Oh, Mummy's in Monaco of course. She gets her drugs through plastic surgery. We both pretend we never notice. Daddy has two other families now, I can never remember the order, so very dreary."

Cormac looked at him. "I don't even want to try stitching it up."

"No," said Barnabas.

"But could you . . . could you consider readmitting yourself? Otherwise you're going to find yourself on the floor of A&E again."

Barnabas waved his hand at Cormac. "Oh, I will, I will. When I'm not so *busy.*"

He picked up his phone and scrolled through Instagram, wincing at many different shots of his own beautiful face. Cormac stood up.

"Well, if you're sure you must go, darling . . ."

"Please, please, check yourself in."

"Oh yes, darling," said Barnabas. "I'll add it to the therapists, the rehab people, the psychiatrist, the art therapist, and the yoga guru list Mummy sent over."

He waved his hand toward a pile of invitations and thick gilt-edged cards.

Cormac was still anxious about him. "Are you in pain?"

"Why, what do you have?" asked Barnabas.

"Not like that. I mean inside."

Barnabas blinked. "No," he said finally. "Everything's fabulous!"

And he heaved himself to his feet.

"Come look."

He grabbed Cormac by the shoulder, pulled him to the window.

"Look out there," he said. "Look at everything down there. Look at it. Look at that old tower . . ."

He indicated the vast sprawl of the Tower of London, dotted with red beefeaters talking to brightly windbreakered tourists.

"See down there? That's layers of living history. Right in front of you. There's Traitors' Gate. That's where they rowed in Anne Boleyn for the last time. You can stand there, feel what went through her mind. Look at that bridge."

Cormac gasped. He hadn't even realized the Tower Bridge still opened up. But there it was, the cars and bright red buses lined up on either side of its bright blue span, as, incredibly slowly, the road itself, markings and all, began to move. It was hypnotic, particularly as a tall ship, sails furled, masts high, was carefully, elegantly, sailing straight toward it. On the banks of the river, all sorts of people gathered to watch—parents pointing for children; well-fed businessmen at expensive Shad Thames restaurants, their expense account lunches forgotten, standing up to get a better look—the sun gleaming off the water and the polished teak of the boat's hull as she glided through, as if impudently unaware of asking an entire city to stop just for her beauty.

"Wow," he said.

"The city is yours for the taking," said Barnabas. "I don't want any more of it."

He collapsed back onto the sofa. He looked very wasted now.

"Do not," he said, "let it use you up and spit you out. But do not waste it. And do not miss its magic."

The bridge was slowly lowering again, the taxis getting impatient, the children pulling at their mothers' skirts. Cormac let himself out and down the luxurious elevator, back to the new mysterious streets so far below.

Chapter 28

Aonghas Collins didn't mean to be frightening; he just had absolutely no idea why someone he assumed was Cormac from the uniform was hanging about his farmyard when they both had plenty to be getting on with, so he lumbered over carefully.

"Aye, whit are you doing, you lazy big jessie?" he said, his brain not being of the quickest sort, not quite getting into gear before he'd hit the fluorescent medical jacket squarely on the back with his good arm, knocking the figure forward and eliciting, to his horror, a loud scream.

The person turned around, black curls bouncing, hand up, ready to slap him in the face, and true terror and panic in her eyes.

"Ah," said Aonghas, jumping back in alarm. "Ach, now."

"What the hell?" yelled Lissa, red-faced and furious. She realized her arm was up and slowly brought it down. "What the hell are you doing?"

"Well, aye, well, this is my farm?" said Aonghas, looking around carefully just in case it might, for whatever reason, not actually be his farm.

Lissa was panting. "Why did you *hit* me?!"

"Aye, well, I thought you were Cormac," said Aonghas, screwing up his eyes apologetically.

"Do I *look* like Cormac?"

"Aye, no, well, no, no, you don't, no."

"Why did you hit Cormac?!"

Aonghas didn't really like being told off in his own farmyard.

"Didn't he tell you I was taking his place?"

It was entirely possible, Aonghas had to concede. Truth was, his mind wandered a little bit from time to time when people were talking too much, to wondering how his cows were getting on. He hadn't done well in school. But it hadn't mattered much. Although he supposed, indirectly, it had led to this, a strange woman shouting at him in his own farmyard . . . His gaze wavered over to the high field, where he'd turned the cows out to enjoy the sunshine; it had rained over the last few days and the grass was so green it was practically fluorescent . . .

"Excuse me, are you listening?"

Aonghas looked at the girl again. She sounded bossy.

"Just . . . don't sneak up on people . . ." she said, as if she'd slightly run out of steam.

He blinked. "But you're in my farmyard," said Aonghas again, stubborn as his own cows when it came to sticking to a point.

They seemed to be at something of an impasse. Lissa, who had been shocked to the point of tears, then furious with both herself and this man for the realization that of course she wasn't any better yet—how could she be?—tried to shake herself out of it and glanced down at her notes.

"A-oooo," she started, then gave up. "Are you Mr. Collins?"

"Aye," said Aonghas, who was thinking it must be lunchtime.

"I'm standing in for Cormac. I'm here to look at your back."

Aonghas didn't want this bossy person—a woman no less—to have anything to do with his wound but didn't quite have the courage to say so in case she yelled at him again.

"Aye," he said.

He looked in pretty good health from what Lissa could see, as she followed him into the farmhouse.

Inside the low building was a nearly bare kitchen with a long, low table. One cup, plate, and knife were neatly washed up on a draining board. Minimal supplies— porridge, flour, a small bowl of apples—were on the surfaces of the old wooden kitchen, a fire was dying down in the corner. Aonghas paced over the flagstones, scowling. He didn't have people in the house very often, and he was never there himself during the day. He led Lissa to the table and sat on one of the ancient wooden chairs.

"Okay," said Lissa. "Can I have a look?"

Aonghas took off his heavy shetland jumper and unbuttoned his frayed check shirt until he was sitting in his undershirt; the air in the dark house was chill, but he didn't seem to notice. Lissa gasped when she took off the blood-soaked bandage: a great curl of skin had come off his back and the top of his right shoulder. It was all on the surface, but it was a horrible thing to see, like he'd been sandpapered. It must have hurt like hell.

"Are you all right? Doesn't it hurt?"

Aonghas shrugged.

"What happened? It looks like a burn?"

"Aye, Maisie got right cross with me."

Lissa rummaged in her bag for the disinfectant and Sudocrem and looked at him. Was that his wife? Girlfriend? Was she going to have to hand out one of her domestic violence leaflets?

"Oh yes," she said, keeping her voice neutral as she always did in these situations. "Did you have a bit of an argument? Had you been drinking?"

Aonghas snorted. "Naw! She just kicked me."

"You know," said Lissa, inspecting it. It didn't smell, which was a good sign; it wasn't suppurating. She remembered suddenly that Barnabas had been on her list today. Oh crap. She really should have warned Cormac about him.

"I'm going to clean it out," she told him. "It might hurt a bit."

"Aye," said Aonghas as if this didn't bother him, which indeed it didn't.

She ran a bowl with very hot water. "So," she said, launching into the spiel, "relationships can be tricky, can't they?"

Aonghas wouldn't know about that, as he had a special lady friend in Inverness whom he saw strictly on market days and the rest of the time got along with just fine, thank you very much.

"Do you find you fight a lot?"

Lissa was abrading a small piece of flesh; Aonghas didn't even wince. Amazing.

"Sorry about this," she said. "So, about the fighting . . . I mean, it's hard sometimes, to live together."

Aonghas was looking out the window, thinking about whether he should sow some more buttercup seed in the big meadow. It was a waste of money, but the cows loved them, and the blooms did look pretty in the sunshine.

"Does she kick you often? Because, you know, there are organizations that can help out there. People tend to think that they're just for women, but they aren't, it's a common misconception. Everyone suffers from violence and there is help available. I can get you a leaflet . . ."

Aonghas turned around. "Whit are you talking aboot?" he said, narrowing his eyes.

"I'm just saying," said Lissa. "Abuse is nothing to be ashamed of. There are people out there who can help, who care."

"That my cow kicked me halfway to kingdom come because I had cold hands?"

There was a pause.

"Oh," said Lissa. *"Oh!"*

Her hand flew to her mouth.

"Sorry," she said. "I thought . . ."

"You thought what?"

"I thought Maisie was your wife."

"Maisie?" Aonghas couldn't suppress a laugh. "I tell you, lass, if I had to marry one of my cows it wouldn't be that grumpy aul bitch!"

Lissa suddenly found herself bursting out laughing.

"Oh, thank goodness," she said. "Sorry. It's a horrible part of my job."

"Aye," said Aonghas reflectively, even as she disinfected the wound area without him even wincing. "Must be.

"Want a bit of lunch?" he said as she finished up with cream and rewrapped the bandage. Normally Lissa would have said no, but she was so unutterably starving hungry. Plus, somehow being around the farmyard and out in the open air had done something to her appetite.

Aonghas got up and stoked the fire, then brought over a stained teapot with fresh tea, a cup of foaming milk, a loaf of fresh white bread, a glass jar full of unidentifiable objects, and a hunk of cheese. He handed Lissa a long, thin metal prong, which she had never before seen in her life. She took it and followed his lead, as he sawed off a rough slice of the bread, poked his toasting fork through it, and held it out just above the flames. Then he did the same with a lump of cheese, until it was melting on the outside, just turning brown around the edges, and starting to drip into the grate, whereupon he roughly spread it on the bread. He opened the glass jar and took out a home-pickled onion, which he took bites of as if it were an apple.

Living in London, Lissa had taken advantage of the many amazing and varied cuisines the capital had to offer. She'd tried kangaroo; she'd eaten vegetarian mango curries with her fingers; she'd watched people throw things in the air at Benihana and lift up glass bowls of smoke and tell her to breathe in straw fumes. Kim-Ange had even once gone to a restaurant where everyone had to eat in the dark and had a very happy evening confusing the other patrons and the waitstaff.

But this was one of the strangest dining experiences she'd ever had. And yet the thick malted bread, slightly charred around the edges; the strong melting cheese; and the tartness of the sour onion all taken together when you were absolutely starving, and washed down with the foamy milk, was one of the most delicious and satisfying meals she'd ever tasted. She sat back in front of the fire with a smile, the sun streaming into the bare room, total silence except for the ticking of an antique clock on the mantelpiece.

"Thank you," she said eventually. "That was very kind."

"You're welcome," said Aonghas. "I'll be sure to pass on your regards to Maisie."

Lissa grinned. "Okay. Listen, don't get it wet, try to sleep on your front, and I think you can take the bandage off yourself in a week. Otherwise call the service and they'll make you another appointment."

Aonghas smiled. "Ach, lass, I think I can manage that."

"I think you can too," said Lissa. "Good luck with Maisie."

"She's an aul bitch," said Aonghas.

And Lissa drove away from the farm and stopped by the side of the field, where a clutch of extremely contented-looking peanut-butter-brown and white cows peacefully grazed in the cold sunshine on a field that glowed with buttercups, and they all looked beautiful.

Chapter 29

After several more house calls, and both of them getting lost countless times—as well as a near miss with a cyclist who called Cormac several names he hadn't heard before and didn't feel he entirely deserved, and Lissa finding that, off-puttingly, people knew more and more about her as she did the rounds so that by the time she got to the last house someone was sending good wishes to her mother—each collapsed at home, equally exhausted. Lissa wasn't at all sure this placement was quite as restful as HR thought it was, although she had rather enjoyed the twenty minutes she'd had to sit stationary in the car while a flock of sheep was herded up the road. She must take a book with her for the next time she found herself waiting, then realized what a long time it had been since she'd even felt unstressed enough to consider reading a book. Interesting.

Cormac by contrast was feeling antsy, oddly full of nervous energy for someone who was normally a pretty laid-back person. It was as if London had this static electricity that buzzed through it, making you wriggly. Maybe that was why so many people here were so skinny.

Lissa had to log on to her Skype session with her Occupational Health therapist next, which she was looking forward to about as much as a plate of snake spaghetti, so she thought she might as well get the emails over with first.

It was a very odd experience, sitting in someone's front room, with his telly and his Xbox and his sofa and his cups and plates, and introducing yourself. Biting her lip slightly, Lissa picked up her laptop and began.

To: cormac.macpherson@npl.nhs.uk

Hi, this is Alyssa Westcott. Thanks for the notes, they were really helpful.

She lied. She would definitely read them later.

The house is cool.

She didn't mention how the idea of having an entire house to yourself, with a garden and a spare bedroom and a stove and a stream, was insane. She was sitting in about five million quids' worth of real estate, if it could only be shifted 583 miles south.

Here's what to look out for tomorrow. James Felixton's dog will try to eat you, but Lee Cheung's is fine. James's is a little dog and Lee's is a big dog. Please don't try and talk too much at the Frasers', they have form for reporting people. And park in the home car park on the Effinch estate but pay for street parking at the Widdings estate, they're buggers.

Cormac looked at it. Well, that was a bit more useful. She didn't seem very friendly, though, which was exactly the message that had been passed on down from everyone who had met her or met someone who had met her or simply liked to have a view on things. He really hoped this wasn't going to turn out more stressful than London for her. Also she hadn't asked him whether he was enjoying London. Probably assumed that he'd absolutely have to love London—who wouldn't? He felt a little bristly about this.

To: alyssa.westcott@npl.nhs.uk

Hi Alyssa, thanks for all of that. Let me know if you need me to draw you any maps, I know some places are hard to find. Also I like drawing. ☺ How are you settling in? Are you liking it?

But Lissa had already moved on to the next thing she had to do, the appointment she was dreading, and didn't reply. *Well, so much for you,* thought Cormac, leaving his phone and moving to the window, trying to open it to circulate the stale trapped air of the heavily populated building. But it kept sticking in the frame, and no matter how hard he tugged, the window wouldn't open.

Chapter 30

Lissa made herself a huge cup of tea. Anything to postpone the inevitable. She knew lots of people had therapists. She didn't see any stigma in it, but she'd never felt the need for one herself. But that was before. And now it was 6:30. It was time.

It took a few moments for the pixels to rearrange themselves, but the figure on the other side finally settled down into a woman of about fifty, well put together, with a humorous tinge around her mouth and a level gaze visible even through the camera lens and the poor reception. She also appeared to be eating something from a bowl.

"Alyssa Westcott?" she said briskly, and rather indistinctly.

"Uh-huh," said Lissa, finding she was sitting with her arms around her knees on the floor in front of the laptop.

The woman put her spoon down and squinted. "Sorry," she said. "All I can see is knee. Do you mind?"

Lissa changed position but suddenly wasn't sure what to do. She moved the laptop onto the coffee table, then found herself awkwardly kneeling in front of it like she was in church, which she didn't like. She tried sitting up and looking down into the screen, but in the little self-image all she could see was her face looming over from above, which wasn't a great concept. She was also increasingly aware of the fact that the more time it took her to make a decision about how she ought to be and sit, the more that would probably mean to the psychiatrist on the other end of the line sitting waiting patiently, which made her start to blush and feel uncomfortable.

"Sorry!" she said, her voice sounding high and completely unlike herself, rather like some posh English woman asking if she was on the right train. "I'm not quite sure where to sit!"

"It doesn't matter," said the woman calmly, which of course convinced Lissa that it did, very much, matter a lot, and she twisted around in a panic. She ended up back on the floor again, her legs tucked under her like a little girl. Then she remembered her tea and had to retrieve it.

Anita the psychiatrist was still smiling patiently at her, even with a quick glance at the upper right-hand quadrant of the screen, which Lissa interpreted, correctly, as a glance at the clock on her computer.

"Um, ha! Hello! Sorry about that!"

"Don't spill your tea," said Anita.

"No! Ha, it's not tea, it's vodka!"

Lissa had absolutely no idea why she just said that. Anita smiled politely, as if it didn't matter to her if it was tea or vodka.

"I'm only kidding! Look!"

Lissa tilted the cup toward the camera, which led to a predictable outcome and resulted in more precious seconds lost in finding a tea towel. She was just about to apologize and suggest they start over when a voice suddenly screamed, "Mummmyyy!"

Anita's face winced, just a little.

"Mummy's busy, darling," she hissed out of the side of her mouth.

"Samosa done fall in the toilet."

Lissa and Anita both froze.

"Um, do you want to go sort that out?" said Lissa.

"No, no, I'm sure it's fine," said Anita, doing her best to look unflustered. "Now, where were we? What we're going to do is carefully go through everything that happened that day, look carefully at the details . . ."

"I just eating it."

There was another long pause.

"Just go," said Lissa, even as Anita jumped up, knocking over a tall pile of notes and case files onto the desktop as she went. Lissa glanced at them as she heard a lot of yelling and negotiation taking place off-screen. "PTSD" was written on hers; she could make it out, bold as brass. She stared at it. Was that her? Was that who she was? Some crazy person? With a label and a padded cell and . . .

Anita came back, her dark hair ruffled, noisy crying still happening off-screen.

"So," she said. She started clearing up the papers, spilling her coffee cup in the process. She screwed up her face. "Sorry," she said. "Some days . . ."

"I know," said Lissa. "You work for the NHS. I know what it's like."

But inside she was burning up with her diagnosis.

"So, I have PTSD?" she found herself saying abruptly.

"What?" Anita's phone was ringing. She glanced at it, hung it up. It started ringing again.

"That's . . . that's what you think I have?"

"I think it's a— Sorry, I just have to get this."

She grabbed the phone.

"Where are you?"

There was a long pause.

"Well, where's your bus pass? . . . But if you don't take your bus pass how can you expect . . . I'm working here! . . . Well, you'll just have to wait. Where are you? Well, what can you see?"

She made an apologetic face at Lissa, who was beginning to wonder whether this was, in fact, the therapy, designed to make her feel better about being all by herself in the middle of nowhere.

By the time Anita had untangled herself from the complexities of the phone call and was nervously eyeing something Lissa couldn't see but could only assume was almost certainly her car keys, their time was almost up.

"Whether it is or whether it isn't," said Anita eventually, "we've found the standard treatment protocol helpful."

"I know the standard treatment protocol," said Lissa a little snappily. "You want me to go over it all again."

Anita nodded sympathetically. "It's certainly something we'd want you to try." Her eyes meandered sideways again.

Lissa saw red suddenly. "But I do. I go . . . I go through it in my head. Every day. All day. Every time I close my eyes. Every time I see a teenage boy, or hear a yell or a shout."

"I realize that," said Anita as patiently as she could. "That's why you have to start from the beginning and go through every inch of it. So it loses its power.

"So. Tell me about that day."

"That actual day?" The knot in Lissa's stomach tightened. She took a very deep breath.

"Uh-huh."

"Right now?"

Anita blinked.

IT WAS PAINSTAKING, painful. Every detail. The sun on the window frame. The saying goodbye to old Mrs. Marks. The noise of the car revving up . . . its speed, faster and faster. The gleam of the phone in the air.

"I was looking at the boys shouting at each other . . ."

Lissa dissolved into sobs. "I can't," she said. "I can't."

"You can," said Anita softly. "You can, Lissa. You were looking at the boys shouting at each other," she repeated. "You were watching them. What did you notice?"

Lissa shook, her face creased with tears. Then she took another breath, opened her mouth . . .

"Mummy!"

A tiny, sweet face appeared, marched up to the screen, seemed to stare directly at Lissa, and then, to the surprise of everyone, slammed the computer shut.

LISSA FELT COMPLETELY stranded. The tears still falling down her face, she stared at her computer screen, but the connection was gone and she couldn't call Anita back; that was how these consultations worked.

She went, dejectedly, upstairs and turned on the taps to the bath. The pounding of the hot water, the fizzing over of the bubbles; gradually the sounds overtook her sobs. But the fear remained. There was something wrong with her. That's why she'd been sent away.

She grabbed her book, retrieved her tea, and sank slowly into the bubble bath. Every time her mind spun back to Kai she forced her attention back to her book and took another slug of tea. As her mind quieted, she listened outside, to the wind whistling through the trees and the calls of distant owls, and instead of finding them threatening, she found them calming.

She knew, even in the brief time they'd managed to discuss the incident, that on one level, Anita was absolutely right. She would have to think about it, would have to be able to work it through in her head, to stop the panic attacks and the anxiety.

But right here, with a warm bath and a book, and almond-scented bubbles and a cup of tea, and the sound of the wind through the trees instead of traffic and sirens and helicopters—well, she wasn't going to think about it. Not right now.

Chapter 31

And Lissa did feel better when she woke up, after another surprising night's sleep. It had to be the fresh air; every breath felt like she'd never properly opened up her lungs before. But then she'd woken up very early, light creeping through, and the fear had returned. She looked out the window at the greenery in the garden, trying to calm herself, then gave up and scrolled through Instagram until it was a decent time to get up.

Her first appointment wasn't until later, so she popped into the little grocers and picked up some amazingly cheap eggs (she didn't know they were cheap, she never bought eggs) direct from Lennox's farm, some local butter and milk, and some sliced bread from the baker, and she had time to make herself some scrambled eggs on toast. The sun was rising earlier; there was a chill wind, but she discovered, out the back of the cottage, the small patio next to the wall was an almost perfect sun trap, warm enough to sit out on regardless of the wind.

She tried to block out what had happened with the psychiatrist the night before, just change the mental subject, and checked in with Kim-Ange, whose Instagram was full of her dressing up and wearing different hats in what looked suspiciously like the millinery department at Peter Jones, where they tended to take a rather dim view of that sort of thing. She missed her, suddenly, missed her old life completely. It was almost the weekend. They'd be up to all sorts. Then she looked at her case file for the day, and her heart skipped a beat.

She knew she wasn't supposed to know. But seriously, you couldn't avoid it. "Young (f), heart and lung transplant," and the dates matched. They hadn't pulled this place out of thin air. Not at all.

Cormac's notes were very straightforward: "Brilliant!" he'd headed them up with. Lissa blinked. It wasn't remotely brilliant, and this was hardly tactful.

She stood up and washed her dishes, then found herself making up a packed lunch—a packed lunch! Who was she? But then it wasn't her fault there wasn't a Pret a Manger for two hundred miles. She took a picture of it and sent it to Kim-Ange to make her smile: a cheese sandwich, augmented with something she found in Cormac's cupboards that she very much hoped was homemade pickle. No tofu. No bean sprouts. No cronuts and no bento boxes. She added a couple of russet apples and contemplated buying a thermos and smiled, just a little, wondering who she was.

IT WAS TRULY a lovely morning, and Lissa decided to walk in—she was going to the center of the village, she could put her medical bag in a rucksack on her shoulders, and it wasn't likely that she was going to be mugged or leave it on a tube train.

And it really was a glorious day; she stopped for a full five minutes across the road, watching a full field of brand-new lambs hop and skip. They were hilarious: tumbling, jumping over puddles, then every so often making bleating noises and skittering back to the comfort and safety of their mothers, who placidly ignored them as they ran rings around them and reached their little pink mouths up to suckle. They were entirely enchanting in the sunshine and hard to watch without your spirits rising at least a little.

She focused on her breathing as she approached the little terraced house. Annoyance leaped in her once again as she wished her psychiatrist hadn't been so brusque or, if she was being truly honest, hadn't allowed her child to hang up the call. Stupid NHS cutbacks, she told herself, throwing her in the deep end like that. And now this.

The door was flung open almost before she had finished ringing it. The woman there, though, looked confused to see her.

"Och no!" she said. "Where's Cormac?"

"Um, he's on secondment," said Lissa. "It's me instead. Sorry."

"Aye!" said the woman, beaming. "Oh, I heard all about you!"

"Yes, I'm beginning to realize that," said Lissa, trying to sound as friendly as the locals, rather than slightly sarcastic.

"Is he liking it?"

"I don't know," admitted Lissa.

The woman looked at her. "But he's doing your job?"

"Yes."

"But you've no chatted about it?"

Lissa shrugged. "Not really," she said. "How's . . ."

She had trouble pronouncing the name, but the woman's face lit up.

"Oh well. You didn't see her before. You had to see her before. That's why I wish Cormac were here."

"Well, he isn't . . ."

"I know. But I wanted him to see this."

Lissa followed, feeling very second best, into the little tidy sitting room.

Sitting in front of *Pitch Perfect* was a very thin, pale little girl with black circles beneath her eyes. The fact that she was sitting up was somewhat lost on Lissa.

"Hello," the girl said softly. Her face screwed up. "Where's Cormac?"

Lissa smiled thinly. "Oh, well, he's in London. I'm standing in for him for a bit. Think of me as Other Cormac."

There was a pause while Lissa wondered if she was going to meet a hostile reception. Then the girl's face brightened.

"Will you tell him? Will you tell him you saw me? Will you tell him everything?"

"Um, of course."

"Will you take a photo?"

"No, that's not allowed."

Islay frowned, but her mother relaxed and went to put the kettle on.

"Take a picture!" the girl insisted bossily, and put on a huge grin and a ta-da with her hands. "Do it!"

Lissa tried to smile patiently. "I'd lose my job," she said.

The girl looked suspicious.

"And so would Cormac."

But already the mother was bustling back in, smiling expectantly. "Och, he'll be wanting a picture," she said. Islay smiled triumphantly and posed again, and Lissa, reluctantly, snapped her.

The girl's blood pressure, heart rate, healing scar—all were fine, totally normal. The parents both lingered at the doorway, fearfully watching Lissa's every move in a way that made the back of her neck prickle. She didn't understand why they were so smug and triumphalist about it all. Didn't they realize? Didn't they know that an innocent boy's blood had trickled out on the pavement for this?

It wasn't until later that night when she got the email back from Cormac that she realized what she had missed.

To: cormac.macpherson@npl.nhs.uk

Um, hi. The Coudrie family asked me to write to you directly and send you a picture.

Oh, and thanks for the house and everything. I took the spare room, by the way. Oh, and I picked some daffodils, I hope that was okay. Hope everything is okay with you.

Anyway, she seems fine, all vitals normal. I'm not sure I even needed to be there. Scar fine and healing fast, patient well in herself, talkative, seems perfectly normal situation. Don't know if follow-up visits will be required as long as immunosuppression initiation continues as normal, but they were very adamant I let you know and send you a picture. PLEASE don't share it. I know I shouldn't send it but she was quite persuasive.

Yours sincerely,
Alyssa Westcott

CORMAC HAD HAD a trying day. He had mixed up the dogs and was slightly perturbed that in discussing the dogs, Alyssa had completely failed to mention that James had a boa constrictor in the house. He hadn't been terrified *exactly;* it would just have been nice to have had a bit of forewarning.

On the plus side, he'd gotten lost only three times and been shouted at by only two cyclists, once for reasons that almost weren't his fault. And he'd gone for a pint after work and been charged £7, and while he didn't think of himself as a stingy man, and certainly didn't want to live up to any kind of Scottish cliché, internally he couldn't help wincing. And it wasn't like Eck's pub, where anyone—hill walkers, tourists, locals, long-lost American cousins searching for their roots—would strike up a conversation with you and where the pub was a convivial meeting place full of dogs and farmers and talk of weather and general hospitableness after a long day. Here there was nowhere to sit and large groups of aggressive young men, and everyone was ignoring everyone else, and there was a slight atmosphere of menace, and the beer tasted like fizz and nothing else, and Cormac had always thought of himself as a man of fairly simple tastes, but he wasn't sure he fitted in here at all.

And the streets were completely astonishing to him. There was a tramp in Kirrinfief, Dorcan. He'd been there longer than anyone could remember; nobody even knew if that was his real name. He came and went, slept in the churchyard, accepted soup and meals left out for him, spoke to no one, but sat on his bench then went on his way again to who knew where. Nobody knew anything about him, and he discouraged chat, even from Judith the friendly vicar, whose garden he was effectively sleeping in. She left the vestry open for him, but he never used it, even on the wettest of nights.

But here—there were people just lying about everywhere, in underpasses and shop doorways, over vents and under bridges. And nobody batted an eyelid. It seemed completely fine. Cormac was entirely baffled by the whole thing but followed what other people did: bought the *Big Issue* when he saw it, blinked in puzzlement. Wasn't everyone here rich? Walking about the city, he'd seen a gold car parked in Covent Garden; restaurants where everything cost £30; shops that smelled of money, with fantastical window displays, Wonder Rooms; and jewelers with watches that cost more than he made in a year.

He knew he didn't understand politics—he'd spent enough time sitting in a desert for reasons he didn't quite grasp to pretend to know anything about anything. But this was so very odd, that everyone had just learned to live with loads of people lying on the ground.

Lissa's email changed his mood in an instant. He pulled out his laptop in the pub and typed back,

To: alyssa.westcott@npl.nhs.uk

I bet she was!!!! That's brilliant! That's just so fantastic! I can't believe she's sitting up! And talking of her own accord! Christ, they must be over the moon—thank you, THANK YOU for doing the house call and reporting back, I've been worried sick.

Amazing. Sometimes this job is really fricking amazing, don't you think? Also, thank you for the dog warning, but if you feel like adding snake warnings at any point, that would also be appreciated.

And he attached a picture of Islay he had taken for her mother, when they thought it might be the very last time they saw her alive: a blue bag of skeletal bones, connected to every tube in the ICU department; a wraith; a frail whisper of an angel Death had already clapped its scaly wings around.

Comparing the two pictures side by side and reading again Cormac's heartfelt joy and relief at the sickly girl back from the very foot of the grave, watching *Pitch Perfect*, eating ginger crunch biscuits, sitting up in her living room, being cheeky, Lissa understood. She stared at the picture for a long time and felt a little spark inside her.

She meant to put the file away. Then she found herself, on impulse, emailing back,

To: cormac.macpherson@npl.nhs.uk

What's wrong with a lovely boa constrictor?

To her total surprise, after a few moments she got back not an email but a photograph of a drawing, and she smiled.

Is that you?

Did you mean, oh look at you, you poor thing, being strangled by a boa constrictor?

That's a terrible picture!

I'll have you know that's exactly what I look like.

You're definitely more scary than the snake.

Thanks very much.

And shaking her head at the odd message, and hoping he hadn't scared James's pride and joy too much, she went to bed.

Chapter 32

The week continued. Even as they both started to get into the swing of things, Cormac peeled a layer of clothes off every day to stop being so hot, and Lissa added a layer every day to stop being so freezing.

Lissa absolutely didn't realize people were gossiping furiously about her and thought she was standoffish, because she generally considered not making eye contact the most polite way of dealing with strangers. But she managed to cover the vast majority of her calls—diabetes management, as everywhere; some quite complex psychiatric treatment she'd called the hospital to talk her through step by step—and Joan seemed, if not exactly over the moon with her, particularly when it turned out she had absolutely no opinion on horse racing, not entirely displeased.

At 6:30 P.M. four days later, though, Lissa was back staring at the laptop.

"Before we start, I meant to tell you, turn off your social," said Anita, who was speaking fast and eating with chopsticks. Lissa watched her hands, fascinated.

"What?" said Lissa. "What's that got to do with PTSD?"

"What have anxiety-creating engines designed to distract, enervate, and worry you got to do with your mental health?"

Lissa frowned. There was a cough on the other side of the computer screen.

"I know," said Anita, but not to Lissa. The forlorn cough came again. "Sorry," said Anita quickly. "I had to keep her home from school."

"I'm sorry about that," said Lissa.

"Iz fine," came a small voice, followed by another racking cough.

"She's not fine. She just wants to watch *Frozen* again."

"Maybe you'll start telling your clients to build a snowman," said Lissa, and the two women smiled briefly at each other.

"Have you got the trial date yet?" asked Anita.

"No. It'll be ages away."

"It probably won't," said Anita. "They fast-track these things, particularly with young lads."

Lissa sighed.

"So you're going to have to be ready," said Anita unnecessarily. "If you can't stand up and tell your story, there might be a mistrial. The perpetrator might be freed. There might be no justice."

Lissa's heart sank again. "Why does that mean I have to give up my social media?"

"Are you on it a lot?"

Lissa glanced at her phone. Kim-Ange appeared to be wearing

a bowl of fruit on her head. "That depends how you define a lot."

"It's going to really impact your recovery," said Anita, slurping. The coughing began again.

"How?"

"It's making you ill. It's making everyone ill with jealousy and self-doubt, and you are particularly vulnerable and in danger from it."

Lissa looked at Anita. She had a large splotch of curry sauce on her cheek, but her expression was serious.

"But I'm out here all alone, and then I'll be even more alone."

"Good," said Anita. "Use your inner resources. Stop trying to distract yourself with tiny pictures and other people's lives. You're distracting yourself from things you ought to be owning up to."

Lissa was biting her lip.

"Feel," said Anita. "You have to feel what you need to feel. Not distract yourself every five seconds. Not be constantly waiting for pings and swipes and likes and enervating yourself. Trust me, Lissa. You are already enervated. You need to get ready to tell this story and you have only four more sessions. Embrace the way you . . . oh."

"What?" said Lissa, but there was no need. Loud and painful sounds of vomiting were coming off-screen.

"Not . . . not on the files!" Anita screamed as she jumped up.

Lissa waited for quite a while, but Anita did not return. Lissa knew she had six sessions of therapy and six only. That was two down already, and they didn't quite seem to have gotten started yet. And the news that the trial would be soon, when she had assumed it would be months and months away, was very worrying. She checked Google, and sure enough the mayor's office was trying to clamp down on youth crime in London by fast-tracking everything through the courts.

She sighed. That was very bad news indeed.

BUT LISSA DID that one thing. She muted her Facebook and Instagram accounts—leaving cheery messages to stop anyone from worrying about her—and removed herself from the conversation. She thought she would be lonely and miserable. In fact, instead—and with the occasional WhatsApp check-in from her good friends—she found it oddly freeing.

She didn't really notice, but she started talking more to the locals, simply because she had no choice. Deirdre in the bakery; Mrs. Murray in the general store. And every day she'd swapped patient notes with Cormac, mostly brisk, but sometimes funny or odd. Irritatingly, he'd normally heard about anything that happened to her, including getting the car stuck up the dyke road, because apparently *everybody* knew you didn't drive up the dyke road after a heavy rainstorm, but nobody had thought to mention it to her and it had taken half of Lennox's lads to pull her out again. He'd also caught her up with how Mrs. Marks had switched to Turkish delight, believing it to be okay.

Seriously? Lissa had written back. Did you confiscate it like I told you?

Yes!

What did you do with it?

Nothing!

And then in the next email:

I am amazed, typed Lissa, that you had to become an NPL instead of a professional artist.

Me too, typed Cormac. An endless and disappointing loss to the art world.

What do people do on the weekend round here? typed Lissa. Have you got anything to do?

In fact, he did. There were people from Kirrinfief in London—not many, and it was his mother's idea, which rarely boded well, as she didn't speak to him that much. But on the other hand it was either that or literally nothing at all, sitting in one small room breathing bad air, so he'd said yes.

That's very unfair, said Lissa. You have a ready-made social life in the greatest city in the world.

So do you. Just go down to the pub.

And make friends with wee Eck?

Well, that sounds like you already have.

Lissa signed off, and Cormac made a mental note that as put off as Jake had been before, it might be worth another shot. Meanwhile, he had the ordeal of a big London night to prepare for. He popped another piece of Turkish delight into his mouth and chewed thoughtfully.

Chapter 33

The night out wouldn't have happened if it hadn't been for Cormac's mum, who did the Rotary club with Larissa's aunt—although Cormac's mum just helped out, and Larissa's aunt, the very posh Tabitha, was the local grandee in charge, who handed out the prizes at the local pet show and chaired the ball committee. Bridie hadn't forgiven her youngest son for ducking out of the army and taking a local job, but she wasn't going to tell Tabitha this; in fact, she made quite the point of him going to London and hobnobbing with the hoi polloi, and wasn't Tabitha's niece there, and perhaps she could show him around, and Tabitha, who was a decent sort underneath it all and terrified of appearing a snob just because her brother was the Duke of Argyll, agreed and passed on Larissa's details.

And, in fact, she'd caught her niece at just the right moment. Larissa was in an absolutely furious mood after being rejected the previous year by the local laird, Ramsay Urquart, who had, in fact, headed off with some guttersnipe nanny who'd inveigled her way sneakily into his pathetic affections—"*Such* a cliché," she'd moaned to her friends, who'd all agreed with her strongly and said he couldn't handle a strong woman with her own mind, and poured more fizz, and complained yet again about how shit all the men were these days, which was comforting.

She hadn't seen a picture of Cormac—he wasn't on Tinder, not that she'd been looking at it or swiping, and anyway Tinder was for absolute losers; it was kind of ridiculous, but they wouldn't let her on Raya, which was a disgrace, all her friends agreed, which was also comforting. Tabitha said he had looked after her knee when she'd gotten it replaced and was quite the hottie, but Tabitha still thought Peter Bowles was the height of hotness, whoever he was, so she wasn't going to take Tabitha's word for it.

And it rather appealed to her to see someone from Kirrinfief. Let that get back to Ramsay, let him see how much she absolutely did not care and was *not* a snob or only after him for his title—as *if.* Who wanted that stupid crumbling house of his when here she was dating a nurse or something? So. Pleasing her aunt, of whom she was fond, and annoying her ex, and bringing a (hopefully) hot new man into her circle, *and* initiating some Scottish rube into what proper London sophistication actually looked like sounded entirely up her street, so she booked a table at her swanky London club and got lots of her girlfriends on board and got the fizz in and was in general in excellent spirits.

BY THE TIME Friday night came around, Cormac was absolutely exhausted from the driving, from the myriad different cases he now had—he'd never treated sickle cell disease in his life before, for example, and was studying up as fast as he could.

He went for a pair of twill trousers he had bought by mistake online once, and never worn out in the village because everyone would laugh at them (they were a little tight, particularly down on the ankles), and a green-gray shirt Emer had bought him that she said exactly matched his eyes, which made him feel like a bit of a prick when he wore it, in case anyone thought that he had bought it for himself because it matched his eyes and because he thought he was terribly good-looking.

Kim-Ange found him ironing in the laundry room. She narrowed her eyes. "Where are you going?"

"I don't know. Some house?"

"Somebody's house?"

"No," said Cormac, wrinkling his face. "It's called a house but it's not a house. But I don't know what it is. I have to give my name at the door."

"Soho House?"

"No. But like that."

"Stockton House?"

"Yes!"

"Oh my God!" said Kim-Ange. "That's, like, a totally cool private members club. You can't just walk in there."

"Why not?" said Cormac. "Is everything free?"

Kim-Ange snorted. "No! Very expensive."

"So why?"

"Exclusive, darling. For the glamorous people!"

They both looked down at the shirt he was ironing.

"No," said Kim-Ange. "You want to stand out."

"I really, really don't," said Cormac.

"This is London, not Buttington McFuckington! You're not going to a sheepdog-shagger trial!"

Cormac gave her a look. "You're being quite rude."

"Come with me," she ordered.

KIM-ANGE'S ROOM WAS as different from Alyssa's as could be, despite being the identical size and shape. Somehow she'd squeezed a double mattress in there, which took over the entire corner of the room next to the window. Purple-and-red cloth with tiny mirrors was draped over the walls and the ceiling, and there were large red-shaded lamps that gave the room a pink glow ("More flattering," said Kim-Ange). Purple cushions were scattered everywhere, and scented candles cluttered up the surfaces, their scent lingering even though they weren't lit. Fairy lights lined the old, faded curtain rails.

"Welcome to my boudoir!" said Kim-Ange, and Cormac had to admit, it was undeniably a boudoir.

"Now," said Kim-Ange. She disappeared into the cupboard, rummaging among tightly stacked boxes, as Cormac looked at a collection of fabulously high-heeled shoes.

Eventually, Kim-Ange brought out an old cardboard box. She smiled at it ruefully.

"Sentimental reasons," she said.

She opened up the box. It was full of carefully saved and beautifully folded men's clothes wrapped in tissue. Designer labels, high-end stuff, all of it. Some of it was garish—bright colors and the occasional rhinestone. Plenty of it was just perfectly normal, but beautifully cut and made.

Cormac blinked as she pulled out a snow-white shirt made of a heavy, billowing material, then shook her head and expertly folded it up again.

"Was this . . . was this yours?" he asked tentatively. Kim-Ange looked at him to check he wasn't being facetious, but he was clearly just interested.

"Yeah," she said. "It's like keeping an old photo album."

She grabbed an exquisite black cashmere jumper.

"Oof," she said. "Dries van Noten. I bought it in Antwerp." She smiled to herself. "What a weekend that was."

She offered it to him.

"It would fit you," she said. "He cuts Dutch."

Cormac didn't know what that meant, but there was no denying it was an exquisitely beautiful piece of clothing, even to him, and he had stopped letting his mum buy his M&S undies only when he joined the army.

"Wow," he said.

"Have it," said Kim-Ange. "Seriously. It's no use to me."

She was wearing a lemon-yellow half scarf, half top, with a pink waistcoat fringed in fake fur over the top of it. Her hair was festooned with pink barrettes.

"I'll . . . I'll bring it straight back."

Kim-Ange waved her hand as Cormac pulled it over his head. It fitted in a way most people would have said was perfect, but Cormac found extremely tight.

"Oh yes," said Kim-Ange. "Have you got a white T-shirt? Brand new, nothing faded or grungy in the wash."

He had a pack of three undershirts, in fact, and Kim-Ange

announced that as absolutely fine. The trousers were still a horror story, but there wasn't much to be done about that, and his black desert boots were passable, if disappointing.

She sent him off for a shower and shave and demanded to see him at the end.

"I'm just going to do your eyebrows," she said. "Sit down."

"You're going to do my what?!"

"Just remove the spare hairs. Tidy you up, nothing dramatic."

"My *eyebrows*? What's wrong with my eyebrows?"

"You just have to be . . . a little groomed, that's all."

Kim-Ange's eyebrows looked like they'd been painted on with Dulux. She caught him staring at hers.

"No, I promise. Just a quick shaping. Let me!"

She didn't say "let me" in a way that sounded like a choice, and he allowed himself to sit down in her dressing room chair.

It hurt like absolute buggery, and it was all he could do to stop himself from swearing aloud. She smiled at this.

"Oh, so much for the big tough farm boy!"

"*Ow!*" And then an indignant scream. "What the *hell* are you doing?!"

"If you don't want that to hurt, don't let hair grow out of your nose" was Kim-Ange's pert response. She took out a pair of scissors and trimmed Cormac's eyebrows slightly straighter and neater across the top.

"There you are," she said. "Isn't that better?"

And as Cormac looked at himself in the mirror, in his expensive jumper, with his fresh shave and tidy, new-look eyebrows, he had to admit that, well, it was different, and Jake would laugh at him—but it certainly wasn't worse, and the jumper did set off the tinge of green in his eyes and his curly brown hair.

"Thank you," he said.

"That's all right," she said, then added with a slight twinge of regret, "And if you meet any of those pretty-boy actors . . . do bring one home for me."

LARISSA GOT SLIGHTLY more nervous about the situation as she waited for Cormac to turn up. What if he was an absolute lout who poured crisps in his mouth straight from the packet and was monosyllabic and a drunk? Perhaps she could write it off as a joke. Maybe she would tell her friends Coco and Zafs that it was something she was doing as a favor for the old Scottish side of the family and he was some kind of village idiot, so they'd forgive her if it all went tits up. But they saw Scottish as something slightly quaint and even exotic, so they'd forgive him if he sounded like a country bumpkin cousin and was completely incomprehensible.

In fact, the large, open-faced man with curly brown hair and a few freckles on his cheeks she found lingering rather awkwardly in the lobby after he'd been buzzed up was a pleasant surprise. She didn't recognize him at all—you saw most people around, at harvest services in the old church or at the village fete, where her aunt was usually judging the pet show or drawing the raffle. But thank God he didn't look too bad, just a plain black top. She'd worried temporarily that he might turn up in a checked shirt and fleece, a pretty common uniform in the Highlands, or, heaven forbid, sportswear. If it had been sportswear, she thought, she would probably just have turned around and texted him that she couldn't make it and pretended not to be there; he didn't know what she looked like either.

"Cormac?"

"Hullo thair," he said in his gentle Highlands accent, very different from the posh-boy London voices she was used to. It sounded nice. It sounded like home.

THE GIRLS WERE sitting around a high table when she got up there, and they all did such an obvious once-over it was annoying. But Cormac didn't seem to notice, apart from going slightly pink, but that might just have been the environment. It was loud in there and of course—*of course*—everyone found it very difficult to understand what he was saying, whether by design or on purpose, because they found him quaint.

"So you're a *nurse*?" said Portia emphatically, as if she'd never met someone who did such a pedestrian job in her entire life, which in fact was quite likely.

"Aye," said Cormac. "I follow up—try and keep people out of hospital. Lot of post-op stuff, wound care, that kind of stuff."

"Oh, so you're not in a hospital?" said Portia, frowning her perfectly Botoxed brow. "Do you ride around on a little bicycle? How adorable!"

Kalitha, a slender art dealer Larissa had met during a course at the Courtauld, simply glanced at him up and down, then turned to Ithica sitting next to her and carried on with the conversation as if he weren't there, which made Larissa feel an anxious tremor of annoyance and shame. She had thought that this would be nice, or different, but instead they were all being rude and snotty, and she was completely annoyed that they were theoretically her friends.

Portia turned her attention to the cocktail menu.

"What do you want to drink?" Larissa asked him.

Cormac was boggling at the prices, utterly astounded. Cocktails were £15! Minimum! £15!! He looked up. If he had to get a round in, that would be £75. Getting a round in at Eck's was £12. He had the money—he didn't spend much at home and his cottage didn't cost much to rent. And he wasn't tight; he was always the first to put his hand in his pocket. It was just the very idea of it; spending so much on so little seemed to him not so much worrying as totally and utterly immoral, when £75 could buy so much or do so much.

A worse thought struck him. He was here with four women, which meant as a gentleman he'd normally insist on paying for all of their drinks. If everyone had four cocktails—and, oh my God, he just realized two of them were drinking from a bottle of champagne—he was going to spend as much as the price of a small car.

It was not Larissa's fault, but it wouldn't have occurred to her in a million years what was going through his mind. Money had simply never, ever been remotely an issue to worry about, and the mentality of adding things up like that had never been a part of her. Plus, she'd assumed she'd be getting it anyway; nurses were really super poor, right? He must know it was her club and her card behind the bar.

"What will you have?"

"I'll . . . I'll just go to the bar," said Cormac unhappily, wondering if he could ask for tap water when he got there.

Kalitha flicked her perfectly made-up eyes to him. "Uh, they'll take your order here?" she said, as if explaining something to a child, just as an incredibly gorgeous, young model-type person in a smart black outfit that patently cost more than anything Cormac himself had ever possessed came up to them, looking at Cormac expectantly.

"Um, pint of eighty shilling?" said Cormac automatically. He could call his bank and make sure, transfer some money over, probably. Yeah. He'd do that. The crushing thought that these beautiful, groomed creatures might snigger to themselves that he fit the stereotype of Scottish people being miserly was so shaming he wanted to bury himself.

The beautiful model-waitress smiled widely. "I'm so sorry, I don't know what that is?" she said, her voice going up at the end. "I can ask maybe at the bar?"

"It's a beer . . ."

"All our beers are imported? We have . . ." And she proceeded to reel off a number of names of beers Cormac had never heard before. Finally Cormac stopped her just to stop things from getting completely out of hand.

"Aye. That one," he said randomly.

The beautiful person smiled. "Wonderful choice?"

Cormac turned to Larissa, but she was emptying the bottle of champagne into a glass and waving the empty bottle about.

"Keep them coming!"

Cormac swallowed carefully.

"Of course!" said the server, and hurried off with another perfect smile.

By the time he had turned back, Kalitha was telling a story about a red carpet that he couldn't really follow but involved lots of squealing, then every so often Larissa or Portia, who seemed slightly kinder than the others, would attempt to bring him in to the conversation by asking him something about Scotland, and he would turn pink and mutter something very unfunny and uninspiring, not feeling like himself at all, and the others would look at him for a second and he could hear Larissa's audible disappointment in him for not being a jolly lad or whatever it was she'd had in mind when she started all this.

It was even worse for the fact that Cormac was a perfectly sociable chap, if a little shy. Not the life and soul, maybe, but he was funny and easygoing and the girls usually liked him, and of course Jake would lead the way. Cormac did think how much Jake would be enjoying himself, telling outrageous stories about people who'd gotten things stuck up their bums, giving cheeky backhanded compliments to Kalitha, and generally being at home everywhere, and he felt completely out of his depth and more and more tongue-tied and awkward than ever. His beer, when it came, was a horrible sweet lager that felt sticky on his teeth, but he drank it determinedly and glanced at his watch so he could work out how soon he could politely leave.

Chapter 34

Jake caught up with Lissa as she left Joan's surgery, exchanging one bundle of notes for another.

"Hi!" he said, and she stared at him as if she couldn't remember who he was (this was not at all the case; she was just still getting used to people recognizing her in the street, which never, ever happened in London).

"Oh, hello," she said, flustered. She held her shopping bag closer to herself in case he wanted to see what kind of groceries she had. She'd never realized how exposing it was, living in a very small village. Mrs. Murray had already remarked more than once on how many Kit Kats she seemed to buy at any one period and she was definitely contemplating getting her Kit Kats online, if she could resist the temptation to buy a box of eighty at a time, which she wasn't sure she could, and that couldn't end anywhere good.

"Jake," said Jake.

"Yeah . . . I know. Ambulance, right?"

He nodded. "Yup."

"Busy shift?"

"In fact, no," he said. "Young boy fell out of a boat on Loch Ness, but he was fine by the time they picked him up."

"Does that happen a lot?"

"More than you'd think. We nearly lost a couple o' bairns last year." He shivered to think about it.

"Do they get eaten by the monster?"

"Yes," he said, totally deadpan. "Monster-related injuries make up about thirty, forty percent of my job most days. It's okay, we have a venom antidote."

She smiled for the first time he'd seen, and he saw her lovely teeth.

"So, you know it's the shows?" he said nervously. He wasn't asking her out, obviously. He wasn't asking her out at all. He was just letting her know it was on, which wasn't the same thing at all, nothing like.

He flashed back to the conversation he'd had the previous night with Cormac.

"You should go see her," Cormac had said.

Jake was still a little sore about being cold-shouldered the last time. "Mebbe," he'd said.

"I think she's a bit lonely," said Cormac.

"Oh, do you? And how do you know?"

"I don't. We exchange medical notes."

"You're practically having a relationship. I'm surprised your mum hasn't been over."

"I'm not," said Cormac.

"Is she still in a mood with you?"

"She is."

"Highland women," said Jake, not for the first time.

"What . . . what does she look like?" asked Cormac tentatively, not even entirely sure why he was asking.

"Oi oi," said Jake, and Cormac instantly cursed.

"Not like that!" he said quickly. "It's just a bit weird not to know who's living in your house."

"Well, get on Facebook then, like normals."

Cormac screwed up his face. "I am on it, remember? It's just my mum sending me pictures of armadillos and my old army pals sharing really, really dodgy stuff. Ugh."

"Well then. You'll never know if she's a frog monster or not."

"Don't say frog monster," said Cormac. "Also, is she a frog monster?"

Jake's voice went quiet for a while. Then he started up again, and it had an uncharacteristically dreamy tone to it Cormac hadn't heard before and certainly not when he was talking about Ginty MacGuire.

"Well," Jake said eventually, "you know Meghan Markle."

"Mm-hmm?"

"Nothing at all like her," clarified Jake. "I mean, not really. I mean, she's curvier, aye, and, well, no she doesn't look . . . but she's got these freckles. And they're . . . they're dead cute. And all this hair! She's just got loads and loads of hair and it's all ringletty and it's everywhere and . . . anyway . . . Anyway. No, I havenae seen her."

"Jake Inglis! You think she's cute!"

"I do not."

"Well, there you go! She's lonely. You can ask her out and thank me later."

"No!"

"That proves it then," said Cormac. "I know how you work. You ask everyone out and run the laws of statistics. If you're not doing it it's because you're sweet."

"I don't," said Jake, although he did and had never seen anything wrong with it. Jake liked women in the abstract and found something attractive in practically every woman he'd ever met. Holding back was very uncharacteristic.

"Well, I'm just glad you're not harassing her."

"I don't harass anyone!" protested Jake. "I'm charming!"

"That is very much a matter of opinion," said Cormac, although several hours later he would be sitting in an overpriced club full of weird squawking beautiful people, wishing he had just a touch of the old Jake charm.

MEANWHILE, JAKE WAS standing in the middle of the village square, tongue-tied for once in his life.

"The what?" Lissa asked.

"The shows?" He shrugged.

"Like, rides and stuff?" She still looked confused.

"And, like, a fun house, and you can win teddy bears on shooting ranges and stuff?"

"Oh, you mean a *fair*?"

"Yeah, all right," said Jake. "There's a fair. And it's mostly run by travelers who do that in the summer but help with the harvest and stuff. We know them all, more or less . . . It's grand."

"Well . . . wait, sorry, do I have to work at it?"

"Oh! No. Nobody's fallen off the Ferris wheel for at least a year."

Lissa wasn't sure whether he was joking.

"I'm kidding. The St. John's Ambulance does it. No, I was just telling you in case you wanted to go."

Lissa smiled to herself. She did love fairs: the bad boys spinning the waltzers, the clashing scents of popcorn and hot dogs and candy floss, the sense of danger as night drew in. She used to go with her girlfriends, slipping out of school, turning up their skirts. She hadn't been in a very long time, as if it had been banned, left behind with becoming a responsible grown-up and a health care professional.

"Um, I'm still here," said Jake, coloring. He couldn't believe this was going quite as badly as it was. Normally a cheeky wink and a story or two about a particularly daring and possibly slightly exaggerated ambulance callout and it was a done deal, more or less, or if it wasn't, well, thank you, next, plenty more fish in the sea.

"Thanks for telling me," said Lissa, slipping out of her reverie. "Okay, well, good to know it's there."

Jake put his hand on the back of his neck. "Actually, I was asking if you wanted to go. With me."

Lissa's eyebrows shot up. It was the oddest thing; another side effect, she supposed. She hadn't been thinking about boys at all.

Of course she'd had the same dating-in-London problems as every other girl she knew, competing for decent men with approximately infinity other people. And then there was Ezra. The ghoster. She had sent him one short, consoling letter about Kai, hoping against hope he didn't think it was another ploy to get his attention. She hadn't expected to hear back from him, and she hadn't. But to be ghosted had been so painful. The internet was just such a tough place to meet men.

So she was extremely surprised and jolted to be "asked out"—London men *never* asked you out. You hung with them or you met via the internet. They didn't just walk up to you in broad daylight and . . .

Jake put his hands up as if he were reading her mind. He'd gone puce.

"Sorry!" he said. "Didn't mean to frighten you! It's all right, don't panic, just a thought, didn't want to trouble you."

And before she could rearrange her face into something vaguely appropriate, he had gone.

LISSA WENT BACK home and called Kim-Ange, who was out with her phone switched off, and of course Lissa couldn't get her on social media anymore. Then she pulled up the laptop and thought she'd like to get Cormac's advice. But he hadn't sent anything over . . . he was out, she realized. It was Friday night and everyone was out except her. She wondered where he was. Surrounded by happy people having an absolutely brilliant time, she imagined. While she was just here.

Perhaps she should say yes to Jake.

Chapter 35

Cormac was very much not having a brilliant time. He got up to use the bathroom—nobody really noticed, he thought, although he wondered if they would all start talking about him as soon as he crossed the room, which of course they did.

He glanced around the large space. Every table was taken up with glamorous people, lipstick shining, hair in bold geometric shapes or tumbling blond or in huge Afros, wearing incredible fashion and big colored glasses. Everyone was laughing and yelling at the top of their voices, or so it seemed. He recognized a few of the faces too; there was someone there who played a doctor on an incredibly popular medical television show that Cormac and Jake watched so they could slag off everything it got wrong about patient care and comment on how they were quite fond of the massive fires and car accidents and extremely not fond of the hard work afterward to get people from simply not being dead to living, functioning humans again.

Well, this was it, he supposed. He wasn't, he thought, suited to being a Londoner after all. He wasn't remotely cool enough: he didn't have any facial hair, he didn't have a bun, and his trousers weren't remotely ridiculous enough.

He vowed to use the restroom—which was pitch black and covered in tiny spotlights and marble and stupidly fancy and impractical, which more or less summed up everything he was feeling—then make up an excuse and go, and he'd have to leave some money at the bar or something, or just pay cash, which would make him feel stupid and cheap, but what choice did he have, really, and okay, it was humiliating but it wasn't, he told himself, as if he'd ever have to see any of these people again. He had never wanted to be sharing a quiet pint in Eck's more.

He walked into the darkened lavatory, had a pee by touch mostly, then was just washing his hands when he heard a deep groan.

He stopped. There was nobody else in the bathroom, or at least nobody at the urinals.

The groan came again.

"Uh . . . hello?"

Silence. Then a weak moan.

Only one of the toilet cubicles had a closed door. A thought struck Cormac: What if it was people having sex in there? That's what happened at these trendy, beautiful places, wasn't it? It was probably two blokes having sex, and he was about to make a bad evening a million times worse by interrupting something and having everyone laugh at him for what a rube he was and how easily shocked.

It didn't sound like a sexy groan, though. He took a deep breath, finished drying his hands, and called out one more time. "Hello? Are you okay?"

There was a long pause. Then: "Heeellllppp meeee . . ."

The voice faded away. If this was a prank, it was a very strange one. But also, Cormac recognized the tone of voice. It was exactly what people said when they came into A&E or when he had had to free them from cars or under walls in the field. He'd heard it a million times.

He ducked into the cubicle next to the closed one and, hoping that expensive places cleaned their bathroom floors more thoroughly than cheap places, put his head down to the floor to look up under the partition.

He got an almighty shock: instead of the pair of feet he'd been expecting, a man's head was lying inches from his, a pair of wide eyes, blown pupils, staring straight at him. It was so dark in there, Cormac used his phone flashlight and could see it already: clammy skin, trembling fingers.

"Oh, for fuck's sake," he said. "Right. Hold on. Hold on, we'll get you out of there."

There was no room to crawl under the partition; he scrambled out and kicked the door open with one foot, a move he had practiced many times, it being an invaluable part of the paramedics' arsenal. He also yelled loudly, although he couldn't imagine anyone being able to hear him over the din of the terrible music and the vulgar self-aggrandizing shouting going on outside.

It was still pitch dark in the loo, though. He dragged the skinny figure through the door and out into the little hallway that led to the toilets. Several beautiful people stared at them suspiciously and stepped over the prone figure, but Cormac wasn't paying any attention; he needed space and room to work.

"Move! *Move!*" he shouted. The man was foaming at the mouth and moving into a fit, and Cormac snapped his fingers at the bar staff, who immediately brought him the first-aid box.

"Call an ambulance," he yelled, but several people already had their phones out. Most were calling. One or two were filming, but Cormac couldn't think about that just then.

He put the man in the recovery position, opened his mouth, and took off his tie. Then, as the man started spasming, he cushioned his head and opened his top button.

"You're fine," he said, promising. "You're going to be fine, you're going to be safe. Hang on."

The man had stopped thrashing but now seemed to be suffocating. He couldn't catch his breath and turned a horrible shade of blue as his head went back, banging onto the ground. Someone in the room screamed; the music had been turned off and the beautiful young bar staff was standing around looking panicked.

Cormac immediately started doing mouth to mouth on the man, feeling for a pulse worriedly. He lifted his head briefly. "Have you got a defibrillator?"

Someone nodded and a yellow box was opened.

"Give it here . . . Is there a doctor around?"

Of course not, thought Cormac, as he continued to perform CPR. Real people with real jobs didn't really belong here. He noticed in his eyeline the man who played a doctor on television approaching.

"You must be joking," he snarled.

"Well, you see, I have done it a lot and performed it, and I feel quite qualified."

"You're fine," said Cormac shortly, relenting. "Okay, hold down his arms."

There was no heartbeat at all now. Cormac knelt over the man's chest and took the defibrillator.

"Right, when I say clear, let him go. One, two, three . . . clear!"

The actor sat back as the body beneath him jolted. Cormac leaned over, listening for a heartbeat.

"Come on," he said. "Come on, wee man. You can do it. Come on."

He shocked him again, fingers crossed. Honestly, once you got into this, he knew—as anyone else who worked in actual medicine, rather than TV medicine, knew—that it was over. He had a horrible, horrible feeling that as well as looking like a cheap, tongue-tied country bumpkin idiot, he was also going to look like a killer or a lazy and useless nurse, according to people who'd only ever watched resuscitations from the comfort of their own trendy leather sofas, in which everyone miraculously returns to life.

"Clear! *Come on*," he almost screamed in frustration, jumping back down to perform mouth to mouth. *"Come on!!"*

Suddenly the man's body jolted. Cormac took nothing from

this; aftershocks were incredibly common in the dead. He bent, though, and lowered his head to the man's chest. The relief he felt when he heard, slowly, first one thump then another, was one of the most gushing feelings of his entire life.

"Yes," he hissed. "Come on, Billy Boy. Come on."

An ambulance crew ran into the room through the now-silent crowd, which had parted to let them in.

"Asystolic?" said the ambulance paramedic, a large, sweet-faced Indian boy.

"Ventricular fibrillation," said Cormac.

The paramedic nodded and threw him an oxygen mask, which he took gratefully with a thumbs-up, placing it over the man's mouth. After several more minutes of working on him, and with both the ambulance crew down, one setting up a drip in situ, they sat back on their haunches as the man, very carefully, opened his eyes.

The three professionals regarded him.

"How you doing?" said Cormac finally.

"You've been taking something naughty, haven't you?" said the paramedic. "Come on. Let's go."

The man, however, once he'd regained consciousness and looked around, realized suddenly where he was.

"Oh *fuck*," he groaned, raising a shaky hand to wipe the sweat off his forehead. "Seriously? In front of these tosspots?"

Worse was to come as the man was loaded onto a wheeled stretcher and it became apparent to everyone he had peed himself in his very expensive suit, then had to be led out in front of everyone. He covered his eyes with his hands. "Christ on a bike," he said mournfully. "No photos. If anyone tells the *Mail* I will *have* you, and don't think I won't."

"Oh my God, was it a speedball?" came a very loud posh voice from the back. "Christ, how terribly nineties."

The man on the stretcher groaned and lowered his eyes in shame.

Cormac blinked as the paramedic thanked him and took his name and address. The man on the stretcher's nose had started to hemorrhage everywhere and a waitress was screaming.

"That's our cue," said the paramedic, wheeling him out. "Will take him forever to get to sleep, then he'll wake up tomorrow and won't remember a thing about it."

"Aye," said Cormac. "Well, his friends all will."

The paramedic laughed. "Yup," he said. "Oh well. Cheers—you performed a miracle."

And as they left, the entire room turned around toward Cormac—who was suddenly extremely worried about the state he'd gotten Kim-Ange's jumper into—and, to his complete surprise, gave him a round of applause, led by the man who played a doctor on TV.

AFTER THAT IT was mayhem. People vied to buy him drinks. Kalitha and Portia were suddenly all over the hero of the hour. Various men came over and announced that they had just been about to do the same thing, or would have done the same thing if he hadn't gotten there first (this was not, to be fair, an attitude confined to London clubland and had happened at pretty much every single incident Cormac had ever encountered).

Finally the manager, an incredibly smartly dressed woman with a brisk manner, took him aside and thanked him from the bottom of her heart for not letting someone die on the floor of their toilets. "I mean, it's terrible for business," she said. "Well, not at first, everyone comes to have a look—rubberneckers— but once that falls off. Well."

Cormac blinked at this. "Well, hopefully he'll let you know he's all right."

"He can't," said the woman shortly. "He's barred. Again."

THEY HAD MOVED from the high table, Cormac noticed, to a booth littered with vodka bottles and champagne. He realized, to his shame, that his biggest relief wasn't just that he'd saved a man's life: it was that he wasn't going to have to face the bar bill.

And then he looked around at the roomful of incredibly beautiful people laughing, joking, gossiping, and yelling at each other and, well, maybe it wasn't what he was used to, and maybe he felt poor and out of place, but, well. A bit of glamour wasn't the worst thing in the world, was it? Everyone dressed up, trying to impress, to get on, to have fun. It might not be real, but there wasn't a lot of fantasy in Cormac's life, not much glitter. He might as well enjoy a bit of it, he thought, even as an incredibly beautiful brunette puckered very puffed-up lips at him and handed him a glass of champagne.

Chapter 36

Lissa woke up on Saturday morning remembering she'd agreed to work in order to catch up on some appointments she'd missed getting lost from one end of Loch Ness to another.

But she didn't mind, she found. She'd be quite glad of the company. And she didn't feel bad, not really. Not stomach-clenchingly frightened. She watched the lambs jumping about the fields from her bedroom window, clutching a cup of hot tea in her hands. In the woods beside the cottage, she noticed something suddenly. She pulled a cardie over her gray *Friends* T-shirt, tied her wild hair back with a wide tartan band, and walked out into the waking morning in her old, soft tartan bottoms. At first she was embarrassed she was wearing her pajamas, and then it occurred to her, with a sudden burst of freedom, that it didn't matter! Nobody could see her on the road! She could wander wherever she liked!

The birdsong struck her first as she opened the back door, the sun illuminating the dew in the grass. It was getting long. She frowned and wondered if she'd have to cut it. She hadn't the faintest idea how one might go about doing that.

Now that she was closer to the trees, she could see it better, and she gasped. Suddenly, all at once, it seemed, the wild grasses had shimmered and completely changed; instead of having bright green shoots everywhere, it was now completely covered with a sea of bright purple bluebells. The color was so ridiculous it looked photoshopped. A sea of them—countless thousands running up and over the hill, to goodness knows where—for nobody, it seemed, except her.

She knelt and breathed in their delicate heavenly scent. It was extraordinary. She found she didn't even want to cut some for the house; they belonged together, a great, secret sea, and she crouched down, still clasping the mug of tea, and took a dozen photographs, but none of them seemed to capture the thick velvety beauty of the sight, so she put her phone away and simply sat still. As she did so, she was rewarded with a startle of movement in the distance, the flash of something white, which she quickly realized was a tail. A doe was bolting through the forest, followed close behind by the most perfect honeycomb-colored fawn, its legs impossibly spindly—the speed of them darting through the wood, as if she'd been visited by magical creatures—and she found herself gasping, then shaking her head, amazed at herself. Next thing she knew she'd be getting wellies.

SHE TOOK THE car, as she had to drive a ways out of the village to a house that GPS was absolutely no use for, as far as she could tell, because the signal burst in and out at unexpected moments. Joan had said something along the lines of "it has its own postcode," which made no sense to Lissa at all until she'd found the road where it was meant to be, more or less, and driven up and down it several times until she'd realized that the rusty gates that looked abandoned were, in fact, exactly where she was meant to be.

She drove up the narrow one-track road, absolutely marveling at the idea of it. Vast woodlands petered away on either side of her—the bluebells had gotten here too, a magic carpet, and daffodils burst into view over the crest of a hill. Coming toward the house, she turned the car around the gravel forecourt—there was an empty fountain that looked rather sorely neglected—and stared at something glinting behind the house before finally realizing it was the loch itself. Imagine. Imagine living here. She couldn't.

She went up to the huge old main door and could hear various banging and music happening behind it, but nobody appeared to have heard her knock. She hadn't been in the country long enough to realize she ought to go around the back until a little voice alerted her.

"Are you absolutely going to give us jabs?"

A small boy with too-long hair was standing by the corner of the house. Next to him was an even smaller boy with olive skin and very long eyelashes. They were wearing identical short yellow dungarees and yellow T-shirts.

"We're absolutely twins," the boy continued.

"Are you?" said Lissa dubiously. On the other hand, she'd seen lots of unusual things and it was very rude to assume.

"*Aye!*" shouted the smaller boy. "We is and all!"

"Okay then, great!" she said. "Is your mother around?"

The boys froze suddenly, then they turned as one and marched around the back of the property. Slightly spooked, Lissa followed them.

A very petite dark-haired woman with a friendly, open face came out of the kitchen door with a tea towel over her shoulder.

"Hello! I forgot you were coming! Well, I thought you were coming the other day . . ."

"Sorry about that," said Lissa.

"That's okay," said the woman, smiling in a friendly way. "I know what it's like when you first get here. Isn't everything huge?"

"I thought Scotland was meant to be a small country."

"I know . . . Shackleton! Get the oven."

A tall shambling teenage boy came out with a tray of cooling scones. "Chill your boots, already done it," he said.

"Excellent," said the woman, introducing herself as Zoe. "Want to come in? And have a scone?"

"You're English?" said Lissa, surprised.

"Oh yes! You too! Ha, we're invading the place. Oh God, Mrs. Murray will have a fit."

"Is that the woman who runs the grocery?"

"Don't mind her, her bark is worse than her bite," said Zoe. "You could say that about a lot of people round here," she continued, as they passed an older lady who was cleaning boots rather ferociously by the sink.

She put an old-fashioned kettle on the stove, then picked up a list from the messy sideboard. What a comforting room this was, Lissa found herself thinking. She started unpacking her kit.

"Hari needs his MMR booster, but I don't think Patrick has had his at all."

Lissa frowned. "But . . . I thought they were twins."

Zoe yelped with laughter. "Boys!" she shouted. "Stop it! Nobody believes you're twins, and you're just confusing people!"

"We are absolutely nearly twins," said Patrick, and Hari nodded solemnly, pointing at his dungarees as proof.

"Isn't it clear they're not related?" said Zoe, still smiling as she poured out tea.

"I've met mixed-race twins before who looked different races," said Lissa.

"Seriously?"

"Yes, absolutely. Fascinating."

"She absolutely thinks we're twins, Nanny Seven," said Patrick.

Zoe rolled her eyes. "Right," she said. "Patrick is five."

"And a half."

"Five and a half, and he's Shackleton's little brother . . . half brother. Did Joan not explain this all to you?"

"She just said it was complicated, then went back to reading a book about cow operations."

"That does sound like Joan," mused Zoe. "Okay. She's right, it's complicated. Hari's mine and the rest are Ramsay's. Oh, actually, that's not too complicated when you think about it."

"Zoe and Ramsay are in love," said Patrick. "And that is why we are now absolutely twins."

"Aye," said Hari, nodding his head to emphasize the wisdom of Patrick's pronouncement.

Zoe colored. "Oh well," she said.

Lissa smiled. "Did you move all the way up here for a man?"

"Quite the opposite," said Zoe. "I moved here to get away from one. Anyway, here we are."

"Right," said Lissa. The scones were delicious, but it was time to get moving. She washed her hands carefully in the big old butler's sink, then looked around for a place to line the children up.

A thin, sallow girl loped in, looking anxious. "I hate medical things," she said.

"You hate everything," said Shackleton. "What? Just saying."

Zoe shot him a look and put her arms around the girl. "It's okay," she said softly. "I'm right here."

"I'm just sick of nurses."

"It'll be quick. But then you'll be safe. And I don't want you to catch the measles."

"Mum didn't either!"

"Of course she didn't." Zoe held the girl closer. "We'll get through this, I'll get some bought cake for later."

The girl smiled.

"Oi!" said Shackleton. "What's wrong with my cake?"

"Bought cake! Bought cake!" the little ones were already shouting, clasping hands in delight.

Zoe smiled. "Sorry," she said. "It's a bit of a madhouse here."

It didn't look like a madhouse, Lissa thought. It looked lovely. A fire burned in the big kitchen grate and a large dog was wandering about aimlessly, and there were pictures on the wall and music blaring and a stew on the stove, and she couldn't help herself feeling envious all of a sudden.

"You like it here, then?" she said.

"Oh yes," said Zoe, sounding heartfelt. "Oh yes, I really do." She saw Lissa's face.

"But it took a while, I promise."

"I'm only here for a bit. But I like it too!"

"Well, try and enjoy it," said Zoe, laughing. "Right, shall we move them somewhere slightly more hygienic than a kitchen with a dog in it and flour everywhere?"

They pushed open the door to a beautiful sitting room lined with books, and Zoe sat all the children on a slippery ottoman.

"Ramsay!" she yelled up the stairway, and just about the tallest man Lissa had ever seen came downstairs and draped his arms over Zoe's shoulders.

"Ah," he said, looking embarrassed. "Yes. I've been meaning to . . . yes. Well."

"Have you got their red books?" asked Lissa.

The very tall man frowned. "Ah. The thing is . . . I have about ten thousand books, and, well, I'm not . . ."

Lissa produced three new health books from her bag— Hari's was in perfect order—and made Zoe and Ramsay fill them all in while the children shifted uncomfortably and Patrick attempted to get into a kicking match with Mary, who finally grabbed a book off a shelf and moved to the window seat to ignore him.

"Shall I put both twins down on the one form?" asked Ramsay wryly as he filled in the forms, and Zoe shot him a look.

"Stop it! You're making everything worse."

"*Yes, twins,*" announced Patrick, and the boys started marching around the room singing a loud song as Zoe gave Ramsay an "I told you so" look.

"Okay, okay," said Lissa, checking the syringes. "We're ready."

Silence fell on the cheery room. Sighing, Shackleton rolled up his sleeve. Everyone watched him as he stoically endured the double injections. Patrick and Hari looked at each other.

"Shackleton's nae greetin'," said Hari in his low growl.

"Shackleton *isn't* greetin'," said Zoe automatically. "I mean crying. Shackleton isn't crying. Seriously. Your dad isn't going to be able to understand you."

"Naw, he willnae."

Patrick had pulled up his T-shirt sleeve and was presenting his arm with the air of a doomed soldier facing the firing squad.

"I will absolutely not cry," he said, screwing up his little face.

Hari watched with interest, then, after it was done, went up and gently wiped away the tear from Patrick's eye then, curiously, licked it.

"Hari!" yelled Zoe, as Lissa reached into her bag and presented Patrick with a sugar-free lollipop.

"Ooh," said Patrick, and Hari's eyes grew wide.

"Oh," said Shackleton quietly. "Only you see I didn't get a lollipop."

"You're thirteen!" said Lissa. The child was enormous; he looked old enough to drive a car.

"I didn't realize there was a legal limit for lollipops," said Shackleton.

Lissa smiled and brought out another one.

"I don't want one," said Mary loftily.

"Can I have two?" said Shackleton.

"No!" said all the adults in the room simultaneously.

Hari might well have cried, even though he needed only his booster, had not Patrick stood in front of him, letting him lick on his lollipop as the needle went in. Mary withstood it with barely a flinch, which made Zoe sad at how used the child was to pain, and she hugged her strongly afterward. And then they were done.

"Okay," said Lissa, straightening up. "Possibly a few cold and flu-like symptoms, but don't worry about them unless they last for more than forty-eight hours."

Patrick immediately started to cough loudly.

"Or are completely made up."

"No, no, it's fine," said Zoe. "Come on, Patrick, straight to bed with you."

"Actually I think I am absolutely fine," said Patrick, eyes wide.

"It was nice to meet you," said Lissa, a tad wistfully. Obviously they lived in a big mansion and were terribly busy and everything, but Zoe seemed like the kind of person Lissa would have liked to have had as a friend.

"Thanks!" said Zoe, and Lissa was halfway to the car before she turned around to find Zoe there.

"Sorry," said Zoe. "I don't know what I was thinking. Sometimes I still have my London head on, where you never talk to strangers. It's an old habit. Also, young people like you I'm sure wouldn't be remotely interested in hanging out with someone else's billion kids. But, listen, would you like coffee sometime? Or we're all going to the fair when it comes . . ."

Normally Lissa would have shut down—smiled politely, backed away—desperate not to reveal that she was dreadfully lonely. But she made a decision, as she went to open the car door, to try something new.

"Yes, please," she said. "Yeah. I'd really like that."

And they swapped numbers, and as Lissa drove away she found she was smiling and decided, being on a roll, to head into the village square and treat herself to a book.

There were a few people gathered around the book bus in the village square, and she went up to have a little look. A pretty woman smiled hello as Lissa poked her head around the door. The bus was like a little TARDIS, far bigger than it looked from the outside, and crammed with every type of book imaginable. It even had, Lissa was amazed to note, a tiny chandelier swinging from the ceiling.

"Hello!" she said. "Oh, you're the English girl! Hello again!"

"The locals think we're invading, one person at a time."

"I know, I met Zoe."

"I'm Nina, by the way. You know, three is definitely enough

for a coven," she said. "It's really going to scare the wits out of Mrs. Murray."

"Why the influx?"

"Well," said Nina, smiling quietly to herself, "the men round here are . . . well, some of them."

Across the square, Wullie, who haunted the pub, and Eck were sitting outside on an absolutely ancient bench, enjoying the sunshine, even though they were still wearing their flat caps and overcoats and high tied scarves. They waved to Nina, who waved back cheerfully.

"My investors," she said, completely bamboozling Lissa. "So, how are you settling in? Are you going to the fair?"

"That's all anyone talks about," said Lissa.

"We don't have *so* much going on," Nina said, looking mildly wistful for a moment. Then her face changed and softened, and Lissa followed her gaze to a tall, sandy-haired man crossing the cobbles with a long stride. In a carrier on his back was a round-eyed baby about six months old, already stretching its arms up in gleeful anticipation of being held by its mother.

"And," she said, "the babies up here are *very* ginger."

She kissed the man and picked up the wriggling infant as his dad unbuckled the sling.

"Hello, John," she said, rubbing the baby's tummy. "How's my best little man?"

"He tried to eat some straw," the man reported.

"Good sign," said Nina. "Moving on from dung. Lennox, this is . . ."

"Lissa," said Lissa, putting out her hand.

"Och!" said Lennox. "You're Cormac!"

"Apparently," said Lissa. "Does everyone know each other here?"

Nina and Lennox looked at each other.

"Well, yes," said Nina. "That's more or less how it works." She kissed the baby, who giggled.

"He's beautiful."

"Thank you," said Nina, pleased. "We like him."

She blew a raspberry on the happy baby's stomach, and he chortled uncontrollably. "My mum still can't believe I came back with a ginger baby," she added.

"God, I can imagine," said Lissa, then: "Oh God, I didn't mean it like that!"

The other two just laughed. "Don't worry about it."

"How's Cormac getting on down south?" said Lennox. "He'll hate it."

"Actually," said Lissa, who'd woken up to a patently drunken and misspelled email and a picture that was just a scribble, "he spent last night at Stockton House and had a totally amazing time."

She had found herself envious. She didn't get invited to many private members clubs.

"*Cormac?*" said Nina. "Ha! Gosh, he's changed. Maybe he'll turn into a socialite and he'll never come back and you'll be stuck here!"

Lissa looked out at the sun dappling the cobbles and Nina

with her happy baby and suddenly felt rather wistful. "What's Cormac like?" she asked.

"Haven't you met him? Oh, no, I suppose you wouldn't have," said Nina. "He's kind. The old ladies love him."

"What about the young ladies?"

Nina smiled. "Oh, he's not an alley cat. Not like that Jake."

Lissa raised her eyebrows. "Oh, is he?" said Lissa, disappointed.

"Oh no! Did he have a crack at you?"

Lissa shrugged. "He wanted to take me to the fair."

Nina grinned. "That's adorable. Well, he's . . . very nice."

"But a bit of a player."

"He . . . has girlfriends," said Nina.

"That's okay," said Lissa. "I'm not after anything serious. I'm supposed to be chilling out anyway."

"Well, you've come to the right place," said Nina. "But he's perfectly safe to go to the fair with. He's a good bloke. Just not marriage material."

Just then a woman darted across the square, looking perturbed. "Lennox!" she yelled. "Lennox, can you come?"

Lennox looked confused. "Aye, Carrie, whit is it?"

"It's Marmalade," she said. "I can't find him."

"Carrie!" said Nina reprovingly. "You can't just ask Lennox every time—"

"Aye, I'll have a look," said Lennox.

Nina gave him a look that turned into a kiss. "You're not the errand boy of the village."

Lennox rolled his eyes and packed little John back into his sling. "Aye, the bairn will like seeing a cat," he said, as the baby waved his fists in the air.

Nina watched him go affectionately, and Lissa had the strange sense, as she had had recently, of watching other people's happy lives as if from behind glass, as if she were watching them on television, taking part in a life that wasn't hers, wasn't a place she could legitimately be in. Why did everyone else seem so sorted and organized? (It would have surprised Nina very much to know that anyone thought this about her; as far as she was concerned they lived on a shoestring, couldn't ever go away because of the farm, and dealt with a myriad of daily ups and downs, just like everyone else in the world. Plus, she was miles from her family. Although when she got home in the evenings to the farmhouse and the log burner was blazing and John was kicking his little feet in delight on the lamb's-wool rug, smelling of baby oil after his bath, grinning and gurgling up at his besotted father—well, nothing else seemed to matter quite so much.)

Would she? Lissa was thinking. Would she ever have something so pleasant and so simple? She sighed. Everything like that, all the trappings of a grown-up life—and they had to be nearly the same age—felt so very far away from where she was.

"You seem pretty settled," she said shyly to Nina, who looked surprised for an instant, then smiled.

"Well . . . it's a pretty nice place to be," she said, and at that moment Lissa could only agree with her.

The next second, there was a terrible screeching of brakes

and a yowling sound. Both the women jumped up, and Lissa dashed out of the bus.

There on the square was an old battered car and, knocked clean to the side of it, a fat, scruffy-looking orange-and-brown tabby cat.

Carrie, following, gasped aloud. "Marmalade!" she screamed.

"Stay here," said Nina fiercely, holding the old woman back. "Can you go?" she said to Lissa. Lissa had absolutely no idea what she could conceivably do with a dead cat, but she tentatively wandered over.

An incredibly old woman, who couldn't possibly have seen over the steering wheel, got out of the ancient white car.

"Noooo," she said. "Och, oh nooooo, is that Carrie's cat?"

"Margaret McLafferty, is that you?" came a loud cracked voice from the bus. Nina obviously wasn't having a great deal of luck holding back Carrie. "Did you just kill my cat?"

"Och, nooooooo," said the woman, leaning faintly on the car door. Lissa went up to her.

"Are you all right?" she said. "Do you need to sit down?"

"Dinnae worry about her!" came Carrie's strident voice. "Save my cat!"

"I'm not . . ."

Lissa moved closer. Her heart dropped. The poor creature was in a bad way: one of her ears was ripped off and her back leg looked as if it were half torn off. The cat eyed her piteously, even as Lennox came and stood next to her.

"Aye, that'll be her," said Lennox shortly. "Tried to fish her out of a tree. She took fright and bolted."

"Can you get the vet?" she said.

"No need," said Lennox. "There's a shovel in the van."

"You're kidding!" said Lissa. "There must be hope."

She crouched down. The cat yowled and tried frantically, claws out, to back away, but couldn't move because of her shattered leg. Her eyes were absolutely wild. It was heartbreaking to see.

Nina came out. "Vet's over Kinross way," she said, and Lennox swore.

"Bloody Sebastian. And those bloody horse shows."

Sebastian was a good vet, but horses were his true love.

"*Fix my cat!*" came Carrie's voice. She still wasn't, Lissa noticed, getting out of the bus. Lissa couldn't blame her for not wanting to see it.

"I feel very faint," said the woman who'd been driving.

"Good!" came Carrie again. "Hope you die!"

Lennox glanced at the surgery. "Where's Joan?"

Lissa winced. "She said she was going to . . ."

"The horse show," said Nina. "Might have known. She'll probably be assisting Sebastian."

"Christ, if we ever needed her."

The cat was yowling, but the sound was deeper and more groaning now.

"I could get the spade," said Lennox helplessly.

"*John Lennox, if you kill my cat I'll have you up in a court of law,*" said Carrie, storming out of the bus, face alight. "*No cat murdering on my watch.*"

Lennox's face was a mask of despair. "You cannae let the

wee thing suffer, Mrs. Brodie. You just cannae do that. It's no right."

The baby started crying, as if to chime in with the miserable atmosphere all around. Nina looked at Lissa inquiringly, who stared back, helpless. She didn't have a clue what to do. Carrie had now burst into noisy sobs.

"Somebody do something! Not you, John Lennox!!"

Lissa fumbled in her pocket for the key to the surgery but then remembered that Joan kept the door unlocked. She couldn't, could she? It was absurd—there was a world of difference between a boy lying on the ground and a cat. They were completely different. But still, somehow, she felt something surge within her. She put her sleeves over her hands and attempted to lift the screaming cat up.

"What are you doing?" said Lennox, still outraged that there was an animal in such pain. Lennox was an extremely conscientious and humane farmer, but he was not remotely squeamish. To his mind, to leave an animal in this state was utmost cruelty.

"We can . . . get her into Joan's," stammered Lissa. "There are supplies there. I could . . . I could take a look."

Lennox looked at her. "You don't know how to treat a cat," he said roughly.

"No, but . . . I can stop her pain," said Lissa, and Lennox calmed down a bit.

"How?" he said, as Nina rushed in to take little John off his dad, with Carrie hurrying behind her, and Lennox took off his jacket and bundled the poor creature inside it.

"It must be the same weight as a baby," said Lissa, opening

the big manse door and then the surgery. She pulled out a huge swath of medical paper and placed Joan's files onto the floor, then put the paper over the top of them. Lennox kept the animal covered with his jacket, but it had quieted now and was making the occasional soft whimper, which they both recognized as being distinctly worse. Lissa scrubbed her hands quickly and put a tiny amount of morphine in a syringe, frantically doing the arithmetic in her head. It slid in easily as she found a tiny vein in the creature's groin, grateful for the amount of times she'd spent taking blood on her various placements.

Then, once the large cat had fallen asleep, she took a look at what they were dealing with. She palpated the cat's stomach—she knew absolutely nothing about animal biology, but it wasn't firm or feeling like it was filling with blood. Neither was the heartbeat thready, although it was fast—"Google cat heartbeat," she told Nina, who immediately complied. There was a leg that was patently broken—there was no plaster of paris onsite, but she could certainly improvise a splint until they could get her to a vet.

The most important thing, though, was the shape of the cat's face. The skin had been ripped away; you could see sinew and bone underneath, and her ear was hanging off. It was a mess. Lissa looked at it carefully. It reminded her of working A&E, in fact. Underneath the fur, it was just skin and sinew and muscle, after all. Nothing she hadn't seen a million times. She looked at it for a long time.

"What?" said Lennox.

"I reckon . . ." She retrieved the stitching kit.

"Whoa," said Nina. "Are you really going to stitch up that cat?"

Lennox still looked dubious.

"She's not in pain right now," said Lissa. "I mean . . . I could have a go . . ."

"*Fix my damn cat,*" came a voice from outside. "I'm holding Margaret until the police come! I've just made a citizen's arrest."

"I'll go calm her down," said Nina. "Also I don't want to watch this part; I'll faint and it'll be disgusting."

So Lennox held down the other end of the cat in silence, while Lissa bent to her work, quickly trying to unravel the ragged ends of severed flesh. It was rather like doing a grisly jigsaw, and Lissa found a certain satisfaction in working away with quick, neat stitches, checking the cat's breathing from time to time, and covering each layer in disinfectant powder. Finally, and carefully, she tried to align the ear correctly. It was always going to be a bit wonky, she figured, but hopefully it would still work.

Once she'd closed the wound, trying to make sure it wasn't pulling in a way that would cause pain, she took a ruler from the stationery drawer and carefully and tightly bound the cat's leg to it.

"It's not going to like that," she observed. "But it'll last until it gets to the vet hospital. Which is where, by the way?"

"Two hours north," said Lennox.

"Cor," said Lissa.

She stroked the cat's head. It was still snoring deeply, out for the count.

"You might just be okay," she said softly, thinking, again, of the time when she couldn't make it okay, when she couldn't control it. "I think you'll be okay."

Lennox looked at her. "Well done," he said.

She shrugged, pleased. "Oh, it's just like being back at A&E," she said. "Except furrier . . ."

There was a huge commotion suddenly at the door, and they both turned around. Nina was walking in with Margaret, who had a black eye.

"What happened?!" said Lissa.

"She tried to kill my cat!" shouted Carrie from outside.

"I thought you were making a citizen's arrest," yelled Lissa crossly, sitting Margaret down.

"I was. Police brutality," came an unapologetic voice as Carrie strode in.

"Right," said Lissa. "You have to get her to the vet hospital, get her leg set properly."

Carrie gave the trembling, cowering figure of Margaret a contemptuous glance. "I'll be borrowing your car."

"You shan't," said Nina hastily. "I've got to visit the warehouse anyway. I'll take you in the bus."

Lennox looked surprised at this but didn't say anything as Nina bundled her out and Lissa carefully tended and cleaned Margaret's eye.

"That's quite nasty," she said. "Do you want to press charges?"

"Against Carrie? She'd bewitch me and throw me down a well!" said the woman. "I'm just glad her cat's okay, otherwise she might have burnt down my house."

Lissa stopped. "There's one more thing," she said, looking severely at the old woman. Joan had an old-fashioned optician's chart on her far wall. "Can you read me the bottom line of that chart?"

"Not without my glasses," said the woman. "I'm blind as a bat without them."

"And were you wearing them when you were driving?"

The woman went very quiet.

"If you don't get your eyesight sorted out," said Lissa gently, because what she was about to say was a complete lie, but she'd used it confidently many, many times before, "I'll have to report you to the police and the DVLA, otherwise I'll lose my license to practice."

"Is that true?" said the woman, looking even more shocked. It had definitely not been her morning.

"It is," said Lissa. "And I'll be watching out for you."

She stood up.

"The swelling should go down—keep this ice pack on it. And I highly recommend going to the bakery and having a cup of sweet tea and a long sit-down. Is there anyone who could drive the car home for you?"

"My son," Margaret said quietly.

"Call him," said Lissa. "Seriously. Nobody wants to get the police involved."

Margaret nodded and left timidly. Lennox looked around the surgery, which appeared as if a bomb had hit it, although not necessarily hugely worse than how Joan normally left it.

"Right," he said. "I'd better get back. Good work."

Chapter 37

After that, although it wasn't, of course, Lennox who'd told everyone about it, the story got out somehow—and, in fact, became rather inflated, till by the end Lissa had single-handedly brought a dead cat back to life while stopping Carrie from performing manslaughter, a fact about Carrie nobody seemed to have the slightest problem believing to be absolutely true. And just like that, it seemed, everyone said hello to her in the morning, and people were pleased to see her when she turned up and weren't so quick to take offense if she looked sad or distracted, and she was amazed, truly, that she wasn't anything like as lonely as she'd expected to be.

Plus, Cormac's email made her smile.

I just want you and everyone else to get this straight, he had typed. That I saved a person and you saved a cat.

That's a cat? Anyway, one, it's entirely debatable that humans are better than cats, and two, whoever saves one life saves the world entire, Lissa had typed with a tongue-sticking-out emoji.

All anyone in Kirrinfief is talking about is you and that stupid cat, and everyone is ignoring my glamorous London heroics.

Sucking face with an overdosing scumbag.

Well, you brought Carrie's cat back to life. You know that's her familiar? You'll bewitch half the town. You're allowing her to continue her reign of terror. When the crops fail and the cows' milk dries up, you'll change your tune then.

I'll be back in London long before then.

Aye, so you will. I'd forgotten. And I'll be back there, seeing what's left of my flowers.

There's a lot of those yellow round ones.

Dandelions?

Yes!

You mean weeds??

I like them.

Weeds!!!!!

Also, I picked some bluebells, I hope that's okay.

Cormac looked out the window. He loved bluebell season.
That heavenly cloud. He didn't want to mention that, though,
for fear of sounding . . . well, whatever.

Sure, just write down how many you've picked and we'll tally it up when
I'm back.

There was no answer, and Cormac wondered whether he
needed to clarify that that was a joke. On the other hand, if
she didn't get it, being told it was a joke probably wouldn't help
matters anyway. He waited, refreshing his inbox.

I think what I'll do is just let you count them when you get back and de-
duct them from the stocktake you already have?

Cormac smiled as he closed the laptop.

Lissa bit her lip and, for the first time, realized she wasn't, at
that precise moment, exactly missing London. It wasn't just the
daffodils that were coming into season; all sorts of plants and
bushes were starting to flower, none of which Lissa knew the
names of, and the wildflowers were tumbling down and crawling up the sides of the road. It was so fast, there was something
new to see every day. And bees! She'd never really seen a bee in
the wild before, and here there were great fat ones everywhere;
butterflies too, orange and black, with eyes on their wings. It
was very slightly amazing.

Chapter 38

Both Cormac and Lissa were rather surprised when they fell out, particularly over someone Lissa had barely met. But Cormac was distracted anyway; he had what Jake would have called his savior face on.

He'd been wandering home late—he would have found it hard to deny that he rather liked the shiny London streets at night: the neon and lights everywhere, the sense of a lot of people with a lot to do. There was always a palpable prickle of excitement in the air; it was never dull. Cormac saw a chap he'd seen before, sitting near the entrance to the nurses' home, over the vent of a posh office building that, judging by the smell, had a swimming pool in the basement. The vent air coming up was warm, and the man lolling there looked about the age of Cormac himself. He felt in his pocket for his wallet. This wasn't right. It was a warm, slightly sticky evening, but even so, everyone needed a place to lay his head.

He put the money down quietly, trying not to disturb the figure, who was very still but had his eyes half open.

"Aye, thanks, man," came a low voice, almost a growl, un-mistakably Scottish, and he stretched out a hand. To Cormac's great surprise there was a badly drawn, but nonetheless recognizable, pinpricked tattoo on the bottom of the grubby pale arm: the clear insignia of his own unit.

"Are you Black Watch?" he asked in amazement.

The dull, lifeless eyes lifted up to him, and Cormac caught a strong waft of unwashed body.

"No anymore," said the figure.

"Where did you serve?" said Cormac worriedly, looking at him carefully in case he knew him.

"Fucking . . . fucking Fallujah," said the man, and Cormac smiled painfully.

"Aye," said Cormac. "I was there too. 2014."

"Fucking . . . fucking shithole," said the man.

Checking which way was upwind, Cormac sat down carefully beside the man. "What happened?"

The man shrugged. He had to be Cormac's age, but he looked far, far older.

"Aye, got stuck in a bit of trouble with the bevvy, aye?"

He looked at Cormac. "Were you really there, man? Or are you after something?"

Cormac didn't even want to think about what something might mean.

"No, I was there," he said grimly. "Did you know that regiment colonel, Spears?"

"Fuck yeah," said the man, almost breaking into a grin. His mouth was covered in sores. "That bawbag."

"I know."

"Fuck it all," said the man. "I lost three mates out there."

Cormac nodded. He had probably worked on at least one of them. "What's your name?"

"Robbie."

"Cormac."

Robbie offered him a bottle, but Cormac declined, instead offering him the last of the money in his wallet.

"I cannae take your cash," said the man.

"Always going to help a comrade," said Cormac. "Have you got a phone?"

The man laughed. "Naw."

"Look, I stay in that building just there. Come find me if you need anything."

Robbie waved him away. "Aye, fine, man."

CORMAC COULDN'T SHAKE the memory, couldn't shake thinking about what had gone on out there on the battlefield that had left Robbie on the pavement, left him treading water in his own life.

But Cormac himself wasn't, he told himself hotly. He was doing something now. He was helping out and being useful, wasn't he?

But he was, unusually, very disinclined to lend a friendly ear to Lissa, who was surrounded by people who wanted her to talk about what she'd been through, who would bend anything to help her get better.

LISSA HAD TURNED up at the appointment—a post-psych-ward discharge, which normally meant a suicide attempt—to be confronted at a beaten-down gate of a very small farmhouse by a grubby teenage boy and a large barking dog with slaver dripping down off its chops, which Lissa didn't like the look of at all.

"Hello!" she said. "I'm from the hospital."

"Shut your pus, you mingebag."

Lissa blinked. "Is your mum or dad home? I'm really just here to change your dressings."

"Feck off, bampot."

Lissa didn't understand any of this, but it didn't sound particularly welcoming.

"Just let me in to have a look," she said. She noticed he was wearing a large, dirty jumper with long sleeves that he had pulled down over his wrists.

"Get to fud," he said, turning on his heel in front of the gate. The dog, however, remained rooted to the spot, snarling at her.

"Cormac knows I'm here," she tried desperately.

"That fannybaws can fuckety bye an' all," said the boy incomprehensibly, disappearing into the tumbledown old cottage.

Lissa frowned. She was used, from her A&E days, to drunk or resistant patients, but it was normally only in the heat of the moment. Working in the community, most people were delighted to see her. Someone like—she checked her notes— Cameron would normally be a social work case. On the other hand, someone needed to take a look at his slit wrists, and that someone was her.

SHE CAME BACK a couple of days later, but the mother was no help. She refused to open the door, shouting through that they were busy. Lissa could hear a lot of yelling and banging around, and a TV and radio fighting each other at top volume, and the dog barking its head off, and she heaved a sigh and thought, you know, sometimes there was nothing more you could do; if the state tried to help you and you couldn't take the help, then there was a limit, truly. But the idea of losing another boy scared her rigid, and she was angry that he wouldn't see a woman, only wanted Cormac.

She knew she'd been lulled into a false sense of security; most of the patients she'd met had been lovely, gentle, and forever pressing her with food: shortbread, homemade bread, cream, and once, memorably, when she'd confirmed Agnieoka's pregnancy, a fresh lobster caught from Loch Ness, which she had given to Joan, who had refused to eat it. The lobster was now happily scrappling its way around the surgery fish tank, terrorizing the other fish, Martina and Billie.

She was gradually getting used to the warmth of the local people, so to be confronted like this was terrifying. And, if she was being honest with herself, was bringing back frightening memories, dialing up her anxiety again. She thought back to what Anita had tried to tell her—to go through the experience again in her head. She hadn't been doing it, and it was show-ing; a common or garden issue had turned into a large problem in her head.

She sighed.

Cormac,

Hi there. I'm afraid I've had to mark as discharged young Cameron Blaine. He wouldn't open the door on third time of asking, won't respond to treatment requests, and is refusing treatment all round. I'm not sure what else to do without breaking and entering the house, so I'm going to discharge him and file with Social Services.

Cormac squinted at it crossly. This was very much not all right. Cameron Blaine had an incredibly difficult family background; he'd been excluded from school, his father was in prison, and his mother was not in prison only to save the council a ton of money on trying to rehome all five of the children. The boy desperately needed help and he had . . . he'd been doing not too badly. Mostly just hanging out with him. He'd gotten Cameron to wash his car once or twice, overpaid him, but tried to make it clear how you did it thoroughly, how you managed not to figure out how to palm the keys in case you wanted to hijack it later. He'd spoken to Gregory Duncan, the amiable local policeman, for whom the Blaine family provided more or less 99 percent of his active work that wasn't about parking, and they both tried to be casually walking by street corners Cameron was on whenever things looked like they might be getting a bit tasty. Cormac also had an old friend in army recruitment, but he thought that might be a step too far for Cameron, at least at the moment.

It had been a couple of years of good, solid work of trying to build up trust, and Lissa was letting it all collapse in two minutes by behaving like exactly the kind of snotty posh woman Cameron had mistrusted all his life. He was angry and emailed back quickly something exactly on those lines, basically instructing her to get back there and get things sorted out.

"He was very grumpy," she complained to Nina in the bus the next day.

Nina squinted. "Cormac MacPherson?" she said. He'd done the health visits for John when he was tiny and had bounced the little creature up and down, then dangled him from his fingertips, turned him upside down to glance at his bum, said, "Yup, perfect bairn, A-one," and gotten him straight up again, while she had watched in horror. Lennox had allowed himself a private grin, given how much Nina fretted about the baby and whether he was all right and if a snuffle meant he was going to die. Lennox knew livestock, and obviously his only son wasn't livestock. But he wasn't exactly *not* livestock, and Lennox knew something bouncing with glorious health when he saw it.

"I know," said Lissa crossly. She was more upset than she'd let on; she'd kind of thought they were becoming . . . friends didn't seem to quite work. Pen pals?

However, she'd made sure every other note she'd sent that day had been entirely professional in possibly quite a passive-aggressive way, and he had, equally passive-aggressively, not gotten back to her at all and left her in quite the temper.

Her face softened, though, as she spied the new Kate Atkinson novel and Nina handed it over.

"Maybe London's affecting Cormac," said Nina thoughtfully. "Making him cranky. Is he happy there?"

Lissa looked pensive. "I don't know," she said. "It never occurred to me to ask. I've no idea how he's getting on."

"Right," said Nina. "Well . . . maybe you should?"

"Hmm," said Lissa. "And what about Cameron Blaine?"

Nina looked around. "Well," she said, "I don't know. I mean, I believe books can fix most things, but . . ."

She had a sudden thought.

"You could try?" And she went to the shelf of classics and pulled out *The Catcher in the Rye*.

"Buying him a book?" said Lissa.

"No need to sound *so* sarcastic."

"I don't want to buy him a present! I want to clip him round the ear."

"Tell me you didn't say that to Cormac."

"No," said Lissa, looking chastened. "He's not talking to me now anyway."

She picked up the familiar book, the edition she knew with the red horse on the cover.

Lissa looked at Nina. "Do you think? It's ancient now."

Nina shrugged. "Does as good a job at reaching adolescent alienation as anything I've ever known."

"I suppose," said Lissa. "Okay, I'll take it. Cormac can pay me back for going above and beyond."

"Bring it back if he doesn't want it," said Nina.

"What if he can't read?"

"That too."

"What if the dog eats it?"

"I think you're procrastinating."

Lissa thought guiltily of everything she should have been doing and felt the anxiety surge again. "Maybe," she admitted.

"That's okay," said Nina. "Most people, when they come across the Blaines, just turn and run. Procrastination is a step in the right direction."

BUT EVEN WHEN she wanted to email Cormac to tell him what she'd done—she'd left a note inside the book, put it on top of the letter box, and, she was ashamed to say, run away— she found she didn't, because she still hadn't heard from him. And then she was puzzled why she even cared that she hadn't heard from him and wanted to stop checking her phone, which was annoying because . . . well, it was annoying. He was being stubborn and irritating and accusing her of not doing her job, and she was furious.

CORMAC WAS FURIOUS. He would have thought that she of all people would understand the vulnerability of damaged young men; she was literally there to try to look after them and make life a bit better. Okay, so they were a bit nasty, but he'd met plenty worse on her beat. He reckoned she thought everyone in the Highlands was just adorable like on a short-bread tin and everything was gorgeous and perfect. She didn't want anything to cloud her judgment of how beautiful the place was, to spoil her vision of loveliness. It was all about her. But there was poverty and deprivation there as there was anywhere else—sometimes worse, due to isolation, stretched services, low wages, and bad public transportation. She couldn't turn her head away just because it wasn't pretty and she had to realize that. And Robbie was preying on his mind too.

London annoyed him tonight; it was hot and noisy, and he couldn't sleep. He wished he were back at home, with the cool breeze coming through the open cottage window, nothing but the rustle of . . . *Ned! Shit!* He sat bolt upright in bed.

Chapter 39

He was still cross with Lissa. He didn't want to email her. And it was late. But he'd forgotten about Ned! How could he? Damn damn damn damn. London had turned his head.

He reached for his laptop and opened it up. Maybe she'd be in bed. Or asleep. He didn't want to type first; it would look like he was apologizing.

He looked at his last sent message and winced a little. Maybe it had been a little harsh. But even so, this was serious.

He sat in his T-shirt and boxers on the side of the too-small single bed, rubbing the back of his neck with his large hand, wondering what to do. Finally he began to type: Are you up?

Lissa couldn't deny being pleased but was also annoyed that a) she was still up, and b) she'd been waiting to hear from him while pretending she wasn't.

Can I help you? she typed rather stiffly.

Can you hear anything in the garden?

What? Why, what is it? Is someone out there??

No. Yes. No.

Slightly fearful, Lissa jumped up. Was it the Blaine family? Were they going to come around, torch the place or something?

She stared out into the garden. She couldn't see anything, but she could hear a rustle. A definite rustle. Her heart started pumping at a gallop.

Do I need to call 999?

Cormac stared at the computer in disbelief, starting to laugh.

God no. DON'T!!! It's Neddie. I forgot he comes about this time
     and I meant to tell you and if you don't feed him he might
     leave.

?????

In the spring. When he wakes up.

????

He's a hedgehog.

A HEDGEHOG??????

Yes.

YOU GAVE ME A HEART ATTACK FOR A FRICKING HEDGEHOG??!!!!!

He's a very nice hedgehog.

I DON'T WANT A FRICKING HEDGEHOG!!!!!!

I'm not asking you to adopt him. Could you leave a saucer out for
 him? Water and honey. Not milk, that's a myth.

You want me to get up right now, go out in the pitch dark and
 freezing cold, and leave honey for a hedgehog.

Is that okay? Only if he doesn't find it, he'll go elsewhere and he'll
 get killed on the road or something.

Lissa looked outside again but couldn't see a thing. There
was some rustling. Oh crap, she was going to have to go outside, otherwise she'd be a hedgehog murderer as well as a "bad
nurse." She rolled her eyes and went downstairs, squeezed some
Huckle honey and water into a little saucer.

THE WORLD OUTSIDE was extraordinary. No cars passed at
this time on the little road; there was no light to be seen anywhere except the dim kitchen lamp in the cottage. A bright,
almost full moon shone overhead, making everything bright
and clear; the stream rippled, full of gold and silver, and the
heavy scent of the bluebells settled over everything. The grass
was wet and cold beneath her feet; it needed cutting, but she
didn't mind. She stepped forward carefully into the enchanted
midnight garden, not a soul in sight, waited for her eyes to
adjust, then knelt down.

 She padded as quietly as she could over to the rustling bush,
then took out her phone and turned on the flashlight. And

there it was! A tiny flash of two bright eyes, then in a blink the little creature was in a fierce ball.

"It's all right," she crooned. "It's okay."

She turned the flashlight off immediately; she didn't want to scare it.

"Here."

She put the saucer down, the moon reflecting straight into the clear ice-cool water, then retreated quietly and knelt down by the back door, absolutely freezing, to watch.

After what felt like a long time, when she could see perfectly well all the outlines of the bushes and the trees, the rustling started up again, and she saw the little shape scamper on tiny feet over to the bowl. It was so cute she nearly exclaimed, wanted desperately to take a photo but knew she couldn't.

Instead she simply sat and watched, feeling incredibly privileged as the tiny thing lapped at the saucer happily; she felt as if royalty had come to tea, as if the universe had bestowed upon her a great secret gift.

EUPHORICALLY, SHE STAYED still until he had had his fill, refilled the saucer, then headed back up to bed, chilled but triumphant.

He's here!!!

Great!!!!

Why is he called Ned?

All hedgehogs are called Ned! Neddie Needles!

His full name is Neddie Needles???

That's what's on his birth certificate.

I've seen worse.

So have I.

How do you know it's the same hedgehog?

I put a splodge of paint on his bristles, did you see it?

Isn't that cruel?

It's a very tiny splodge. Right, I'm going to bed, you can report me to the
    Royal Society for the Prevention of Paint-Based Hedgehog Cruelty.

There was a pause.
Sorry for being hard on you about Cameron. I'd had a tough day, Cormac typed eventually.

No, you were right. I just wasn't expecting it. I bought him a book!

Have you been hanging out with Nina Lennox?

Might have.

She thinks that's the answer to everything.

Maybe it is.

If he can read.

I'll pop back in.

Cheers.

Well, good night.

Good night.

And then a short time later:

Part III

Chapter 40

Neddie was gone the next day, but Lissa refilled his saucer anyway. She'd have liked to have taken a picture. On the other hand, she had a drawing. She pushed on through the garden and out into the field behind the house.

Lissa found herself wandering through the waist-high meadowsweet grass, breathing it in. When it wasn't absolutely hosing, there was no doubt the landscape was completely ridiculous. She supposed the rain was what made the green so vivid as to be luminous and the clumps of wildflowers—and nettles, as she discovered when wandering off trail and being glad she hadn't gone the whole hog and opted for shorts—so vibrant and full, the bees dancing among the tall purple flowers.

She found a stream rippling through the woods past the bluebells and, worrying slightly as to whether she'd be poisoned (she checked for sheep pooing in it: there didn't seem to be many nearby), finally filled her water bottle—the sun was warm on her back—and took a long pull.

The freezing bright freshness of it made her gasp; she could feel it coursing down her throat, so pure and clean and bracing she felt her eyes dazzle with it. As she straightened up, almost drunk on the frozen light, she found herself face-to-face with a huge stag at the opposite end of the clearing.

She blinked and stretched out her phone to take a picture, almost as if it wasn't real until she did . . . but as soon as she moved her arm, to her great regret, it turned and bounded, crackling through the bracken, the speed of it astonishing until it was gone and she felt like she'd dreamed it.

She carried on, walking almost without direction, off past the village and onto a long road overshadowed with trees. It was farther than it looked, and she realized quickly that she was out of condition. She'd just been sitting, she thought. Sitting, and fretting, and obsessing, and fiddling with her phone, just to put off . . . well, everything. Looking at pictures of other people's parties. It had been a distraction, but it hadn't helped. Anita was right. Coming off it was the best thing she'd done.

SHE HIT THE roadway eventually and was about to turn back, when she saw trundling toward her a pale blue van and recognized Zoe, the woman with all the children, driving it, although she was alone for once. She waved, and Zoe immediately pulled over.

"Hello! Want a lift?"

Lissa almost smiled: it felt as if the universe had answered her so quickly. "Um, yes, please. Are you heading to the village?"

"Nina needs to do the banking. Hop in!"

"It's weird to see you by yourself."

"I know! Having both hands to myself is very strange."

Lissa pulled herself up into the van's tall carriage. Zoe passed her a bag of tablet.

"What is this stuff?"

"Keeps your energy levels up."

It was a hard, sugary fudge that, once you got over the insane pitch of sweetness, was incredibly delicious.

"Oh goodness," said Lissa.

"I know," said Zoe. "Shackleton made it. Then I confiscated it in case they all get diabetes."

Lissa looked at the bag.

"Yes, please eat more," said Zoe. "Seriously, it's going to kill me. It's going to kill us all."

"We should have one more piece each then hurl the rest out of the window," said Lissa bravely.

"You'd kill the first bird that found it," said Zoe mournfully. "Stone dead. Nobody's body can absorb that much sugar without consequences."

They both looked at the bag again.

"Perhaps if we just finished it and got it out of the way, we wouldn't have to think about it again," said Zoe.

"We could keep some for Nina."

"She can't have it. It would kill John if he got it through her breast milk."

Giggling mightily, they put the absolutely delicious vanilla-flavored lumps of tablet in their mouths to happily dissolve as the van trundled down the country road, not another car in sight, the sun streaming through the van's open windows, the radio playing a jolly song with fiddles and lyrics Lissa couldn't make out.

Nina was pleased to see them as they rounded the farmyard.

"Watch out for that chicken," said Zoe to Lissa as she stepped down. A particularly beady-eyed specimen was lurking, stepping from side to side in a corner of the farmyard. "She's a total nightmare."

Lissa looked at the chicken, who glanced back at her, then directed her gaze straight back to Zoe. It was almost as if she was looking at Zoe specifically, in a threatening fashion, but that couldn't possibly be true.

Anyway, Nina was sitting cheerfully on the steps of the book bus and waved them over. "Kettle's just boiled."

"Where's John?"

"Out with Lennox," said Nina, rolling her eyes but looking proud at the same time. Her bonny boy and his dad were rarely parted. "Have a good morning?"

"Yes!" said Zoe. "Those cuddly Nessies are flying off the shelf."

Nina rolled her eyes again. The tension between her beautifully curated bookshop and Zoe's more touristy shop—Zoe parked up at Loch Ness—was sometimes there, but it didn't matter. They were both making a living, and now, sitting out in the cool shade of the beautiful farmhouse, with three huge mugs of tea, Lissa reveled in their chat, especially what it was like coming from an English city to such a remote part of the world.

"My mum thought I was coming to the moon," said Zoe. "And also that I would be kidnapped by my new employer."

Nina smiled in response. "At least you weren't the first English girl ever to set foot here. The silence in Eck's pub!"

Zoe laughed.

"I think Eck thought you were going to seduce Ramsay," Nina continued.

"Evil English temptress," agreed Zoe.

"So what do you think?" said Nina, turning to Lissa. "Are you going to stay for a bit?"

"I can't," said Lissa. "It's just a placement."

"Why did you choose here?" said Nina curiously. "I mean, I kind of got stuck . . ."

Lissa shrugged. "The . . . I mean, this is where it came up with Cormac."

"Good old Cormac," said Nina. "I bet he's having an absolute ball down there."

Lissa wondered what she meant by this but didn't pursue it in case it meant, as she suspected, "getting lots of girls," some of whom might even be her friends. She thought of her hedgehog picture and smiled, then dismissed it. He obviously did that for everyone.

Instead she leaned forward. She was glad she was off the internet, but she did miss just having people to chat to. And she felt she ought to be a little brave. After all, they'd all made the move.

"I . . . They kind of sent me here to . . ."

The other girls went silent, sensing she had something to say.

"I had a rough time in London," Lissa confessed. "I was a witness to a hit-and-run and . . . it all got a bit much for me."

Nobody said anything.

"So. I'm kind of supposedly on a quieter beat for a bit. The NHS equivalent of basket weaving."

She attempted to smile, but it didn't quite work.

Zoe leaned forward. "Was it awful?" she said gently.

Lissa got that awful about-to-cry feeling again. She couldn't speak, just nodded.

Nina, who was next to her, patted her gently on the hand. "God, that must be awful. The worst that's ever happened to me was a paper cut."

Lissa half smiled.

"Is it helping?" said Zoe.

"I wasn't . . . I mean, I wasn't, like, traumatized or anything. But I was stressed out and miserable, and coming here . . ."

A flock of swallows lifted up from the far field across the road, in one great swarm. Lissa watched them go.

"I think so."

"Hang on," said Nina, standing up and going inside. She came back with a small book with a woman standing on the cover. "Here."

Lissa picked it up.

"I got two copies by accident," said Nina. "You can have it."

"*The Accidental Tourist,*" read Lissa. "What's it about?"

"Healing," said Nina. "Best book ever written on the subject."

Lissa looked up at her, touched beyond measure. "Thank you."

"You're welcome. *Oh*." Her face changed. "Here they come!"

Lennox was bouncing the baby on his shoulders, heading down from the fields for lunch. In the old days he'd have taken a lunch box and thrown a sandwich in his mouth in the barn. Now, he knew there was warm bread in the kitchen from the baker, good cheese, and ripe tomatoes, and if he wasn't mistaken, Nina had bought some ironic ginger beer that they were both enjoying entirely unironically. Seeing they had company made him clam up slightly, as usual, but the girls talked enough for them all, as they sat out on the first clear warm day of the year, watching John try to crawl on the rug, as the chicken pecked sinisterly at the corner of the barn. Eventually Lissa headed off, clutching her book gift as if it were a treasure.

"Oh," said Lennox as she went. "Are you talking to Cormac at all?"

Lissa flushed. "Um . . . only professionally, you know, patient notes and stuff."

Lennox wasn't interested in that. "Tell him I need harvesters, I'm not kidding. Barn's all set up. Ninety squillion lads in London, they can surely spare a few."

Lissa blinked, then nodded and carried on her way.

Chapter 41

Cormac headed out, taking Robbie his breakfast. To his surprise Robbie was sitting up, staring into the distance; normally he was unconscious at this time of day, and Cormac would leave the food near him.

"Morning," said Cormac.

Robbie looked at him, and it wasn't the usual unfocused look he had. The sun was out and could just be glimpsed behind the roundabout underpass. Robbie scratched his head. "Man," he said. "Can I ask you something?"

"Sure," said Cormac.

Robbie looked uncomfortable. "Can I . . . can I have a shower?"

Cormac thought about it. Sure, nobody was going to mind. The only person he was going to have to deal with was . . .

"MORNING," HE SAID.

The grumpy porter looked up and grunted. Then he focused on Robbie, looking disgruntled. There was, undeniably, quite the whiff.

"I brought you this," said Cormac. "I just had too many."

And he handed over a bag of fresh pain au raisins. Being able to go out and buy pretty much whatever you liked whenever you felt like it remained quite the novelty to Cormac, and he was enjoying it.

"Try them," he said. "I think they're French. They've got custard in them!"

The man sniffed, then without another word took the bag off Cormac, who quickly shuffled Robbie inside.

CORMAC BUNDLED ROBBIE into the showers with a fresh towel, some of his clothes, and instructions to stay in as long as he wanted; the hot water was limitless, even if the tiles were cracked.

Kim-Ange caught him at the basement laundry door and stood there, arms folded. "Who's that in the shower?"

"A . . . friend," said Cormac.

Kim-Ange beamed. "A lover?"

"No!"

She frowned at him and he realized he'd gotten it wrong again. London was teaching him a lot.

"I mean, that would be obviously fine, aye . . ."

Kim-Ange nodded more appreciatively. "But it isn't . . ."

"Not on this occasion, no," said Cormac, feeling increasingly stupid.

"Okay then," said Kim-Ange. "So he's a friend of yours?"

Cormac explained. Kim-Ange raised her eyebrows.

"You've let a homeless guy into a nurses' home?"

"I thought you were meant to be the tolerant one."

"Well, have you left your wallet in your bedroom?"

Cormac had, of course. He turned around, then turned back. "I'm sure it's fine."

"Yes, all right, country bumpkin," said Kim-Ange.

"Oh, for heaven's sake," said Cormac, as she followed him back upstairs.

THE ROOM WAS empty, the shower too. Cormac called out Robbie's name, but there was no response at all; he'd done a runner, taking Cormac's clean clothes but leaving his dirty ones behind. They were, truly, only fit for the bin.

Cormac looked around for his phone, but it was in his pocket—there was a new message from Lissa, something about Lennox looking for harvesters. Well, he was hardly going to manage that, was he? He scrabbled around the room, trying not to let Kim-Ange see that he was worried or reveal the huge relief he felt when he saw his wallet, untouched, on the desk, and his watch next to it, likewise, and he felt both instantly guilty and dreadfully sorry for Robbie running away. He sat down on the bed, defeated. Kim-Ange made a decision.

"Come for a walk with me," said Kim-Ange. She was wearing a bright gold sleeveless jacket with fur trim over her wide back, tight black leggings, and high-heeled gold Timberlands, with gold eye shadow to match. It was a little alarming to the uninitiated.

"What time is it?" said Cormac.

"Going-for-a-walk time," said Kim-Ange.

Cormac groaned and went over and washed his face in the

small sink. "Are you sure you don't just want me with you so you can lean on me when your feet get sore in your very stupid shoes?" he said.

They were quite stupid shoes, with a dangerous-looking stiletto heel.

"I do," said Kim-Ange. "And bare your teeth if anyone starts shouting."

"Who's going to shout at you?" said Cormac, drying his stubble. "And even if they do, you won't hear them up there, you're about nine feet tall in those."

"Catwalk," said Kim-Ange sagely. "Come on, we'll go up to Tate Modern. They're all arty up there. I shall be *appreciated*."

She smiled at him.

"Well done for this morning. Risky, but you pulled it off."

Cormac didn't feel much better, though.

Although once they got outside, into what Cormac considered to be a terrifying heat wave and everyone else thought was a perfectly normal day, he felt that something had changed. At first when he'd gone into clothes shops or walked through Soho, marveling at the looks, the fashion, the different types of people—male, female, and everything in between—he'd found it embarrassing. Why would anyone dress like that? Why would people want to stand out and have everyone stare at them, giggling and pointing?

Now, as he started to get more used to the ins and outs of the inner city, he'd realized something that would have completely surprised him: he liked it.

He liked the individuality of people's dressing. He liked the

effort that went into having silver hair, or wearing a wig or
something incredibly uncomfortable, just so that everyone else
didn't have to look at the same boring jeans and fleeces all day.

He also had a theory: In Scotland, the colors and the world
around you changed daily, hourly even. The pink of the blos-
som bursting, the gold of the daffodils, the deep greens of the
grass after the rain, and the soft lavender of the heather on
the hillsides. Bright yellow fields of rapeseed; fresh white lambs
dotting the place like clouds; sunsets that stretched uninter-
rupted for miles.

Here it was gray pavement, gray buildings, gray pavement,
brown buildings, everywhere you went. Always the same, never
changing. Harsh electric lights burning yellow, over and over
again. You could barely see the sky from the street, couldn't
see anything bursting into life and color, changing day by day.
Nothing changed. Everything was at the same temperature,
everything was built upon, and anything that wasn't had a
crane sitting on top of it.

So people dressing colorfully, wearing yellow spectacles or
bright turquoise suits or pointy red shoes, they were all adding
to the brick urban landscape, giving you something beautiful
and interesting to look at, because, in Cormac's mind, they
were so unlucky as to be trapped somewhere they couldn't look
at the sea, and the trees, and the sky.

They walked along the embankment of the vast sludge-
covered river. It being the weekend, the sidewalks were absolutely thronged with people: families; people on bicycles and
scooters, mostly ridiculous grown men with funny beards;

brightly colored groups of young Italians with large rucksacks; self-satisfied people stepping out of the curious Globe Theatre. There were just so many people. How, thought Cormac, did you ever get used to it? He understood completely now why you couldn't say hello to passersby, couldn't even make eye contact. It would be impossible, exhausting. Except, as he got carried along by the throng, he found himself thinking, *You know, if anyone was looking at me, they wouldn't necessarily think that I came from a tiny village, that I'd never spent time in the city before. They would see me walk and not think anything of it, think I'd lived like this all my life.* And he found, to his surprise, that he rather liked that sensation.

"We're going to look at some art," announced Kim-Ange.

"I don't know anything about art," said Cormac.

"You doodle all day long!"

"That's different. And modern art is weird. It looks like a kid did it."

"What an original and valuable insight," said Kim-Ange. "You're in the middle of one of the best centers for art in the world and all you want to do is sit in steak house windows in Leicester Square."

Cormac wished he'd never told her that. "Shut up."

"No, you shut up! You might learn something!"

Cormac trailed after her like a reluctant child as they entered a huge factory building with high brown chimneys right on the riverbank. There was a low, wide set of glass doors along the back end, and small children with scooters and tricycles were gleefully careering about the open space.

Inside, away from the sunlight, it was gloomy and cool. The sloping concrete floor opened onto a vast underground chamber filled with odd shapes and sizes. Cormac folded his arms and announced that he couldn't tell a piece of sculpture from the sign for the toilets, but Kim-Ange oohed and aahed. Cormac nodded patiently and wondered whether there was a fast-food restaurant nearby, because in Kirrinfief the closest McDonald's was fifty miles away, and he found it something of a treat; it reminded him of birthdays when he was a child, when the entire family would make a special trip, and Jake had been bugging him to find out what KFC tasted like.

"Come look at this," said Kim-Ange, recognizing a bored person when she saw it. "These are cool. It's a guy who went mad. And he painted pictures of his madness. And they're the best insights into trauma I think we have."

Cormac was expecting something weird and surreal—melting clocks maybe. He wasn't expecting what he saw. The upper galleries were dimly lit, practically dark, and he found himself in a small room, shaped like a pentagon, with large canvases hanging on each felt-covered wall. The effect was close and claustrophobic.

The first thing he noticed was there was nothing on them: no shapes, no drawings of anything at all, just great blocks of pure color looming above him. What on earth was this? What a complete waste of his time. He didn't understand modern art, and that was that. Kim-Ange, meanwhile, was off to the side, staring, utterly rapt.

He peered closer, then took a step back, so he could take in the whole of a canvas at one go. It was three blocks of color, but it could—did, in fact—look like the ground, the sea, and the sky. The sky section was a deep rust color, like dried blood or the warning of something ominous; the blue section below was battered and rough, as if the sky was upsetting the sea, because something terrible was coming; and the earth was brown and dry, as if everything was hopeless and everything had need; it was unutterably bleak, extraordinarily beautiful. *How?* Cormac thought. *It's just some paint on a wall.* But it filled him with deep and heavy emotions.

"Oh my God," he said finally.

"I know," said Kim-Ange, who had a look of fervent reverence on her face, as if having a religious experience. "Aren't they amazing?"

Cormac looked at another one. Here there was a diseased yellow, the color itself, the very pigment, like a howl of disgust and misery. It had the ability to spear his mood, get right to the heart of him; he felt the artist was crying out, personally, for help, straight to him.

"Who *is* this artist?"

"Mark," said Kim-Ange, respectfully. "Mark Rothko."

"Is he still alive? What happened to him?"

Kim-Ange looked at Cormac and he immediately knew the answer.

"Suicide," he said. "It's written there."

"Plain as day," said Kim-Ange, with an uncharacteristically grim tone.

Suddenly Cormac found himself thinking: of Robbie, yes,

but also of Lissa. Is this how she had felt? Why she'd had to move?

"Amazing," he said, gazing at the paintings.

They passed through halls and rooms of modernism, of the world sliced up and twisted around.

"Why did they start doing this?" he said.

"Why do you think?" said Kim-Ange, pointing out a Braques. "Look when it all started, a hundred years ago."

Cormac blinked. "After the First World War."

"After the war"—Kim-Ange nodded—"when the world got ripped apart. After Hiroshima, it got torn up again. You couldn't look at life the way people had looked at it before."

Now Cormac couldn't see enough of it. He wandered through the galleries of Picassos, Dalís, mouth open.

"They're all soldiers."

"We're all soldiers," observed Kim-Ange, eventually pulling him away. "Art is amazing," she added perkily. "*And* you get a slice of cake at the end of it. Shall we?"

And Cormac was just about to enthusiastically agree, and concede that, okay, London maybe *did* have a bit more to offer than he'd originally thought . . . but his phone buzzed, and he took it out and stared at it, disconsolately, reading a message.

"Oh, bugger," he said.

Chapter 42

Why didn't you call me?" he almost yelled down the phone.

"It's just a broken wrist," said his mother, equally crossly. "I called a taxi. Honestly, don't worry about it."

"What were you doing?"

"I was on the trapeze."

"Mu-um."

"My stupid bicycle. How's London?"

"So who set it for you?"

"Some nine-year-old up at the hospital."

"I'll pop up," said Cormac.

"You won't 'pop up,'" said Bridie. "I am perfectly fine and Yasmeena is coming over."

Yasmeena lived in Inverness with Lewis, the middle son.

Cormac sighed. "I can get a flight."

"You can do nothing of the sort! You've got a job to do. I am totally fine."

Cormac took stock. After his father had died, his mother's default was "totally fine," and she took any insinuation to the contrary as a total insult.

"Okay," he said. "Well, at least there'll be someone to check it for you. I wouldn't have been allowed."

"It's fine!"

"I mean, I would anyway . . ."

"It's fine! I'm busy anyway."

"Which wrist is it?"

"My right," admitted Bridie.

"Mum!" Cormac tsked. "It's okay, I'm going to get the new girl who's standing in for me to pop in."

"I've seen her," said Bridie. "She has hair all over the place."

"So I hear," said Cormac.

"And she's a bit standoffish."

"You think everyone who doesn't come from Kirrinfief is standoffish! Remember what you said about that woman with the book bus?"

"Aye, she's all right, Nina."

"She is!" said Cormac. "So is Alyssa. I'm pretty sure."

"Mm-hmm," said Bridie.

Which is how Cormac found himself writing a note on Monday morning asking, as politely as he knew how, if Lissa could possibly go and visit his mother.

LISSA WAS CURIOUS, she couldn't help it. Cormac sent her stupid little pictures, but he didn't give that much away. Not that she'd been thinking about him, but given she was living in his house, she couldn't help but wonder, couldn't help being slightly aware of the smell of someone else's aftershave, shampoo, pillowcases. She hadn't snooped. But she'd considered it.

She picked up the notes from Joan, although there was nothing in them—a sixty-four-year-old woman in absolutely tremendous health with a snapped wrist from falling off her bicycle—and went around, faintly nervous.

The woman didn't answer the bell of the small neat Victorian stone house with its arched porch and pretty pathway, and Lissa eventually found herself pootling down the little close at the side until she got into the immaculate back garden, filled with neat rows of daffodils, bluebells, and rhododendron bushes and grass so perfect it looked like someone had trimmed it with nail scissors. The woman was trying to weed with one hand, the other in a sling, and it looked like she would topple over at any moment.

"Um, hello?" said Lissa, trying not to startle her.

Mrs. MacPherson stood up with a start. "Hello?"

"I'm Lissa Westcott . . . the nurse liaison? I just came to check up on you."

The short woman with steel-gray hair cut close to her head—no room for vanity here—looked at her beadily. "Yes, I know who you are. You're doing my son's job. Why are you here?"

"Well . . . because it's procedure?"

"It's a broken wrist! Have you come round to give me a lollipop?"

"No. Although if you'd like one . . ."

"Or perhaps I count as geriatric now, and you're here to move me into a home where you can't have a hot bath for health and safety reasons?"

Lissa shook her head. "Cormac asked me to come take a look," she said honestly. "He's just worried about you."

"So he sent a *spy*?"

Nonetheless Bridie bustled inside through a small set of French doors built into the back of the house. After a moment or two, Lissa started to follow her.

"Beautiful garden," said Lissa.

"Is this truly the best use of NHS resources?" grumbled Bridie.

Lissa could see it was an effort for her to fill the kettle. Once that was on she looked around. There were pictures of little boys everywhere—she hadn't known he had brothers. It was impossible to tell which one was Cormac from the three sandy heads and toothless grins, and Lissa was suddenly too shy to ask. She did feel like she was spying—but not on Bridie.

"So can you wiggle your fingers for me?" she said, taking Bridie's hand, once she'd made them both tea. "And put some pressure on my hand here . . . and here . . . good, good."

She moved her head closer, performing the embarrassing bit where she had to sniff the bandage for evidence of rot or bad skin healing without looking like that was what she was doing.

"Are you *sniffing* me?" said Bridie rather crossly.

"So is Cormac enjoying himself in London, then?" asked Lissa quickly.

Bridie shrugged. "I dinnae ken. Is he staying in your hoose?"

"Well, my digs," said Lissa. "It's a nurses' home really. Nothing like as nice as his place."

"A nurses' home. I'm so proud," said Bridie dryly. Lissa caught sight of a photo of a handsome man wearing a smart army uniform, including an elaborate hat that came over his chin, with a younger Bridie and a stooped man on either side.

"Is this him?"

"Naw," said Bridie, her voice softening a little. "That's Rawdon."

"He's in the army?"

"So was Cormac once. Now he's busy living in a nurses' home, apparently." Her voice sounded raw.

"He didn't like it?" ventured Lissa.

"Not everyone can cut the army," said Bridie sharply. "He's just like his father. Anyway. Here it is. It's a broken wrist. Well done. Can you tick your ninety-five file boxes, give me some nonsense survey, and be on your way, lass? I'm busy."

She didn't, to Lissa's practiced eye, look remotely busy. The house was immaculate.

"Is anyone helping you out?"

"Aye," said Bridie. "This is Kirrinfief. We help each other oot. Dinnae worry about me. I ken you English types don't really believe in friendship, but we do round these parts."

"All right," said Lissa, knowing when she was beaten. "Okay, I'll tell Cormac you're fine."

Bridie sniffed. "Well, make sure you don't interrupt him being too busy in the *nurses' home,* filling in all those forms."

Lissa blinked. She glanced out the window into Bridie's spectacular garden, where a pair of starlings was pecking on the lawn. Then she got up.

"There is nothing wrong with you, you're healing fine," she said. "Do you want me to tell Cormac I'm popping in every day and then not come?"

Bridie smiled. "That would be perfect."

IN A FUNNY way, although she had learned nothing about him, Lissa was actually quite happy. It was easy, when you were having a difficult time, to think of everyone else's lives as absolutely perfect and straightforward. This was why coming off Instagram had been, on balance, a good idea. So although she felt slightly sorry for Cormac having a grumpy mother—her own mother had pretty high expectations of her too—she also felt a little comforted.

She's fine, Lissa typed. Big army fan.

She is, said Cormac, but nothing more.

Were you in the army for long?

Eight years.

That is a long time! Why did you leave?

Why did you leave A&E?

How did you know I was in A&E?

Kim-Ange told me.

That's very unfair.

You went to my mum's house!

You asked me to!

This was straying into the realm of a very personal conversation, and Lissa was worried, suddenly, that she'd gone too far. She was, after all, sitting in his house. It wasn't really fair; it was just a professional swap.

How were the Lindells? she typed suddenly, anxious not to offend him.

Cormac mentally groaned, although at least he was on safer ground. He did feel uncomfortable, wondering what his mother had told Lissa, what she told everyone else in the village. She didn't know what he'd seen, what it was like out there. Neither did Lissa, neither did Emer. Nobody did.

He wrenched his memory back to his unpleasant afternoon.

It was horrible to see.

I know.

THE ODDEST THING had been that Cormac had just been thinking how surprised he was by the city, how it wasn't at all what he'd expected. From the papers you'd think it was all pollution and crime, but instead he found himself daily impressed by the layers of history, from the Roman walls in the City to the mudlarks down by the Thames, searching for ancient coins and treasure from the two thousand years' worth of boats that had traveled up and down the river. And the contrasts, like where he was now, with the shining modern glass towers and the beautifully preserved old Georgian buildings of weavers and artisans past. Walking to his next appointment, he had passed an ancient building where they made up coats of arms and that housed the great merchant companies of the cities, then, being characteristically early, he had taken a detour to see the extraordinary inns of Chancery, with their fountains and gardens, mysterious shops selling wigs and pens, and signposts to the "Yeoman's Office." Cormac had never been academic, but even he was quietly taken aback to walk past the redbrick Middle Temple Hall and read a small plaque modestly mentioning that Shakespeare's *Twelfth Night* was first performed within its walls; he had then passed the famous circular church of the Knights Templars, with its gray stone effigies laid to rest.

It was a completely different world from any he had ever known; he felt there was a surprise behind every corner in London, a sense too of the huge weight of history, commerce, and grandeur that made it easy—perhaps even necessary—for Westminster to send a bunch of young lads from small towns far, far away to fight and die in a distant desert.

He was in a thoughtful frame of mind when he reached his next appointment, and what happened next did not change it.

The house, some distance away, was located down a quiet residential street, tucked away just across from the river, where the great steel towers met the Georgian byways of Shoreditch. It had big, flat-fronted windows, with brightly polished panes of ancient glass in freshly painted pale green frames, and neat potted plants of lavender and small orange trees. It was a beautiful house, immaculately restored, and Cormac could only wonder about the amount of money invested in such a project. He'd double-checked the address, but no, it was here all right.

An incredibly beautiful woman answered the door: tanned skin, blond hair tumbling over a pretty, flowing dress. It was a sunny day, and the yellow light pooling into the lane made her appear to glow.

"You're from the hospital?"

Cormac showed his badge.

"Not the Social?"

The way she said "the Social" sounded odd with her posh accent; it wasn't, in his experience, the kind of thing women who looked like that and lived in multimillion-pound houses normally said. They normally never met with Social Services at all.

"Just the health worker," he said, almost adding "ma'am" to it, her tone was so imperious.

She sighed. "I'm sure you feed back to your spy network," she said.

Cormac wrinkled his brow and tried to imagine what that might be like. "Sorry," he said. "Is this a bad time?"

She shrugged in bad grace and let him in.

INSIDE THE HOUSE was even more beautiful: architecturally designed, full of light and slick lines. Expensive-looking art books were piled up heavily on the tables; abstract pictures hung on the walls, which Cormac eyed with a newly found interest. It was a haven: it looked like a magazine shoot. Inside the vast light-filled kitchen, which had been extended back over the glorious garden, were folding doors that today were flung open, meaning the indoors and outdoors mingled, and you could hear birds squawking and bees buzzing—the first time, Cormac realized with a start, that he'd heard these things since he'd gotten to London. A tall, incredibly handsome man wearing tortoiseshell glasses and a perfectly ironed linen shirt was making a green juice in a blender. He turned it off and gave the same distant smile to Cormac. The pair of them were so tall and beautiful they could be in an advertisement, or identical twins.

"Right," said Cormac. "So . . . the patient?"

The woman rolled her eyes. "She's *fine*."

The woman led him upstairs, past more pictures and books, set off with expensive lighting and polished wood shelves and the scent of posh candles. She took him into a second-floor bedroom, a beautiful, hand-painted room full of friezes of flowers and fairies dancing, with a soft pale carpet on the floor and a huge armchair, stuffed full of books and toys, including a large dollhouse propped underneath the window. It was a dream of a room for a little girl.

Lying there on the bed was a pitiable figure.

Soaked in sweat, bright red in the face, was a little girl of around eight or nine. She was completely covered in red dots. Cormac looked at her, telling himself not to let the horror show in his face. A Filipino woman was sitting by her head with a rag she periodically soaked in iced water, wringing it and placing it over the child's forehead.

He moved over.

"Hello . . . Titania," he said, worried he'd pronounced it wrong. "Hello. I'm Cormac. I'm a nurse and I'm here to see how you're getting on."

In response the child burst into tears. Cormac gently took her temperature, then looked at the mother.

"Have you been giving her the ibuprofen?" he said as gently as he could.

"No!" said the woman. "She's my child! I think I know what she needs! I'm treating her homeopathically!"

"I think that can be very useful," said Cormac, who thought nothing of the kind, "when given in conjunction with other medicines. And when it comes to beating back a fever, ibuprofen can really help."

"Well, you would say that," hissed the woman. "You're part of Big Pharma."

Cormac wished that he were and Big Pharma would top up his salary once in a while. The woman's calm, beautiful expression had gone; she now looked tight-faced and pinched.

"Are you giving her plenty of fluids?"

"Yes!" said the woman triumphantly. "This is Kona Nigari"— she held up a fantastically complicated-looking bottle —"it's collected from a Hawaiian spring and is the purest water in the world. We get it flown in specially. There's nothing we wouldn't do for our precious Titania."

She smiled beatifically at the child, but made no move to actually comfort her.

Cormac wiped the girl's forehead with a cloth, propping her up a little.

"You're going to be fine," he said to the moaning child. "It's just not very nice for a little while. But soon you'll be able to watch *Hey Duggee* again."

"Actually we believe screen rays are dangerous for children," said the mother in a sharp voice. "We don't believe in them."

Cormac was reasonably sure he'd seen the husband on his phone downstairs but didn't mention it. Instead he made notes on the form, saw that her temperature was down a little and that she was probably on the mend. But seeing a child suffer for no reason was almost more than he could bear.

"And afterward," he couldn't help asking—it was his duty— "when she's well, will you consider vaccinating against other diseases?"

"Well, she can't get measles again," said the mother as if he, Cormac, were being quite the idiot.

"No," said Cormac. "But you would maybe want to consider rubella?"

"But God knows what the government puts in vaccinations!" she said, almost screaming. "Have you ever seen an autistic child?!"

Cormac, of course, had seen many.

"If you think I'd subject my perfect daughter to something the government—the *government*—thinks is okay, you have another think coming."

Her face was now bright red, and Cormac didn't think she was anything like as beautiful as he had when they'd first met.

"It can protect other people who can't be vaccinated," he said gently.

The woman stared at him. "You've been totally brainwashed," she said quietly.

The child moaned on the bed.

Cormac held up his hands. "I think Titania needs rest. She's going to be fine."

"Of course she is!" said the woman. "She's being treated. Naturally! By me!"

And the great city had looked a little meaner to Cormac as he'd headed back home.

> For no stupid reason! Because of some stupid woman who thinks
> she knows better than hundreds of years of medical science!!!!
> Stupid spoiled spoiled spoiled cow.

> Then ten seconds later he realized.

> Shit! This is our official NHS account!!!!

> I know!!!!!!!

> Shit! Can you delete that? Please? Quickly?!

> It's NHS IT. They can't tell the arse codes from their elbow codes!

> I know. But!!!

> I know.

And that was how they moved on to text messaging and swapped telephone numbers.

Chapter 43

Jake finally plucked up the courage—much to the disappointment and the rather unkind remarks, if we're being honest, of Ginty MacGuire in the hairdresser's, who also might have mentioned in passing that if that new nurse thought that she, Ginty MacGuire, was going to do her hair for the big night, she had another think coming—to ask Lissa to the farmers' dance that took place before the fair arrived.

It was a big affair around their neck of the woods, and with the typical Highlands imbalance of men to women, it wasn't like Ginty MacGuire hadn't already been asked four or five times by shy, sturdy red-cheeked young men; but that didn't matter. She wasn't the least bit interested in them and very interested in the dark-eyed Jake Inglis and the excellent time they'd had last summer, but he seemed to have time for no one these days but that exotic-looking incomer, which was men for you.

In general her clientele agreed with her (it is wise, incidentally, if you live in a very small village, not to get on the wrong side of its only hairdresser). Lissa, to them, still seemed a little strange and standoffish, always looking as if she was in a hurry to get places, dashing here and there. That was English folk for you. And now (once Jake had, while slightly drunk in Eck's, revealed his intentions to ask her to the dance) here she was, waltzing off with the most eligible man in the village, now that Cormac MacPherson was down south too. Talk about having your cake and eating it.

Then Jake had asked Cormac for her number, and Cormac had found himself slightly awkward about passing it on.

Jake asked me for your number, he sent, which was better on the text as they'd just been exchanging notes on anal polyp medication and he wasn't sure they weren't together.

I know, said Lissa.

I was going to ask you if it was okay to give it to him.

Of course.

Of course? thought Cormac.

Mrs. Murray and some very angry hairdresser told me he was going to ask me out. The hairdresser is quite scary.

She is. Are you going to go?

Cormac loved the farmers' dance. He thought back ruefully to the previous year, when he'd drunk a load of cider and let Emer do what she'd been pretty clear she wanted to do for some months, given how often she happened to be walking past the cottage in full makeup. He wasn't God's gift, Cormac would be the first to admit, but when girls liked him, they *really* liked him.

I don't know. Should I?

You should. It's at Lennox's farm, they always put a good spread on. And what else are you doing for fun?

Is this the bit where you show off about going to that private members club again?

In fact, Larissa had texted him, but Cormac had pretended he hadn't seen it. It wasn't really his scene. He didn't tell Lissa that, though.

Well, maybe you should up your game then.

What game?

The "Who's Having the Best Secondment" game.

That's not a game!

That's exactly what someone losing a game would say.

Lissa looked at the screen, slightly annoyed and amused. A tiny bit of her was, she thought, possibly—just a tiny bit, not really—hoping he might be jealous.

All right. I will go to your stupid dance. What should I wear?

Piss off! And that looks NOTHING LIKE ME!!

I'm relieved to hear that.

And what's the music going to be like? All fiddle-de-dee twiddly-dee
    "I would walk 500 miles" stuff?

Cormac didn't answer and Lissa wondered if she'd offended him.

She absolutely had.

AFTER HE DIDN'T reply, she glanced around the room and
noticed something she hadn't noticed before: a small stereo system, exactly the kind of thing that a well-meaning but otherwise utterly clueless auntie would buy you for your fourteenth
birthday. She had the exact same make and model, but it was in
the attic at her mum's house. Next to Cormac's, however, was
a line of CDs. Nothing as cool as vinyl, she thought, pictur-
ing her London hipster mates with their vintage record players

and independent record shop habit. Who still bought CDs? She leafed through them. Runrig, Orange Juice, Deacon Blue, Biffy Clyro, Del Amitri, Belle & Sebastian. Then she pulled out one with a picture of two identical men wearing glasses and playing the guitar. *Ah,* she thought.

Can I play some of your music? she typed, trying to placate him.

It's a bit "twiddly-dee" for you, came back.

She had offended him! Oh no! Boys and their music. She would hardly be offended if he didn't like hers, e.g., her mum's calypso music (this was a total lie; she would have been completely offended).

Maybe I'll give it a shot, she said.

Don't put yourself out, came back.

Lissa smiled. For a moment she found herself thinking maybe she could tease him later when she saw him . . . And then she remembered that he was in London and she was here and this was a professional work placement, and she rolled her eyes and went to look at her very limited wardrobe and do her best.

JAKE WAS INCREDIBLY pleased Lissa was coming out with him, even if it did mean bad haircuts for the rest of his life. And Cormac was good enough, listening to Jake's boasting, not to mention that he had had a little something to do with it. And he didn't tell Jake, or even himself, how much, in fact, he maybe would have liked to have been there too.

Tentatively, Lissa texted Zoe. It was really awkward, trying to make a new friend. She felt like she was fourteen and asking out a boy, and more or less expected not to hear from her. Instead Zoe immediately texted her back and said why didn't she come and get dressed up at the house. Ramsay could drive them there, seeing as he wasn't going, for the male-female ratio was already hopelessly skewed, which meant he wouldn't get five minutes with his girlfriend without her being asked to dance all the time. Plus, he had a deep and abiding horror of having to stand around in front of everyone from the village, who would undoubtedly have much to gossip either to or about him.

Also, he had to bend over so hard to hear anyone it gave him a sore back, and the only person he liked to dance with was Zoe, because she was so little he could pick her up and stick her legs around his waist, then carry her straight home, something that he assumed would be rather frowned upon by other people.

Chapter 44

W here is your *happy face*?!" demanded Kim-Ange loudly as she ran into Cormac that evening in the old battered lift.

"Ach," said Cormac. "It's the village dance coming up. Was just thinking about it."

"Ha, God, I can't imagine Lissa going to something like that."

"She is going!" said Cormac. "I made her!"

"Seriously? *LISSA?*"

"Yes."

"At a *village dance*?!" Kim-Ange burst out into a peal of loud laughter.

"It's not that weird," said Cormac.

Kim-Ange shook her head. "I know. It's just . . . until she's had a few, Lissa's not much of a dancer. She's far too shy."

Cormac blinked at this. It hadn't occurred to him that Lissa might be shy. She didn't seem shy to him. Of course, they'd never been face-to-face.

They made their way through the dingy common room. Kim-Ange looked around it.

"Well," she said, "why don't we have a village dance?"

Cormac gave her some side-eye.

"We could have it here! They let people use it if you book it. Get some music, you can teach people to dance. Sell tickets. They can set up a bar."

"Who'd come to a ceilidh in a nurses' home?"

"Every drunk Scotsman in London! And there are a *lot* of them."

Cormac thought about it. "I suppose I could design a poster."

"Give me some," said Kim-Ange. "I'll take them up to the hospital."

THE RESPONSE WAS absolutely extraordinary and immediate, partly because on the whole when Kim-Ange suggested you do something, it was normally easier just to do it. They sold out all their tickets, and Cormac had enough money to hire a small ceilidh band with a caller to tell people what to do and to stock the small bar with additional Tunnock's tea cakes and caramel wafers.

Kim-Ange took over the decor and, amazingly, with a few meters of tartan cloth and ribbon and a vast amount of Ikea twinkle lights, transformed the scuffed hall and battered old tables into something rather magical. From seven P.M., hordes began pouring in. Cormac had absolutely no idea there were so many Scots in London. Although most of them were from Glasgow and Edinburgh, he still found it comforting to be surrounded by familiar voices, red hair, freckles, loud laughter, and the sound of people calling each other "tubes" and "bawbags."

But there were also all the nurses who lived there, who came from everywhere—all over the world. One after another they came up to him, giggling and pleased, often telling him what their local dances were like.

The band set up in the corner, and the caller was absolutely excellent, marshaled her forces extremely effectively, which meant that the Scots who had been taught the dances at school and knew them back to front and the girls from the halls could partner up extremely well. The lights flashed as Nethmi, from Sri Lanka, bounded around the eightsome reel, her small hands in the great meaty paws of Tam Lickwood, one of the hospital porters, a proud Govan man. There were consultant surgeons from the hospital (thin, austere men who'd learned their trade in the chill sea winds of Aberdeen and St. Andrews); a young radiographer from Elgin, who'd brought his entire team; a clique of Glaswegian nurses who'd trained and moved to London together, who gathered and fussed around Cormac like he was a new puppy (something, he felt very strongly, that must be of enormous comfort to their patients); a girl called Yazzie, whom he'd noticed in the halls and who now seemed clamped to his side whenever he needed a partner.

Kim-Ange wore a yellow Buchanan tartan dress, a pattern so loud that many Buchanan descendants who had arrived in Scotland on the track of their ancestors and had been shown their family stripe had turned away, deflated. She had also tied large bows of the same material into her hair, which meant wherever Cormac was in the room, he could usually spot her, clearly having an absolute whale of a time, enthusiastically twirling in the arms of a faintly concerned-looking porter called Piotr. Cormac smiled to himself and agreed to make up the third member of a Dashing White Sergeant team with Chi-Li, who lived down the corridor and had never so much as nodded to him before, but now, wearing a bright red dress with a tartan trim, looked glorious and danced beautifully on tiny feet. He did, in fact, survey the entire scene with some satisfaction and quickly sketched it in his head to send to . . . ha, that was odd. Why he was thinking of Lissa right then. He wondered how she was getting on at hers.

Chapter 45

Lissa was sitting absolutely flat on her arse, her skirt splayed around her hips, howling with laughter.

She hadn't realized, to be fair, quite how formidably strong the elderflower wine was—it tasted like cordial—even as Zoe had given her a few worried glances.

And it had been so very long since she'd been able to cut loose. And it was, the tiny insects in the air notwithstanding, the most utterly beautiful evening. Lissa couldn't believe how light it was, was convinced it couldn't be past six P.M., even as the clock ticked on deep into the night.

The whole village was there in a flood of different colors and kilts, everyone cheerful and laughing—many was the night when they had had to hold the ceilidh in Lennox's barn and dash about in the mud, when there was absolutely nothing to be done about that except to deal with the fact that you were going to get very muddy indeed. But on a night like tonight, the heavy sun hung in the sky like syrup, slowly and patiently lowering itself; the midges buzzed and hummed imperceptibly; the fiddlers played wilder; the grass came to your ankles; and the elderflower wine tasted like nectar and could persuade even a nervous, slightly uptight Londoner, Lissa was explaining to all and sundry, to dance.

On the straw in front of the barn, she could see Joan hoofing merrily up and down with Sebastian the vet (in real life they were everyday nemeses, as she was constantly second-guessing his diagnoses and making his clients crazy), galloping the pair of them to the same reel that was taking place in slightly more cramped conditions five hundred miles to the south.

The contrast was stark: there, different people from different backgrounds were taking a shot and throwing themselves into things and having a laugh. Up here, it was a deadly serious business, like people playing a sport. The fiddlers played fast and clean. There was no caller, just a brief announcement— "Flying Scotsman!" "Cumberland Square Eight!"—and then people would immediately dissolve partnerships or join up with others, pull the awkward-looking teenagers off the walls they were leaning against. And Lissa had danced every one.

Lennox had strode up, little John on his shoulders, and was watching cheerfully, leaning on a barn gate—he wasn't much of a dancer. But Lissa, emboldened by the music and the alcohol, was watching everyone else and suddenly was determined to join in the fun. It was just fun, in, of, and for itself—not showing off, not spending a lot of money (it was five pounds for entrance and a pound a glass), not wearing clothes they couldn't afford that would get returned in the morning, not queuing for hip restaurants in the rain only to be jostled into a tiny space in return for handing over vast amounts of money for bao. Yes, people were taking photos—but only snaps in which they were laughing, not making puffy-lipped pouts for Instagram, nor were they insisting on taking the same pic one hundred times. They didn't have time for that; they were too busy having fun in the hazy, dripping golden light, with a drum, two fiddles, and a big double bass.

And then Jake approached, his shadow passing over the grass. He was wearing an open-necked white shirt made of heavy cotton and a pale green-and-gray kilt. Lissa wished more than anything else Kim-Ange were there; she would have fainted, she would have fainted clean away. Obviously it was just totally normal around here, but it was pretty hot stuff regardless.

"Stop there," said Lissa, smiling and taking out her phone camera. "I want a pic. You look like you're in *Outlander.*"

Jake smiled bashfully but, in fact, was pleased and secretly felt like cheering. He spotted the empty glass of elderflower wine by her side. He should probably warn her a bit about that.

"Okay," said Lissa. "I'll send it."

"Don't you want to be in it?" said Jake. "Hey, hi, Ginty, can you take a picture of us?"

Ginty scowled but stepped forward nonetheless. She wanted to take an unflattering picture of Lissa, but Lissa was so happy and, for once, carefree and utterly amazed at just how great she felt, she couldn't stop grinning, and the sun shone through her light floral dress, and Jake leaned in and just ever so gently put his arm around her to touch her opposite elbow, ever so lightly, and he was grinning too, and Ginty could have hurled the camera back at the pair of them.

"Ooh!" said Lissa, and she sent it immediately to Kim-Ange.

"AW, LOOK AT this," said Kim-Ange, who was hot and sweaty from all the dancing, and she passed her phone over to Cormac. She had absolutely no idea he'd never seen a picture of Lissa before. Taking pictures of everyone and everything was one of the cornerstones of Kim-Ange's life.

He saw the shot and winced. He'd been right about the curly hair.

Well. Good for Jake. They looked incredibly happy.

"That's the first time I've ever seen her," he said.

Kim-Ange looked at him crossly. "You don't follow her Insta? Although her Insta *is* very boring," said Kim-Ange, whose Insta was not in the slightest bit boring.

"Ach, I don't really go in for that stuff," said Cormac shyly.

"You're sleeping in her bed!"

"I know," said Cormac, still staring. Her smile beamed. The screen faded to black on Kim-Ange's phone and he handed it back, somewhat reluctantly.

He had kind of known what she looked like, from what Jake said. But from her missives, her slightly short, occasionally sarcastic emails, he'd been expecting someone a little . . . more uptight. The girl in the picture, she was radiant.

"She looks happy," said Kim-Ange. "Good. It's been a while."

"Yeah," said Cormac. "Good."

And they tried to take one together to send back, but Kim-Ange wasn't happy with the angle and insisted on nine more, and then Cormac got called away to pay the bar staff, and it never happened after all.

Chapter 46

Lissa fell, got up, danced, and still constantly felt she was absolutely fine because it was still light outside, even as everybody else started to drift off. She wanted to dance on and on. The relief of it all was quite something.

Finally, there was a massive circular "Auld Lang Syne," and when the music stopped, you could feel, at last, the chill of the spring night come on them, and she found herself shivering. Jake immediately took one of the blankets off the hay bales and put it around her shoulders. She smiled at him gratefully.

"Thanks," she said. She looked around. The previously shy teenagers were now snogging their heads off by the side of the barn. Cars had vanished from the fields, and the lowing of cows, disturbed by the recent noise, reached them across the distant fields.

"Walk you home?" said Jake, handing her a large glass of water that she downed in one.

"Oh, thanks," she said. "I needed that."

"Fierce stuff, the elderflower," said Jake.

"Uh-huh," said Lissa.

They headed out, and she put her foot into a massive muddy

rut on the road and nearly stumbled over. Jake put out his arm to steady her and, once he had done so, left it there.

"So," he said. "You had fun."

Lissa's tongue felt thick in her mouth, the way it did when you're trying to explain something but can't quite remember how, but somehow feel that regardless, it's still very important to get out what you mean. In other words, she was a little drunk. Pinpricks of stars were appearing overhead.

"I *did*," she said. "I did, you know. And for the first time . . . for the first time . . ."

She heaved a breath.

"I wasn't . . . It was like I was just feeling lighter. Just living in the moment. Not anxious, not scared every second of the day. Not terrified for whether I was safe."

"Is that because you were pished up, though?" said Jake with a smile.

"Yes . . . *No!*" said Lissa emphatically. "It's because when you're dancing you can't really do anything else. Not when you're trying to remember the steps and how they go."

Jake kindly did not mention that not one single time had Lissa managed to remember the steps and how they went.

"You just have to get on with it. And then you manage it, and it's fun, and it's just different from everything, and everything else falls away, and all you're doing is dancing."

She attempted a pirouette in the middle of the road. Jake steadied her again.

"Oh! Sorry!" she said, realizing she was blundering. "But," she went on, "it's been so hard . . ."

"Cormac said," said Jake, and Lissa blinked suddenly, realizing she wanted to tell Cormac, wanted to tell him she wasn't feeling so cranky anymore, wasn't so annoyed with everything. She picked up her phone, but she had to shut one eye to read anything off it so decided against it.

"So," she said as they reached the door of the little cottage, the roses starting to bud in the beds alongside it. "Thank you. That's what I wanted to say. Thank you."

She looked up at him, but Jake could see her mind was elsewhere. And she was definitely rather on the squiffy side. It absolutely wasn't, he thought, the moment to try to kiss her, even though her eyes were sparkling, her smile wide. She'd regret it tomorrow, he thought. And he wanted to see her tomorrow, and after that if he could.

"Drink some water," he told her, taking back the blanket. He could drop it off in the morning. "Lots of water. Take some aspirin."

It was true; just in that moment there had been, Lissa had felt, a tiny bit of magic in the air, a definite sense that she might say, *Screw it. Give me a little bit. Give me a little bit back of being young.*

Give me back my fearless side that violence has stolen away. Give me some carelessness, where I am not worried, and scared, and trying to please people.

Give me tonight, with a handsome man in a kilt by my side, and a heavy warmth, and a short night, and a pair of fiddles, and a glass of sweet elderflower wine, and let me dance.

Jake saw it in her eyes. But he knew—or suspected at least—what anyone would: that her wild mood was dangerous.

And, he had to admit to himself, he liked her. He really liked her. He didn't want her to wake up, head pounding, full of regret, too embarrassed to see him again after a night's wild fancy.

"Go to bed," he said. "Let's have coffee in the week."

She smiled flirtatiously at him, and he turned away quickly before he changed his mind and followed her into the house—Cormac's house, he reminded himself.

Ah well, thought Lissa later, trying to brush her teeth and making a bit of a mess of it. If she'd lost her ability to seduce a guy, that was one thing. But still. She drank a pint of water; the freezing freshness of Scottish water never failed to make her gasp and splutter. Still. It had been good. It was a small country dance in a tiny village clinging to the edge of a loch. To Lissa it had been everything.

FIVE HUNDRED MILES south, Cormac finished tidying up the common room, its plain walls looking duller than ever as the ribbons and fabric came down. Countless people besieged him to tell him what a great night they'd had; a few invited him for a drink or to go on up to their rooms, in the case of a particularly jovial bunch of Spanish nurses, all of them raving beauties out of their scrubs, and Yazzie, who'd been constantly trying to catch his eye.

He smiled blankly at them all, then went upstairs and fell

asleep with the sound of the drums beating in his ears and the faint outline of the photograph—he tried drawing it but couldn't make a fist of it—in his head.

There was a shy knock on the door. He opened it to Yazzie, the girl from downstairs who'd wanted to dance, and he felt suddenly lost, and empty, and sad, and homesick, and confused, and he let her in.

Chapter 47

Cormac couldn't believe how hot it was. It was ridiculous, worse than Spain. Practically as bad as . . . well, he wasn't going to think about his old job. But he disliked the heat, didn't trust it. And London felt oddly feral when it got hot. The bins stank. The people were out in the streets more; you felt how crowded the city was, how constantly everyone managed to bubble along, but sometimes, it felt precariously close to boiling over. Cars with windows open blasted out incredibly loud music with rumbling bass lines you could hear coming a mile away. Groups of young people sat and drank pints on the sidewalks of the bars, looking for a place outside even when there wasn't anywhere to sit, getting, sometimes, aggressive and yelling at the passing cars, who circled, shouting at the girls.

It was oppressive; Cormac had never known anything like it. There was no air-conditioning in the nurses' home, so he managed to pry his window open, which meant all night he could hear police sirens screaming and helicopters going and voices and music and smell drifting barbecues. How, he wondered, could people live like this all the time, piled on top of one another, without going mad? He was naturally calm, but this was making him anxious, wound up. His patients were fretful, full of complaints about the hospital and their injuries and illnesses; for the housebound it was unpleasant—stuffy rooms in stuffy houses, dreaming of fresh air that was nowhere to be found. He tried to be particularly kind, to not get upset when the tar was practically melting on the roads, when drivers were screaming at each other, confronting each other in jams and accidents; the frustration was never far away, the shouts and howls.

Once again Cormac felt homesick, less interested in shaking up all the new experiences London had to offer him—he felt completely nonchalant now, strolling down the south bank, crossing Tower Bridge.

He didn't see Robbie, although he looked for him every day, for another week, and then he recognized his old trainers, sitting in one of the underpasses.

"Hey," he said.

"Hey yersel," said Robbie.

"How's it going?"

Cormac couldn't help thinking of Robbie leaving his wallet, of how difficult it must be for someone with nothing not to have taken it. But to imply he would have would have been so awful.

Robbie shrugged.

"Listen," said Cormac, wondering. He'd need to ask Lennox, but it might be worth a shot. It wasn't like Lennox wasn't used to all sorts coming along to help with the harvest. "If I knew of a job, would you be interested?"

Robbie shrugged again. "I've got a record," he said. Then he glanced up at Cormac, his eyes wild and haunted. "Not for anything bad! Just a bit o' street drinking and that . . ."

He trailed off.

"Nothing bad, you can check."

Cormac believed him. "It's hard work. Just harvest. But there's a bed and three meals a day."

"I'd like to work hard again," mumbled Robbie.

"Let me have a word," said Cormac.

Back at the nurses' home, it didn't help that Yazzie, while absolutely delightful, was proving slightly difficult to avoid, seeing as they lived in the same building, and much as he was generally pleased to see her, it did seem to be mounting into something he didn't quite have the full inclination for and he was relieved when she went on nights.

Jake, uncharacteristically, was furious when he heard about this.

"What?" said Cormac. "I thought you'd be thrilled I'd kind of started seeing someone."

"No," said Jake. "You do this all the time! You're out do-gooding." (Cormac had told him about Robbie.) "And you use that as an excuse so you don't make any effort, and some girl moves on you and you just go for it because you are lazy as shit and they get upset. You should see Emer moping about the village."

"Um," said Cormac, surprised he was getting a telling-off from Jake of all people.

"Well, I'm not," said Jake. "There are lovely women out there in the world . . . lots of them nurses . . ."

His voice took on a slightly dreamy turn.

". . . and all they want to do is do good in the world and help others, but it doesn't mean they block out other people . . . and they deserve someone who is absolutely crazy about them."

Cormac paused. "Who are we talking about here exactly?" he asked. It wasn't like Jake to be quite so romantic.

"No one," said Jake sullenly. "I'm just saying. If you want her you should treat her right, and if you don't you should let her go politely, it's not fair."

"Yeah," said Cormac. "Also, can you tell me how much ransom money you want for holding Jake?"

"I'm just saying!" said Jake.

"Jake, if I want disapproval I can call my mother."

"And you need to call your mother. I saw her the other day."

"I do call her! All the time! She says she's too busy and then makes sarcastic remarks!"

"She's an old lady with her hand in a sling," said Jake.

Cormac sighed. Outside, the sun was beating through the window and his little room was uncomfortably hot.

"Do you think I should come back? It's the Fordell Fair this weekend."

"No!" said Jake quickly. "No, it's fine."

"Jake," said Cormac, unable to keep the smile out of his voice, "is there someone doing my job and living in my house who is, in fact, herself a nurse that you might be rather fond of in a very un-Jake-like fashion and you really don't want me around?"

"You could not," said Jake stiffly, "be further from the truth."

And Cormac was still chuckling by the time they rang off and rather cheered. Though Jake, irritatingly, was right about Yazzie, and Cormac vowed to do better. Once he got Robbie on the coach. Lennox had a certain amount of tolerance for wounded birds, and though he was worried about the drinking, he'd agreed to give him a trial. Cormac walked him to Victoria bus station, bought him new clothes from Primark, a toothbrush, and a washcloth, then could do nothing but wish him his best.

"Nemo me impune lacessit," he said as Robbie turned to go.

"Black Watch," said Robbie in return. Then, falteringly: "I'll try."

"They're good people," said Cormac. "Go well."

Chapter 48

Nina called Lissa, and they went together.

"If you could just check him over," Nina said. "He's going to live out in the barn . . ."

"If he's an alcoholic, he shouldn't be coming off drink right away," said Lissa. "That could be worse. I'll check him over, sure."

She tried to make her voice sound neutral.

"So, this is a friend of Cormac's?"

"I think so . . ."

The coach steamed up to the little stand at Inverness bus station, and a few road-crumpled people got off. The girls were both a little nervous; Nina had left little John behind at the farm.

Nina smiled. "The last time I was here, I was picking up Zoe and Hari."

"Really? What was she like?"

"Very, very dirty," said Nina, grinning. "Gosh, I thought it was going to be a disaster. She was just so miserable."

Privately Lissa thought Zoe was one of the happiest-looking people she'd ever met. But even she had turned up battered and bruised by life.

"Maybe Kirrinfief is magic," said Lissa, which was precisely the wrong thing to say to a dreamy bookworm like Nina, who immediately got a distant expression and started talking about Brigadoon.

Robbie was the last passenger to disembark, everyone else swallowed up in a mass of happy families welcoming home students or grannies who'd been on a trip to the Big Smoke. Robbie emerged barely looking up, as if he never expected to be greeted anywhere, his few belongings in an army-issue canvas bag.

"Uh, hello," said Nina.

Lissa looked at him curiously. Was this what Cormac was like? Shaggy around the edges, covered in homemade tattoos— an old soldier by any measure? Robbie didn't look frightening, though, or violent. His eyes were haunted; he looked very, very tired.

"Did you sleep on the coach?" asked Nina gently, and he shook his head.

They led him to the book bus out front. He looked at it inquiringly but didn't say anything.

"Things been tough?" said Lissa, and he nodded sadly, and she looked at him and suddenly, piercingly, felt simultaneously ashamed of her own trauma and more determined to push through it. Because when you couldn't, it could consume you. She was lucky; she had a loving family, friends, and a job that had given her an amazing opportunity to start over. Robbie had been unlucky. But maybe Scotland gave everyone a second chance. "Let's get you back and checked over."

ROBBIE WAS QUIET as a lamb as she examined him in the room next to the barn after he'd washed up. He had scabies, but that would clear up with permethrin. He'd shaved his head, which would probably help with lice, and his skin wasn't as yellow as she'd feared; hopefully he wouldn't present with liver complaints, but it was too early to tell. Then they discussed withdrawal and alcohol management.

She had done this many, many times working in A&E. Sometimes, though, she felt that it might work. Robbie might be one of the lucky ones. She directed him to the nearest group, gave him every leaflet Joan had, and added him to be checked up on by her twice a week.

"And now," she said with a slight smile, "I think they probably have work for you to do."

Lennox had already arrived at the doorway, little John in his carrier on his back as usual, carrying two trowels in his pockets and two cups of tea in his hands.

"Three sugars," he grunted. "We've got a few poison berries on the upper field to get rid of. The buggers eat 'em, then we're really in trouble. You up for it?"

Robbie's face, however, had completely changed when he saw the baby.

"Aye, look at yon bairn," he said, a half smile revealing his rotten teeth, and Lissa made a mental note to get him on a dentist's list. Little John beamed and waved in response. "Oh, he is bonny," said Robbie, moving closer.

He put out a yellowing finger, and John grabbed it tightly, grinning at the game. Then Robbie nodded.

"Aye," he said, and followed Lennox out into the sunny farmyard, scattering chickens as they went, and Lissa watched them both go and crossed her fingers.

STILL VERY THOUGHTFUL, Lissa went back to the cottage. She had an hour before her next appointment. Looking for something to listen to while she made lunch, she pulled out Cormac's CDs and, smiling when she remembered how cross he'd been, slid in the Proclaimers.

She had been expecting the bouncy song she half remembered. Instead a piano was starting a slow waltz. A soft, lamenting voice started to sing, joined by another.

"My heart was broken . . . my heart was broken."

Then it simply repeated,

"Sorrow. Sorrow. Sorrow. Sorrow."

Lissa turned around, frozen. It sounded . . . it sounded exactly like someone voicing what she'd been feeling for so long.

"My tears are drying . . . my tears are drying."

By the time she got to the bursting, heartfelt, hopeful chorus, she was an absolute wreck. It felt as if, in some odd way, the song was a tiny key, unlocking something very important.

Lunch forgotten, she listened to it over and over again. Then she texted Cormac.

I might have been wrong about that band you like, she wrote.

Aye you were, came the response, quick as a wink.

Chapter 49

Y ou won't believe this!"

Kim-Ange was gasping down the phone to Lissa, who had woken up to a cool, foggy morning and was warming herself in front of the smoldering peat fire. She couldn't believe Kim-Ange was actually boiling hot when they inhabited the same landmass. They were busy being jealous of each other's weather; Kim-Ange did not take to the heat well. It played havoc with her makeup regimen, which was prolonged and highly technical.

"You'd know if you were still on Instagram and Facebook."

"I explained," said Lissa patiently. It was true. She had felt more at peace since she'd closed her social media, was amazed at how pleasurable a novel and hot bath could be. Plus, she could always rely on Kim-Ange to let her know what was really happening. Like now, in fact.

"Well, Yazzie's been all over it. Him. It! After he had a man in too!"

"What are you talking about?"

"Your Scottish boy!"

"He's not 'my Scottish boy,'" said Lissa, feeling slightly un-comfortable. "I've never even met him. I don't even know what he looks like."

"You can see half his arse on Yazzie's Instagram. I think she took the picture while he was asleep," said Kim-Ange mus-ingly.

"Well, that doesn't sound very nice . . . What, they're going out together?"

"Well, she hasn't changed her Facebook status . . . and he doesn't really use his, so . . ."

"Not even to 'it's complicated'?"

"Nope."

Lissa was annoyed at the fact that she felt slightly relieved. "Maybe it's just a casual thing."

She was still disappointed in him. She hadn't thought of him as a player like that. Mind you, wasn't that the point about players? They were really sweet and fun—that's why they reeled you in every time. But she'd definitely thought he was different.

Kim-Ange was still talking. "Yazzie *is* a filthy mare. Of course, I approve of that."

"And gorgeous," said Lissa.

"What do you care?" said Kim-Ange. "Haven't you got a date?"

Lissa thought of cute Jake. "I do," she said, smiling wryly.

"Well then."

"What about you?"

"*Yes!*" said Kim-Ange. "See, this is a lot of news. I like catching up like this."

"It's almost as good as having you here," said Lissa. "Not quite, though."

"Well, spray a shitload of Jo Malone perfume around and it will almost be the same."

"Almost too much."

"What?"

"*Not at all too much! Who is your date with?!*"

"Piotr."

Lissa had to think for a minute. It wasn't just nurses in the home; it was more a general backup housing facility for anyone who had to work at the hospital and couldn't quite manage on the wages the hospital paid.

"Piotr the porter? Amazing!"

It was indeed the diminutive porter Kim-Ange had spent the evening dancing with at the ceilidh, who was completely overwhelmed.

"Is he nice?"

"I don't care," said Kim-Ange. "There are no men in this town and I haven't had a proper date in eight months. As long as he doesn't eat weasels, I'm probably going to let him get to second base."

"What if he licks weasels?"

"First base."

Lissa smiled. "I just can't believe we've all got dates!"

"I know," said Kim-Ange. "Skype me later and I'll tell you why you're dressed all wrong."

CORMAC SENT OVER the last of the week's notes to Lissa and couldn't stop himself from adding at the bottom, seemingly innocently, Going to Fordell Fair?

Lissa saw the line and smiled, then frowned. Word got around. She took another bite of her russet apple.

Maybe. What about you? Busy I believe?

Cormac squinted at the message. Oh, obviously she'd heard. Kim-Ange would have been all over it. It felt very odd—were they . . . were they *friends* now?

Oi! he typed, throwing the core of the russet he was eating into the bin.

There you go, all Eastenders again. Where are you going?

Some hot new restaurant.

You'll be queueing for an hour and it'll be full of snotty types and all anyone does is take photographs of the food, and the plates will be too small and you won't get enough to eat and it will be filthy expensive.

Well YOU might throw up on the big dipper.

Shan't! AND Kim-Ange has a date! It must be almost summer.

So we all have dates.

Cormac grabbed another apple from the bag.

Good!

Good!

Lissa decided on another apple and bit into it, trying not to betray how cross she was, and went out to feed Neddie Needles.

Chapter 50

The fog rose on the little town of Kirrinfief that Saturday and they had, by noon, one of those days in the Highlands also known as "you should have been here last week."

It is a fact—sad but true—but please, don't ever let it put you off visiting our beautiful country; we would be so happy to see you, I promise. Nonetheless, it remains a fairly hardwired truth that if you want to plan a visit to Scotland, or a wedding, or a barbecue, even simply planning it is an act of hubris that upsets the weather gods of Scotland. Lugh, he of the one eye and the ability to summon storms, will be displeased, and at the very least there will be light drizzle and ominous gray skies, and if you are in a place that has a beautiful view, you will have to put up with people telling you there is a beautiful view, because you will not be able to see it.

But take Scotland by surprise and you might just get a day like this, in early June, when the sun warms every nook and cranny, and the breeze gently pootling over a loch as calm as glass will keep you from getting too hot; when the stillness of the air means the cries of the many birds can be heard more loudly than ever, as well as the lightly tapping hooves of the deer in the forest. The sky is a freshly washed blue, the green of the meadows far greener than anything you would expect to find without a heavy filter on it; fat bees buzz merrily among the meadowsweet and long grass, and the evenings last forever.

IN LONDON, YAZZIE had persuaded Cormac to come out with her to a new restaurant and he had said yes, because he didn't know what else to do and Kim-Ange was mysteriously unavailable.

Kim-Ange was going for a walk with Piotr, who was both excited and slightly concerned about it.

And Lissa Westcott was going to the fair. She was in a blue dress that, for once, she was wearing without a coat or a cardigan. It was a plain dress, but it suited her, and she had left off the makeup apart from a little pink lipstick, and her hair was bouncing down her back, and she felt . . . not fine exactly. But, as Kim-Ange gave her the thumbs-up from the laptop in the corner of the room, she reminded herself again and again, *It's only Jake, it's only Jake,* then she couldn't feel worse.

They were all of them out, in the warm of a British evening as beautiful as she makes them; hundreds of miles apart, but each with the same combination of butterflies and cheerfulness and a slight aura of dread and considering just canceling the entire thing and never mentioning it again and running away to the sea to be a sailor, which characterizes the process of dating. But they were all young*ish,* and it was a beautiful evening, and there was potential magic in the air, so you couldn't be too worried for them, not really. Tonight, even for Lissa, the bad things felt a little further away, warded off by the magical sweetness of the air, a late spring's caress, a new pair of boots; by expectation, possibilities, aftershave, and checking wristwatches and best earrings and chewing gum.

Chapter 51

The fair was easy to smell, coming in on the old farm track. The normal scents of pine and bracken in the air—with an undertone of cow that at first Lissa had been averse to but now rather liked—had been overtaken by smells that were familiar and strange all at once: the fairground mix of candy floss, popcorn, diesel, and dirty old engines.

Lissa remembered her mother hurrying her past it, refusing to let her go, completely uninterested in the entire affair. She recalled not wanting to catch the eye of the rougher girls in case they teased her later (which they did anyway, calling her stuck up, which was hard to disagree with because her mother was so very insistent that that's exactly what she was).

And then another time, when she was a little older, she did exactly what her mother was so scared she would: pretended she was going around to Majabeen's house to study, whereupon the two of them slipped out to "the library" and rushed down to the common, pooling their money, which was just enough to share candy floss and have one ride. The scrawny boy on the waltzers had a tooth missing, but to them he just looked even more exotic, like a pirate. He came and hung off the back of their car as they screamed their heads off. The evening was dark and the music was incredibly loud, and as she spun around and around, her neck hurting from the pressure, she couldn't remember feeling more alive, more naughty.

Of course one of the girls from school saw them, and even though she was friendly enough, word got around and someone's mum ran into her mum at Sainsbury's and the worst came to the worst and she was grounded for a solid month.

It had been so worth it.

JAKE WAS STANDING there, wearing an open-necked blue shirt that suited his hair. He'd had it trimmed, Lissa noticed, for the occasion. It looked ridiculously sharp and contoured and gelled and she wasn't crazy about it (fearing retributive ear cutting, Jake had gone into the nearest town, forty miles away, and gotten it done by somebody who hadn't known him his entire life).

He grinned at her nervously. She looked lovely, her curls bouncing behind her and the smile he never normally saw in the daytime.

They awkwardly attempted a social kiss, which went a little wrong, and Jake would normally have taken her hand but, suddenly shy, he didn't. Instead, he gallantly offered her his arm, and she took it rather tentatively.

"Okay," he said. "So what do you want to do first? What's your favorite thing?"

"I don't know," said Lissa. "I've never been to a fair before. Except the waltzers. I like the waltzers."

"You've never been?!" He was incredulous. "Were you brought up in a cupboard under the stairs?"

"No," said Lissa.

He stopped himself suddenly. "Sorry, is it . . . like, a culture thing?"

Lissa gave him a sideways glance. "How would that work, then?"

"I don't know!" said Jake, lifting his hands in horror in case he'd said the wrong thing.

"No," said Lissa slowly. "We have fairs in London. My mum just didn't really approve."

"Because . . . ?"

Lissa thought about it. "Oh . . . I suppose she was a bit of a snob."

This was such an out-of-character thing to say that Lissa lifted her hand to her mouth.

"Oh my God," she said. "I can't believe I just said that about my mum. She's amazing, a really inspirational character, very . . . all of that."

Jake smiled. "She sounds . . . terrifying. And amazing, obviously," he added hastily, horrified at how he was doing.

Lissa smiled again. "Oh God," she said, and swallowed. "Okay. She is both of those things."

She wondered, suddenly, why she hadn't confided more in her mum. Would she even have needed to come here? Would her mum have been disappointed?

She thought of Cormac too, and his mother, fussing about

him. It was odd, sometimes, just a little, the strange things they had in common.

"Well then," said Jake after a long pause, trying to get her attention. "Where shall we start? I really need to win you a large soft toy."

"I don't need one of those."

"You don't need one," said Jake, who had, truth be told, been practicing, "but I think you should have one. To make up for all the ones you missed when you were a child."

And he bought her a large candy floss, which immediately got stuck in her hair and was just as sticky and ridiculous a concept of foodstuff as Lissa remembered from nearly half a lifetime ago and was messing up her lipstick, but she found she didn't care and they both laughed. She wondered briefly if she didn't care because she was so relaxed or because she genuinely wasn't that into the guy she was with, but soon she told herself to stop bothering and just enjoy herself. And she did.

They passed Ramsay and Zoe with their clutch of children, the two little boys wearing identical Spider-Man costumes, holding hands, and looking absolutely terrified.

"What about the ghost train?" Zoe was saying, and the taller of the small children said, "We absolutely do not want to meet any more ghosts, Nanny Seven," and the littler was shaking his head in terror, and Zoe said, "What do you mean 'more ghosts'?" rather nervously, and Patrick and Hari just looked at each other.

"Hello, you two," said Zoe, and Lissa felt odd to hear them referred to as a couple.

"Hello," said Lissa, smiling.

"Lollipops!" hollered Patrick. "You're the lady with all the lollipops. And jabs. And lollipops."

He narrowed his eyes as if trying to work out whether seeing her was a good or bad thing.

"I don't have any lollipops. Or jabs," said Lissa reassuringly. "Are you having a good time at the fair?"

Patrick and Hari shook their heads firmly.

"They won't go on anything," said Zoe in despair. "They think this entire fair is a plot to kill them."

"Mary said so!" said Patrick.

"Oh, Mary," said Ramsay, holding the girl. "Well, at least it's cheap."

Zoe agreed vigorously.

"Ah disnae want to die," said the tiniest of the children.

"You're not going to die!"

A large ride that tipped people upside down about forty meters in the air suddenly did just that, and a huge amount of screaming rent the air. Both the lads looked absolutely petrified.

"Perhaps the spinning teacups." Zoe grimaced, marching them off.

"Hot tea absolutely no thank you" was the last thing Lissa heard of Patrick as the oddly shaped family vanished into the crowd.

"They probably will die now," predicted Jake. "Just to be ironic."

"Did you bring your med case?"

"I am technically off duty," said Jake. "So don't let me go too near the St. John's Ambulance tent. They are all madly in love with me."

"That's very cocky," said Lissa, but she had to eat her words when they passed the tent, Jake notably skulking, only for a large older lady to come fluttering out. She had very small feet in very high-heeled shoes, given the ground was still pretty muddy.

"*There's my favorite ambulance man!*" she trilled. Other women in the more familiar green outfits poked their heads out of the tent. One appeared to be busy attempting to cut candy floss out of a small child's hair; another one was comforting a child sobbing his heart out.

"What's the matter?" said Lissa instantly.

"Och," said the woman thoughtfully. "I'm not sure if the ghost train is getting scarier or bairns are getting more scared."

"The world is getting scarier," guessed Lissa. "We probably don't need ghost trains too."

"*Aye,*" said the wee lad whose shoulders were shaking.

Jake had been bustled away and was being fed sandwiches.

"You know this lad. Always ready to help out," said the first woman, handing him a plate piled high with sandwiches and chocolate biscuits.

"Well, it's his job," said Lissa, watching him, amused.

"Here you go, Jakie, tea just how you like it," said another one, piling sugar into a large enamel mug. He looked at Lissa rather shamefaced.

"Would *you* like a sandwich?" said one of the women, not in a particularly friendly way. "Only they're really just for the volunteers."

"I'm fine without a sandwich, thank you." Lissa smiled. "That's okay. Jake, you eat your fill."

Chapter 52

Cormac popped next door in response to a loud banging on the thin wall. It was definitely a summoning banging, though.

Kim-Ange was standing with her hand behind her shoulder, waving uselessly.

"Can you zip me up?" she said. She was wearing a bright purple chiffon dress with a chain belt around her waist. Cormac stood behind her as she looked at herself in the mirror. Her purple eye shadow matched exactly, as did her high velvet boots.

"Well?" she said, turning around nervously.

"You look beautiful," said Cormac, and he meant it. "Knock him dead."

"Not literally, like, by accident or anything?" Kim-Ange sounded uncharacteristically worried.

"No," said Cormac. "By being your gorgeous self."

And she was about to say something sarcastic, but she grabbed her purple clutch bag, kissed him on the cheek, and left instead.

"You didn't wish me luck with my date!" shouted Cormac behind her.

"No, I didn't," said Kim-Ange, whose opinion of Yazzie was

unsisterly, but it was too late, as Yazzie was already standing there, her large eyes looking at Kim-Ange tremulously. Kim-Ange decided, again uncharacteristically, to suddenly take the stairs.

THERE WAS SOMETHING about standing in a very long queue that was not conducive to a good date, however beautiful Yazzie looked—which she did, in a long orange dress that perfectly set off her dark braids and huge dark eyes.

London was still ridiculously climate-change hot, and people were walking about in shorts, red-faced, an aura of vaguely suppressed threat in the air. They walked past the skateboarders under the Royal Festival Hall, who shouted and entranced children cheek by jowl with expensively dressed older people on their way to concerts and the theater; frozen-still mimes standing in the middle of the street, balancing on poles and getting in the way; art and books for sale; hawkers; jugglers; people yelling and handing out leaflets—the whole noisy cacophony of life. The smog hanging above the water and the great towers of the east took on a pink tinge in the early evening.

The air smelled of food vans and garbage and fuel, and he felt stuffy and hot in his best checked shirt, which had made Kim-Ange pretend to vomit but then decide was good enough after all. No designer borrowing tonight, he noticed.

Yazzie was chatting about someone she'd seen on her ward rounds, and he listened cheerfully enough, as they dodged and weaved around the hundreds of other people on the narrow bridge that cut its way up to Charing Cross station, next to thundering trains on the track beside them, above gray water filled with pleasure boats and dredgers, odd flat structures covered in cement, and a lifeboat station. The clouds seemed to seal the heat to the ground. He accidentally bumped into one group of tourists, fell back, and jostled a large man who looked furious with him and swore under his breath.

His newfound fondness for the big city was muted tonight; he was thinking about how the fair was always such a fun time. He'd normally go a couple of times. Jake would get in with the St. John's Ambulance ladies, who got free passes to everything but never wanted to use them—it was obviously a scam, they should have gone to a much more deserving cause, but Jake had the gift of the gab and that was that.

He hoped he was nice to Lissa. It would be cool there tonight. Bright as well, you wouldn't get a whiff of sunset till ten P.M. There'd be a breeze probably; the right kind of evening for just a shirt and a jumper and being totally comfortable wherever you were, with fresh air and the sweet smell of the last of the bluebells on the air, as well as the gorse, warmed by the sun through the day . . . he could almost feel it. And smell the candy floss on the air, and feel you couldn't be happier . . .

"So, anyway, we drained about a liter of bile from his abdomen," Yazzie was saying.

Cormac blinked. "Is that right?" he said.

She looked worried. "Sorry, is that gross? Before dinner?"

"Naw, naw, not at all," said Cormac.

In fact, it wasn't before dinner at all. Lissa had been right, they'd had to queue; what she hadn't been correct about was it certainly wasn't an hour. It was at least ninety minutes.

Something happened in the queue. Looking around, Cormac could see most people on their phones; some had been left to hold places while their presumably more popular mates whooped it up in a local bar somewhere. Some couples were tight in conversation, as if they were as happy to be in a queue together as they would be anywhere else, and some groups of friends were doing that slightly nervous loud thing groups do at the beginning of a night out, before they've all managed to have a drink and settle down. They were whooping at each other and shouting performatively and welcoming more and more members to their group, until Cormac started to doubt whether they were ever going to make it to the front of the queue.

"What do they sell here?" he said, realizing that both of them were actually finding the conversation a little slow and stilted; that even before they knew each other, they kind of looked like one of those couples with absolutely nothing to say to each other, once she'd told him about old Mr. Haber's drained cyst.

"Buns," said Yazzie, pointing to the menu in the window.

"Buns?" Cormac screwed up his face. He didn't want a bun; he was starving.

"Bao," said Yazzie. "They're like Chinese street food. They're filled with meat and stuff."

"Meat buns," said Cormac. They had already been there for forty-five minutes. His shirt was sticking to his back and his neck felt grimy, simply from standing on a narrow sidewalk with cabs and trucks squeezing past him every second.

"Apparently they're amazing," said Yazzie sullenly, because she had bought a new orange dress for this and told all her mates about how she'd managed to pull that hot Scottish NPL they all liked, and now she was standing on a sidewalk with a guy who looked like he'd rather be on the moon than here.

If it was warm in Kirrinfief, there was a little hidden bay down by the loch where you couldn't drive, only walk, and as long as you took all your rubbish away, the police (Gregory Duncan from Hart's farm; they'd all been to school together) would turn a blind eye to it, and they'd light a bonfire and drink cider and watch as the sky barely darkened as the hour neared midnight, and they could play their music as loud as they wanted, nobody was anywhere near to hear them, not for miles, and they watched the stars pop out, one by one, never too bright, for the night wasn't long enough for them to shine; the north of the planet had tilted too far on its axis.

Stars were for a different season; this was their season of light. Someone would sometimes bring a guitar, and everyone else would groan and throw stones and call them a James Blunt fud, but even so, if the gentle chords of "Caledonia" or "Sunshine on Leith" started up, well, it wouldn't really be possible not to sing along to that, would it, as the moon reflected on the calm waters of the loch and its endless rippling glory. And as soon as the sun was sunk on one side of the dark shapes of the mountains, it felt the lightest rays of the dawn were just appearing once more.

They had been such happy nights. Cormac found himself wondering if that's where Jake would take Lissa and whether she'd like it. Just a bonfire, some cider, a bit of music, some hamburgers and marshmallows. Nothing fancy. Occasionally a soft toy someone had won at the fair, which would get to sit on a proper throne made of sticks, after the year Gordon Lowrie had thrown one in the fire, and the nylon had sparked and melted horribly and the plastic eyes had dropped down the edges of the pink bear, and all the girls had screamed and gotten upset with him. After that, stuffed animals had pride of place.

He smiled to himself. Yazzie cleared her throat crossly.

"Ach. Where were we?" he said, looking up. The queue hadn't moved at all.

"Meat buns," she said.

Chapter 53

Meanwhile, three miles across town, two people had, amazingly, found a very quiet space.

Piotr had arrived in London with absolutely no money whatsoever, nothing more than the bus fare to Victoria station. He had spent the first six months, when he couldn't afford even to eke out a beer, at the Polish Centre and walking around and around the huge, terrifying, expensive city, walking for miles along unfamiliar sidewalks with foreign signs and extraordinary monuments and strange things. So he was taking Kim-Ange to somewhere he really liked, because you could be a tourist for only so long before you started getting deeper and deeper into what was around you, and one of his endless drizzly Sunday walks had taken him to this enchanted spot.

Piotr wasn't 100 percent up on the difference between South Korean and Japanese but thought she might like it, and he was right, she did.

Buried deep in Holland Park, well off the main thoroughfares and hard to find unless you already knew it was there, was Kyoto Garden, its colors burnished and bright in the West London evening, full of exotic plants and knotted trees and streams with little bridges. There was nobody there, but a pair of cranes nested at the water's edge, just below the waterfall. It was breathtakingly lovely.

Piotr opened the rucksack he had been clunking all the way from the tube station, and he pulled out one large bottle of brown beer, one smaller one of vodka, a bag of dumplings one of his substitute aunties at the Polish club had rustled up for him, a box of sushi just in case, and a family-sized bar of Dairy Milk. Kim-Ange grinned widely and grabbed the vodka and the chocolate.

"Normally I hate picnics," she said, looking around at the tranquil site, the water trickling through the curves of the beautifully made little streams with wooden bridges, smooth rocks, and carp. "But I might make an exception for you."

And some time later, Piotr was sitting giving bits of dumpling to the fish until Kim-Ange made him stop and they found their two hands together, and their heads even closer, and suddenly, as the fish bubbled in the water and the waterfall tinkled overhead and there was a faint rustling of perfectly manicured fronds, but nobody else at all, they kissed, and even if there was a whole London, a whole eight million people, around them, they were not aware of another soul.

STROLLING BACK TO the tube station, giggly, tripping over their feet, clutching hands, Kim-Ange whispered something into his ear. Piotr shook his head.

"To me, you are only yourself," he said stoutly, for his diminutive figure, his narrow hips and short height, belied a man with the heart of a lion. "Only yourself."

Chapter 54

Lissa supposed people liked fairground rides for the same reason they liked scary films: the freedom of knowing that you felt a little frightened but you were actually incredibly safe.

But these rides—these were more than watching a horror film. It was stupid, and she felt she was making up for her childhood, but it was the wind in your hair and, in fact, the view you got, even when the ride paused for only a little bit at the top—it was like a double-edged sword, and everybody else was screaming their heads off with delight or horror.

She, by contrast, liked to try to hold the sight in her head; it was the best view she had had of the absolute vastness of the loch. It seemed to go on forever, and even though the day was still bright, the center of it was pitch dark. No wonder, she thought. No wonder they thought there was a monster in there. It was magical. She almost forgot to scream as they plummeted like a stone, until it looked like they would hit the ground, then just in time brushed past it and were on the rise again, and the view would unfold like a magnificent carpet, and she could see farther and farther as she turned her head: the rolling roofs of the little cobbled village, undulating over the fell; the neat layout of the farmers' fields stretching ahead; the long line of the railway with a dark red train hurtling down its tracks; and the great body of water. She felt like she could touch the clouds. She wanted to stay up there all day.

Jake thought he'd have to put his arm around her—it was, he was finding, a very intense ride indeed, particularly when you'd just eaten three Scotch eggs and four Penguin biscuits, as pressed upon him by the good ladies of the St. John's Ambulance. He felt distinctly queasy and wished the damn thing would stop. He shut his eyes to make it pass.

Lissa, meanwhile, couldn't have enjoyed it more and wished it had lasted longer. She was absolutely blown away by the beauty and drama of the landscape; the ride had made her feel as high as the mountaintops, as close to the birds that circled in the updrafts. She sighed with something perilously close to happiness.

"That was amazing," she said, when they finally got unclipped and rejoined the music and flashing lights and commotion of the fair at ground level. "I'd be happy just to be up there all the time!"

Jake couldn't answer; he was very busy simply trying not to throw up and wiped the sweat off his brow.

"Are you okay?" said Lissa.

Jake nodded, wishing he could sit down.

"Do you need . . ." Lissa smiled. "Do we need to go back to the St. John's tent?"

The thought of more Scotch eggs was simply too much for Jake. He held up a finger and charged off into the woods.

Lissa, surprised, smiled to herself. Then she glanced at her phone—out of habit, more than thinking anyone would be in touch. She wasn't missing Instagram and Facebook, not usually. But she would have liked to have posted the view. It was quite something.

There was nothing there, of course, except a little dot on her WhatsApp. She opened it. It was a picture of three white spherical things, hard to make out.

Meat buns, she read, 90-minute wait. Excellent!!!!

She put her phone back, smiling. Well. Someone was having a good date, she supposed.

CORMAC COULDN'T HELP it. He was distracted, and that wasn't fair. Ironically, of course, it was Jake who had told him all along: don't be distracted, stop just falling into things. Think about the person you're with.

He looked up at Yazzie, who smiled back at him nervously, aware this wasn't going very well. She'd started a long story about the worst wound she'd ever seen, which, on balance, she really wished she hadn't, especially as she had to shout above the insane noise levels in the bar. They were crammed into a tiny corner space. At least, she thought, the food was amazing—and it truly was, Cormac had never tasted anything like it; every herb and flavor superbly delineated, tasting fresh and light—so that was something.

"This is amazing," he said. Then found his thoughts, once again, straying north and wondering if the hot dog stall was

there and if Lissa was enjoying herself. He resisted the urge to
check his phone; this was awful. He was behaving like some
kind of bounder.

"So, wounds, huh?" he found himself saying as Yazzie picked
unhappily at the delicious food.

"Did you always want to be a nurse?" she asked him.

Cormac half smiled to himself. "Ach, not quite," he said.
"Everyone in my family joined the army, so I joined up too.
Became a medic."

"Ooh," said Yazzie. "That's interesting."

Cormac shrugged. "A bit too interesting at times," he said.

"Did you get shot at?"

Cormac blinked. He almost answered the question and then
reined it back. But why . . . why? Why did he suddenly feel
almost ready to tell someone . . . but then had held back? This
was ridiculous.

It was the newness, he decided. Everything being new. He
could see, for the first time, the benefits of the big city: shaking off who you were, where you were from, what you came
with, the baggage. That you were free to start over, to ditch
everything, to feel lighter. He nearly told Yazzie, but something
stopped him. He shrugged. The people in the queue were doing
exactly what they had done, stared ferociously at people who
had already managed to sit and get fed, and he felt the weight
of their hungry eyes on him.

"Nah, it was fine," he said briefly. "Shall we head out?"

That was the problem with the food: it had come served in

little wicker baskets, each a perfect box of steaming heaven—
but the buns had come quickly, and they'd eaten them even
faster, and now the waitress was eyeing them up and making
it very clear that if they were sitting and not actually stuffing
their faces, they were costing her money, and would they mind
terribly moving straightaway?

Cormac paid the eye-watering bill, and they hadn't even gotten up from their seats before the next couple of hipsters were
on top of them, photographing and uploading selfies to Instagram before they'd even sat down.

It was still light when they hit the noisy streets.

"We could go somewhere else?" said Yazzie, but neither of
them knew where to go and all the bars and pubs were stuffed
to the gills, spilling all their clients out onto the pavement. A
warm Saturday evening in central London was not in any way
conducive to quiet chatting, even if he could think of anything
he wanted to say to her.

Yazzie was growing increasingly irritated and very ready to
go back and complain to all her friends about how that Scottish boy might be hot, but oh my God, he was the most boring
man in the universe and a total waste of time.

She wouldn't sleep with him again, she vowed to herself. This
was going nowhere, and she wanted a boyfriend, not someone
who lived on the next floor with benefits.

On the other hand, the sleeping with bit had been pretty
good. Better than pretty good.

No. Definitely not.

"Um, I'm not sure where . . ." said Cormac, looking at a street crowded with young Londoners on a night out.

"Actually," said Yazzie, "I'm working tomorrow, I'd better get an early night."

It was irritatingly insulting how quickly he agreed with her.

Chapter 55

Jake came out of the bushes looking slightly greenish but more or less recovered.

"Gum?" he offered her, and Lissa smiled and politely refused. They walked on in silence. Lissa wanted another shot on the rides, but she felt under the circumstances it wouldn't be very tactful.

Instead Jake insisted on going to a ridiculous shooting arcade and attempting to hit enough traveling ducks with a toy rifle to win her a huge tiger, despite her protesting she really didn't want a huge tiger and probably wouldn't have anywhere to put it.

They couldn't agree on that, but also hitting the ducks proved—particularly if you were feeling a little wobbly to begin with—rather more difficult than Jake had anticipated, and he kept missing. Unfortunately, once he'd started, he was not the type of man who, like Cormac, would simply have raised his hands and laughed about it; instead he gave the carny more and more money, while Lissa stood at the side faintly embarrassed, and Jake's ears got redder and redder, and the anger made him even shakier on the trigger and the entire thing went from fun to awkward rather quickly, particularly when a small group of boys appeared from nowhere to laugh at him.

"Aye, gies it another one, mister! You're a really good protector of ducks, aye!" shouted one.

"Aye, he's one of those environmentalists," said another. "Protecting species everywhere."

Jake cursed at them and looked ready to lose his cool altogether, until at last, after paying out far more than the cheap nylon toy could possibly have cost in the first place, he retrieved the white tiger and handed it over, looking bashful.

"Well," said Lissa, trying not to smile too much in case it looked as if she were laughing at him. "Thank you, I suppose."

"S-so listen," said Jake, stuttering slightly. "There's a wee barbecue happening down by the loch. You fancy it? There's a nice bonfire and that . . . um . . . music, I think . . ."

Just then Ginty and her friends appeared out of nowhere. Lissa still had only a vague idea of who she was. She was looking absolutely impressive, that much was clearly true, in a pair of skintight black leggings, enormous wedge heels, an off-the-shoulder cropped pink top that showed off her nice round shoulders and vast bosoms, and more hair than Lissa had ever seen on a human person. It tumbled down her back in great blond waves, all the way to her bottom. There seemed to be no end to it; it looked like at least four people's hair. Coupled with the breasts (natural) and lips (much less so), in the normally dressed-down life of the village and the beginning chill of even the sunniest of Highland evenings, she stood out like a rare orchid. It wasn't a look Lissa could have ever worn herself, but she couldn't help but be impressed at the commitment it took. Ginty's huge pneumatic lips were polished to a high sheen, and her eyebrows were perfectly shaded brown geometric shapes that looked carved into her forehead.

"Hi, Jake," she said seductively, tossing her hair over her shoulders.

Lissa smiled. She clearly expected Jake's tongue to unravel like a cartoon fox's.

Jake, meanwhile, had been having a profoundly disappointing evening. By now, in his personal schedule, Lissa would have been incredibly impressed by how he knew everyone, she'd have been terrified on the very high ride and he'd have had to comfort her with an arm around her, and she'd have thrown her arms around his neck when he'd easily won her the biggest toy in the fair, and well, it was a pretty short trip from there back home, he reckoned. But it was worse than that. His entire gift of the gab had deserted him. He'd always found it easy to chat with women; they always liked him. He had treated it like a game, and it had worked.

Lissa hadn't felt like a game, and that had made it absolutely impossible. He couldn't think straight. And now Ginty MacGuire was throwing another wrench in the works.

"Hi, Ginty," he said, in a resigned tone of voice.

"Who's this?" said Ginty, as if she didn't know.

"Oh, you know . . . this is Lissa? She's doing Cormac's job?"

"Where are you from?" said Ginty.

"London," said Lissa, putting her hand out. The other girls looked at that and sniggered.

"No, I mean, where are you really from?" said Ginty.

"London," said Lissa shortly, bristling. The evening, which had started so promisingly, had taken a sour turn. The brightly painted machines and stalls of the fair suddenly looked tawdry, chipped under the bright lights, grubby and cheap.

"Mm-hmm," said Ginty, undaunted. She liked to think of herself as someone who was straight with others and told them what she thought of them to their faces. Not everyone saw this as quite as much of a virtue as she did.

"So, Jakes, are you coming down to the bonfire? Everyone's going."

Too late, Jake remembered that the previous year he had spent the evening of the fair—several evenings, in fact (it wasn't as if there was so much entertainment that came to Kirrinfief that anyone went only once)—down in the sand dunes, rather close to Ginty. Extremely close, in fact.

"Um . . ."

"What's the matter, didn't have a good time last year? Don't you remember?" Ginty was pouting now. She turned to Lissa. "Jake and I have always been . . . friends . . ."

The other girls sniggered on.

"They've lit the bonfire," Ginty went on. She bit her lip seductively. "It's pretty hot down there."

Jake was absolutely scarlet.

"Do you know," said Lissa, "I'm feeling pretty tired."

"I'll take you home?" said Jake desperately.

"But you'll miss it!" said Ginty.

Lissa looked up. "You know what?" she said. "It's okay. You go."

Chapter 56

The music of the fair faded away as Lissa made her way along the still-light road, stopping to watch a baby rabbit make a desperate plunge across it in front of her. She smiled, then pulled out her phone, then put it away again. He was on a date. With Yazzie. She shouldn't be even thinking about him. It was just that she didn't know him, that was all. And she was in a strange place and dealing with a lot of crap in her life, and of course she'd glommed on to the nearest person who seemed okay and not a terrible loser. She knew nothing about him, not really, didn't have a clue even what he looked like. It was a fantasy in her head, that was all, and starting talking to him at ten P.M. on a Saturday night was . . . well, it was ridiculous. A conversation that had started about someone else's snake.

She had pulled out her phone again and was looking at the screen when, to her amazement, a text popped up.

Hey?

She replied with fumbling fingers. Hey.

Cormac had been staring out over the lights of London. He was amazed how electrified he was to hear from her. He'd texted Lennox too—they'd picked up Robbie, who had apparently gone to work with a will. Fingers crossed it would last. The news had made him feel happy and anxious all at once, and he wanted to talk to someone about it.

Someone specific, he realized.

You still out?

Nearly home. You?

Cormac felt a huge gush of relief. This was ridiculous. He didn't even know this girl. But somehow, he'd found, she was the one he wanted to talk to.

I'm back too. It's hot out there

But what about the delicious meat buns?

It turns out I'm quite quick at eating meat buns.

Lissa felt her heart beating faster as she reached the little cottage. She went into the back garden to try to take a picture of Neddie Needles, but he hadn't appeared.

So what's on your mind? she found herself typing.

A bit of her, the tiniest bit, thought she should call him. But somehow, in the absolute stillness and quiet of the night, it seemed strange, such a boundary crosser. She was too nervous. This was safe, and she needed to feel safe.

You know when you were at that accident?

Yeah.

How did you feel?

You sound like my therapist! SHIT I need to skype my therapist!

Had you forgotten?

Yes!

I wonder if that's a sign.

Of me being a coward, probably.

Of you getting better, maybe.

Lissa looked around the garden, the evening scents of the cooling grass hanging heavy in the still air. It was lovely, even if it was getting horribly overgrown. The stream tinkled prettily.

This place is quite special.

It is. So is London.

Is this about meat buns again?

Yeah probably.

Anyway, why are you asking?

I just . . . I think it might be a bit the same as the army.

Lissa didn't say anything, just sat and waited, the little glow-ing phone in her hand, the center of her world right then. And Cormac poured it all out, typing as if his life depended on it, his spelling all over the place. Telling her about the hideous injuries, the pointless pain, the children caught in the cross fire; the waste of all of it. How he couldn't sleep, couldn't stop worrying about it. How he had come home, and his mother was ashamed of him, and he felt like a coward for leaving his comrades. She read it all, patiently and carefully. And at the end of it, she typed just two words.

I know.

And she signed it off with a kiss. And Cormac held his phone to his chest, close, just as, five hundred miles away, Lissa was doing exactly the same thing, as if they were holding each other's hearts in their hands.

Chapter 57

Oh, the luxury, the rare luxury, of waking on a sunny Sunday morning with nothing to do and someone else to think about.

Once upon a time this would have made Lissa panic. She would have felt lonely and worried that she was living in the center of the greatest city in the world and not making the most of it. She would have been entirely concerned that she was wasting time, desperately checking her Insta to see if her friends had been up to something fun that she would have wanted to go to; pinging her mates immediately to see if anyone was up to anything, while trying not to look too needy; worrying if her mother was coming into town, who would want to complain about her hair or her living conditions, or why she didn't just look at these brochures for research chemistry—she'd been so *good* at chemistry at school, and there were all sorts of interesting careers that could spin off it now, it wasn't just in labs you know, you could travel all over the world . . .

But there was something about living in Kirrinfief that had changed all that, she could tell. Something about being perfectly content with your own company—you had to be in a region the size of London but with eight thousand people living in it instead of eight million. If you wanted company you could simply wander into the village and someone you knew would come along immediately; you could head down to the fair or the pub and find yourself caught up in whatever came along. If there was anything to do—a fiddle band playing, a community play, Nina running a book reading—everybody went automatically. And if there wasn't, you stayed in and suited yourself. In the middle of nowhere, she found, she didn't feel lonely at all. She was so far removed from everything she couldn't possibly be worried about missing anything. And what was she missing anyway?

Nonetheless, she thought, stretching luxuriously, the sun making panes on the duvet. She would putter into town, buy something nice, and actually cook for herself; pick up some of the Lennox farm eggs, which were fine, fine things indeed; buy a book from Nina and sit in the sun; maybe see what Zoe was up to. Zoe always seemed happy to have her around, even if there was never a moment when Zoe didn't have about five people climbing all over her. She didn't seem to mind a bit. Lissa occasionally wondered if she didn't actually bother counting up however many people were in her kitchen at any one time. Then tonight she'd open a bottle of wine and call Kim-Ange and see how her date had gone and they could laugh about hers being a bit of a disaster, which would help, and maybe— *maybe*—she would tell her about her and Cormac. But tell her what, truly? That they emailed and texted a lot? Kim-Ange had met plenty of men who were happy to chat online, but when it came to meeting, everything changed.

She walked across the quiet kitchen, which she had grown to love in its understated way, and boiled the kettle and was briefly startled by the rattle of the postman at the letter box. Little arrived for Cormac except bills and circulars. She needed to send him his statements, actually. She smiled to herself. The post office was open until lunchtime, so she would go and do that. She liked the women who worked there, and they also sold incredible cheese and local bacon on the side (nobody in the Highlands had only one job really), so that would give her a little purpose to her morning, which would somehow allow her to spend the entire afternoon lazing around, having completed her errand. And maybe, she thought. *Maybe* talking to Cormac.

She picked up the letters. Two political leaflets for parties she'd never heard of, one in a language she couldn't read, and then, to her great surprise, a letter to her. It was in a white envelope, her name and address typed, with a redirect stuck over it in Kim-Ange's flamboyant handwriting. She frowned. There was a crown printed on the envelope, and suddenly she realized what it was.

She put it down on the table incredibly quickly, as if it were hot, and stared at it.

The Crown Prosecution Service.

Instantly she could feel her every muscle tighten; her fingers curled. Her throat felt like it was closing over. She was suddenly gasping for breath. Every ridiculous claim she'd made the night before, about feeling better, about getting over things: it was all nonsense.

No, no, she kept telling herself. *No.* She stumbled toward the door, opened it wide, and drew in as many deep breaths as she could. The fresh, bright air stung her lungs as she told herself, *Calm down. Calm down.* The road was empty, and she walked across it to the copse on the opposite side.

Oddly—and she felt faintly ridiculous—holding on to one of the trees seemed to sooth her. The deep heavy scent of the bark and the sap, the bright overwhelming neon greenness of the new leaves, filled her senses; the shade and the height of the great oak made her feel strangely safe. She leaned against it, hands on her knees, and took great deep breaths; gradually, her back against the trunk, she felt her heart rate steadily return to normal. She had known this was coming, of course she had. She always did. Anita had told her about it, over and over again, but she had been too resistant. Classic health professional: terrible patient.

But she had been stupid, and arrogant, and frustrated at having to pay attention, to think about the thing she didn't want to think about—and now she couldn't cope with this, not at all. And she had thought she was getting better, had genuinely truly believed it. And now she felt back at square one.

Cormac?

Yes?

I got the letter from court. I have to testify.

Cormac couldn't help it; his heart started to beat a little faster.

You're coming to London?

I have to go to court.

When?

Next week.

What's going to happen?

I have to stand up and . . . go through it again.

That will be okay, won't it? Help put it to rest? Isn't that what we're
meant to be doing?

I'll have to see his mother. I'll have to see the boy who did it.

He's not going to get off. He's not going to come after you.

His friends might.

She felt her heartbeat rise again, felt the panic rise.

I think you'll feel sorry for him more than anything else.

I don't know what I'll feel.

There'll be a lawyer with you.

Oh God.

Honestly, don't panic. I promise. You got this.

How do you know? You haven't met me. I might be completely
  useless.

Not according to my sources.

She half smiled at that.

Have *you* been in a court case?

There was a long pause.

Yes.

What was it?

Friendly fire.

Lissa blinked.

Did you shoot someone??

No. It was a friend of mine. A translator, working with us. Out with
his friends. Some of the squaddies got a little . . . well.

He got shot.

Everyone got shot.

He deleted that last message, but it was somehow worse now
that he'd deleted it; it made it clear that it had had a big impact
on him. Which it had.

Lissa looked at it for a long time.

What are we like? she typed finally, adding a row of screwy-face
emojis.

Cormac looked up at the gray river and smiled to himself.
Suddenly in the midst of eight million people he felt incredibly
close to someone very, very far away.

Eejits, he typed.

Lissa smiled to herself.

Eediats, she typed back.

And that was the moment Cormac nearly called her. He almost pressed the button. But what if he called her and she
didn't pick up? What would he do then? What if he broke the
connection, ruined everything. He thought of Jake telling him
he didn't behave well with women. He thought too of Jake,
who, he thought, was dating her. Oh Lord. Well. He put his
phone back in his pocket so he wasn't tempted.

He was so tempted.

Lissa stared at the screen. Maybe he would just call? Throw caution to the wind? Call and talk and tell her everything? She wondered if he sounded like Jake, with that melodious Highland accent. Maybe deeper; Jake said he was taller than him. She sighed. This was ridiculous. She was building it into something it absolutely wasn't. The wind rustled through the trees.

But just connecting had worked somehow. He had calmed her down, made her feel better. She straightened up again, looked around her. The birds were calling, high up in the fresh bright air. Their days, she supposed, were all the same. The world was awake around her.

And it wasn't going anywhere. The trees had been here for hundreds of years. The wood had stood through wars and great changes, but had never been uprooted. The foxes and rabbits lived their lives; the deer ran; the trout still jumped in the stream; the seals still flapped along the lochside.

For the first time Lissa started to wonder: Could she build a life here? Not with Cormac of course, that was ridiculous, they hadn't even met, she didn't even know what he looked like. Of course he wasn't going to like her—how could he? It was a silly crush, that was all, a good distraction from the anxiety and the pain. Plus, she had his job.

But even without that . . . might this be a place for her? She thought of Nina's friendly face behind the piles of books she organized so beautifully. She had found a home here. And Zoe too, even if she was trailed by what looked like six or seven children at all times and, if Lissa's professional opinion was not mistaken, what looked like another one on the way.

They had found a place here. Could she?

She would read the letter. She would read it, and she would face up to it, and then, when the secondment was over—then she would see.

She glanced, sadly, once more at the phone. She missed him already.

Just as she crossed the threshold, it pinged. She grabbed it delightedly. Was it him?

It was.

So, it said.

Cormac had thought about things. He'd heard from Jake about Ginty MacGuire, which was patently terrible news for Jake, who was stuck somewhere with a terrible headache and deep regrets.

And he'd thought about everything. About everything he'd learned in London, where people were bold and not shy, where people came to get what they wanted, to try everything out there. He knew he'd been lazy in relationships, had always preferred to think of humanity in the abstract, rather than people in particular. He wanted to change that. Starting now.

So. Wanna meet in London then?

Chapter 58

The letter had been short and straightforward, with a date a week hence and a time she was due at Southwark Crown Court. It warned her that the timings might be off and she may have to wait, and there was a form for expenses.

The lawyer had rung her just as Lissa was trying to pluck up the courage to ring her, and she, Roisin, talked her through what would happen. Lissa would be given the opportunity to read the statement she'd given at the police station the first time around to refresh her memory for the small details, then Roisin would walk her through it on the stand. Then the defense lawyer would ask her a few questions.

"But honestly," said Roisin, "you're a noble, trustworthy health care worker who happened to be walking past and did her absolute best to save the life of a child. They'd have a devil of a job making you look bad in front of a jury, and I would be very, very surprised if they bothered to try. They'll probably get you off the stand as soon as possible. All you're doing is confirming the perpetrator. The person you've already picked out of the lineup."

"What if I can't remember his face?"

"I'll ask you if you recognize the person driving the car. If you do, say yes."

"But what if I don't . . ."

"Alyssa," said Roisin, "don't panic. It's okay to be nervous. He'll be in a suit, but it's the same person. The police had to pull him out of his car, remember? When it was surrounded by the lads from the estate?"

"Okay . . ." said Lissa, swallowing hard.

"Who is also on the CCTV that is going to be played to the jury."

"Can I watch that?"

"Nope. I'm just saying. Don't worry about it."

Lissa sighed.

"It's all right," said the lawyer. "You're going to be fine. Honest. And you'll be back in London. Enjoy that, surely!"

Lissa bit her lip. She couldn't help it; something about a tiny thing to look forward to. A tiny green shoot. And she'd teased Cormac about it: he'd suggested going to Borough Market, which made him *such* a Londoner—it was an incredibly expensive, very chichi food market just on the south bank by London Bridge station that sold all manner of exotic and organic foods at incredible prices.

But it was still a lovely place to roam around, smelling the cheeses and the coffee beans and seeing the beautiful cakes that were practically works of art and the unidentifiable (certainly to Cormac) spiky fruits. It was an oasis of beauty in the big granite city, and Cormac had liked it straightaway; it was so different from the very solid, decent farmers' market in Kirrinfief, where you could buy the freshest local brown hen's eggs with great big melting yolks, half a dozen for a pound. Here you could buy a single ostrich egg for £7. At the Kirrinfief farmers' market you could buy basket after basket of fresh strawberries, huge, some a little battered, falling over, from the fields all around them for miles and miles. Here you could buy six perfectly curated strawberries in an artisanal basket and they would cost almost a pound each.

But Cormac liked it anyway. It reminded him a little of home and people who took their food seriously, even if he had been slightly taken aback when asked to pay £8 for a toasted cheese sandwich.

And it was a ten-minute walk away from the courthouse. Her stomach fizzed.

SHE HAD TOLD herself not to get carried away, not to build it up too much. She had failed miserably.

"You look very distracted," said old Joe Cahill the previous Thursday.

Seeing as she was checking his foot operation post-wound care, and seeing as, distractingly, he had a set of the most gnarled and twisted hobbit-feet toenails she'd ever encountered, it wasn't, Lissa thought, as she came back to herself, the worst place to lose her concentration. She straightened up.

"Your wound is fine, Mr. Cahill," she said. "But did they not tell you to cut those nails?"

"Aye, they did, aye," he said mournfully. Then he looked down at his expansive stomach. "Och, it's not that easy, no," he added with a sigh.

"Could they not get someone to do it there?"

"Aye, they tried, but they couldnae work it with the scissors, eh."

It was true, they looked like sheep's horns.

"Let me have a shot," said Lissa. "You'll never get walking with those on."

But Joe had been quite right; there was absolutely no shifting them. Outside, a brief shower had made everything sparkle and bounce in the light. She could see the sheep nudging their way around the luminous green field. Suddenly she had an idea.

"I'm just going to see if Joan's about," she said.

Joan did, in fact, happen to be in the general area (which she gauged as being within fifteen miles) and came over immediately.

"I wondered," said Lissa, "if you knew if there was a technique that they used on, like, boy sheep and stuff."

"Boy sheep," said Joan, her lip curling.

"Um, yes," said Lissa.

"I'm not sure we're going to make a country girl out of you. But your thinking isn't bad. Joe!"

"Whit?"

"Stop eating pies, this is ridiculous." She prodded at his round stomach.

"Actually I was taught not to fat-shame patients," said Lissa quietly, feeling Joan had been unkind.

"More's the pity!" boomed Joan. "Come on, Joe."

"I do like a pie," said Joe.

"You can have a pie! Just don't have all the pies!"

"Um," said Lissa.

"Okay," said Joan. "Where's your hacksaw?"

"His what?"

"It's a small saw people use for cutting things," said Joan.

"No, but I thought you would have some animal thing . . . some technique they use on animals' horns."

"I do! It's called a hacksaw."

"There's one in the lean-to," said Joe.

The lean-to was a ramshackle space utterly filled with junk and tomato plants.

"If he can get around he can tidy up," muttered Joan. "You did the right thing to call me in."

She peered at Lissa over her spectacles.

"Just as you're getting the hang of it, you'll be heading back, eh?"

Lissa shrugged. "The court case is soon."

"Yes, I saw on the roster."

There was a pause as they rummaged through a large pile of seed catalogs, a lot of ancient *Farmers Weekly*s, and a medium-sized stuffed owl.

"I never thought you'd manage up here," said Joan finally, "with your London ways, but I think you've done rather well. I think people are finally taking to you."

Lissa blinked. "Except Ginty."

"Yes, except Ginty. She hates you. I heard all about it last time I was in."

"Oh good."

"I wouldn't worry about it. Everyone feels sorry for whoever is in Ginty's firing line. That poor Jake . . . Aha!"

Triumphantly she pulled a small hacksaw from the bottom of a teetering mass of unpleasant soil samples.

Lissa followed her back into the bedroom.

"I feel like I'm taking off someone's fingers for frostbite! Again!"

Lissa checked to see if she was kidding, but she didn't appear to be.

"Right, Joe. Feet up. Lissa, you hold him."

Lissa took one ankle at a time. It was a ridiculous business, but Joan worked quickly and carefully, sawing through the long, twirly nails, then Lissa neatly clipped what was left over and swept it up with a brush and pan.

Joe couldn't stop staring at his toes.

"Well," he said. Then he walked a few paces and a few more. "Well," he said again, scratching his head as if he couldn't quite believe it. "That is quite something. That is really quite something."

His eyes lit up.

"I feel like I could . . ."

"Do *not* dance," said Joan quickly. "You still have a foot injury."

"Och, just a jig . . ."

"No dancing. For a week. Then dance a lot. It'll help. And *no more pies!*"

"Aye," said Joe. "But noo I can dance I dinnae need pies."

He did an experimental twiddle.

"I am warning you!" said Joan. "No dancing. Some mild tidying up I would absolutely suggest to you."

"I need to find my dancing shoes," agreed Joe.

"Fine."

"Thanks, lass," he said, looking at Lissa. "This was your idea. You know, for a Sassenach, you're not that bad."

THE SUN WAS still high in the sky as they left, and the sheep pootled around, completely disinterested in them, as they headed toward their respective cars. It was a glorious evening, though, the breeze ruffling Lissa's hair. Joan marched straight to her high car, the dogs as usual going bananas in the back.

"Um," said Lissa just as she was about to get in. "Just . . . just . . . When Cormac comes back . . . just . . . Do you think—do you think there might be another opening here? For another person? I mean, I'm qualified for community nursing too."

Joan frowned. "Oh, I don't think so, dear. We're a shrinking region, there just aren't enough people here to support two NPLs. But there's absolutely loads of places in the Highlands that would snap you up . . . and I'd write you a good reference."

"Okay. Right. Thanks," said Lissa. But she didn't want anywhere in the Highlands. She wanted here.

Well, it was worth asking. Maybe getting back to London would make her feel more homesick; she'd always assumed that she would be. Once she saw all her friends and got back into her commute and with her life there . . . feeling lonely among crowds, making herself busy because somehow not being busy was associated with failure, cramming her calendar full of events she didn't really want to do, because she lived in London and how else was she supposed to manage?

No more wandering down into the village on a morning when she could see the changes from the day before: the new colors and flowers pouring out of the sides of the roads, the trees getting thicker every day, the loch mist burning off before she'd had her second cup of coffee. The noisy quiet of the countryside—the birds and the occasional growl in the woods, the sound of the wind in the fireplace—and the sweet smell of burning whisky wood. Pigeons eating old McDonald's leftovers didn't have quite the appeal of the herons that took off from the very tip of the loch like ballerinas.

Well. There was a lot happening. A lot coming up. She should just get through it a bit at a time.

Chapter 59

Lissa looked around the little cottage. It was as if she'd never lived there at all, now that she'd neatly packed her black carry-on case and emptied out the jam jar full of wildflowers.

Why, she found herself wondering now, had she not put up a picture? Set the books up on shelves rather than scattering them underneath her bed? She must have been in such a bad state when she arrived. The cottage was beautiful, and she could have made it even lovelier. Especially now that she knew Cormac wouldn't have minded.

She thought about him briefly, imagined him walking in. In her head, he was alternately very tall and very short and stocky; sometimes he had a beard and then he absolutely didn't—nurses never had beards anyway, in case they had to do mouth to mouth. Also, if he'd been in the army . . .

He hadn't mentioned Yazzie again, might even still be seeing her anyway. And she hoped he hadn't discussed her with Jake . . . They wouldn't, surely? They were Highland blokes—surely they'd just be discussing who'd won at the shinty.

She realized she'd actually had the conscious thought *Who'd won at the shinty*. God, she had changed.

When she got back from London, she vowed. She would make it beautiful, for the time she had left of June, when it never got dark and the air softened, and she was so looking forward to it, although she reminded herself to bring super-strength midge spray back with her. They must sell something in London for people going to the tropics. Something must kill those pesky mites.

She couldn't help it, though. Imagining. What it would be like if he walked through the door and grabbed her and . . .

She was being ridiculous, she realized. But also it was good: good that she was thinking about a chap again. It had been so very long since her mind hadn't felt closed, confused, frightened all the time. Even her ability to daydream, to fantasize, seemed to have been turned off by the anxiety; the luxury of even believing in a brighter future for herself. That had been lost; now it seemed to have been found. Even if, of course, it was nonsense.

Still. They were meeting. After the trial. Better than that: he had promised to take her out to lunch and she had (and she felt guilty about it) not even told her mum or Kim-Ange, even though she knew they were both longing to see her. This was bad, but it was going to be such an awful day, and only the thought of Cormac was keeping her hanging on.

Her Skype bonged, and she groaned.

ANITA WAS FULLY dressed and had two suitcases by the side of her kitchen table.

"Is this a bad time?" said Lissa, not wanting to point out that Anita had called her.

"Pfft," said Anita, glancing nervously at a pile of paperwork on the kitchen table. "Apparently I'm passport monitor and it's making me very nervous."

"Perhaps try some deep breathing exercises," said Lissa, then immediately felt bad. "Sorry, I'm sorry."

But Anita was looking around anxiously. "Where is that sodding cat?" she was saying to herself.

Just at that exact moment, a cat shot past the screen, so fast it was just a blur, pursued by two rampaging children.

"Not on the road! Not on the road!"

Lissa found herself thinking about Nina and Zoe, baby John pottering about the farmyard with his dad and Zoe's little tribe cavorting about the fields. Anita obviously lived in a nice terrace house in South London; it was probably worth more than the entire village up here. But as the children sped around the nice, expensive kitchen, it couldn't help crossing Lissa's mind if it was worth it. How much it must cost to pay the mortgage; how hard it must be to raise children you couldn't let out on their own.

"Honestly, I can—"

"No, you have these sessions paid for and I need to complete them before you go." She looked crestfallen. "Sorry they've been a little rushed . . ."

"It doesn't look easy, your job," said Lissa mildly.

"I know," said Anita, as little shoes pattered overhead. "I'm sorry . . ."

Lissa shook her head. "Actually," she said cheerfully, "turning off my social media . . . it really helped."

"Did it?" Anita brightened.

"Yup. And so did you telling me to go over it in my head."

"Did you?"

"No, but I thought the idea was solid. So . . ."

Outside Anita's door a taxi honked its horn and her face fell.

"Tell me quickly," said Lissa.

"It's quite strong," said Anita.

"I don't care. Call it efficient and I'll give you a good feed-back form."

"That would be good," said Anita, looking stressed.

There was a pause.

"Okay," she said, then took a deep breath. "If you don't go over this right now, out loud, whether to me or somebody else, this is your last chance. You'll be in the witness-box. And the perpetrator is going to be staring straight at you. Possibly his mates will be there. Staring at you. Threatening you. I'm not trying to scare you, Lissa. But what if you freeze? Clam up?"

"Oh, actually this is quite harsh," said Lissa.

The honking grew louder. Anita paused.

"I won't freeze," said Lissa suddenly.

"You might."

Lissa blinked back tears. All at once, the gray day outside the window didn't look soft and welcoming: it looked ominous and oppressive.

"And I have to warn you. You could cause a mistrial or let the offender go free, if you can't explain clearly what you saw."

Lissa could barely speak; the lump in her throat was huge.

Upstairs, Anita's children were yelling their heads off. Anita leaned forward.

"Lissa, I have black sons. One day you might too. The streets of the city have to be safe for them. You know that. You know that, right?"

And her voice was intense and serious and not at all distracted. All Lissa could do was back away from her gaze, nodding slowly. The taxi honked for the last time, and Anita straightened up.

"And now I have to go," she said, and Lissa simply nodded.

THERE WAS ANOTHER honking sound, and Lissa belatedly realized it was her own cab. Her heart was racing. She knew Anita was right. She knew. But suddenly it seemed harder than ever.

Chapter 60

I won't know what you look like, Lissa had typed as she set off for London, after she'd been driven through a bright and golden dawn.

They hadn't been communicating beyond the professional in the last week, mostly because both of them, without mentioning it, were extremely nervous. Lissa nearly wrote "it's a blind date" but managed to delete it just in time because it wasn't a date, it was a meeting with someone she had been doing a job share with—professional, if anything. They had already discussed dates they'd had with other people. So. The fact that she hadn't mentioned it to Kim-Ange had . . . nothing to do with anything.

Cormac also hadn't mentioned their meeting to Kim-Ange. She would just make a big deal out of it. Plus, she and Piotr were madly in love and snogging up a storm at breakfast time every day and frankly making everyone a tiny bit sick, and nothing would make her happier than to think of the two of them . . . going for lunch, no more, no less, he told himself, nonetheless ironing his best shirt, a yellow check.

He glanced at her message and typed, I'll recognize YOU. You'll be the one loudly complaining about diabetic prescribing.

It just makes everything else MORE DIFFICULT, started Lissa, a bugbear that always made him smile.

ROISIN HAD TOLD Lissa to look sensible in court, so she pulled her hair back into a tight bun that made her look more professional than the curls everywhere and put on a sleek houndstooth check skirt suit that she never really got a chance to wear. Paired with a blouse and some smart earrings her mother had sent her (as well as the suit), she looked surprisingly professional, particularly after having spent the last two months either in uniform or wrapped up in woolly jumpers and thick tights, even through the Highlands spring.

She had brought her overnight bag; she was coming back on the night train, which she was rather excited about; it stopped just up the road from Kirrinfief and was patently the best way to get there, even if it was expensive.

All she had to get through was the trial.

Her heart was beating hard all the way to the airport. Being in Scotland had felt safe, protected, away from everyone else. Not having to face what had happened. There weren't any teen gangs in Kirrinfief, at least not that she'd heard of. Children ran around practically free range, something that had surprised her when she'd first noticed it, but then realized that everyone knew everyone in their small corner of the world; their children were everyone's children. It was nice, to see children playing in the streets and down on the little shore and not have to worry about them.

As the little twin prop plane burred its way down the length of the country, Lissa looked at the patchwork fields through the window, unable to concentrate on the book Nina had pressed on her, worrying more and more about coming face-to-face with Kai's family again. Would they be mad at her? Would questions be asked about that dreadful night at the hospital? No complaints had ever been filed; nothing had happened to her except the secondment, and that hadn't ended up feeling like a punishment, not at all.

Maybe, she thought, it would be straightforward, would take two minutes. And there would be . . . the Loch Ness monster. She bit her lip. It was nice of him, that was all. And no doubt he wanted to cast an eye over the person who'd been sleeping in his spare room, would be trying to work out whether she'd killed all his plants or broken his fridge. At least he probably knew she hadn't exactly been having wild parties.

Then another two weeks to pack up and then . . .

Well, she'd think about the future when she had to. She had had a little fantasy, it was true, of possibly renting the guest room, if he was keen—imagine living somewhere where you could afford to have a spare room on an NHS salary! It still beggared belief. A fantasy of finding a job nearby. Maybe not what she was doing, but there must be something. Of, dare she say it, escaping once and for all. The pressure and the racing and the craziness of the city. Just turning her back on it. Leaving the new restaurants and the high heels and the hot new thing to other people. People who got more out of it than she did. People who wouldn't be constantly worried every time they heard an ambulance whoop, sirens go off, or a helicopter pass overhead.

She blinked. She had barely slept and the drone of the engines was making her want to drop off (everyone else was comfortably snoozing), but every time she came close to doing so, she remembered, yet again, what the day was for, and bolted back upright again.

SOUTHWARK CROWN COURT was a squat, ugly brown 1980s building, put up by someone who had obviously taken their inspiration from a supermarket. It was faceless and bureaucratic, neither terrifyingly grand nor trying to be welcoming. It simply was. Lissa supposed in some way that was the point.

It was boiling. A damp, oppressive heat. Lissa couldn't remember the last time she'd been so hot. She was wearing far too many clothes, it was ridiculous. She pulled off her large coat and jammed it on top of her wheelie bag, making it unwieldy and hard to get past the crowds on the tubes. She'd forgotten about those too. So many people! How did anyone get anywhere? And could she really have forgotten about this in such a short space of time? She felt herself begin to sweat. This was the last thing she needed, to look damp and flustered.

Roisin—short, businesslike, and dressed in a smart black suit and heels that looked like absolute torture to march about in all day—met her at the side entrance. People were milling around and Lissa was anxious, concerned about seeing the boy's mother again, jerking back to the memory of everything that had happened before, again and again.

She looked around nervously. How would the family of the defendant be? Angry? Frustrated? Violent?

Instead she saw a mixed lineup of smartly dressed solicitors and barristers hurrying in and out of entrances; clerks with huge bundles of papers and files, sometimes rolling them along in carrying cases; and other people, some dowdily dressed, smoking patiently by the bins or sitting staring into space. It did not feel like a cheerful place, nor was it meant to.

"You'll be fine," said Roisin, sitting her down in the witness waiting room after they got buzzed in. It was completely plain and bare, and the coffee was absolutely disgusting, served in a thin white plastic cup. Lissa kept forgetting and took automatic sips of it.

She read over her statement again. It was just as she recalled it, and she felt her heart begin to thump. The day, the person she'd been visiting. Seeing the boys in the walkway. And the flash, the hideous flash, of the phone, glinting in the sun; the crunching of bones; the squelching of flesh.

The rush. The ambulance. The sitting. The begging, the bargaining. The faces.

She started to cry.

"You'll be fine," said Roisin, glancing at her watch. "Come on! You've been a big tough A&E nurse! You're used to all sorts! How come this one is bothering you?"

She remembered the boy's soft face lying on the hard pavement. "It just does," she said.

"Well, distract yourself," said Roisin. "How's country life treating you?"

At this Lissa felt herself turn pink. "It's all right," she said.

"Seriously? Lots of cows to talk to?"

"Yup," said Lissa. "Lots of cows."

"Isn't it freezing? I couldn't handle the weather."

"It's fresh," said Lissa. "I quite like it. It's better than . . ."

She indicated out the tiny window: the heat shimmers coming off the pavement, the scent of rubbish rising into the stuffy air, smoke everywhere.

"Well," said Lissa, "I quite like it."

"I see your point," Roisin sniffed, and Lissa bent again to the black-and-white sheet of paper.

Chapter 61

Cormac woke early that morning, the room stuffy already, excited about something before he remembered exactly what it was. He sat up, grinning to himself. Then he stopped and felt worried instead. Today was the day. He was going to meet Lissa.

He told himself to stop being daft. He was a grown man, and he felt like a teenager on a first date. Getting overexcited was only going to lead to disappointment. Plus, she was stressed out and worried anyway; the last thing she'd be thinking about was him. But he could be there, take her to lunch—he was proud of discovering somewhere lovely to take her—listen, get to know her. That was all. Yes.

He still couldn't keep that infernal smile off his face as he got into the shower and pondered the new, slightly flowery shirt Kim-Ange had persuaded him to buy. It wasn't his style at all and had been to his mind hideously expensive, but Kim-Ange had been extremely persuasive on the issue, and sure enough, nobody had pointed and laughed when he'd worn it to the pub for half an hour just to give it a tryout.

The way he was thinking about Lissa, though . . . nothing

about Emer or Yazzie had ever come close to. No. He was being ridiculous. Overthinking everything.

But it was the first time in such a long time that he'd just felt so . . . so alive.

He thought back to Robbie. He'd better call Lennox and see how he was doing, although so far no news felt like good news. And Lissa would be seeing him, of course . . .

Don't go overboard, he told himself. She was in for such a tough day. Testifying in court. Reliving that awful time. He had to play it cool.

Or, he also found himself thinking, he could turn up early, go support her in court. It wasn't right she had to be in court by herself. He could just say hi, just let her know that he was there for her. Would that be weird?

It was a glorious day out there. Perhaps he would take a stroll—just a casual stroll—in his new shirt along the south bank, a place he had come to . . . Well, it wasn't Scotland. But it definitely had *something*. So. He could take a stroll. Get a lovely cup of coffee that took someone quite a while to make grinding beans and stuff, and, well, he could see where the day took him.

THE CURVACEOUS WOMAN with the thick spectacles and the tightly pulled back hair barely gave the man in the flowery shirt who held the door open for her a second glance as she marched toward it, head down, anxious beyond belief about what was coming.

Cormac didn't notice the woman either; he had meant to

look around for someone who might be Lissa, but his phone had rung just as he was walking in. He recognized the number, grimaced, and picked up.

"Hi!" came the English-sounding voice. "Is that the life-saver?"

Cormac frowned. "Larissa, hi."

"Hi! Listen, darling, beautiful day, we've got lunch booked on the roof of Coq d'Argent. It's beautiful and you'll be able to save anyone that falls off it. See you there, yah?"

Cormac passed the door to the girl behind him, who took it with muted thanks and dived past the annoying man walking too slowly in a flowery shirt.

"I'm a bit busy today," he said quite happily.

"Oh, don't worry about that, darling, we'll be there all afternoon. Ciao!"

But Cormac's thoughts were still on a laughing girl with tumbling curls. Plus, he had realized to his slight annoyance that he was absolutely miles too early—bursting, truly, from turning up, too excited and over the top—and was contemplating going back out again to find another coffee, but then he'd have had far too much caffeine and that really wasn't an ideal situation for meeting someone either, so he decided to go fill up his water bottle from somewhere and sit and stare out at the passing boats and, hopefully, calm the crap down before he ruined everything.

Chapter 62

Are you ready?" Roisin asked. "You do know this is a murder trial?"

"Why isn't it manslaughter?" said Lissa.

"Because we have evidence the defendant thought Kai was a gang member from a rival group, even though he wasn't. It was mistaken identity, but we're fairly clear it was deliberate. Kai was the youngest of his friends; he was only fifteen. They thought he was a runner. He wasn't. The driver never meant to get caught, but he did mean to do it."

Lissa thought again of the car speeding up. *Speeding up.* This was worse—not a hideous accident, but a deliberate attempt to extinguish a young life. The wrong life. It was almost unbearable.

Lissa took a deep breath and bent her head to the paper. The words swam in front of her eyes.

"*. . . I saw the car swing round the corner and mount the curb . . .*"

She saw the boy again, his phone glinting as it was thrown up and fell, thrown up and fell, spinning in the sunlight

"*. . . and when I got to him . . .*"

She remembered the trickle of blood dripping down from the side of his mouth; the shouts and yells of the rest of them chasing the car down; the cries and the shrieking of brakes and the *drip drip drip* of the blood.

Blindly panicking, unable to breathe, her heart trying to burst out of her chest, she stood up, leaving everything behind her, and ran out of the room.

Chapter 63

Cormac wandered back into the courthouse, figuring he needed to use the bathroom and surely the case would be starting soon. He was still annoyed at how restless he felt. When someone pushed past him . . .

It was a flash, nothing more; he didn't catch sight of the person . . .

He dismissed it as the fact that he had curly hair on his mind, but then it struck him, as the figure dashed past in a blur, ringlets bouncing out of their tight band, that she might well be here by now, and by the time his heart had suddenly dialed up to a hundred miles an hour and he'd turned around, there was a loud bang, and he realized that the figure had disappeared into the disabled toilet and locked the door behind her.

AH. NOW HERE was a thing. Lurking around the loo was . . . Cormac tried to think of a worse possible way to meet Lissa for the first time—if it even was her; it might just have been his mind playing tricks. How would he even know?

The corridor was empty and he backed away carefully, concerned at the loudness of the bang she had made and the speed she'd been running. Whoever it was, she was clearly upset.

He took out his phone and was about to text her, then he put it away again. If it wasn't her, it would be very weird. If it was, saying "have you locked yourself in the toilet right now?" was hardly going to come over well.

He was about to go over to the courtroom, check if he could see her there, when he heard a noise coming from the door. Just a sob. The tiniest little sob.

Cormac stopped in his tracks. Whether it was her or whether it wasn't . . . someone was really upset. And it just wasn't in him not to pay attention to that.

He went over to the door and knocked gently.

LISSA FROZE. SHE had tried to keep quiet, but it was almost impossible; the lump in her throat was overwhelming. Oh God. She couldn't believe it. Someone needed in. She was gasping for breath, didn't know what to do. She tried to calm herself down.

"Um . . ." Cormac listened. He could hear heavy breaths. If she was genuinely having a panic attack, adding an extra stressor by identifying himself was probably the worst thing he could do. If it even was her.

Lissa put her hands on her knees, tried to suck in some air. "Just a minute," she managed weakly.

She straightened up slowly, trying to breathe properly. She didn't recognize her face in the mirror. She was being ridicu-

lous. This was nuts. She had to go and do this. She had to . . .
she had to . . .

She felt the tears welling up again.

"Are you all right?" came a soft voice.

She froze again. She hadn't even thought so far ahead, just
knew she had to escape that airless little room, the words in
front of her, the memories.

But time was moving on; they were going to call the case.
There was a whole roomful of people waiting for justice, waiting for her to help Kai. She had to be there. But she couldn't.

THERE WAS A silence. Cormac cursed to himself. He couldn't
believe he'd spoken. Now what kind of trouble was he in?

If he said who he was, she might get really upset or take um
brage, or it might be just incredibly weird. If he didn't and she
found out later, that would be awful too. But he couldn't run
away. She needed help. He knew she did. He couldn't leave.

That was when Cormac MacPherson, in a split second, made
possibly the most ridiculous decision of his entire life.

"Yeah, awright, luv, tell me what's up, duck."

He winced at himself. He sounded more Welsh than Cock-
ney, probably. Or just downright insane.

Lissa squinted. The voice—she couldn't tell where it was
from—sounded kind. She threw some water on her face, trying to make her heart stop racing. She couldn't stay like this,
she couldn't.

Snuffling slightly, she moved a little closer to the door, tried
to catch her breath. "I have to . . . I have to testify."

On the other side of the door, Cormac blinked. He wished he could go inside, hold her, tell her everything was going to be all right. But he didn't know this person. He didn't know her at all. Instead, he found himself saying, "Oh yeah. Innit?" Then wincing all the more.

"I . . . It should be straightforward. Just . . . just say what happened."

"Yeah, that sounds awright."

"And . . . I'm just so scared."

"Wot 'appened, then?" said Cormac. "Tell me . . . duck."

He wasn't at all sure about "duck."

"Weren't rude or nuffin'?"

Lissa slumped to sit down, her back to the door. Cormac sat down too, his back on the other side, separated only by a few centimeters of wood.

"Oh . . . no," she said, half smiling. "No, nuffin' rude."

She squeezed her eyes together. A kind stranger on the other side of the door . . .

"Sorry, do you really need the bathroom?" she said, suddenly gripped by the worry that it might be an actual wheelchair user outside.

"You're awright, luv," said Cormac, begging himself to stop talking.

There was a pause. And somehow, Lissa found her heart rate slowing a little, as everything went quiet.

"I just have to tell them . . ." Lissa began.

Cormac pressed his head against the door to hear her better.

"I just have to say . . . that I saw the boys shouting and arguing. And then I saw the car. And the man in the car. And I saw
him hit the boy. That's it. That's all I have to say. That's all . . ."

Her voice caught as she saw once again the phone whipping
through the air, heard the hideous clunk of Kai's head on the
concrete.

"Yeah," said Cormac. "You can do that. You can tell the
truth. Telling the truth should feel easy."

"I saw . . . I saw the car come round," said Lissa again, her
voice still wavering. "I saw it come round too fast. I saw the
color of it. I saw it."

"Yeah," said Cormac, more encouraging now.

"I saw it hit . . . I saw it hit the boy. I saw it. I *saw* him. I
saw him hit the boy, and Kai . . . Kai's . . . the boy's Kai's
phone. Went up. In the air. I saw it. And he went up, he was
thrown up, and . . . and he killed him. I saw it. I did. I saw it.
I was there."

"*'Scuse me.*"

Cormac blinked, the spell broken, and looked up. A large
girl with a lot of straw-colored blond hair and a crop top that
seemed slightly unusual in a court situation was glaring at him.

"Need to use this loo."

She didn't seem obviously disabled, but Cormac knew better than to judge that. On the other side of the door, Lissa
had gone totally silent, just, Cormac thought, as she needed to
speak up.

"There's just someone in," said Cormac. "Is it urgent?"

"Fuck off," said the girl.

There was a slightly awkward standoff. Cormac stood up carefully. "Could you just give us a minute?"

"No," said the girl. "I'm gluten intolerant?"

"Oh," mumbled Cormac. "Oh, okay, I see . . ."

On the other side of the door, Lissa struggled to hear what was going on outside. She had been so caught up in the moment. She stood up and threw some more water on her face.

Oddly, she felt better. She'd said it. Aloud. She'd said it, seen it in her head as she spoke aloud.

Even talking to a stranger—or perhaps exactly because she *had* been talking to a stranger—had let her say the words out loud, the words she needed to say; to prepare to point the finger she needed to point, to get justice for the Mitchells, to see justice be done without letting anyone down.

She decided to open the door, thank the odd chap who'd been there, start to move back . . . Roisin must be wondering where she was; she'd left her phone on the table. And her bag. She couldn't decide if your handbag would be safer in a crown court or much less safe.

She took a deep breath and moved toward the door. Which was the precise second the fire alarm went off.

Chapter 64

Weeeeeeeee!!

The round girl eyed Cormac crossly. "Did you just set the *fire alarm* on me?" she said, looking murderous.

"What? No!" said Cormac in consternation. If Lissa burst out now . . . well, awkward didn't quite cover it . . .

There was a loud pummeling noise and shouting barreling down the corridor, and as Cormac stepped toward it, he realized what he was looking at.

The hallway was full of fighters, gang members—the boys who were there as witnesses—and the huge and intimidating family of the defendant himself. The court was specially set up to absolutely avoid this kind of thing from happening, to keep families and gangs apart. Cormac didn't know what had broken down today, but something obviously had.

The woman waiting for the bathroom turned around. "Oh, for fuck's sake," she yelled. "I told you all to stay in your rooms!"

Ah, well, that explained a lot, thought Cormac, as the melee bowled ever closer, and a high-pitched squeal burst from someone. Cormac didn't hesitate: he headed straight toward the trouble.

Chapter 65

Violence had burst out in the constrained space of the corridor: a mass of youths against a family of mixed ages and sizes, many blond. Screams and curses filled the air. Cormac saw one boy unleash a huge fist and start punching a man full in the face, unusually not immediately pulling back his hand with his fingers broken. He obviously had boxing experience. The smaller and older man beneath him was cowering, his nose squashed to a pulp. As the huge boy raised his fist again, Cormac jumped on him from behind, took his arm, and tried to twist it upward in a restraining position.

"Come on, lad," he said, in as reasonable a tone as he could manage. "Settle down."

There was considerable swearing from all sides at this. Someone glanced a blow off Cormac's ear, but he didn't let go of his grip on this chap who was far too big for him. Terrible tragedies were caused by young men who didn't know their own strength, who didn't know they could fell a man or break a neck with one punch; that they could spend the rest of their lives in jail for one fatal white-hot moment. The man on the other side, with the jelly nose, was whimpering and trembling and didn't seem able to move at all. Cormac had seen a million fights, in the army and in hospitals. They were always like this and never like the movies: slightly pathetic, very noisy, and completely confusing for everyone involved.

"Come on!" he said, as the big youth spun around trying to dislodge him, and one of his other mates grabbed Cormac's ear, which was ridiculous, though it also hurt like hell.

"GERROFF!" shouted Cormac, in what would have surprised him to learn was an exceptional London cabbie accent.

They stumbled backward, hitting the wall, and Cormac was about to give up, hissing at the man in front to move out of the bloody way before he got punched again, when the worst thing happened.

Chapter 66

Lissa unlocked the door, and as soon as she did, the other woman pushed her way in and locked it behind them both.

"It's kicked off," she said.

The two women in the loo looked at each other rather awkwardly as the shouting and fighting continued beyond the bathroom door.

"Weird sort of panic room," said Lissa in a waver, attempting to break the ice.

The fire alarm was still going off, but nobody was moving. Lissa assumed, correctly, that someone had set it off on purpose to get everyone out in the corridors. Certainly you couldn't smell anything. The woman had her phone out and was tutting loudly.

"Sorry," said Lissa. "Did you really need to use the loo? I can stand in the corner if you like."

"You don't look very disabled," said the woman crossly.

"I know," said Lissa. "I'm sorry about that. I was having a panic attack. I know that doesn't count."

The woman shrugged. "Oh. Well. Maybe that should count."

"Not if other people need it."

"I'm gluten intolerant."

"*Oh,*" said Lissa. "Oh, well, I *am* sorry to hear that . . ." Her voice trailed off.

"Why were you panicking?" said the other girl eventually, giving up tapping on her phone.

"I . . . I'm meant to be giving evidence. It's scary to think about it," said Lissa. She couldn't believe she'd even managed to say that out loud. "I never used to be frightened about stuff. Then I saw a horrible accident and it really knocked me over."

She paused. This was . . . this was exactly what Anita had told her to do. Talk about it, over and over. Relive it till she couldn't be scared of it anymore. That guy too.

"The guy outside . . . the guy I was talking to. He said I should just talk about it."

"He's probably right," said the woman. "Mind you, he went off to have a fight, so God knows."

"I know . . . bit weird taking advice from a bloke on the other side of a toilet door."

"Take it where you can get it, I say," said the woman, looking at her face in the mirror and adjusting her carefully painted-on eyebrows. "I have some advice for you. If you're meant to be sitting with five lads in a jury situation, don't go to the toilet."

It took Lissa a minute. "*Oh God,*" she said. "Is this . . ."

The woman looked at her. "Shh," she said. "I'm a youth worker, yes. But I really did have to go."

Her brow furrowed.

"Not so much now."

"I mean, please do . . ."

"I can't now, I'm too uptight."

The alarm stopped going off.

"Phew," said Lissa, feeling oddly better now that she was comforting somebody else. "How about now, without the alarm?"

"Nope," said the woman. "Still not feeling it. It's like all the pee has hopped back up me."

She frowned.

"This is going to do nothing for my gluten intolerance."

"Well, no," said Lissa truthfully.

They both approached the door. The noise seemed to have died down.

"Do you think it's safe?" said Lissa.

"Well, either that or they're just a pile of corpses out there," said the woman. "I'm joking! I'm joking! Wish me luck!"

She paused.

"And listen. I know they sound rowdy. But they're just lads. Tell the truth and shame the devil, and it'll all be fine."

"That's what Toilet Guy said. He said I should talk about it."

"Well then."

And they smiled tentatively at each other, and Lissa turned the handle on the door.

Chapter 67

But I was just passing by!" said Cormac uselessly, as the two policemen marched him into the van.

"That is what they all say," said a slim, bespectacled police officer with a wispy mustache.

"I know!" said Cormac. "But I'm a medical professional."

"And I am the uncle of a monkey," said the policeman—unnecessarily, Cormac thought. The local copper in Kirrinfief knew every single person in the village and spent a lot of time posing with tourists and trying to stop toddlers escaping from the nursery.

There was a paddy wagon ahead. Surely not, thought Cormac. This was a joke. But there it was. He was being arrested, as was everybody else.

He remembered back a few short hours when he had woken up with the sun on his face, full of happiness and feeling like singing out loud. What a wonderful day he had planned. Surprising Lissa at the courthouse, and seeing her lovely face beam the same smile on him as he'd seen in the photo . . .

Rather than, of course, what had actually happened, when he'd ended up sitting down in a dirty corridor doing a fake accent while she sobbed uncontrollably. Not exactly what he'd had in mind.

Oh, and now he had handcuffs on.

It struck him that this wasn't remotely funny, and also that he should probably let her know that he wasn't coming for lunch. He scrabbled around in his back pocket for his phone, which promptly fell on the floor.

"I'll have that," said the young officer, taking it peremptorily and putting it in a bag.

"What! I need to call someone!"

"You'll get your call at the station. Until then, all phones are confiscated."

There were general growls of annoyance all around. Cormac blinked. If he had only one call . . . could he call someone he'd never met to come bail him out? That really was an almost worse introduction to someone than meeting her for the first time when she was collapsed sobbing on a dirty bathroom floor. Oh God.

"Seriously, I'm not involved!" said Cormac in desperation.

"This is why we had to pull you off someone in the fray," said the constable. "Okay. Got it."

Cormac winced. This could be bad.

And who the hell was he going to call?

Chapter 68

Once order had been more or less restored, Lissa crept back to the witness room. Roisin was waiting for her, arms folded.

"Well, you're here now," she sniffed.

"Sorry," said Lissa.

"I'm sympathetic," said Roisin, sounding anything but. "But you're lucky it got delayed. We can't do this without you. You're the only witness who wasn't involved!"

"I know," said Lissa, breathing deeply. "But I think . . . I think I'm all right."

"Good," said Roisin, as a number flashed up on the wall. "Okay, that's us. Let's go."

THE COURTROOM—A windowless room with stained cheap carpet and pinboard walls, that smelled of stale coffee and dusty lighting—was not remotely impressive. The judge sat looking half asleep, not a flicker of interest on her face as Lissa entered.

The big group of Kai's friends had all gone, likewise the family of Marcus, the defendant, who stood defiant in a cheap suit and a razor-sharp haircut, swaggering in the dock facing the judge's podium. A stern-looking lawyer was sitting behind him, scribbling; a hodgepodge lineup of people sitting expectantly to the side, she realized, of course would be the jury.

"Alyssa Westcott called to the stand," said a bored-sounding woman on the side.

Lissa took a deep breath. She wished that she'd asked her mum to be here—or even, she thought suddenly, Cormac. He would have come. Still, she would see him after this. All she had to do was to get through with this and . . . she checked her mobile phone. She hadn't heard from him, but that's okay. She'd WhatsApp him when they were out and then—well, she'd probably better redo her makeup and, Christ, her hair. But then . . .

"Phone off!" hissed a court clerk, and Lissa immediately passed it on to Roisin.

But she still held on to the idea as she walked slowly up the stained carpet toward the chair with the microphone, where she swore an oath, her hand a little shaky on the faded Bible they offered her. *Just think of what happens next,* she told herself. *Just think about what happens next.*

"Can you tell us what happened on the nineteenth of March of this year?" said Roisin.

And slowly, haltingly, Lissa told the story all the way through, even though the man with the razor-cut blond hair stared at her menacingly, as if he could beam malevolence and fury toward her, even as she avoided his gaze. And when Roisin asked her very clearly whether the car slowed down or sped up as it turned the corner, she answered carefully so she could not be misunderstood by the jury, the judge, or anyone else.

"Yes. He sped up."

"And can you see the driver in this courtroom?"

"Yes. He's over there in the box."

The man hissed at her, actually hissed, and was immediately disciplined by the police officer standing to his left. Lissa was suddenly very relieved none of his family was in the room to see her.

"You're sure."

"I'm sure."

"But the car was going quickly," said the defense lawyer, when it came time for questions. "You can't have gotten more than a glimpse."

"He stared straight at me," said Lissa. "I remember everything about it. I'm a trained A&E nurse. We see a lot of potentially dangerous situations. Sir—he grimaced at me. Just like that. It was him. He drove round the corner, he sped up, and he drove straight toward . . . Kai. He knocked his phone out of his hand, then his body went straight up in the air and landed on the concrete. Then he sped off."

She took a deep breath.

"That's what happened."

The defense lawyer looked at her. A young nurse, calm, clearly telling the truth, who had absolutely no reason to lie and absolutely no reason to be here except for justice. He could sense the waves off the jury of how much they approved of her. He looked at Lissa one last time, glanced at the jury, cast his client a slightly apologetic shrug, and stood back.

"No further questions."

Chapter 69

Unable to quite believe she was free, Lissa walked slowly down the aisle to leave the courtroom. At the end she caught sight of a face she recognized. Quickly and without ceremony, Mrs. Mitchell, Kai's mother, nodded briskly.

Lissa felt relieved but chastened: glad that she had managed to do what she needed to do and overwhelmingly guilty because she was feeling happy now, like she was in a position to get on with her life. And Mrs. Mitchell never, ever could. She gave a half smile of apology and regret; but she had to leave, and the court had to carry on with its work, as human misery spilled out from courtroom after courtroom, in town after town.

It felt like a breath of liberty as Lissa pushed through the doors of the sour-smelling courtroom. The security guards were wired and buzzy after the fight that morning, everyone twitchy and tired and stressed.

She headed into the normal bathrooms this time, to reapply a whole face of makeup, and curled her eyelashes right out, something she almost never did. Her eyebrows were a mess, her not trusting Ginty on this issue, but she'd done the best she could, and she added a pretty rose-colored lipstick to her lips and a little blush to her cheeks and let down her hair, then laughed at herself for being so over the top. Then she squirted on some more perfume just in case.

Still nothing on her phone from Cormac. She frowned. Well, it wasn't far to Borough Market. Maybe he thought court would run later. She'd been surprised how quick it had been, in the end. She'd been a good witness, Roisin had told her, which had felt so good.

Or perhaps he'd be waiting there . . . sitting in the sun. She reminded herself that he might be five feet tall and three feet wide, then wondered how much that would really— *really*— matter, as much as she looked forward to talking to him, how his messages were the highlight of her day.

The sunshine hit her full in the face, dazzling her. She practically bounced along the south bank, cutting through side streets to avoid the crowds, walking straight past the police station Cormac was currently being held in.

Chapter 70

Cormac sat in the holding cell with two other kids from the courthouse, both of them cursing and swearing.

"We were just there to support Kai," complained one, whose name was Tim. "Just to show him he isn't forgotten."

"By kicking the lumps out of some guy," said Cormac. "Come on, lads. You must know that isn't helpful."

"Are you Scottish?" said Tim. "I thought Scotch folk *love* kicking lumps out of people."

"He was doing a good job with Big Al," pointed out the other boy, who presumably had a name that wasn't Nobbo, but Nobbo seemed to do.

"So you were," said Tim.

"I was trying to stop him accidentally really hurting someone. And ending up in prison," said Cormac.

"We're in prison now," said Tim.

"I realize that," said Cormac.

BOROUGH MARKET WAS absolutely heaving, every stall was rammed. And Lissa didn't know what he looked like. She glanced around. What kind of thing would Cormac like? She didn't even know, she realized. She knew so little about him.

Finally, right at the back, she spied an empty table at a little hole-in-the-wall tapas bar. That looked absolutely perfect. She slipped into the bar, smiling at the man serving, who showed her to the table with a wave of his hand.

"For one?"

"Two," said Lissa, beaming nervously. "I'm waiting on someone."

The man smiled. "Lovely. Can I bring you a negroni?"

Lissa looked around, still feeling excited and nervous and so pleased with the fact that she'd managed to do the right thing. It wouldn't bring Kai back, but she'd been able to look Mrs. Mitchell in the eye as she'd left.

"Yes, please!" she said. Then she took a picture of the bar sign and texted it to Cormac.

She also sent Anita a Skype message to say she had done it and to say thank you: the woman had been right all along. Anita responded by sending her a picture of an ice-cream cone and Lissa smiled to herself.

SHE FINISHED HER drink and immediately declined another, the idea of being drunk when Cormac arrived too hideous to contemplate. She considered a coffee, then worried her breath would smell and settled for a fizzy water. The waiter looked a tiny bit concerned. A cloud passed across the sun.

She thought whenever Ezra hadn't been in the mood to see

her, he'd just not answer any of her messages or texts. It happened to Kim-Ange all the time, when she met guys and then they got cold feet. Ghosting was awful.

But that wasn't going to happen here. Not with Cormac. He'd asked her to lunch, after all. They'd arranged to meet.

Although they hadn't picked anywhere specific, had they? They hadn't actually said, "This restaurant in this place." Just Borough Market. It was fairly nonspecific after all when you thought about it.

She shook herself. Come on. She was catastrophizing, overthinking, everything a therapist would say was unhelpful. She'd gotten through one thing today. She was going to manage. She was.

She tried not to drink all her water too quickly. Her battery was running a little low. Still no message.

Chapter 71

"So you came to meet some bird," said Tim scornfully. "That you've never even met."

They had been in the cell together for some time and were trading stories.

"Yeah," said Cormac.

"What if she's, like, a fuckbeast," said Nobbo.

"I'm sure she's not a fuckbeast," said Cormac carefully.

"Well, did she send you pictures? Of her tits and that?"

"No, of course not! Women don't do that."

"Fuckbeasts don't."

"Could you stop using that term? It's really unpleasant."

Tim sniffed a bunch of phlegm up his nose and, with one finger closing a nostril, hocked it into the seatless metal toilet at the side of the room. Cormac didn't necessarily feel this was an improvement. He paced up and down, feeling worse and worse—she must be there; or had she left by now? Stormed off, furious with him? Maybe she'd never speak to him again. Maybe that was his chance and he'd muffed it. After all, there was only another couple of weeks to go . . .

And he'd be back home, which was . . . well, it was fine of course.

But the cottage could feel a little empty on those long, dark evenings that came in the wintertime.

"MacPherson?" came the guard at the door, unlocking it. "You can make your phone call now."

"Are you charging me?"

"We're going to have a word, so hold your horses."

"He was just pulling off Big Al!" shouted Tim, and Nobbo agreed vociferously, while laughing like an eighteen-year-old at the same time.

Cormac sighed as he followed the officer down the hallway. Who on earth was he going to call?

Chapter 72

Kim-Ange shook her phone crossly. "Oh, for goodness' sake."

There was a blubbering noise.

"Stop crying," she said, as Lissa tried and failed to stop crying down the telephone. "Come home immediately. You know I didn't have him pegged as a loser. Mind you, he treated Yazzie pretty shabbily. And I never saw his 'friend' again."

"I mean . . . I keep thinking maybe he's here, but nearly everyone's gone and all the stalls are closed up and the vans have driven off, and I've drunk a liter of mineral water . . ."

"Well, that's good," said Kim-Ange encouragingly.

". . . so I keep thinking I'll miss him every time I go to the toilet and . . ."

"Are you freaking out?"

"It's been a very long day."

"Take deep breaths."

"I've been trying that. The waiter is looking at me funny. He was friendly three hours ago."

"Don't tell me you waited for him for three hours."

There was a pause. "I can't not tell you that."

"Would Beyoncé wait for Jay-Z for three hours?"

"No," said Lissa in a quiet voice. "Although Kim probably has to wait for Kanye for three hours all the time."

"Three hours?!" said Kim-Ange again.

"I . . . I really thought I liked him," said Lissa.

Kim-Ange bit her lip. "Come over," she said. Then: "Hang on, let me just make sure he's not here."

"Oh God," said Lissa. Then, more hopefully, as if the thought had just occurred to her: "Maybe he's fallen asleep or something, just lost track of time!"

Kim-Ange couldn't bear to hear the forced casualness in her voice. "Mm-hmm, give me a minute."

She banged loudly on her side of the wall, their normal method of communication.

"Nope," she said finally. "That always works. He's not here. You're safe, come over."

Lissa felt her heart plunge. That was her last hope. Well, that or him being wounded with something painful, but not aesthetically disfiguring, in the hospital somewhere where she could tenderly nurse him back to health, but she didn't really want to say that one out loud.

"But then he'll find me sitting there when he gets back like some kind of mega stalker! He's already in hiding from me!"

Kim-Ange sighed. "I am taking you to the gin bar. That is the only way out of this situation."

"Can we talk about him?"

"No. Just gin."

"Can I cry a little bit?"

"Gin only."

"ENGAGED," SAID CORMAC ruefully, hanging up the phone. Kim-Ange would almost certainly be talking to her parents again, something that took place, on and off, quite a lot of the day.

"Mm-hmm," said the policeman, uninterested. Cormac was still worried about whether they were going to charge him.

"Want a solicitor?"

On a list of things Cormac wanted, a solicitor was so far from being something he wanted he nearly cried. Instead he said, clearly, no, he didn't and hoped he'd made the right decision.

The interview room was horrible, small, with a tiny cracked reinforced glass window set high above their heads and a revolting stale odor made no better by the heat of the day. What was lovely outside in London was very muggy and unpleasant in a basement near the River Thames. Feet were just visible above his head, walking back and forth in freedom. He watched them pass, feeling defeated, which he imagined was the point of the place, after all.

"I WAS TRYING to stop the big lad hurting anyone," said Cormac for the fourth time to the two police officers opposite him. "I was using army defense methods to restrain him, nothing more. They went slightly wrong. But you know the trouble these big lads get themselves into. We were already there because of a horrible accident. Really wasn't in the mood for another one."

He sniffed.

"Also, sorry to point this out, but we were in a courtroom facility crawling with police officers and security guards. Why was I the only person in there trying to sort something out to stop them killing each other?"

The police officers looked at each other for a moment.

"Okay," said the policeman finally. "Well, Big Al said to say thanks. He could have killed that guy and he did feel very bad about that."

He was reading from a piece of paper.

"He's pleaded guilty to brawling. Shouldn't get him into too much trouble—slap on the wrist if he's lucky."

"Anger management? He needs it."

"I hope so," said the female officer. "Perhaps a medical professional could write a letter of recommendation."

"Happy to," said Cormac.

They all looked at one another. Cormac tried desperately not to glance at the clock.

"Ex-army, huh?" said the police officer, checking the files on her computer. "Says here you served in Fallujah?"

Cormac nodded.

"But you've never been in trouble?" She smiled rather wryly. "My brother was out there."

She gave him a shrewd look.

"He found it quite tricky coming home."

Cormac found himself swallowing suddenly. "Yes, ma'am," he said, in a quiet tone of voice.

"But you're doing well."

"Apart from being in prison," said Cormac, thinking of everything that had happened, everything he'd learned and seen in the last few months.

"I'd say . . . nae bad." The officer stood up. "Right. Off you go. Stay out of trouble."

Cormac ventured to say his piece. "They're just lads, you know. And they've been through a lot."

"They have," said the woman. "So have a lot of people who don't start punch-ups in public places."

"They started . . ."

Cormac realized quickly he was going to get himself into trouble again as a frown crossed the other officer's face. He stood up fast.

"Thank you so much."

THE SARCASTIC POLICE officer looked practically disappointed to see Cormac ready to walk out. "Leaving so soon?" he said.

"Aye," said Cormac. He was handed back an envelope containing his wallet, watch, and phone. The battery was completely drained. Shit. He winced when he saw it. Then he realized he didn't have a lot of time to lose. The other lads had already been released; he was the last one.

"Good luck with the fuckbeast!" shouted Nobbo as he ran out of the police station at top speed. They had found a pub next door to the police station, which seemed to Cormac unwise, to say the very least, but he didn't have time to do much but wave quickly.

Chapter 73

I have been ghosted," said Kim-Ange dramatically—she had quickly put on a large black head scarf to chime with the somber feel of the occasion—"twenty-seven times. It has been terrible every single one of those times."

"Perhaps he's dead," said Lissa hopefully.

Kim-Ange had bought four massive balloon glasses full of a gin concoction, to save time, and she was drinking it, Lissa realized, rather like she'd drink beer, just because the glasses were so big. This was unwise. On the other hand, screw absolutely everything.

"*To death,*" said Kim-Ange, and they chinked glasses.

Lissa sighed. "Was he really tiny, though? Did he look like a mole? Did his nose come straight out of his neck?"

Kim-Ange sighed in turn. Shook her head. "I had no idea you liked him so much."

"Neither did I!" burst out Lissa. "Until I literally found myself *right here, saying this.* I think I just . . . I needed a little crush."

"Are you sure it isn't his house you like?"

"I *do* like his house," said Lissa, thinking of the cozy fire and the little wooden staircase.

"That's what you've done," said Kim-Ange comfortingly. "Projected the idea of home ownership onto some bloke. It's the idea of owning your own house you are in love with."

"Maybe," said Lissa a little dreamily. "So, he's a loser, then?"

"He has," said Kim-Ange, crossing her fingers to try to save her friend from more pain, "seven toes on each foot and ears bigger than his head. He comes up to my waist and sheds hair like a pony. And oh my God, the smell."

"Really?" said Lissa, approaching the bottom of the vat glass. The house didn't smell at all. Nice, if anything—that little scent of almond shampoo, the same type she'd started using.

"Yup," said Kim-Ange. "Lucky escape if you ask me. Another?"

Chapter 74

*K*im-Ange?!"

But nobody was answering the door. Cormac slumped in the doorframe, sweating. He had run all the way there, and even though it was later, the heat was still dense and humid, unpleasant, as if all the buildings were holding it in, storing it all day like a battery, then giving it back into the evening. Cars had honked and people had yelled as he tore past, his lungs ragged with what felt absurdly like freedom. She had to be at the nurses' home, she had to be. Where else would she go but to see her best friend?

There were a million places she could go, of course, but he couldn't think of that right now, only that she'd be there; he had charged through Borough Market, but the stalls were closed and the bars full of couples and groups, and as if—*as if*—she'd have waited all day! It wasn't even possibly or remotely likely. Nobody noticed him as he ran past, tension on his face, except for one waiter, clocking on to his second shift, who looked at him and wondered . . . just wondered. And hoped it would be okay for the sweet girl with the sad face.

AND HERE HE was. Stav the doorman had smiled happily at him—it had taken a quarter of the year, but Cormac had worn him down eventually with a very expensive pain au raisin habit—as he'd hopped up, sweaty and disheveled, and banged on Kim-Ange's door, even thinking he really ought to take a shower but unable to wait, completely unable to wait even one second more to see her.

Yazzie walked past.

"Hey!" said Cormac.

She sniffed loudly at him, which he found slightly puzzling, as he had absolutely no idea she was annoyed with him.

"Have you seen Kim-Ange?"

"She's got a boyfriend," said Yazzie pointedly.

Cormac blinked. "Aye, I know that . . . I just wondered if you'd seen her."

"You look filthy and awful," pointed out Yazzie.

"Thanks," said Cormac.

"Just call her," said Yazzie.

"Could you? I'm almost out of charge," said Cormac. "Please? *Please!* Tell her if she's with Lissa I can explain . . . please? Tell her I'll call."

"Sure," said Yazzie, walking off and pretending to put her phone to her ear.

He glanced at his watch. Shit! It was after eight o'clock already. Lissa's train left at nine. Euston station was half an hour away.

Chapter 75

Did you call your mum?" said Kim-Ange, pouring Lissa into a taxi. "Don't call her now, I mean. Just . . . call her."

"I didn't tell anyone I was coming today," said Lissa. "Because I didn't know if I could manage it . . . and because I wanted . . . I wanted to spend it with . . ."

Lissa's lip was wobbling. Kim-Ange leaned into the cab and gave her a big full-body hug.

"Don't worry about it," she said. "You did the right thing. Go back to Scotland, pack up, and I'll see you back here in a couple of weeks. Don't worry about that loser. I will make his life absolute hell also."

"Don't put prawns in the curtains, because when I come back they will still be my curtains," said Lissa.

"Okay."

Lissa checked her phone again.

"*Put your phone down!* You know you *will* hear from him. Tomorrow, with some bullshit excuse," said Kim-Ange fussily. "Then it'll all pick up again, the flirting and the little jokes and everything, until it comes time to meet again and then the same thing will happen. Trust me. I know men."

"I know," said Lissa.

"Is she going to spew in my cab, love?" said the taxi driver.

"*No!*" they both said together.

"Give me the phone," said Kim-Ange. "Come on, hand it over. You're pissed and in possession of a phone, it's a deadly weapon."

Lissa sighed. Kim-Ange grabbed it and hit a few buttons. She'd done this before.

"I've blocked his number. Stopped any recriminatory texts."

"I've got his number at home."

"Yes, but that will be in the morning and then you can *think about what you're doing.* In between sending me a thank-you bouquet."

The meter ticked on.

"Don't . . . don't lose the messages," mumbled Lissa.

"Messages are saved, but you can't send any more and neither can he," said Kim-Ange. "Not till you sober up."

"Thanks," said Lissa, flinging her arms around her again. "You're a great friend."

"I am," said Kim-Ange grimly. "Now I am going back to set fire to his bed."

"*It's my bed!*"

"Oh yes. I'll think of something."

It felt suddenly unbearably unfair to Lissa that Kim-Ange was going back to Cormac and she wasn't.

"Maybe he is dead," she said, "from saving a bunch of children from a burning orphanage. Even then I still hate him."

"In you go," said Kim-Ange, slamming the door behind her as the cab shot off into the night.

Chapter 76

There are several ways of getting from South Bank to Euston in half an hour: Thameslink, the Northern line, the number 63 bus, a black cab, which will do puzzling things around Bedford Square—but if you are in a tearing hurry and, frankly, a bit of a panic, you could always try running it. I wouldn't, personally. But then it very much depends on whether you are thinking straight.

Cormac wasn't thinking straight at all.

But as he flew down the stairs, out into the humid night, and hit the great river and charged along, he felt better running—feeling free, rather than jiggering about in a cab stuck in the sticky traffic or the tube inching forward. He couldn't have borne it.

To his surprise, he realized he knew where he was going. Across the bridge at Embankment, through Trafalgar Square and into Covent Garden, passing hordes of Lycra-clad tourists looking confused and buskers looking tired, then cutting toward Bloomsbury with its pretty red mansions and well-trimmed squares. He felt the ground under his feet and felt, at last, the pull of the city—that it could be your city, that it was expensive, yes, and grubby, and strange, but you could belong too; skirt the crowds, find your corner; experience the whole world on your doorstep.

And even as he ran, Cormac couldn't help but feel a little comforted, as he crashed across Tottenham Court Road, skirted the sofa shops, grabbed little alleyways he thought would get him through, passed the big hospital, and emerged, panting, utterly exhausted yet somehow exhilarated too, in Lissa's great city, as she got closer with every step. Up now the great throbbing gristly artery of Euston Road, filthy black with traffic, Euston station squat and grim across the road. Not all of London was beautiful. He glanced at his watch. Ten to nine. At home it would have been bright daylight still; here the streetlights were coming on.

He couldn't cross the road. Six thundering lanes of traffic were roaring without a break. He hopped from foot to foot at the traffic lights. Stop. *Stoppp!!*

Chapter 77

There was something almost motherly in the way the attendant on the sleeper train greeted Lissa and, worn out as she was, she almost started to cry.

"Have you had a nice day, hen?" said the woman, and it was a familiar accent to Lissa, and she bit her lip.

"Mm-hmm," she said, as her name was ticked off on a list and she found her way to her own tiny bedroom on the train.

She sighed happily as she opened the door. A bed was made up with a fresh white duvet and white sheets, two pillows and a tartan blanket. There was a sink at one end and a shelf for her clothes and a bottle of water, and it felt at that moment like the ultimate in luxury. A place to shut herself in, lock the world out, and lick her wounds.

The window showed the dank black interior of Euston station. She didn't want to see it. She turned away and opened her bag to finally—*finally*—get into her pajamas and forget about today altogether.

"I'M AFRAID YOU need a ticket, son," said the woman on the reception desk at the train, now looking not quite as nicely at the large, rather sweaty figure in front of her.

"Where can I get one?!"

"From the booking office . . . if it's still open."

Cormac looked back in dismay. The booking office was miles away. They both glanced at the clock. It was four minutes to nine.

"Am I going to make it?" he said.

The woman looked sad. "You can get the eleven fifty to Edinburgh," she said brightly. "That'll be fine."

"If I was going to Edinburgh that would be fine!" said Cormac in anguish. If he didn't get on that train, that would be it, it would be over. She'd never trust him again.

"It's nice," said the woman.

He gave her a level glance. The train started to make noises, the engines huffing up.

He screwed up his eyes. "Is there . . . Someone I really need to see is on this train. Can you call her for me?"

The woman protectively hid her clipboard with her hand. "What if you're a murderer?"

"Okay," said Cormac desperately.

Doors were slamming up and down the train now, and a guard was raising a whistle to his lips.

"Can I . . . can I just run up and down the train to see if I can see her?"

"Am I going to let you, a murderer, run up and down the train and peer in everybody's windows?"

"Pleeeease! This is someone . . . this is someone really important to me. Please. *Please.*"

The woman looked at him sadly. "I cannae," said the woman. "Health and Safety. We've had a lot of training."

"Me too," said Cormac ruefully.

Peeep! blew the whistle.

LISSA STOOD UP and leaned her head against the window of the little cabin, peering out into the world of the sooty, fluorescent station beyond, smelling of fast food and filled with the shouts of cheery or drunken commuters. When had London started to feel so strange?

Funny, it was almost as if it were calling her name. But as she strained her ears to hear, there was another sharp blow on the whistle, and the train began, smoothly, to chug its way out of the great black dirty station.

Chapter 78

T hat," said the woman on the reception desk, covering her ears, "is quite the shout you've got there."

And she lightly stepped onto the platform as Cormac, throat ragged, cried out, "LISSSAAA!!!!" one last time, to no avail. As the train took off, he tried to run alongside it, even as security hailed him, and he stopped, put his hands on his knees, utterly out of breath, utterly defeated.

EMPTY, EXHAUSTED, FEELING foolish, simply ridiculous, for having pinned so many hopes and dreams . . . Lissa sank down on the bed, feeling the soothing motion of the train beneath her. She glanced at her phone . . . no, no, no. Of course.

She had been so stupid. Well. This was modern life, she supposed. She sank back against the pillows. No way was she going to sleep. She was going to have to lie awake in a frenzy of embarrassment and recrimination all night, then have to get straight back to work the next day, which was the only reason she'd been bought a sleeper ticket in the first place.

She turned her face into the pillows. Well. Tomorrow was another day, she supposed. But somehow—and having her phone off definitely helped—the slightly jolting motion of the train, the fresh white linen, the sheer exhaustion, and, let us be honest, the several gins somehow worked their magic, and within moments, Lissa was utterly and completely asleep.

OUTSIDE IN THE streets of London it was dark, and the corner pubs were starting to take on a more aggressive turn; there was distant shouting and omnipresent sirens and a helicopter somewhere overhead, the faint, tense feeling that there were too many people, hot and drunk and angry, in too small a space. King's Cross was absolutely heaving, its restaurants and piazzas overspilling with people.

It crossed his mind; it absolutely crossed his mind. That Larissa might still be in her fancy restaurant with her fancy mates. That he could at least sit and lick his wounds surrounded by sympathetic company.

But it was strange. Those girls didn't appeal to him. Not at all. Not Larissa, not Yazzie. Nobody did. Nobody except the person who thought he'd dropped her. After all, who these days didn't have their phone? Who would ever believe it? Only a very stupid person, and he knew she wasn't that.

Cormac turned blindly south again. Retracing the steps he had run with so much hope in his heart was bitter and exhausting. A group of cabaret performers shouted at him as he accidentally trod on the tail of someone's feather boa, and he recoiled and apologized. A drunk heckled him from the street, and instead of stopping, he passed on by, head down. *Stop trying to care for everyone and just care for one person*, he thought bitterly. *Well, look how brilliantly that had turned out.*

It seemed so far now, through endless paved roads, past endless taxis at endless junctions, their yellow lights glinting into the distance. He considered taking one, but there was no benefit to arriving home any earlier, was there? His phone battery was almost dead. By the time it charged she'd be over the border, cursing him forever. And "I was in prison" wasn't exactly the excuse he'd been hoping to give.

He sighed, passing, finally, the police station for what he hoped would be the last time ever. The lads were still, to his utter amazement, at the pub next door and increasingly merry, and, he was astounded to see, the coppers were now drinking as well. A mass cheer greeted him as he stumbled past.

"Did you find her? The fuckbeast?" shouted Nobbo.

One glance from Cormac convinced him otherwise.

"Aww," said the group in chorus.

"What's this?" said the sarcastic copper, and to Cormac's horrified amazement, they immediately started telling him the entire story, while someone fetched Cormac a pint, which he declined in favor of a very large glass of water. The absolute last thing he needed was to get maudlin.

As the story unrolled the copper screwed up his face. "He's never even *seen* her?"

"Naw, mate!"

"That's nuts!" He pulled out his phone. "What's her name? She's got to be on Instagram."

But he found nothing.

"Look for her on the police database," said his colleague.

"Do *not* do that!" said Cormac.

"Well, you tried, you failed," said Tim. "Might as well just hang out with the rest of us . . ."

"No!" said the sarcastic policeman. "If you want her, go get her! That's what I had to do with Gus!"

"Where did Gus go?" said his colleague.

"Um . . . West London," said the policeman, and everyone gave a sharp intake of breath.

"Well, I tried that," said Cormac. "Didn't quite work."

"Hang on!" said Tim, possibly somewhat overrefreshed. "Where is Scotland anyway? If you drove would you get there faster?"

"Where is *Scotland*?"

"Focus on the question, mate, not your national pride."

Cormac glanced at his watch. "Well, maybe. But I haven't got a car at the moment."

"We've got a car!"

The policemen immediately looked up.

"You have?"

"It's insured!" said Tim instantly. The others nodded.

"I won't be on your insurance," said Cormac. "And youse are all too pished up to drive."

"Yeah, we are," said Tim thoughtfully. "But the insurance covers everyone."

"Otherwise we can't afford it," piped up Nobbo. "We had to pool it between everyone."

"You have a shared communal car?" said Cormac.

"Rotas are a nightmare," said Tim.

"I'm going to run the plates," said the police officer.

"Leave 'em," said the other copper. "You're off duty, Nish. Just leave it. For once."

"Okay," said Nish.

"You're a great copper. You just need to know when to relax. Switch off. Do a bit of self-care."

"You're right."

"Just . . . do your job. Don't let it consume you."

"Thanks, Harry."

"Don't mention it," said Harry, looking sadly at Nish's wedding ring.

The lads were getting up.

"Okay, let's go," said Tim.

"You're not coming," said Cormac.

"Course we are! It's our car!"

"Also we're not doing anything else," said Nobbo a little sadly.

"Road trip! Road trip!"

Cormac looked at them for a second, about to say don't be ridiculous, everyone had to go home to bed and work to go to. Except they didn't, did they?

"Road trip! Road trip!"

Then he thought about Lissa. And then, unexpectedly, he had another thought.

He took out his dying phone. He knew Lennox went to bed early, all farmers did. But it would be there waiting for him when he woke up.

I can't promise, he typed. But I MIGHT have solved your harvest crisis.

Chapter 79

Unsurprisingly, the boys bantered and chugged beer and yelled and tried to honk the horn for at least all the way to Birmingham. He'd explained there might be jobs up there for them, and they'd agreed instantly. Whether they'd feel the same in the morning was another story, of course.

Then, like the lads they all still were, they fell asleep, snoring loudly on the back seat, Tim up front.

Cormac had managed to plug his phone into the charger in the car—at last—and watched anxiously as the battery charged.

There were messages up till about four o'clock, jolly at first, then increasingly curt (from, in fact, Lissa and Larissa too), but they stopped fast (this was when Kim-Ange had gotten hold of the phone). Nothing recriminatory, nothing drunken or angry.

This was the worst thing of all. If there had been upset texts, he could have convinced himself there was still a chance that she cared for him, that this had meant something to her too, not just some stupid fantasy he'd concocted in his head.

He couldn't help it. He pulled over onto the hard shoulder and texted her. Just a simple hey.

It pinged back immediately. Number blocked. His stomach plummeted.

HE WAS, HE realized, halfway between London and Scotland, 250 miles to go. Before he could fall down at her door. Or not.

He could turn around, work out his exchange, never see her again, only talk briefly about the cases. They never had to meet at all. He could go back, professional relations would be resumed; she'd succeeded in what she had to do and given her evidence. Everything would go back to normal, as if it had never happened.

LISSA WOKE SUDDENLY on the train, not sure why. At first she was completely disoriented, couldn't remember where she was. Then she went to the window. They were flying through moonlit valleys and dales, not yet in Scotland, somewhere in the heart of the UK, between two worlds. London and Scotland. She sighed. That was what it felt like, to be in different places at once. Her heart was in Scotland but her life . . . well, her life was in London. She knew that now. She could thank that Cormac, she supposed. Whoever the hell he had turned out to be in the end.

CORMAC'S PHONE PINGED. He leaped on it, his heart beating.

Up for baby. Good news, desperate need.

His heart sank. It was Lennox, expecting him to be turning up with lads who would work for a bit. Maybe he could drop them off and turn around. Have a quick nap and head back.

Nobbo snorted and turned over. Cormac thought of them all, young lads, nothing to do, hanging about on street corners, starting fights. How much they might change; how much they were capable of. He already knew how well Robbie had settled in, and he had been in a much darker place.

He glanced at his phone again. She'd blocked him. Maybe Kim-Ange had dissed him, he hadn't even thought of that. Told Lissa what a rube he was, how many mistakes he'd made. Maybe they'd laughed themselves silly at the narrow escape she'd had. Oh God.

He took a deep breath.

He drove on.

IT WAS STRANGE; he didn't feel tired. Even though it was the early hours of the morning, he felt strangely alive, crossing the fells through the beautiful lake district, climbing higher and higher through Cumbria, till he finally crossed the border, and on and on they went, through a blissfully snoozing Glasgow and up north, ever north, across the Campsie Fells, and now when he opened the window the air was fresh and freezing, and clouds passed across the moon as the stars began to vanish, one by one, and at first it was the faintest passing of black to navy and navy to blue and a very thin line at the horizon to his right, promising a new day.

Chapter 80

It was just after six when Cormac reached Lennox's farm, but everyone was up already, Lennox beaming broadly when he met the lads stumbling out of the car, blinking and rubbing their eyes, some of them already regretting their drunken plans of the night before. Nina had gotten up too and prepared a large breakfast for the incomers.

The train didn't arrive till seven. Cormac was edgy and itchy and couldn't put his phone away. Nina noticed.

"Can I use your shower?" he asked awkwardly.

"Why don't you go to your own lovely house and use your own lovely shower, Cormac MacPherson?" she said.

"Because . . . there's a girl in it," he said.

"Oh, she's lovely, Lissa," said Nina. "I'm sure she wouldn't mind."

Cormac turned bright scarlet and tried to answer, but couldn't. Nina gave him a very shrewd look.

"Here, I'll get you a towel," she said, John on her hip as she went toward the airing cupboard. "You can borrow a shirt of Lennox's too, if you're desperate."

"Uh, thanks," said Cormac.

"If you see her," said Nina, bustling off, "tell her I've got that copy of *Daddy-Long-Legs* in I ordered for her. Actually here, take it yourself."

And she went back downstairs, to pour thick cream and honey on the porridge and to brew fresh coffee for the new batch of harvest boys.

CORMAC FOLLOWED HER outside. "Actually, I might just . . . head back to London," he said, head down.

Nina looked at him, frowning. "Why?"

"Um, long story. But I need to get packed up down there. Head back here. Just . . . tie up some loose ends."

"Are you okay?"

Cormac shrugged. "Ach. There was a girl. It didn't work out."

Nina smiled sympathetically. "English girls," she said. "We're terribly tricky."

"I might as well go back, get it sorted out. Plus, I think the lads share that car with about twenty other people. Don't want to get anyone into trouble."

"Are you sure you don't want to sleep?"

"Neh, can't really miss a shift. I'll be fine."

"Okay then," said Nina. "See you in two weeks."

He paused. "I don't think the streets of London really are paved with gold."

Nina looked around the bustling farmyard. In the corner, a quiet Robbie was on the ground, crawling up to little John and pretending to be a bear, while John cackled hysterically. He had adjusted to the quiet of the farm so quickly, Nina hadn't seen him take a drink since he got there. He ate with the other laborers every night, kept to himself, but the relief in his face was obvious, and Nina always dug him up an extra slice of bacon from somewhere. Little John adored him; Robbie always made him smile, and he crawled around after him half the day. If it hadn't been ridiculous, Nina would have thought he understood that he was needed.

At a long table set up in the barn, the South London lads were nervously joshing with one another, showing off, talking about who had the biggest muscles for working in the fields, while eating large second helpings of porridge and thick-cut bread with marmalade and surreptitiously texting their mums to let them know they were all right.

"Oh, I don't know," said Nina.

Chapter 81

The long, rambling bus had toured the hills at dawn, and Lissa felt it was very unfair, listening to the elderly couple behind her, who were clearly having a massive argument, because it was in Gaelic, and it sounded completely beautiful to her ears anyway.

Scotland was doing this on purpose: ray after ray of sun breaking through the morning clouds, revealing fields so green they could have been made of neon; nearly grown lambs tearing about in joy; towering peaks overhead sheltering little stone villages huddled around market squares in their lee. The air had a catch of cold early-morning mist in it; you could feel it in your throat, but also you could smell, feel, a warm day ahead, when the scent would rise off the heather, where your hands would trace the high, high tops of the wildflowers, intertwined everywhere with butterflies and bees.

Groggy still, as well as feeling the aftereffects of the gin—plus, the shock of the change between grimy Euston and here was like jet lag—she stared out the window, her chin on her hand. What a privilege it had been, in the end, she supposed, to get to come here. It was annoying in a way that the human resources people and the therapists and her friends had all been right. It had done her good. Okay, she didn't get everything . . . but that had been a silly fantasy. It shouldn't—it mustn't—define her stay, define her, take away what she had gained from the amazing country.

She stepped out into the early pink morning, Kirrinfief still quiet, apart from old Mrs. Whirter trundling up with her cart to hit the newsagent first. She waved to Lissa and, completely ignoring the fact that the girl looked exhausted, was carrying an overnight bag, and obviously just wanted to go home, immediately jumped into the bunion conversation again.

Three months ago, Lissa would have given a half smile and hurried on. This morning, she put her bag down and let the whole story—involving evil daughters-in-law and, for some reason, an Irn-Bru margarita—unfold, before promising to squeeze in an extra appointment and pop in later once she'd gotten herself squared up. Mrs. Whirter smiled broadly and said that wouldn't be necessary, a chat with Lissa was a tonic in itself, and wasn't it a terrible shame she had to leave?

Fortunately her eyes weren't quite good enough these days to see the rapid tears forming in Lissa's.

THE ROAD TO the little cottage was wildly overgrown, the hedgerows riotous and crazy from the never-ending sun and rain, sun and rain. Lissa took in their morning scent as the sun began to slowly rise, lifting the mists off the loch. The birds sounded in the trees; barely a car passed to disturb them, or her thoughts, as she trundled her suitcase behind her.

The little house looked sweeter than ever to her as she stepped up to the doorway, put the big old key in the lock.

For the oddest moment as she turned it she wondered . . . No, of course not. She was being ridiculous. And the kitchen was just as she had left it—was it really only twenty-four hours ago? Yes. Twenty-four hours before, one cup and one plate all by themselves neatly on the drying rack. Nothing had moved; nobody had been there. It was just her, alone, again. Her phone pinged. She couldn't help grabbing at it. Her mum.

She smiled. I'll call you later, she texted, and made a promise to herself to do so and invite her mum up, invite Kim-Ange. Everyone should get a chance to enjoy the cottage before she had to leave.

Lissa left her bag as it stood, went to the sink, and threw that icy water on her face and drank a large glassful of it. Okay. She was straight back to work today; she was due at the surgery in half an hour. Time to wrap things up. She could send . . . well, a formal email to Cormac she supposed. Signing off on all the patients so ideally they could slip seamlessly back into their own lives, pretending nothing had happened, pretending she hadn't changed . . . And one day, Scotland would be just a distant dream, a memory that she told her children in some faraway future, where she had a place of her own and a partner and a grown-up life. "Once upon a time," she would say, "I visited a magical land . . ."

She stopped suddenly, her heart in her throat. She was standing in front of the large window at the back of the kitchen, and out in the garden, there was a dark shape.

She took in a deep breath, fighting her panic response. This was Scotland, for God's sake, not central London. The biggest crime here was someone crashing into the bus shelter when they'd had a few.

She took another deep breath, then glanced around for something to use as a weapon. Perhaps someone had thought the house was empty or abandoned.

The dark shape was on the lawn, crouching. She stepped forward, then turned around, looking for a knife. She could find only a bread knife. She wasn't sure how effective that would be, but she took it anyway, then found herself ducking and crawling to the door at the back of the house. The figure was stockstill. Was it staring at the house? Had it seen her?

Heart palpitating, she stood by the back door, closed her eyes, took another deep breath, remembered that she was meant to be a braver person these days, whether it felt like it or not—and flung open the door.

Chapter 82

H e-hello?"

Her voice was trembly and weak. The figure didn't move. Lissa edged forward a little bit, then a little bit more. It was like a statue.

She moved cautiously to the end of the garden. "Hello?"

It was a man she had never seen before, fast asleep, curled up with a hedgehog in his lap.

CORMAC HAD THOUGHT he would just pop in, grab a change of clothes, feed Neddie, and go again. He knew what time the train got in; then she had to get the bus, so he wouldn't disturb her. He toyed with leaving a letter saying sorry but figured it might be creepy and decided against it. He had let himself get completely out of control; it was a silly crush and there was no point pushing it any further.

The sun was streaming in the garden, and he realized, as he fed Neddie little grubs with his hands, suddenly just how exhausted he was from driving all night. The hedgehog snuffled as Cormac slumped down onto the stone by the undergrowth, steadily warmed by the sun. He would get up and head out in just a minute . . . but it was so soothing simply being home. Just to breathe the air of his homeland, just to let all the stress and pressure of the city rush out and fade away . . .

HE DIDN'T LOOK at all as she'd expected.

But the hair was the same as he'd drawn in the pictures: curly, overgrown, a little unruly. And it would take quite a burglar to fall asleep in a garden not his own.

Apart from that, he was much larger than she'd imagined: not fat, but solid; broad shouldered, heavy legged, more like a soldier or a rugby player than came across when he wrote. She couldn't see his eyes, but dark lashes left shadows on ruddy cheeks, and there was bristle on his strong chin. He wasn't at all like she'd conjured in her head. But . . . but there was something in the large bulk of his shoulders, the careless tangle of hair, the wide mouth that looked as if it would laugh easily.

She couldn't stop staring. He was breathing evenly. The little hedgehog snuffled in his lap, entirely comfortable in his presence. What on earth was he doing here?

HE NEVER KNEW what woke him. One minute he'd been to see Neddie, the next—the sun was beaming straight into his eyes, and Lissa was standing over him, her face hidden by the sun. All he could see was a full head of bouncing curls. He squinted upward, confused: Was he asleep? Dreaming? Where was he? What was happening?

Suddenly:

"YOW!"

He jumped up. He had somehow woken Neddie, who had responded in the only way he knew how, and now he had a big jab in his hand.

Lissa couldn't help it. She dissolved completely in giggles. Neddie was still hanging on to Cormac's hand for dear life, his tiny paws scrabbling in the air.

Cormac would have sorted it, but he was transfixed by the laughing sun-touched face, the exact face he'd seen in the photo, in his dreams. Lissa jumped forward with her coat, scooped up the tiny creature, crooning, "It's okay, you're all right, you're all right, little one," in a softer voice than the one he'd heard yesterday, through the door.

He was about to say something, but suddenly it struck him that the words "you're all right, little one" were, somehow, so much what he'd wanted to hear for so long, and for a moment, he couldn't quite say anything at all.

LISSA, HEART POUNDING, took a step forward and gently put the hedgehog down, whereupon it instantly scurried away.

"Are you okay?" she said, as Cormac clutched his hand, a very confused look on his face.

Not taking his eyes off her, he raised his hand to his face. It was bleeding, very slightly. They carried on, just staring at each other, Lissa feeling her heart beating in the agony, in the dancing, buzzing, swishing noise of the garden.

Slowly, infinitely slowly, a smile began to spread across his face. It transformed his face completely. Lissa still hadn't taken her eyes off him.

"Well," he said, in the soft Highlands accent she had dreamed of. "Well noo, I don't suppose you ken anybody in the medical line?"

Chapter 83

Work was still out there, but, after calling in to London, Cormac made a plan to divvy up the calls, so they could finish by lunchtime and spend the day together.

Lissa flew through her rounds, bestowing huge smiles on everyone. Cormac, of course, took far longer, as he was corralled by every single person he met and forced to repeat more or less everything he'd done down south, while also listening to them tell him how they didn't trust that London and how nothing good ever came out of it, until he found himself getting more and more defensive of his adopted city. Plus, he had to pop in and see his mum, and was touched by how delighted she was to see him. Breaking her wrist, he realized suddenly, had made her more vulnerable than he'd known, and he gave her a huge hug, as she told him how the strange new nurse hadn't been as bad as she'd expected for an English, and he wondered how on earth they were going to break the news to her.

They met up back at the surgery. Cormac watched her crossing the market square. Without even thinking about it, he put his hand out, and she took it. It was the strangest thing; he had barely had to apologize, had barely had to explain himself at all. Which was a relief, as he'd decided to keep the bathroom incident to himself. Just for now. There'd be time for all that.

The dogs set off a melee of barking as they arrived, and Joan let them out, so Cormac and Lissa were both pawed half to death.

"Oh, good, good," she said, noticing immediately. "Always good to mate outside the pack."

Lissa and Cormac were both so startled, they laughed in surprise.

"Anyway, also good, I have a puppy available soon. You two can have it."

"Um, we've literally just met," said Lissa.

Joan waved her away. "Are you telling me I don't know anything about the natural world? Oh! Speaking of which." She peered at Lissa. "You know I said there were no nursing jobs?"

Lissa stared at her.

"Wait, you asked?" said Cormac, beside himself.

"No!" said Lissa. "Well, maybe. Just an inquiry. Um, I wanted a puppy."

"How much midwifery experience have you had? Ever since you English started invading, there's babies all over the place. They're hiring a community midwife."

"Oh," said Lissa, her face falling, "that's not what I am."

"You could manage, couldn't you? Also there's occasional lambing. It doesn't say that on the ad, I'm just telling you that there is, round here."

Lissa shrugged. "Not really."

Cormac looked thoughtful. "Well," he said, "there's something I wanted to talk to you about. There's an outreach project in London . . . helping people on the street. They're looking for part-time. It would mean I'd be looking for a job share."

"You're kidding," said Lissa. "Oh my God, I could kiss you."

Cormac blushed. "Would it be a wee bit forward to invite you into my hoose?"

"I'll have to go with you anyway," said Lissa. "I don't know how to unblock your number from my phone."

"Good," said Cormac. "You'll just have to stay very, very close by."

BOTH OF THEM were trembling as they stood in the little cottage in front of the fire, which Cormac admired, which made Lissa feel rather proud. It was so exciting, frightening, and strange all at once. He put some music on and moved a little closer to where she was standing at the sink, filling the kettle for tea. Lissa didn't want any tea; she just didn't know what to do with herself.

He moved even closer behind her. "Is this okay?" he said in a very soft voice, and she nodded, without quite being able to turn around.

"Normally this should be late at night and we should be very drunk," complained Lissa. "That's the English way. *And* the Scottish way, I have observed."

Cormac smiled. She could feel him towering over her, smell the almond shampoo. He took his left hand, put it around her waist. She stood stock-still, and, very gently, he bent his shaggy head and kissed her on the nape of her neck.

"See, this way," he said gruffly, "you still don't need to see me."

Lissa grinned then and turned around. "Maybe I want to do that," she said, reaching up on tiptoes.

"Braw," he said, and the fresh clear Scottish water ran up and over the top of the kettle, and neither of them noticed at all, and soon the Proclaimers were singing to an empty room.

Chapter 84

Three months later

There had been a short, violent rainstorm the night before, but by the time the train got in the next morning, the world was bright again, shining. Lissa had warned Mrs. Mitchell to wear a coat, and the woman stepped off the train into the September glow in a brand-new Artic-level North Face jacket. They were both there to meet her, holding their hands out to her, their faces grave.

They pulled up by the little quiet row of houses just beside the town square.

"Are you ready?" Lissa said, Cormac helping her down.

Word had gotten around in Kirrinfief, as it so often did, and there was quite the crowd who happened to be passing.

Lissa rang the bell, and Mr. Coudrie opened the door, more people spilling out on either side.

The house's inhabitants and Mrs. Mitchell stood, staring at each other curiously, respectfully.

"I . . . I don't know what to say," said Gregor finally.

"I understand," said Mrs. Mitchell without smiling.

He was about to invite her in when, suddenly, there was a whirl of noise and movement, and Islay burst out of the house onto the pavement. She was wearing a new dress, bought in honor of the occasion, and had a ribbon in her hair and was delighted there were so many people about, and in the mood to show off. Her parents still couldn't get used to the fact that she could work off her natural energy without them being terrified.

She stopped when she saw Mrs. Mitchell, though, who had made a small sound.

"Do you want to come inside?" said Gregor.

More people were crowding around. Mrs. Mitchell didn't even hear him. Lissa steadied her with her arm.

"This is . . . ?" she asked, in just above a whisper.

Lissa nodded.

"I'm Islay!" said Islay cheerfully.

Mrs. Mitchell looked at her for a long moment, tears rolling down her face. "Can I . . . ?" she said suddenly, looking at Islay's parents.

"Do you mind, Islay?" said Gregor, realizing instantly what she was asking.

Islay, who had been well briefed by Cormac, opened her arms wide.

Mrs. Mitchell took one tottering step forward, then another. Then she quietly pressed her head against the little girl's chest and held it there, Islay for once standing still, so she could hear her son's heart beating, beating, beating.

The street turned silent, and when she straightened up again, tears in her eyes, Islay grinning her usual toothy grin, Islay's mother walked up to her.

"I am your child's mother now," she said calmly. "And you are Islay's. Your child is my child. And my child is yours."

Mrs. Mitchell nodded. And together they disappeared into the house. And Cormac and Lissa squeezed their hands together, hard.

Acknowledgments

It is incredibly useful for a writer to have her two best friends from school be a doctor and a lawyer, and I unabashedly hit them up for free help on this book (although all errors or simple fiction smoothing —few cases come to court as quickly as they do here, alas—are of course mine). So huge thanks— and love, as always—to Karen Murphy, FRCS, and Alison Woodall, BA (Hons) Law.

Also thanks to Muriel Gray for plant help, Claire and Fredi Melo for helping me out with Albanian (faleminderit!), and Rona Monroe, my secret Plot Fairy Godmother.

Huge thanks to Jo Unwin, Maddie West, Lucy Malagoni, Milly Reilly, Donna Greaves, Joanna Kramer, Charlie King (NICE BABY YOU GOT THERE), David Shelley, Stephanie Melrose, Emma Williams, and all at Little, Brown; Deborah Schneider, Rachel Kahan, Jennifer Hart, Dan Mallory, Alexander Cochran, Jake Smith-Bosanquet, and Kate Burton.

And finally, as they deserve top billing: I am so thrilled we were allowed to use not only lyrics from "I'm Gonna Be (500 Miles)" but also lines from "Sunshine on Leith" in this book. Thanks to one of the best bands in the known universe, the

Proclaimers, and the best management in the business, Braw Management. Massive thanks also due to Sandra McKay and the estimable Kenny MacDonald, as well as to Sarah Sharp at Warner Chappell Music and, of course, the amazing brothers themselves. (I apologize for the shocking illustration.) If the Proclaimers is not a band you're familiar with, you're in for such a treat.

About the Author

JENNY COLGAN is the *New York Times* bestselling author of numerous novels, including *The Bookshop on the Corner, Christmas on the Island,* and *The Bookshop on the Shore*. Jenny is married with three children and lives in Scotland.

ALSO BY JENNY COLGAN

AMANDA'S WEDDING

MY VERY '90S ROMANCE

THE BOOKSHOP ON THE SHORE

CHRISTMAS ON THE ISLAND

THE ENDLESS BEACH

CHRISTMAS AT LITTLE
BEACH STREET BAKERY

THE CAFÉ BY THE SEA

THE BOOKSHOP ON THE CORNER

SUMMER AT LITTLE BEACH
STREET BAKERY

LITTLE BEACH STREET BAKERY

THE CHRISTMAS SURPRISE

CHRISTMAS AT ROSIE HOPKINS'
SWEETSHOP

CHRISTMAS AT THE CUPCAKE CAFÉ

WHERE HAVE ALL THE BOYS GONE?

DIAMONDS ARE A GIRL'S BEST FRIEND

500 MILES FROM YOU

WWW.JENNYCOLGAN.COM